S0-BNJ-493

THE STRANGER . . .

It was late at night.
John Sayer's car was the only one on the turnpike.
What possessed him to pick up the stranger? It was a foolish, dangerous thing to do.
Even as he let the man into his car, John Sayer knew something beyond his own power made him do it.
For the stranger was someone very special. Very special indeed. And from that moment on, John Sayer's life took a perilous turn into his past . . . a past that had never released him from the nightmare of memory.

ANOTHER FAWCETT CREST BOOK BY
JEROME WEIDMAN:

Other People's Money

WORD

OF

MOUTH

JEROME WEIDMAN

A FAWCETT CREST BOOK

Fawcett Publications, Inc., Greenwich, Conn.
Member of American Book Publishers Council, Inc.

THIS BOOK CONTAINS THE COMPLETE TEXT
OF THE ORIGINAL HARDCOVER EDITION.

All of the characters in this book are fictitious, and any
resemblance to actual persons, living or dead, is purely
coincidental.

A Fawcett Crest Book reprinted by arrangement with
Random House, Inc.

© Copyright, 1964, by Jerome Weidman. All rights reserved,
including the right to reproduce this book or portions
thereof.

Library of Congress Catalog Card Number: 64-17938

PRINTING HISTORY
Random House edition published August 24, 1964
First printing, July 1964
Second printing, September 1964

First Fawcett Crest Printing, May 1968

Published by Fawcett World Library
67 West 44th Street, New York, N. Y. 10036
Printed in the United States of America

*For Peggy, Jeff
and John*

I thought the time had come to declare myself.
"*I* am the captain."

I heard a "By Jove!" at the level of the water. The phosphorescence flashed in the swirl of the water all about his limbs, his other hand seized the ladder.
"My name's Leggatt."

Joseph Conrad
The Secret Sharer

WORD

OF

MOUTH

Part I

1

THE WINKING LIGHT was small. So very small that, for several moments after it attracted John Sayer's attention, he did not think it was a light at all, and he made no attempt to check his speed. Then, when it was too late, he saw the frantic man on the grass divider. John realized, as he whipped by, that the man was signaling by waving a flashlight. John slammed on the brakes. The tires shrieked and the motor stalled. While his mind struggled with a vague feeling that he should back the car up and see what was wrong, John heard running footsteps approaching from behind. He leaned out of the car and looked back. It was a cloudy, dark night, but the Turnpike was brightly lighted. John could see clearly that it was the man with the flashlight. He came running up to the car and stopped.

"Whee," he said, or rather whistled, blowing out the sound in a panting puff. "Just catch my breath a sec." He stood there, one hand on the car window, looking down at the asphalt, until his body stopped heaving. Then he lifted his glance, shook his head, smiled ruefully, and said, "Wind's not what it used to be."

John's mind felt helpless. The thoughts with which he had left the parking lot in New Haven, and the decision he had reached shortly after he came out of the side roads onto the Turnpike, seemed to be sitting on his brain like a massive paperweight on a piece of flimsy tissue. He struggled with a tangle of once familiar words that seemed to have lost their meaning for him, and he came up with a totally uninflected and completely disinterested, "You in trouble?"

"Well," the man said, "I need a lift."

He poked his hand through the open window, toward John, and turned the flashlight beam down on his own palm. The man was holding out a worn piece of leather to which was pinned a silver badge. The massive paperweight inside John's head shifted slightly.

"Oh," he said. "You're a policeman."

His voice sounded strange in his own ears. John wondered if he was already dead but had not yet been deprived of the capacity to hear. Was he picking up his own words the way, when he was a boy, he used to pick up distant voices on his home-made crystal set?

"You could call me a policeman, yes," the man said. "I've got to get down to Edesboro."

He said no more, as though no more was necessary, and walked around the front of the car to the other side. John wondered if he should protest, but the decision, made only a few minutes ago, sat there in his head, making everything else seem totally irrelevant, and the policeman opened the door. In the glow from the ceiling light, John saw a pleasantly ugly man wearing a soiled raincoat. On his head sat a jaunty, narrow-brimmed, greenish Swiss mountaineer's hat. A cockade of colored feathers was tucked into the black band. He was odd looking for a policeman, John thought, but the thought carried with it a modifying footnote: John had not, in his thirty-five years, met many policemen. The man slipped onto the front seat and pulled the door shut. The ceiling light went out.

With it seemed to go John's sense of continuity. He had the utterly preposterous feeling that he did not know what to do next. A flashing image of school, when he was small boy, darted through his mind: morning Assembly was almost over; the Pledge of Allegiance had been recited; "The Star-Spangled Banner" had been sung; a boy had come to the platform and read aloud the Twenty-third Psalm. All the familiar items of the morning routine having been ticked off, the unfamiliar was about to start. What it was, precisely what the next step would be, depended on Mr. Tristram, the teacher, who was sitting up front. When the teacher rose, and made the announcement, John and the other boys would know what to do. Meanwhile, they waited. Thirty years later, seated beside a total stranger in the car that had been carrying him from New Haven to New York, John Sayer did the same thing. He waited.

"Do you think you can drive?" the policeman said.

"What?" John said, and then he realized the stranger's words were not a question. "Oh, yes," John said. "Sorry."

He twisted the ignition key. The motor caught. He moved his foot from the brake to the gas pedal. As the car picked up speed, it seemed to shift the enormous weight inside his head. Around the decision, which was all that mattered, a question that did not matter seemed to escape and float upward, like a bubble from beneath a rock jostled underwater: *Why is mine the only car on the Turnpike?*

"It's better this way," the policeman said quietly. "If there was a lot of traffic, cars passing us, traffic whizzing by on the other side, going toward New Haven, it would be distracting. Hard to talk when you've got to watch the road every second. About serious things, anyway. You agree?"

"Yes," John said. The enormous weight inside his head seemed to shift again. Another bubble escaped. How had the stranger heard the question John had asked inside his own head? He had not spoken it aloud. But this question, like the other, did not seem to matter. Not enough, at any rate, to interest John in a reply. "Whatever it is you want to talk about," he said, "I don't mind."

"You sure?" the policeman said. John, who was not sure, wondered why he wasn't. He realized that a sense of inevitability had closed in on him. From the moment he had made the decision, shortly after he turned off the side road into the Turnpike, he had been invaded totally by a feeling that everything was now out of his hands. Other hands had taken over. They would do what had to be done. With the feeling had come a sense of relief, almost of pleasure, as though a great pain had been eased away.

The winking light on the road, John began to grasp slowly, had cut across this sense of relief. The entrance of the stranger into the car had stopped the pain from easing away. It was as though a spigot, from which were pouring the slowly rising waters that were about to float him away to the peace for which he yearned, had been turned off. The peace that had been within his grasp was in danger. Unless he fought, everything would be thrust back into his hands. John did not want that. He wanted the hands that had taken over to remain in control.

With an effort that took all his strength, he shifted the weight inside his head and managed to say, "No, please, I don't want to talk."

The policeman shook his head sadly and said, "I'm afraid you'll have to. So let's begin with the basic stuff and get that out of the way. First, you're John Sayer. Right?"

"That's right."

"Home address: One West Seventy-first Street, New York City?"

"Right."

"Age thirty-five? Profession, lawyer? Offices on Lexington Avenue and Fifty-fourth Street?"

"Correct," John said.

"Married? Wife named Ellie? Two sons? James and Samuel? Eight and nine? Both attend the Porte School on West Seventy-sixth Street?"

"Right," John said.

"Born in Dutchess County, upper New York State? Educated, Harvard and Harvard Law? Served with Eighth Air Force during war?"

"All correct," John said.

"You've just been up in New Haven? To see the tryout of a musical play called *Deucalion?* Because you're the lawyer for the producer? And now you're driving back to your apartment in New York?"

"That's right," John said.

The policeman on the seat beside him blew out his breath in a small, tired sigh.

"That much is okay, then," he said. "I've got the right man."

John opened his eyes, and blinked with surprise. He had not realized his eyes had been closed. Seeing the long asphalt ribbon of road rushing up toward the car and then under it, he had a stab of panic.

"It doesn't matter," the policeman said. "Once you made your decision, back there when you came out of the side road onto the Turnpike, once you decided to kill yourself, you can't die in any other way."

"But the way it's going to happen," John said. "I haven't decided that yet." The crystal set picked up the touch of irritability in his voice. "The only decision I made, I decided there's only one way out, that's all." The touch of irritability turned to anger. "That's all I *did* decide."

"I know," the policeman said. "That's all anyone ever decides. The rest is done for you."

The stab of panic made John's stomach knot. His hands jerked the wheel sharply to the left. Terrified, involuntarily, he twisted the wheel back to the right.

"You see," the policeman said quietly, "people aren't always sure. They think it's the only way out. They decide to take that way out. Then when they realize what the decision means, they panic. The instinct to live, to go on living, is very strong. Take you. Just now. The realization that it's

more than a decision, that it really means the end, that realization is so overpowering, it's saved many lives. What you
just did, for example, those two twists of the wheel, they
were the result of that realization. But if this car were still in
your control, those two involuntary jerks of the wheel, the
car would have cracked up, and you'd now be dead."

John stared straight ahead, regretting the sense of inevitability that had vanished, wanting again the pleasure of the
cessation of pain, yet aware of something new: a flicker of
hope.

"Then I'm not dead?" he said.

"No," the policeman said, "not yet."

John fought back the new stab of terror. His palms, he
realized, were damp on the wheel. He tried for a rational, ju-
dicious tone. As though he were doing something perfectly
normal, part of his regular day's work in the courtroom, putting a question to a witness on behalf of a client.

"But I'm going to be dead?" John Sayer said.

"That's up to you," the policeman said.

"I don't understand."

"It's simple enough," the policeman said. "Most people
who decide to commit suicide think they also decide on how
and when it will happen. This is natural enough, since there's
usually a gun around, or a bottle of pills, or they happen to
be near an open window high up somewhere, and very often
the act seems to take place immediately following the decision. But it only seems so. Between the decision and the act
—there's me."

"Who are you?" John said.

"Your second chance," the policeman said. He glanced at
his wrist watch. "Between now and the moment you are
scheduled to die, you have fifty minutes. Fifty-one, to be precise."

"Scheduled?" John said. "But I didn't make the decision
until a few minutes ago. How could—?"

"The moment you made the decision," the policeman said,
"the method and time were assigned, and I was sent to inter-
cept you and offer you your second chance."

Thrusting up through the fear, like a trapped child slowly
lifting with his frail shoulders an enormously heavy manhole
cover, came the moment of curiosity that no terror could resist or smother.

"What method and time were assigned to me?" John said.

"You are scheduled to go through the cabled rails of the

Turnpike where it crosses the Saugatuck River just outside Edesboro," the policeman said. "That's about halfway between New Haven and New York. Your time is eight o'clock sharp, and it is now nine, no, ten minutes after seven, so you have exactly fifty minutes."

The decision, which when it was made had seemed to solve everything, now seemed merely to have complicated the agony out of which it had come. John Sayer did not want fifty minutes. He wanted oblivion.

"I'd rather not take the fifty minutes," he said. "I want—"

"I'm afraid you have to take the fifty minutes," the policeman said.

"Why?"

"So you can relive the events that led up to the decision, and thus decide—"

"No," John said firmly. Anything¹ but that. He did not want to relive the events that had led up to the decision. He wanted them never to have happened. With two synchronized movements, John tramped the gas pedal down hard, all the way, and jerked the steering wheel savagely to the right, all the way, toward the cement pillars guarding the road from a Fallen Rock Zone. His stomach knotted again. The muscles in his arms and legs stiffened. The short, shaved hairs on the side of his jaw tingled. He leaned back, eyes closed, waiting for the crash.

After a while, his arms and legs began to ache. John opened his eyes. The car was rolling along smoothly, as before. And it was still the only car in sight. The policeman on the seat beside John blew out his breath in the small, tired sigh.

"You've got the next fifty minutes whether you want them or not," he said. "Don't make it tougher for yourself than you have to," he said patiently. "Please go back to the beginning. When you got involved in this *Deucalion* thing. A year ago."

John hesitated, testing the weight of the decision in his head. All at once it didn't seem quite so heavy. The curiosity that had come through his terror to ask the place and time of his death now came through again. Perhaps if he did as he was told, if he used the fifty minutes to relive the events that had led to the decision, perhaps the decision could be avoided. It didn't seem possible, but—

"Everything is possible when you've reached this point," the policeman said.

John hesitated again, wondered why, and then had it.

"You know my name," he said. "What's yours?"

"Mancini," the policeman said. "Nick Mancini. It doesn't mean anything. On the table of organization I'm just listed as a conductor. But that's always made me feel sort of naked. So I invented a name for myself. Nick Mancini sounds like a policeman, doesn't it?"

"Yes," John said as he sent the car down the Turnpike toward New York.

"It's a year ago," the policeman said helpfully. "November sixth. You've just stepped out of the elevator on the twelfth floor of the Hotel Stanton at Sixty-fourth Street and Park Avenue."

John nodded and said, "Yes, that's right. I'm on my way to see a man named Arnold Zucker. I've never set eyes on him before. I've never heard of him. I don't know what his business is. All I know is he called me on the phone, asked me to come see him, and I've come."

"Didn't the whole thing strike you as being a little unusual?" Mr. Mancini said. "I mean going to see a total stranger just because he called you up?"

"Sort of, yes," John said. "I thought maybe he's a potential new client. Somebody my firm had been recommended to. But the fact that it was more than unusual, almost weird, frankly, that didn't occur to me until the door of Mr. Zucker's apartment opened and I saw the person looking out at me."

"Come *in*, Mr. Sawyer," the huge woman said crossly. She sounded as though she had been repeating the invitation for some time and she was finding it difficult to restrain her annoyance with John's refusal to comply. He stepped in quickly. As the woman closed the door, from an archway at the other end of the foyer came a soft, purring, scarcely audible and yet remarkably penetrating British voice: "Not Sawyer, Ilsa, *Sayer*."

"I'm sorry," Ilsa said. She dipped in a bow that John guessed was at least an 8⅞ head. This reduced temporarily her seven feet or better to his just slightly less than six. "Go in there, Mr. Sayer," she said, pointing toward the far side of the foyer. "It's Mr. Zucker."

"Thank you," John said, and he did start to go as directed. But as the maid wheeled and marched off to what he supposed was the kitchen section of the apartment, he could not resist stealing another glance at the towering figure. Wrapped in the voluminous starched apron and the turban-like starched cap, the maid reminded him of the eunuchs in the *Esquire* cartoons.

"Mr. Sayer?" the British voice purred.

John turned and moved across the foyer. He stepped into a small living room, and said, "Hello" to a round, bald man in a red satin robe. He was sitting in the center of a sofa under an elaborately framed painting of some very bright green sea water.

"Hello," the man said, or rather murmured. For a startled moment John did not realize the word had been addressed to him. "I'm Arnold Zucker. Sit down. With you in a moment."

John sat down in a chair facing the sofa and realized why he was startled: Mr. Zucker's head looked like that of a boy suffering from mumps in a comic strip. Except that he had been bandaged not with the traditional white but, because some joke was afoot, with swathes of black toweling. A moment later, settling back in the chair, John saw that the illusion was created by something he had often heard about but, in actual fact, had never seen *except* in a comic strip: Mr. Zucker had two phones clamped to the sides of his head. Even though John felt it couldn't possibly be true, Mr. Zucker seemed to be carrying on two conversations simultaneously.

"Yes, I know about the pearl necklace," Mr. Zucker murmured. He sent, or rather dropped, the scarcely audible words impartially between the two mouthpieces. "Gallagher said seven and a half, ten, and then twelve and a half on everything over forty thousand. He said that would be all right." Somewhere between John's chair and the sofa a telephone bell tinkled. John watched, fascinated, as Mr. Zucker murmured, "She has a quality, yes, there's no doubt about it." At the same time he moved his left hand perhaps two inches, so that his grip on that telephone shifted to a cupping support under his several chins of both instruments. His right hand, thus freed, descended into what first seemed to John the depths of the red satin dressing gown. From it, to John's astonishment, Mr. Zucker now brought a third telephone. He placed it against the right side of his head, parallel with the instrument already lodged there. Without the slightest change of inflection, he said, "Hello. Who? With you in a moment, Beatrice." Then John saw that the third telephone had come not from Mr. Zucker's robe but from a recess under the coffee table across which John was watching his host. The murmuring British voice was saying into all three instruments, or so it seemed to John, "Cultured pearls in a pinch, yes. But the fact that they are cultured would have to be stated. Because of Larry's special knowledge of the field." Then John became aware that Mr. Zucker was examining him with direct, unabashed, unblinking interest.

Feeling his face flush, and resenting the fact that it should, John stared back resolutely into Mr. Zucker's eyes. They were, he saw, small and had a delicate Oriental puffiness along the lids. The irises were so distressingly ice-blue in color that, for several uncomfortable moments, John had the feeling he was staring into empty sockets. Then Mr. Zucker's head moved slightly. "The mood of Zarathustra, yes, Beatrice, but not the ambiance," he said. Dropping these words into all three telephones apparently involved the use of a number of only rarely employed facial muscles. As a result, the light from the Park Avenue window behind John's chair shifted on his host's face. He saw that Mr. Zucker's direct, unabashed, and unblinking examination had become an almost preposterously charming smile.

"You will excuse me, won't you?" dropped, syllable by syllable, onto the wine-colored necktie inside the red satin robe. John realized, with a start of surprise, that Mr. Zucker was addressing him. "I won't be but a moment, Mr. Sayer, really I won't," the round man said. "Would you like a cup of coffee?"

"No, thanks," John said.

"Something stronger, perhaps?" Mr. Zucker murmured. But John could not tell whether the round man was murmuring to him or to the people at the other ends of the three phones laced like ivy to his host's head. Without pause, the low-keyed British voice rolled right on with: "I've had my office work out the figures, Max, and they run as follows."

The murmuring, now reduced to a recitation of numbers and percentages, lost much of its fascination for John. He felt free to examine the rest of the room. He found it surprisingly unexciting, in spite of several features that were not exactly ordinary. As his roving glance absorbed these, John wondered why he should expect excitement, or feel surprise because of its lack.

On his right, filling at least one-quarter of the room's not very ample floor space, was a Steinway grand. It was congestedly covered with photographs in silver frames racked tightly one against the other. It was possible to make out the faces of the people only in the front row. The effect was that of a suspended mobile representing a forest of silver birch trees in miniature. Distributed around the walls were what at first glance looked like six reproductions of the elaborately framed painting of bright green sea water behind Mr. Zucker's head. A second glance, however, revealed that they were not reproductions. They were variations of the same scene. At the far side of the room, under the windows that faced Sixty-fourth Street, stood a long, wide, unpainted pine table. It was not unlike a carpenter's bench. On it were stacked, in neat little piles of varying height, an enormous number of what could have been school composition notebooks, all with bright red covers. John had the feeling he was looking at a display of student stationery in a college campus book store. Then his glance returned to the couch against the wall facing him, and John understood why he found the rest of the room surprisingly unexciting: everything suffered by comparison with Mr. Zucker.

The other parts of the room were just parts of a room. But the corner inhabited by Arnold Zucker was touched by something special. The plump, bald man in the red satin robe cast a glow.

"Beatrice, dear, Ziegfeld is dead, and has been for almost thirty years, or hasn't anybody told you?" he was saying in the measured tones of a man dictating a telegram. John wondered what in God's name Mr. Zucker was talking about and to whom. He wondered even more about the nature of Mr. Zucker's glow. At first glance he looked not unlike the German proprietor behind the counter of a delicatessen on Columbus Avenue. Here John occasionally picked up the cold cuts and potato salad for the Sunday supper he and Ellie decided on the spur of the moment every now and then to have in front of the television set when Sam and Jim went out to a Porte School week-end basketball game. Mr. Zucker's accent, on the other hand, was unadulterated Gaumont-British.

The combination of the salami slicer and the dubious duke, John saw, was not unlike, if he remembered his college chemistry, the accidental meeting of two recognizable and not very exciting elements that resulted in the creation of a totally unrecognizable and wildly exciting new element.

"No more calls," Mr. Zucker said. To whom? John wondered. He watched as Mr. Zucker peeled the phones away from his head, one at a time, slowly, gracefully, almost *too* gracefully. "Now, then," Mr. Zucker said. He folded his now unoccupied hands in the lap of the red satin robe as though he were with great care fitting together the two halves of a cantaloupe. "You are John Sayer?"

"I am," John Sayer said. He found he was getting up out of his chair, moving across the room, and reaching to take the hand Mr. Zucker was holding out across the coffee table. "I'm very glad to meet you, sir."

"Not nearly so glad, no, not even remotely so glad, I assure you, as I am to meet the son of Sennacherib Sayer," the round man said. Even in the moment of shock, John's stunned mind recorded the irrelevant fact that Mr. Zucker's hand, which looked like a lump of tallow, had the surprisingly rough, hard feel of a piece of dried asphalt. Then the eyebrows rose a fraction of an inch over the puffy Oriental lids. The cinema version of an Etonian voice intoned, on a faintly rising note, "You *are* the son of Sennacherib Sayer, are you not?"

"Oh, yes. Yes, of course," John said. He settled back in the chair with the disturbing knowledge that what had created the moment of shock was his realization of an almost incredible fact: he had not heard his father's name spoken aloud since the earliest days of the war, in 1939.

"Sennacherib Sayer was one of the great heroes of my youth," Mr. Zucker said. At once, to the round man's special world-weary glow, a new dimension was added in John's mind: disbelief. Arnold Zucker did not look the sort of man who had ever had a hero. "I was just a boy in school, of course," he said, "and I didn't really know what a trust was, but the word trust-buster had a ring to it, like Indian scout, I suppose, or secret agent. And of course the alliteration of the name made its contribution, too. Sennacherib Sayer. Buffalo Bill. Thrilling combinations of sounds. Yes, it's a great pleasure to me, Mr. Sayer, to meet the son of Sennacherib Sayer."

"Thank you," John said. He was wishing at once that he had not come and, a moment later, he was angry with himself. He was having a reaction that, as a man of thirty-five, he felt he should have outgrown long ago. He was a father himself now. If in that role he was going to discharge his obligations properly to Sam and Jim, he had damn well better stop nursing a childish grudge against the man who, he felt, had failed to discharge those obligations to him. In an effort to lift himself out of the confused moment of anger, John said, "But I'm sure you didn't ask me to come here today, Mr. Zucker, to discuss my father."

"My dear Mr. Sayer, that is *precisely* why I asked you to come here today," the round man said. He spoke through a slight rearrangement of his lips. John supposed Mr. Zucker intended his visitor to consider this a smile. "I want very much to discuss Sennacherib Sayer."

"But why?" John said. "Aside from the fact that he was my father, it strikes me as somewhat like asking someone to come to see you in the middle of a business day to discuss Admiral Byrd."

The dead, ice-blue eyes flicked to momentary life in the pale round head. It was as though the wheel of a cigarette lighter without fluid had been thumbed. Then the spark vanished, but John sensed that something in what he had said had taken Mr. Zucker by surprise.

"I know this will surprise you," Mr. Zucker said, "but I have asked people to come and see me on at least three, no, four, yes, four different occasions to discuss Admiral Byrd. And I want to assure you that even though the discussions came to nothing, they were not initiated for the purpose of wasting a part of either my business day or the business days of my visitors. The same, I assure you, Mr. Sayer, is true in this case. While it is a pleasure to me to talk with his son about one of the heroes of my youth, the intent of this talk about Sennacherib Sayer is strictly business."

"In what way?" John said.

"You are a lawyer, sir?"

"Yes," John said. "Of course. I thought that was clear when you called my secretary and asked me to come here?"

Mr. Zucker nodded and smiled and said, "Perfectly clear. I have some people who are interested in the life of Sennacherib Sayer. Their interest, if it becomes activated, will involve a certain amount of legal work that might prove extremely lucrative. It seemed to me not merely sensible but only fair for the fees to go to Sennacherib Sayer's son. That is, if Sennacherib Sayer's son is interested and wants to earn the fees."

"Being a lawyer," John Sayer said, "I am naturally also a businessman, so of course I am interested in earning new fees. Provided."

"Provided what?" Mr. Zucker said.

"Provided I am not asked to do anything to earn them that is inconsistent with my principles as a lawyer and a businessman," John Sayer said.

The lips rearranged themselves in the round face to create the illusion of a smile, and Mr. Zucker said, "Spoken as one would expect the son of Sennacherib Sayer to speak. May I ask, sir, what it is that has given you the impression that, to earn these fees, you might conceivably be asked to do anything inconsistent with your principles as a lawyer and a businessman?"

The answer was clearly irrelevant as well as ludicrous: I have never been in a room like this, John wanted to say; met a man like you; or seen a maid like the giantess in white starched muslin who opened the door for me.

"Absolutely nothing," said John. He sometimes felt he had not learned as much about life as a man who has lived through thirty-five years of it should have. Among the few things he *had* managed to pick up, however, was a conviction that irrelevant and ludicrous answers to sensible questions were better left unuttered. "It's just the sort of routine precautionary statement that I suppose most businessmen make."

Mr. Zucker said, "Not in *my* business."

"Which is what?" John said.

The round face was suddenly creased by a curious expression. Not quite uneasiness, not exactly displeasure, and yet somehow compounded, at least in part, of both. "You see, my recollections as a boy of Sennacherib Sayer the great trust-buster are so vivid," Mr. Zucker began, "that I—"

Sensing that he had somehow gained an advantage, although he could not imagine how or over what, John pressed it by saying again, "What proposition?"

The curious expression sank deeper into Mr. Zucker's face. The round man cast two hasty glances across his red satin shoulders, one to the left, another to the right, as though scouting for intruders in the small living room. John grasped what was wrong: Mr. Zucker felt cornered.

"Well, I have these people," he murmured vaguely. He underscored the vagueness with a short, indecisive wave of his hand, as though he were talking, not about some men or women who had asked him to present a business proposition to John Sayer, but about a few shapeless figures glimpsed in the dead of night at the window of a passing train. And all at once John grasped something he sensed was basic about the man he had come to see: Mr. Zucker's business, whatever it was, functioned in a climate where its practitioners equated the act of being pinned down with the fact of death: both had to be faced ultimately, of course; but it was better to postpone facing them as long as possible.

"What people?" John Sayer said, enjoying the politely relentless note in his own voice.

"These people who came to me," Mr. Zucker said.

"Came to you from where?" John said.

"Oh," Mr. Zucker said. Again the plump hand lifted from the satin lap, thought better of it, came back to rest, tried again, and thought better of that, too. "Does it matter where they came from, Mr. Sayer?"

"I don't know," John said. "I don't know who they are or what they want, and since you seem reluctant to tell me, even though you've asked me to come to see you presumably so that you *could* tell me, I thought I'd try to pin down just one small fact in what is beginning to look and sound, if you will pardon my saying so, Mr. Zucker, like one of the weirdest business meetings I have ever attended."

"Well, you see, Mr. Sayer, it's not really *my* proposition," Mr. Zucker murmured. "Although, of course, I am the one who has been asked to present it to you."

"Go ahead," John said. "Present it."

A flicker of distaste raced across Mr. Zucker's plump features.

"Do you know Vinnie Howe?" he said.

"Who?" John said.

"Vinnie Howe," Mr. Zucker said. "Vincent Howe."

"No, I'm sorry," John said. "Should I know him?"

"Not necessarily," Mr. Zucker said. "Although he *is* one of the better known managers."

"Managers of what?" John said.

"Theatrical managers," Mr. Zucker said.

"Oh," John said, not with comprehension but with relief. It was as though he had been wandering around helplessly in a darkened attic, telling himself as he pawed for the door that there was no occasion for panic. Suddenly a beam of light had cut through the unsettling blackness. "You are in the theatrical business, Mr. Zucker?"

Even as he said it, John's mind leaped to the pine table at the far end of the room. Abruptly he knew that all those mounds of red notebooks undoubtedly were bound scripts of plays. Then his mind followed his glance to the dense forest of silver-framed photographs on the piano. His eyes poked about among the cluster of still indistinguishable but now suddenly glamorous faces. He was trying to see if he could recognize any of their owners.

Mr. Zucker gestured toward the piano. "The one behind and to the right, that's Vinnie Howe."

"This one?" John said.

"Yes," Mr. Zucker said.

John picked up the silver frame. It enclosed a glossy print, obviously snapped by an army press photographer. The print showed a smiling, fragile-looking man of perhaps fifty. His thin, sandy hair was tumbled about by the wind. A topcoat hung across his arm. He had been caught by the camera in the act of descending from the small plane with USAAF markings at an unidentified airport.

"That's Croydon, during the war," Mr. Zucker said. "You can tell by the grass. They were still taking off and landing on grass in those days. Vinnie had gone over to have a look at the Redgrave production of *A Month in the Country*. He didn't like it much. Not enough to bring over to New York, at any rate."

"But he likes the life of Sennacherib Sayer?"

John was pleased to see that his stab at bringing the tangled strands of Mr. Zucker's evasive business method to some sort of seizable knot of comprehension had worked. The round face under the painting of angry waves looked pained.

"I didn't say he *likes* the life of Sennacherib Sayer," Mr. Zucker said. It occurred to John that this was the first time he had ever heard a murmur with a cutting edge. "I didn't say *anybody* likes the life of Sennacherib Sayer. I said I have these people who are *interested* in the life of Sennacherib Sayer."

"Is Vincent Howe one of these people?" John said.

Mr. Zucker squirmed slightly inside the magnificent red satin robe. Like most lawyers, John always began to enjoy the question and answer exchange when it passed the invisible line that told him he had his man cornered. He had to restrain a smile as he said again, "Mr. Zucker, is Vincent Howe one of these people?"

Reluctantly, as though he were being forced at the poker table to relinquish a valuable card, the round man on the couch said, "Yes, he is."

"Who are the other people?" John said.

"They're not important at the moment," Mr. Zucker said. "You will meet them in due course. If you are interested, that is, in their proposition."

"Leaving aside the rest of these people you seem eager not to talk about, Mr. Zucker. Let's stick only to the one hard fact you have divulged, namely, that Vincent Howe is interested in the life of Sennacherib Sayer. May I now ask, and could I please have a straight answer because my lunch date is creeping up on me, may I now ask what is the nature of Mr. Howe's interest?"

"Well, it isn't really only Vinnie's interest, you understand. As I said, there are these people—"

"*Mister* Zucker."

"Yes?"

"A straight answer, please."

In the pause that followed John was assailed by the thought that perhaps Mr. Zucker didn't know how to utter one.

"Mr. Howe," the round man said, paused, scowled, and started again. "Vinnie," he said, but that didn't seem to help him, because once more he paused. "It's like this," Mr. Zucker said. Now there was a sudden breathless quality in the murmur. "Vinnie is not interested in *all* of your father's life. What Vinnie Howe is interested in is the time your father was running that place upstate, that place called Deucalion, if I'm pronouncing it correctly?" The question, coming like the sting in a scorpion's tail at the end of the breathless murmur, hung in the air. John knew he should bat it down. A word or even a nod would have done the trick. He was, however, capable of neither. The cutting edge reappeared in Mr. Zucker's voice. "Is that how it's pronounced? Or was? Deucalion." John fought, and won: he nodded. The victory did not, however, seem to satisfy Mr. Zucker. A small scowl pinched the smooth skin of the round, bald head. Why, John thought helplessly, why couldn't Mr. Zucker scowl the way other people did, with their faces, not with their scalps? "Mr. Sayer, what's wrong?"

John shook his head, fought again, and won again.

"Nothing," he said, but did not relax. He fought on, clawing at the escaping memories, cramming them back into the locked box Mr. Zucker had smashed open with his Gaumont-British pronunciation of the word John Sayer had not heard spoken aloud for more years than he had not heard his father's name. The word he had heard only once before pronounced in that curious, haunting way.

"Tell me something, Mr. Sayer." The man on the couch paused. John knew why. Mr. Zucker had suddenly been assailed by a terrifyingly fundamental doubt. It was as though he had come to a dentist, allowed himself to be placed in the chair and then, looking up at the man bending over him with the drill, realized he had come to the wrong office. The edged murmur said, "Do you remember that place, Mr. Sayer? Deucalion?"

It was like asking Ulysses if he remembered Troy.

"Of course," John said.

Mr. Zucker's expressive scalp resumed its polished smoothness.

"Vinnie thought you would," he said. "Vinnie's information was that you were actually born at Deucalion."

"Not quite," John said. He found relief from his bout with the box of memory in correcting simple factual points. "I was born in the hospital in Wellesville. That's the town near Deucalion, about four miles away."

"Is that how you pronounce it?" Mr. Zucker said.

"That's how everybody up there pronounced it," John said. "Dew-*kayl*-yin, with the accent on the middle syllable, Deucalion."

"No wonder you looked so irritated," Mr. Zucker said.

"Did I?" John said.

Mr. Zucker nodded, clearly with relief, as though he had found himself in the right dentist's chair after all.

"Very," he said. "A few moments ago, when I pronounced it Dew-kally-yon. You looked positively pained. I can hardly blame you. It's almost like having one's own name mispronounced. The place where a man is born and spent the first dozen years of his life."

"I see where Mr. Howe has done a bit of research," John said. "But again he's just slightly off. I spent the first ten years of my life at Deucalion, not dozen."

"Oh, well, you know," Mr. Zucker murmured. He swept his plump hand back and forth across the coffee table laden with phones as though he were slapping whitewash on a fence. "Vinnie didn't actually do any research. He's about my age, you see, and so he, too, remembered Sennacherib Sayer, the great trust-buster, and that extraordinary colony he founded up there in Dutchess County right after the First World War. He's always felt there's a great musical in Deucalion. Excuse me, Deucalion."

"A musical?" John said.

That small look of pain, like a pinch of pepper at the center of a large fried egg, appeared on Mr. Zucker's face.

"Why, yes," he said. "What do you think Vinnie had in mind?"

"I'm beginning to wonder if he has one," John said.

"What?"

The word erupted in the room like a pistol shot. John was aware of a moment of glee. The human being on the couch had been jolted out from under the concealing layers of British accent, expensive satin, and controlled facial muscles. For a moment Mr. Zucker looked like an angry delicatessen store proprietor who has been accused of cheating his customers by using a doctored scale. But only for a moment.

"I'm afraid I don't quite understand," he murmured. As each layer of the façade fell back into place, each word in the sentence became more vigorously British. "Are you casting aspersions on Vincent Howe's intelligence?"

"I can hardly do that, since I've never met him and know nothing about him," John said. "I merely expressed the opinion that a man, any man, who wants to make a musical comedy, and when you say musical, Mr. Zucker, I assume you mean a musical comedy—"

"I do."

"—out of the place where I was born, that man can't be very bright," John said.

"One of the odd things about the theatre," Mr. Zucker said, "is that everybody's opinion matters. Even people like you, Mr. Sayer, who know nothing about the theatre. The reason for this is that people who put on plays are engaged in one of the most unpredictable enterprises ever conceived by the mind of man. They are trying to catch the wispiest of will-o'-the-wisps, namely, the public fancy. Since nobody knows what will do the trick, everybody is constantly seeking everybody else's advice, analyzing everybody else's experience, trying to find reassuring fragments to assist his own upcoming experience. I'm sure you, as a lawyer, Mr. Sayer, would never even dream of asking your bootblack for his opinion of a brief you have just written. Yet I have never known a playwright who has not at one time or another asked his bootblack what he thinks of the second act. In such an atmosphere, to uncertain people inhabiting the most uncertain of worlds and lusting fiercely for certainty, instinct takes on many of the dependable certainties of, let us say, a tested chemical formula. Vinnie Howe has proved his theatrical instinct is a sound one. Did you see *True North*, Mr. Sayer?"

"Was that the one about the R.A.F.?"

"No," Mr. Zucker said. "You're thinking of *Near the Wind*. *True North* was a musical about a paper-box factory. *Gathering Dust*. Did you see that?" John shook his head. Mr. Zucker said, "A musical about a janitor in a Brooklyn apartment house. How about *A Lick and a Promise?*"

"I didn't, but I think my wife did," John said. "The one about the Civil War?"

"No, that was *Reduction in Force*," Mr. Zucker said. "*A Lick and a Promise* was a musical about the New York City Sanitation Department. Street cleaners, Mr. Sayer. *Slow Leak?*"

"Never even heard of it," John said.

"Well, it was during the war, and you may have been overseas."

"I was."

"Your tour of duty must have been a long one," Mr. Zucker said. "*Slow Leak* ran almost eight hundred performances at the Shubert, just short of two years, and it toured for two more. A musical about automobile racing. I could go on for quite a while."

"Mr. Zucker."

"Yes, Mr. Sayer?"

"You have made your point."

"Permit me to underscore it," Mr. Zucker said. "All these shows had three things in common. When first announced, most people around Broadway felt their subject matter was wrong and even preposterous for musical comedy. When they opened, all these shows were hits. And third, all of them were dreamed up and produced by Vincent Howe."

"My God," John said.

"Precisely," Mr. Zucker said.

"Has he ever had a flop?"

"Many."

"When did he have time?"

"Between hits," Mr. Zucker said. "Vinnie feels a show about Deucalion will be a hit. If he didn't, he wouldn't try to get it off the ground. To you, since you were born and raised on the place, Vinnie seems crazy because, and I hope you understand the spirit in which this is said, because you have no perspective on it. Very few of us have about the places where we were born. But if you can stand outside yourself, so to speak, if you can look back on the place impartially, Mr. Sayer, what do you see?"

John had never been able to look back on the place impartially. That was why he had forced it, and everything connected with it, into the locked box in his mind.

"I don't really see anything," he said.

"Let me tell you what Vinnie sees," Mr. Zucker said. "And what I see, too. A wonderful period in America's recent history that has been exploited endlessly in song and story, has nonetheless never lost its fascination, and has never been seen from the angle Vinnie and I see it, the angle you don't see, Mr. Sayer. People talk glibly about the twenties. The Jazz Age. The Era of Wonderful Nonsense. The Long House Party. The Big Hangover. And so on. The twenties were all that, yes. Of course they were. But they were also a time of hope, a time of courage, a time of experiment. Nothing, it seems to Vinnie, is more typical of this aspect of the twenties than Sennacherib Sayer's great experiment in Upstate New York called Deucalion."

"The experiment failed," John said. The remark seemed utterly pointless, yet he could not stop himself from making it.

"So did Hamlet's," Mr. Zucker said. "That, however, did not prevent Mr. Shakespeare from making of the failure the greatest play in the language. To the artist, Mr. Sayer, failure and defeat are infinitely greater themes than success and triumph. Who can even remember what William the Conqueror said about his great victory at Hastings? But who can possibly forget Harold's words as he lay dying on the field of battle?"

"What were they?" John said.

"They escape me at the moment," murmured Mr. Zucker.

So I thought, thought John. All at once he knew why he had made the utterly pointless remark about Deucalion's failure. It no longer seemed utterly pointless. He had learned in the courtroom the truth of the rule Professor Thompkins had laid down in the classroom: *Always try to keep salesmen out of the jury box.*

The man whose contribution to society is not that of hewing wood or drawing water, but extolling the virtues of the wood hewn and the water drawn by others, has a tendency to think highly of the extolling process. The salesman who finds himself in disagreement with his fellow jurors is not swept by the suspicion that they may be right, but rather by the belief that it is his duty to convert them to his own conviction. Too often he does, not because they see the light, but because his powers of persuasion are greater than their powers of resistance: they are, after all, customers.

Until Mr. Zucker was well launched into his passionate description of the aspect of the twenties that he seemed to believe only he and Vinnie Howe had ever before noticed, John had not realized that inside the carefully constructed magisterial presence of the skillfully evasive maneuverer in the red satin robe there lurked an equally skillful salesman. John did not mind being sold. The receiving end of the process could be pleasant, not unlike a manicure or a massage, if what the process aimed at was no more than a corner of your wallet. But Mr. Zucker, who obviously believed he was doing precisely that—who probably believed, in fact, that he was aiming at fattening John's wallet—had no way of knowing that he had invaded a jealously guarded corner of his visitor's heart.

Out of the instinct to repulse the invader, to stop what one of his classmates would have called the mellifluous but corrosive flow of the swinging bullshit artist, had come John's statement that the Deucalion experiment had failed.

"I'll be glad to look up Harold's dying words, if he left any, and send them on to you," John said. "For the purpose of this discussion, couldn't we leave the Battle of Hastings out of it, and stick to your client Vincent Howe?"

"I didn't say he was my client," Mr. Zucker murmured hastily.

"What is he?" John said. "Your chiropodist?"

"You are a wit, Mr. Sayer."

"Not really," John said. "I'm just getting to the end of you know what."

"What?" Mr. Zucker said.

"My tether," John said.

Mr. Zucker's eyebrows rose like the hints of twin sunrises on the wide expanse of forehead.

"Have I left anything out?" he said.

"Not much," John said. "Just what Mr. Howe wants with me. And how you are related to Mr. Howe. And how you will be related to me. And what I will be supposed to do as a lawyer to earn the fees you imply will come flooding my way if I join, approve of, attach myself to, or perhaps only give my consent to this project. Things like that, Mr. Zucker. That's all you've left out."

"Very well," the round man said. "In order, Mr. Sayer. One at a time. As follows. Mr. Howe wants to see you and talk to you. I am not related to Mr. Howe in any way. Except for what I trust will blossom from this first pleasant meeting into a lasting friendship, I will not be related to you in any way, Mr. Sayer, and what you will be expected to do to earn your fees, why, I think Vinnie Howe can tell you that much better and more accurately than I can." The plump hand swung back and forth again across the telephones on the coffee table in the whitewashing-a-fence gesture, and Mr. Zucker murmured, "Have I omitted anything?"

"Yes," John said. "Who are you?"

The shoulders shrugged under the satin robe.

"A friend at court, you might say," Mr. Zucker said. "An interested observer. An ambassador without portfolio. A rooter for the project. Take your pick, Mr. Sayer."

"I'd rather not," John said. "Because they don't answer my question. Who are you, Mr. Zucker?"

"Why, I should think that's obvious," the plump man said. "I am a resident of the Hotel Stanton."

"Mr. Zucker, are you ashamed of what you do?"

"Do?"

"For a living," John said.

The plump face stretched as the lips turned down in a shrug that did not involve the body beneath them.

"Oh, I make a few phone calls," Mr. Zucker said. "I see a few people."

"Is it legal?"

"What?"

"These things you do," John said. "Are you within the law, or outside the law?"

"Mr. Sayer, in a lifetime of some sixty summers, I have never had so much as a parking ticket."

"Then why are you ashamed to tell me what you do?"

Mr. Zucker hesitated, as though there were several answers available to him, and he wanted to choose the one most appropriate.

"It isn't shame," he said finally. "I think calling it shame is unfair."

"What would be more fair?" John said.

"Reticence, perhaps," Mr. Zucker said, and then his face brightened. "Reluctance would be more accurate."

"All right," John said. "You admit you're reluctant to tell me what you do. Would you now tell me why you are reluctant?"

"To name something that has many ramifications is to diminish its stature," Mr. Zucker said. "I want you to think highly of me."

"The best way to do that," John said, "would be to tell me in a word the name of your profession or trade or whatever it is."

"I can't do that," Mr. Zucker said. He sank one plump hand into a lumped hill of red robe at his side. "But I can tell it to you in *three* words. Would that do?"

"I am listening," John said.

"I represent people," Mr. Zucker murmured. The plump hand came out of the hill of satin with a small white card attached at the end of the pursed fingers like a flag of truce in a toy soldier battlefield. "Here is Vinnie Howe's office address and phone number. Why don't you give him a call, tell him of our talk, and decide between you where you want to go with this. Any further questions?"

"Just one," John said as he stood up. "Those paintings." He nodded toward the angry waves above Mr. Zucker's head and gestured toward their several framed variations on the other walls. "Do they have anything to do with the practice of your profession?"

"A great deal," Mr. Zucker said. "Without them I would be nought. Samson shorn of his tresses. These, Mr. Sayer," the plump man murmured proudly, "were all painted by my wife on the porch of our summer place in Cape May. You will, of course, call Vinnie at once, won't you, Mr. Sayer? And then get back to me?"

"Of course," John said, but he didn't. This, he found when he came into his office, was not necessary.

"Do you know a Mr. Howe?" his secretary said, and then glanced at the message slip in her hand. "Vincent Howe?"

"Not yet," John said. "Why?"

"He called about half an hour ago—" Miss Faille hesitated, then said, "I'm going to read this off exactly as I took it down, Mr. Sayer. He said, quote, that is *Mr. Howe* said, quote, *Arnold Zucker just told me he saw Mr. Sayer and Mr. Sayer said he's going to call me, but to hell with all that formality and fencing around waiting for him to call me, so here I am on the blower, wanting to talk to Mr. Sayer,* and when I told him you were out," said Miss Faille, who apparently felt she could convey the rest of the message without help because she looked up from the slip, "Mr. Howe said would I ask you to call him back as soon as you came in."

"Okay," said John. "Anything else?"

"Mrs. Sayer called," Miss Faille said. "She wanted you to

know that the ballots were finally counted this morning, and
your son Sam has won. Wait." Miss Faille looked down at another message slip, nodded, smiled, and looked up. "Yes, Sam
has been elected Fifth Grade representative to the Porte
School's Student Council."

"No kidding?" John said. "Get Mrs. Sayer, would you?"

"Well," Miss Faille said, following him into his office,
"Mrs. Sayer said you were not to bother calling back because—"

"No, please," John said. He tossed his hat on the leather
couch under the window. "I want to talk to her. How about
that? There were four kids running against him, you know."

"Yes, I know," Miss Faille said, smiling happily. "He's
such a bright boy."

"Loaded with personality, too, obviously," John said with a
laugh. He dropped into the chair behind his desk. "You
wouldn't think from the way he drops his dirty clothes all
over the house and fights with his brother that he's potentially
another Jim Farley."

Miss Faille laughed, placed both message slips on the desk
in front of her boss, and went out. John stared out the window, his eyes fixed on the other side of Lexington Avenue,
seeing none of it, allowing himself to dunk up and down, like
a lazily floating swimmer, in the pleasure of Sam's victory.
The phone rang. John snatched it up eagerly.

"Hey, Ellie," he said. "How about that? That kid is going to—"

"Oh, I'm sorry," Miss Faille's voice said. She did sound
sorry, as though she felt it was her fault that she had to cut
off his pleasure by admitting she was not Ellie Sayer. "I
haven't had a chance to get Mrs. Sayer yet," she said. "The
phone rang when I sat down to it, and it's Mr. Howe again.
Will you speak to him?"

John hesitated. As the joy drained out of him, he could
feel the worry seeping back. It filled him again, slowly, inex-
orably, with the uneasiness and fear he had carried with him
from Mr. Zucker's office.

"Well," he began. He wanted to say no. He was aware that
he needed Ellie's voice on the phone to carry with him into
whatever his meeting with Mr. Howe would be like. With a
weariness he tried but failed to conceal, at least completely,
John Sayer said to his secretary, "Sure, put him on."

Mr. Howe came on like a clown who has been kicked out
of the wings, tumbles head over heels across the stage, and

comes to his feet clasping to his ear the telephone he has snatched from a table he passed on the way.

"Mr. Sayer?" he bellowed.

"Yes," John said, wincing as he pulled the phone away from his ear. "Hello, Mr. Howe."

"How are you, fella?" Mr. Howe demanded and, like Pilate, did not stay for an answer. "Boy, kid," he roared, "if Arnie Zucker knew I was doing this, he'd bust a gut."

"Doing what?" John said.

"Calling you," Mr. Howe screamed happily. "Don't you know about Arnie?"

"I met him only this morning," John said. "A couple of hours ago."

"Well, he's the Scarlet Pimpernel and Secret Operative ZX42 rolled into one," Mr. Howe shouted. He sounded as though he were in the final heat of a hog-calling contest. John wondered why he found the voice vaguely pleasant. "With Arnie Zucker it's all secret panels, and don't put anything on paper, and never say anything so nobody will ever be able to have anything on you. The old *misterioso* act, but I'm different. I'm not that kind of guy. With me it's all out in the open, fella. When I like somebody, I say so. Right out. Like that. When I want something, I go after it. Straight from the shoulder. No double talk. I just go. Arnie says to me on the phone you and he had this talk this morning, and he thinks he's got you interested, let's wait until we see if you're interested enough to make the call to me that you promised Arnie you *would* make. But I said to hell with that. You know what I mean, fella?"

"Well," said John. He suddenly knew why Mr. Howe's rasping, high-pitched voice had struck him as vaguely pleasant. It reminded him of Ike Ten Eyck, the hard-drinking old handyman who had tended the furnace in the main building at Deucalion and made most of the repairs in the outlying cottages. When he drove the Ford truck into Wellesville either to pick up groceries for Mrs. Loring, the cook, or to meet the train on which John's father came up from New York every Friday afternoon, Ike would be allowed to take John along. Provided the handyman first passed Mrs. Sayer's own private drunkometer test.

"I mean what the hell, fella," Mr. Howe shrieked into John's ear. John suddenly smiled with pleasure. Across the years, almost thirty of them, he had once again heard Ike Ten Eyck's shriek of protest as Mrs. Sayer, hands on hips, insisted that either he successfully carried the two walnuts, one sitting on the back of each of his two outstretched hands, from the south entrance of the main dining room to the north entrance, and by successfully, Ike, I mean without dropping them, if you please, or you will have to drive down into Wellesville without the benefit of John's company.

"What?" John said, thirty years later, into the phone on Lexington Avenue. "Sorry, Mr. Howe. I missed that."

"I said what the hell, fella," Mr. Howe said. "I want to do this show, and this John Sayer is the guy who can help me get it off the ground, so why all this secret operative stuff, and let's wait and see if he calls me like he promised Arnie Zucker he would. I want to do it? Okay, what the hell, nuts to wait and see. *I'll* make the call, which is what I'm doing right now. How you fixed, fella?"

Startled, as though he had been approached on a dark street and offered a pinch of heroin or a packet of feelthy pictures, John said, "In what respect?"

"You got nothing on now, I could come right up to see you, fella," Mr. Howe said. "I'm just around the corner."

"Well, now, wait," John said.

"It's no inconvenience, fella."

John had not been thinking of Mr. Howe's convenience. He decided, however, that he preferred thinking of that to thinking his other thoughts, and said, "I'm all the way over here on Lexington and you're—"

His voice stopped. First, because it had suddenly occurred to him that perhaps he was wrong in assuming Mr. Howe's office was over on the West Side, in the theatrical district. Second, because Mr. Howe was screaming again.

"No inconvenience at all, fella. You're in the Erbst Building. Sit tight. Be right over, fella."

Replacing the dead phone, John was only mildly amused by the emotion that now assailed him: a desire to lock his door; to call Miss Faille and order her to bar the outer door; perhaps even to call the building superintendent and ask him to tell everybody who entered the lobby for the rest of the day that he had moved from the building and could not be reached until further notice. The exaggerated desire to prevent Mr. Howe from getting to him settled down into a more sensible need to gird his loins, as it were, against the imminent visit. John picked up the phone.

"Miss Faille, get Mrs. Sayer, please," he said. "And Miss Faille?"

"Yes, Mr. Sayer?"

"That Mr. Howe? The one who just called?"

"Yes?"

"He's on his way over here now," John said. "When he comes, bring him right in, but first I'll speak to Mrs. Sayer."

As it turned out, he didn't speak to her for very long. Ellie had given him the exact figures on the Porte School voting that had resulted in Sam's victory; and John had confessed cheerfully to her accusation that he was acting like a foolish doting parent; and Ellie was reminding him that the Heemuths were coming to dinner, so would he please not be late, when her voice suddenly stopped. There was a pause and then, not quite anxiously, but with a hint of tension, Ellie said, "John, is anything wrong?"

"Wrong?" he said. "You mean here? With me?"

"Yes."

"No," John said. "Why do you ask?"

"I suddenly had the feeling you weren't listening to me."

"Must be the acoustics," John said. "That damn building going up across the street."

There was another pause. It increased his uneasiness. It was broken by Ellie. "John, you're sure?"

"Of course I'm sure," John said. Then he hesitated, wishing he could recall the words, or the emphasis with which he had pushed them into the mouthpiece. He had, after all, called to gain sustenance from her, to gird his loins, as he had put it, against the invasion of the present he had fashioned with Ellie by the past that had been thrust upon him. But he was too late. The door had opened and Miss Faille was coming in. She was followed by a jaunty little man who looked so much like Ike Ten Eyck that John's first startled thought was: *No wonder he sounds like him!* "Ellie," he said into the phone, "I've got a visitor. See you tonight."

"All right," Ellie said. "Take care."

Of what, John wondered as he rose to meet his visitor. The feeling that he was on the brink of trouble, which he had carried with him out of Mr. Zucker's apartment in the Hotel Stanton; the apprehension that had filled him from the moment he realized Mr. Howe was on his way to this room—all had vanished abruptly now that Mr. Howe was in it.

Mr. Howe came forward, his hand out straight at the end of his rigid arm, as though he were measuring the space available for a piece of furniture he contemplated bringing into the room. He said, "How are you, fella?"

"Great," said John, and indeed he felt he had never used the word more accurately. "Nice to meet you, Mr. Howe."

"Same here, fella," said Mr. Howe. Even though John knew he should ask his visitor to sit down, he delayed making the request. He indulged himself in another moment of the pure pleasure he was getting from the sight of Mr. Howe standing up. Like Ike Ten Eyck, who according to John's mother had done it because he was always half seas over, Mr. Howe stood at a slant. He resembled one of those hitching posts for gondolas in the canals of Venice. The illusion that he was leaning to one side was underscored by Mr. Howe's clothes and his features. The bold stripes on his brown tie went in the direction toward which he inclined. His tan felt hat, surrounded by the sort of narrow brown band John associated with Texans, was cocked rakishly on the side of his head nearest the floor. His long, pointed nose, the direction of which looked as though it had been rearranged in a youthful fight, followed the lines of Mr. Howe's tie. And his infectiously crooked grin was crooked in the same direction. Then Mr. Howe took off his hat. His thinning hair, which Sam had guessed from the framed black and white photograph on Mr. Zucker's piano was sandy, proved to be somewhat lighter. John had to resist the impulse to hug his visitor. Ike Ten Eyck's hair, when Ike had been Mr. Howe's age, had been exactly the same color.

"Something wrong, fella?" Mr. Howe said worriedly.

"On the contrary," John said. "Forgive me. Please sit down. I didn't mean to stare. It's just that you reminded me of someone I know. Someone," he added as Mr. Howe sat down, "I used to like very much."

It did not surprise John Sayer that he had almost said: *Someone I used to love very much.*

"That's great, fella," Mr. Howe said. The worried look vanished. His delightful smile resumed its crooked, downward slant. "If I remind you of someone you like, that's a step forward with the project. If I'd reminded you of someone you *didn't* like, fella, then I'd be in trouble, boy."

"Well, you're not in trouble," John said. "At least not in that respect."

Mr. Howe's appearance, manner, and even tone of voice seemed to have been put together by Norman Rockwell. He belonged in a *Saturday Evening Post* cover depicting the simple, homey, but rugged and enduring virtues of the Yankee temperament. Nevertheless, John noticed that Mr. Howe was giving John's office—swiftly, efficiently, and with no visible damage to the overall impression of an open-eyed, eager, affable country scoutmaster examining strange surroundings —what John's sons called the hairy eyeball. Bringing his glance back to John behind the desk, Mr. Howe somehow managed to convey the impression that, under the engagingly innocent smile, his busy little mind had raked up, from the darting survey of the room, the equivalent of a Dun & Bradstreet report on the financial status of Heemuth & Sayer.

"Mr. Sayer, I don't think with a man like you, fella, I'm ever going to be in trouble," Mr. Howe said. John felt a glow of warmth for Ellie and the things she had put into the room when he rented the suite. The small Miro lithograph (marked in one corner XXXIV); the unframed blue grapefruit, curiously and for some reason movingly dented at the top, that had come off the fence of a Washington Square outdoor exhibit; the Bahooli burial figure Ellie's aunt had brought back from a visit to Tangier; all were inexpensive, but quite obviously, because in a lawyer's office they were unexpected, Mr. Howe had assumed the contrary. He said, "The percentages on these deals are cut and dried. All worked out by the Dramatists' Guild. So even if a man wanted to be greedy and cause trouble, he couldn't."

"You mean the Dramatists' Guild has worked out the terms of legal fees?" John said.

Mr. Howe looked thoughtful, as though he had been asked to phrase the handful of words that were going to be inscribed on a silver cup. Then he smiled.

"No, but what it comes to, we figured it this way," he said. "You join the project, you fix your fee. What you feel as the lawyer for the thing you're entitled to. For your services, I mean, and okay, you've got a figure. But if instead of a fixed fee, if we cut you in, or your firm, if we cut you in for one per cent of the gross, you get that piece of money every single week the show is running. Not only here in New York, but all over. On the road, other countries, everywhere. And then later, stock and amateur rights. Every time for the next fifty-six years, as long as it's in copyright, which is twenty-eight years plus one renewal for another twenty-eight, as I'm sure I don't have to tell a lawyer, all those fifty-six years, whenever *Deucalion* gets played, you get yourself a piece of money, fella. And if you're gone, the wife and kiddies get it, if you know what I mean."

"I'm not sure that I do," John said. "When you say *we* figured it this way, do you mean you and Arnold Zucker?"

"Well, sure," Mr. Howe said. "Arnie represents Gwen."

"Who is Gwen?"

Again Mr. Howe looked thoughtful, as though the people for whom he had prepared the inscription that was to go on the silver cup had asked him to shorten it. This time, to the smile that terminated his musing, Mr. Howe added a chuckle.

"That Arnie," he said. "He'd make a secret out of his own name, if you'd let him. Gwen is Gwendolyn Quill, the director. She's going to do *Deucalion* with me, and she's a client of Arnie Zucker's." Mr. Howe paused. He seemed troubled by what he saw on John Sayer's face. The jaunty little man shifted the angle at which he normally leaned. He said anxiously, "You've *heard* of Gwen Quill, haven't you?"

The anxiety in his voice, plus the shift in position, was like a moment of the past thrown on a brightly lighted screen. This, John remembered, was the way Ike Ten Eyck looked and sounded when, having sent the boy up to the commissary back of the main house to sneak a bottle of grape tonic from Mrs. Loring's stores, he would peer out from behind the lilac bush at the foot of the hill to see if John had succeeded.

"I'm afraid I haven't," John said. "I suppose I should, but as I explained to Mr. Zucker this morning, my contacts with the theatre have been limited."

"What Gwen is, she's a phenomenon," Mr. Howe said. "There have never been many women directors in the theatre. Don't ask me why. And until Gwen came along last year with *Fig Leaf*, I don't think there'd been one for years and years and years. I mean a real active one."

"Oh, did she direct that?" John said. *"Fig Leaf?"*

"She sure did," Mr. Howe said proudly. "Some job, hey, fella?"

"I don't really know," John said. "I haven't seen it. But friends of mine, *they* saw it, and they said it's wonderful."

"That's the word, wonderful," Mr. Howe said. He pulled a small black leather book from his pocket. "When would you and Mrs. Sayer like to go?" He plucked a tiny gold pencil from a loop on the side of the book. "I'll send you a couple of house seats."

"Oh, no, wait, thanks," John said. "You don't have to do that."

"I *want* to do it, fella," Mr. Howe said. As the producer toyed with the little book, John saw, fastened to the leather cover like a brooch to a woman's dress, a reproduction in gold of a scrawled signature. It was completely illegible but it matched a similar, smaller scrawl imbedded in the golden bar that held Mr. Howe's striped tie fastened to his shirt. "You and Gwen are going to work together," he said. "You ought to see the kind of thing she does. When would you like to go?"

"I'll ask my wife and let you know," John said. "How do you mean I'm going to work with her? Miss Quill, is it?"

"Yes, like in John Hancock signing the Declaration of Independence," Mr. Howe said. Then he grinned shyly and said, "I'm quoting Gwen. She always says that when people ask about her name. You have a name like that, it's so short and simple, Quill, you'd think people would get it right off. But they don't, so Gwen always makes that joke."

"I take it then that what you and Miss Quill have in mind is not a funny play?"

"Oh, no," Mr. Howe said, and then he looked troubled. "I didn't mean that that's the only kind of joke Gwen is capable of," he said. "That's just something she always *says,* fella. You know what I mean?"

"Of course," said John. He didn't, but was beginning to suspect, as he compared this meeting with his earlier meeting in Mr. Zucker's suite at the Stanton, that in dealing with theatre people, at least those engaged in the managerial end, it was probably best not to press too hard for total comprehension in the early phases of a discussion. What he had in the morning suspected was deviousness on Mr. Zucker's part, John now saw, from watching and listening to Mr. Howe, was probably no more than the deeply imbedded knowledge, undoubtedly gleaned from experience, that to say too much was to end up saying nothing. Until all the elements of a "project" were assembled, there was no project. And the assembling process was apparently so complicated and delicate that, by a word spoken too soon, a fact revealed before the revelation should have come, the project as well as the assembling process might vanish forever like a puff of smoke in a gust of wind. John said, "I got the impression from Mr. Zucker this morning that what you had in mind was a musical comedy, and perhaps, like most laymen, I've been interpreting the word comedy much too literally."

"Well, you know, a few laughs never did any harm at the box office," Mr. Howe said. "And I'm sure by the time Gwen has this one finished, there will be many a chuckle in *Deuca-*

lion. But basically, what she's after, what we're *both* after, Gwen and I, we want a play of stature. Something worthy of the kind of man Sennacherib Sayer was, and what he was shooting for up there in Dutchess County thirty years ago. You agree, fella?"

Wondering what Mr. Howe's reaction would be if he said he disagreed, John said, "Naturally, of course, yes. But do you mind if I go back a bit? You say by the time Miss Quill has this one finished. Finished how? I assume with a musical show you need a composer and a lyricist and a writer. For the nonmusical scenes, I mean. I assume you need all those people in *addition* to a director. Isn't that so?"

Mr. Howe seemed to find the question troublesome, as though it were a clause in a treaty that had been sprung on him at the conference table without warning. Like Ike Ten Eyck when, peering around the lilac bush at the bottom of the hill, the handyman saw that John had succeeded in pinching a bottle of grape tonic, Mr. Howe's face suddenly spread in a smile.

"Look, I got an idea," he said eagerly. "How's about you and me, Mr. Sayer, how's about the both of us, right now, we go round the corner to see Gwen? She lives on East Fifty-fifth between Lex and Third. She's dying to meet you, and I know you'll like her, and she can answer all your questions." Mr. Howe jumped up. He snatched his hat from the desk. He fitted it to the side of his head at the angle that synchronized with the stripes in his tie and the slant of his smile, and said, "How about it, fella?"

Amused by the response to his simple question, John ran back over it in his mind, and decided there was no reason why the question could not be answered here, in his own office.

"Mr. Howe," he said, "all I asked was won't you need these other people?"

"Let's walk around the corner to see Gwen," Mr. Howe said. "She knows more about all this than I do."

John said, "But I thought you are the producer?"

"I am," Mr. Howe said. "Sure."

"Then how can Miss Quill know more about it than you do?"

"It's her idea," Mr. Howe said. "She brought it to me."

John thrust from his mind the irrelevant image of Miss Quill carrying the idea into Mr. Howe's presence like a page boy bringing the wedding ring on a satin pillow to the groom. John said, "From where?"

Mr. Howe hesitated, leaning steadily to the left. Then, slowly, he removed his hat, placed it on the desk, and sat down.

"You know the U.S. Foundry Hour?" he said.

The wild irrelevance of Mr. Howe's reply sent John's thoughts scattering. Then, as he began to pull them together, he realized that the words had meaning.

"You mean the television show?" John said.

Mr. Howe nodded, smiling encouragingly, like a teacher urging on to greater effort a backward child that has suddenly begun to display surprising signs of intelligence.

"That's right, fella," Mr. Howe said. "The U.S. Foundry Hour." A muted but proud blare of trumpets seemed to carry the six syllables across the desk toward John. The name of this television show seemed to stir in Mr. Howe the sort of emotions that had once elicited from Stephen Decatur his famous statement about his feelings for his country. "The U.S. Foundry Hour is the greatest single program in the whole history of television, I don't have to tell you," Mr. Howe said. Perhaps he didn't, but Mr. Howe went right on and told John nonetheless. "In spite of all the ups and downs of the industry, the scared sponsors, the ass-licking advertising agencies, the crappy westerns, the dirty-raincoat private eyes, the hoked up medicos and what not, in spite of all that, the U.S. Foundry Hour has gone on, year after year, week after week, giving the American public every seven days a fine, serious, important play. *Live,* not on film. Real actors, like you're in a theatre, produced right here in New York. A serious play every damn week. A play that every week it's *about* something. Real people. In a real situation. Facing real problems. Like you and me. That's quite an achievement, fella, quite an achievement, and it's no secret on the street that the reason for the success of the U.S. Foundry Hour, what made it tick, what kept it going, what gave it *life,* for God's sake, was Gwen Quill."

John had seen a few of the U.S. Foundry Hour plays. He wondered uneasily about Miss Quill's definition of life. He remembered that, when he was in his teens, after he had left the farm in Dutchess County and was going to Norcross Academy and regularly visiting New York, he had been caught up along with his classmates in the excitement of the new drama that had erupted on the American scene in the early thirties. The fact that so much of it was rooted in and dominated by a left-wing political point of view had seemed perfectly natural at the time. Then, since his interest had been only that of a spectator, just as his interest in books had been no more than that of a reader, John had forgotten all about the new drama as his life had been caught up first by the war and, after he got out of the army, by the problems of earning a living. It was not until he was married, and had settled with Ellie in Stamford to raise their two sons, a process inevitably involving the purchase of a television set, that John began to remember the plays he had seen in the early thirties. What reminded him were programs like the U.S. Foundry Hour. The plays put on the air by these programs were disturbingly reminiscent of the turbulent dramas John had seen on Broadway in his teens. For a long time he wondered why he should find them disturbing. Then, one morning, reading his paper along with the other commuters on the train into New York, John happened to glance at the television page and saw a review of the U.S. Foundry Hour show he and Ellie had watched the night before. "A Drama of Inner Conflict," said the headline over the review, and all at once John knew what had been bothering him about all those television plays. They were *too* inner. They were the work of people who had been frightened away from looking outward. The left-wing point of view of the thirties had become unpopular and dangerous. The playwrights who wrote for television, being human, wanted popularity and disliked danger. So they had taken the left-wing plays of the thirties and were rewriting them to suit their special needs. They eliminated all references to dangerous and unpopular political points of view. Relentlessly they forced their characters to live in a world apparently devoid of politics. A world in which people did not function in relation to a surrounding world of many other human beings whose existence and problems affected the existence and problems of every human being. The television playwrights had invented for their own convenience—or perhaps for the convenience of the sponsors who wanted no traffic with the unpleasant problems of the real world—a totally unreal world in which all that mattered, or so the audience was told, was the problem of the character or characters about whom the playwrights were writing. Since almost none of these characters was particularly complex, the process of continuing to dig into them, long after it was obvious that there was nothing more to be found worth watching or discussing, had a tendency to become repetitious. It was like continuing to hunt desperately for money in a suit after it has been clearly established that all the pockets are empty. The only way out of the dilemma was, therefore, to treat the act of repetition as an admirable end in itself. Therefore, since the characters in one U.S. Foundry Hour play explored pretty much the same shallow emotional terrain as the characters in every other U.S. Foundry Hour play, it was the backgrounds against which the exploration was conducted that received the attention of the producers and directors. Watching this process could be interesting, even amusing. The swimmers churning away so industriously in an empty pool, looking for all the world like real people immersed in real water, were they going to be put through their act this week against a background of Southern California palm trees, Bushwick Avenue garbage cans, or Harlem fire escapes? It could be interesting, even amusing, as long as you were not involved. But John was being urged to become involved. And John was suddenly wondering if he wanted to become involved through someone who, according to Vincent Howe, had made the U.S. Foundry Hour tick, had kept it going, and had given it life.

"Has Miss Quill given up television?" John said. "I mean, now that she's directed *Fig Leaf,* and it's such a big hit, and that percentage of the gross you were just telling me about, coming in as it does every week, as you said, I should think Miss Quill would consider television pretty small potatoes now?"

"She certainly does," Mr. Howe said. He smiled happily, as though the backward child had demonstrated signs of catching on that were beyond his wildest dreams. "Gwen is finished with all that crap," he said. Then some fragment of experience seemed to nudge him into a recollection of the hard and often dismal fact that burning one's bridges could prove to be an unprofitable as well as an exhilarating business. Mr. Howe added hastily, "Not that all of television is crap, fella, if you know what I mean. After all, hell, look at the great things the medium has done." Mr. Howe looked thoughtfully at the Miro lithograph, as though in the seemingly pointless but acutely delicious arrangement of circles and squares he could read a list of the great things television had done. Perhaps because the list eluded him, Mr. Howe said, "The thing is, everybody wants to move onward and upward, and Gwen is no exception. She learned a lot in television, and she gave back a lot, as anyone who knows what she did for the U.S.

Foundry Hour will agree. But the theatre is her real love, as *Fig Leaf* has demonstrated, and now she's ready to move onward and upward from *that*."

"From *Fig Leaf?*" John said.

Mr. Howe's charming, crooked smile took on a boyish touch.

"From *Fig Leaf*," he said, nodding happily. "And Gwen figures *Decaulion* is it. That's why she came to me with it."

The light, which had been cowering shyly in the background, as for so long it had cowered that morning in Mr. Zucker's apartment, suddenly began to dawn. John said, "You mean it was a television idea?"

Mr. Howe seemed to find the question so distressing that for a moment he leaned—smile, nose, tie stripes and all—in the opposite direction. But only for a moment.

"What's wrong with that?" he said.

John hesitated, then decided to tell him.

"Mr. Howe," he said, "I don't like to think that what my father tried to do up in Dutchess County thirty years ago, even if the experiment failed, amounts to nothing more than a U.S. Foundry Hour television show."

Mr. Howe went back to leaning in the direction nature had quite obviously decreed was best for him. He also smiled.

"Neither does Gwen," he said. "That's why she brought the idea to me. All those years she was doing the U.S. Foundry Hour show, Gwen was coming up with ideas like Mickey Mantle with homers. One after the other, bang, bang, bang. But not all of them got on the air. The system is brutal, fella. First she'd have to get the idea through the producer. Then he'd have to take it to the network. And the network had to take it to the advertising agency. And the agency had to take it to the sponsor, where with these sponsors, a cigarette company, say, or like U.S. Foundry, there could be a dozen vice-presidents, maybe more. Not to mention their wives, every one of them they put their two cents in to say no, the idea stinks. So that with her best ideas, which were naturally about real things, issues that affect the lives of real people, I mean, with those ideas Gwen was going crazy. All the way up the line, no matter how many of these monkeys she'd get through, there was always another guy higher up who could say no. Sacco and Vanzetti, for instance, that one got killed by a sponsor's wife."

John said, his voice rising slightly, "Miss Quill wanted to do a U.S. Foundry Hour show on the Sacco-Vanzetti case?"

"Sure," Mr. Howe said. "She was full of ideas like that. Sacco-Vanzetti? Out, said this vice-president's better half. They were a couple of anarchists. The Battle of Jutland? No dice. In the agency itself they killed *that* one. On account, this guy said, we've had enough German war stuff on the air. You know why they killed Gwen's Lewis and Clark idea? The network itself? It never even got to the agency?"

John wondered if there was enough justification for the feeling of respect for the unknown Miss Quill that had suddenly invaded his sense of distaste about her background. He said, "Why?"

"This guy in the network had a wife who was Alcoholics Anonymous," Mr. Howe said. "And he'd read somewhere, it turned out later he'd made a mistake, he'd read it about somebody else, but by then it was too late. Gwen's Lewis and Clark idea was killed dead. He'd read somewhere, this network guy, he'd read Lewis, Meriwether Lewis, Gwen says his name was, he'd read somewhere Meriwether Lewis had been a lush. Can you beat that?"

"No," John said. "Not in the television field, about which I know very little. But I once lost an accident case because my client's wife, he was suing a railroad, I lost the case because his wife came to court in slacks."

Mr. Howe's eyes narrowed. John was not surprised to notice that they narrowed at a slant that matched the stripes on the tie, the smile, and the general inclination toward the left.

"I don't get it," Howe said.

"The judge was offended by a woman coming into his courtroom in slacks," John said. "And he said so, and I could tell the jury was affected by his statement."

Mr. Howe shook his head ruefully at the incongruous surprises imbedded in the human landscape. He said, "Christ, and I thought *I* was in a crazy business."

"You *do* think that?" John said.

The rueful look on Mr. Howe's face changed to a grimace of worry.

"How do you mean, fella?" he said.

"*Is* the theatre a crazy business?" John said.

The grimace of worry vanished into the creases of the Norman Rockwell smile.

"No more so than any other business," Mr. Howe said. "You take a thousand people, you put them all together in a room, *any* kind of people in *any* kind of room, and let me tell you something, fella. One of those thousand people will say *anything,* absolutely *anything.*"

The incontestable truth of this statement, which John had suspected for years but had never before heard expressed in quite this way, caused him to look at the jaunty little slanting man with admiration.

"What you're saying, Mr. Howe, is you don't think the theatre is any crazier than any other business?"

"I'm saying don't worry about the craziness of it," Mr. Howe said. "What counts is not the craziness. What counts is you come up with a hit. Take *Fig Leaf.* That was one of Gwen's ideas for the U.S. Foundry Hour. Adam and Eve. What could be more natural? The original love story of all time? You know what killed it?"

"Too difficult to cast the part of the serpent?" John said.

Mr. Howe wagged his forefinger in the air. "Arnie Zucker said to watch out for you," he said with a chuckle. "This boy makes with the jokes, Arnie said."

"Mr. Zucker is too kind," John said. But he was not unaware of a small glow of pleasure. "Why did the U.S. Foundry Hour turn down Miss Quill's *Fig Leaf* idea?"

"Sponsor's wife again," Mr. Howe said. "This vice-president had taken a cruise with his wife to the Near East, and it seems they'd seen some actual fig trees, and when Gwen's idea for the Adam and Eve show was bumped upstairs, step by step, it gets to this vice-president, and he happens to mention it to his wife that night. She says nothing doing, you saw those fig leaves when we were in Beirut or Lebanon or some such place. Fig leaves, she says, are much smaller than I thought."

John felt his eyelids blink up and down, very fast, and then he heard himself burst into a sharp guffaw. He said, "Mr. Howe, you are kidding!"

Mr. Howe glowed as though he had received a Presidential citation. He shook his head and said, "Fact. That's what the lady said, so Gwen figured to hell with this. She'd had a bellyful. She gets hold of Leonard Lawrence, he's one of the writers on the U.S. Foundry Hour, and she says Leonard, I am fed up but up to here. How about we get out of this booby hatch and try a piece of the real world? In short, fella, she got Leonard to do the Adam and Eve idea as a play, all on spec, of course, and when it's finished Gwen brings it to me, and me, I flip, of course, and, well, the rest is history. Good old *Fig Leaf.* Fifteenth month at the Plymouth. Not an empty seat. Not an empty standing room slot in all that time. Every week, like clockwork, the gross is forty-two thousand eight hundred and sixteen bucks. And it's going to be that way another eight months, maybe a year, believe me. By which time, fella, I expect to have *Deucalion* running across the street at the good old Imperial. How about it, fella? Shall we all get rich together?"

"If you don't mind answering a couple of questions first," John said.

"Shoot," Mr. Howe said.

"How much of that weekly forty-two thousand eight hundred and sixteen dollars gross does the lawyer for *Fig Leaf* get?"

Mr. Howe took John by surprise. The leaning man's face seemed so constructed that it was incapable of reflecting anything that resembled even remotely an expression of distaste. Yet now it reflected annoyance.

"There *is* no lawyer for *Fig Leaf*," Mr. Howe said curtly. "The papers were drawn by my regular lawyers, who get a yearly retainer from me, and anything extra, extra work they do, they bill me. They don't get any percentages of any grosses."

"Then why should I get a percentage of the gross of *Deucalion?*" John said.

"Because *Deucalion* is different," Mr. Howe said. "And so are you."

"In what way?"

"*Deucalion* is a play about a man and a place that really existed," Mr. Howe said. "You're the son of that man, and you were born and raised on that place. You can contribute more to this project, fella, than any lawyer can contribute to any other project. Gwen will be asking you, for example, while she's writing it, she'll be asking you to check her on the facts."

"Oh," John said. "Miss Quill will be writing this play as well as directing it?"

"That's right," Mr. Howe said.

"What happened to Leonard Lawrence?"

"He's got another project."

"One he likes better than *Deucalion?*"

"*Deucalion* was never offered to Leonard."

"Why not?"

"Gwen wanted to do this one herself right from the start."

"Because she felt Mr. Lawrence was not right for it?" John

said. "Or because Miss Quill wanted, as you put it, Mr. Howe, to move onward and upward?"

"What's the difference?" Mr. Howe said.

"I don't know," John said. He didn't, but he had a nagging feeling that the knowledge was important. "Has Miss Quill done any writing before?"

"I don't know how that matters," Mr. Howe said.

"Only in the way you pointed out yourself," John said. "What you are proposing is a play about a real man and a real place. A man who was my father. A place where I was born. It seems to me it matters a great deal whether the person who is going to write the play has had any experience as a writer."

"Gwen is convinced she can do this job," Mr. Howe said.

"How do you feel?" John said.

"I'm convinced Gwen can do it," Mr. Howe said.

"Then the only person left to convince is me," John said.

All the slanting lines of Mr. Howe's face and figure joined in a Q.E.D. smile and gesture.

"That's why I been asking you to come around the corner to Gwen's apartment and meet her."

"Meeting her won't convince me of her ability as a writer, will it?" John said.

"She's done an outline," Mr. Howe said. "Scene by scene. It's very complete and I think it's great. Gwen wants to read it to you."

John was not quite sure why he should feel this was the last thing *he* wanted at the moment. He wondered how the discussion, which he had felt was under his control, had been snatched away from him. Firmly, trying to keep out of his voice the sense of defeat that puzzled and alarmed him, John said, "I'd like to hear it, but I'm afraid I can't make it today." He leaned forward, glancing at his desk calendar, and added, "I'm booked solid for the rest of the afternoon. But how about tomorrow?"

"Gwen will be disappointed," Mr. Howe said. "She's waiting."

"I'm sorry," John said. "You gave me no warning, and it's too late to call off these other appointments."

"In that case," Mr. Howe said, getting up and again taking his hat from the desk, "I guess tomorrow it is, fella. What's a good time for you?"

"What's a good time for Miss Quill?" John said.

"You pick it," Mr. Howe said. "She said to suit your convenience."

"I'll call your office tomorrow morning," John said. "Say ten sharp, and we'll fix the exact time."

"Good enough, fella," said Mr. Howe. All of him leaned into the movement with which he thrust out his hand. "I have a feeling this is the start of something big."

John wished, as he saw his visitor to the door, that he could discard the same feeling. The trouble was that, while he felt something was indeed starting, he was not sure that he wanted it to start. On the other hand, he felt no strong desire to stop it, whatever "it" was. John was amused to realize that his feelings were not unlike those he'd had years ago, during his first experience with girls, when, both eager and afraid, he could at one and the same time be excited by, and blush for, his crude fumblings with buttons and zippers. He shrugged the thought away.

Why did everything draw him back into the past? He couldn't relive it. He couldn't change it. What was done was done, Ike Ten Eyck used to say as he took another swig from the pilfered grape tonic bottle. It was hardly the greatest of philosophical truths, John knew. Yet it was a truth nonetheless. What diluted it, of course, to the point where it seemed almost a lie, was the stubbornly unreasonable belief that the past *could* be changed. That what was done could be undone. If only the moment of the wrong turning could be recaptured. If the fork in the road could be faced once again. If the opportunity to make the choice could once again be presented.

Miss Quill had an outline. Scene by scene, Mr. Howe had said. John did not know where the scenes had come from, but he could imagine. The facts about Deucalion, which most of the world had forgotten, were a part of many public records. Miss Quill had had at her command the research staff of the U.S. Foundry Hour. She had no doubt unearthed most of these facts. John, who knew them all, knew no reason why he should be reluctant to hear them. Yet his reluctance was as real as his eagerness.

What he needed, John suddenly realized, was some form of reassurance. Even as he turned toward the phone to call Ellie, he knew she could not provide it. Ellie had not been a part of the past.

"Miss Faille," John said into the phone, "I'm going out. An appointment I almost forgot. Would you call Mrs. Sayer

and tell her something unexpected came up, so I might be a
little late for dinner, but I'll try not to be."

The attempt involved getting to Grand Central in eleven
minutes. John managed to do this by not even trying to find a
cab or wait for a bus. He had discovered long ago, in his
days as a commuter, that by walking at a normally brisk
pace, he could cover a city block, including the short wait for
passing traffic at the curb of each cross street, in sixty seconds. By putting on the pressure when he was late or in a
hurry, he could reduce this to forty-five seconds. Thus, the
distance from the front entrance of the T. Turner Erbst
Building at Fifty-fourth and Lexington to the Forty-third
Street entrance to Grand Central on Lexington had long ago
become for John a journey of either eleven comfortable minutes or slightly more than eight mildly uncomfortable minutes.

He did not realize, until he dropped into a window seat on
the Stamford local, that what had made this most recent walk
down Lexington a mildly uncomfortable one was not the feeling that he was late, and therefore had better put the pressure
on, but his uneasiness about whether the 2:10 was still running. It jerked into life immediately, as though the engineer
up front had been waiting to be told Mr. Sayer had come
aboard. John had heard nothing about the 2:10 for two
years, ever since he and Ellie had moved in from Stamford to
the city.

John's knowledge about the habits of the 2:10 had all been
gleaned from Ellie. She used to take it back to Stamford on
days when she dropped Sam and Jim in Miss Willett's Country Day School on Dearborn Lane at 9:00 and then dashed
into New York on the 9:35 for a morning of shopping. If all
went well, the 2:10 would get her to Stamford at 2:55, just
—but only just—in time to get to Dearborn Lane and pick
up the children as the final strains of "Farewell, Dear
Teacher, Farewell to Thee," the song with which Miss Willett
closed each day at her school, were rolling out onto the sand-
box and the seesaw.

John hummed the almost insanely banal but infectious
melody as he looked out the cracked train window. He had
picked up the tune years ago, like measles, during a Parents'
Day visit to his sons' first school. Between the two layers of
window glass the trapped remnants of an old rainstorm
sloshed back and forth, creating the impression in John's

mind that he was peering out through a porthole in heavy weather. In a way, he was. He knew that the weather was of his own creation. He knew also that the porthole was a lens he had deliberately interposed between the events of the morning and his memory of their origins. This knowledge did not change John's feeling that his destination was obscure. A phrase from one of the posters the government had slapped up all over the country during the war in an attempt to get the civilian population to save fuel slid into his mind: IS THIS TRIP NECESSARY?

John didn't know. He knew only that a part of his life, which had long ago been laid away neatly like a bundle of old love letters in the attic of memory, had been dragged out unexpectedly by Arnold Zucker and Vincent Howe and their project. Tomorrow morning Miss Gwen Quill was going to read the old letters aloud. John guessed that what he was doing was not unlike the games the kids of the Deucalion Children's Guild used to play during recess. The games were all different, of course, but in some basic respects they were always the same. They always seemed to involve hiding behind trees and bushes and corners of the Children's Guild building; sudden dashes from hiding places to tag people; chanting in a disguised voice to fool the boy or girl who happened to be "it"; and always, before the fortunes of the game could shift in your favor, there was the wild race to touch home base ahead of your opponents. John Sayer, aged thirty-five and father of two, guessed, as the train slowed down and he rose to walk toward the door, that what he was doing was trying, before he listened to Miss Quill read those letters aloud in the morning, to touch home base.

John walked down to the taxi hut. The man reading a comic book in a chair tipped back against the wall looked up and said, "Oh, hi."

"Hi," said John. He was doing the same thing the man was doing: trying to remember the name that went with the face he had just recognized. "Could you take me out to the Dogwood Lane Rest Home?"

"Glad to," the man said. He bumped himself away from the wall and stood up. He shoved the comic book into his hip pocket, stepped down to the Pontiac at the curb, and held the rear door open until John got in. Then he slammed the door shut, came around to the front, and slid in behind the wheel. As the car pulled away from the station, he said, "You Mr. McGonnigle from over to Powder Horn Hill?"

"No, Sayer," John said. "I used to live on South King's Highway."

"That's right," the driver said. "Thought I recognized you. Been away?"

"Yes," John said. He wondered, as he looked out at the familiar streets and buildings, if he had ever been here. It didn't seem possible that he could have lived in this community for almost eight years and have left behind no reservoir of emotion, however small, on which he should now be drawing. It didn't seem possible, but it was. Not only did he feel nothing for this place to which he had brought his bride and in which his sons had been born; John found it difficult to believe he had ever lived here. This capacity to close off a piece of the past, to wipe out a part of his life as though it had never existed, was all at once terrifying. It was as though he had been suddenly told, by a doctor whose diagnosis could not be dismissed or even questioned, a monstrous truth about himself. Had he done with the years of his youth what he had done with his recent years here in Stamford? If so, why? What was he afraid of? Aside from the act of commuting, which had been at first irksome and later exhausting, the years in Stamford, when the children were growing up, had been brightly hued. If the desire to obliterate the weariness of the daily act of travel had carried away with it all of the happy time in which the act had been imbedded, what had been carried away with the desire to forget the shadowy areas of his youth? Turning irritably from the terror of what might have been lost, John said sharply, "You go down the Post Road to the second light, then turn left at the Congregational Church."

"I know," the driver said. Then, as though to establish the credentials for his knowledge, he said, "Nice place, the Dogwood Lane Rest Home." John nodded. The driver seemed to interpret his silence as criticism, because he added hastily, "Not that I mean it's nice to have to go to one. I mean people get sick, especially old people, it's nice to have a nice place to go to where nice people can take care of you." He cocked his head, looking up into the rear view mirror as though to see how his remarks were being received, and said, "That Miss Sidcup, she's a wonder."

"Nice woman," John said, "yes."

Encouraged by his fare's more relaxed tone, the driver said, "Did you know she served with the Red Cross in the First World War?"

"Really?" John said.

"Fact," the driver said. "They say she invented a special kind of tourniquet, it saved hundreds of lives at that battle, Château Thierry, if I'm pronouncing it right? French?"

"Sounds right to me," John said.

"She was so famous, Miss Sidcup, this Admiral Byrd, those expeditions to the South Pole? Remember?" John nodded again. The driver said, "They say Admiral Byrd wanted to take Miss Sidcup along, but on account of it was no women, only men, she didn't get to go."

"Too bad," said John. He wished he could concentrate on what the driver was saying, because the man's voice had a soothing effect.

"But she got to go to lots of other places," the driver said. "Scotland, Africa, even out there in the desert, Arizona, I think, those Indians. She was out there working with them. We're mighty proud of her here in Stamford. Miss Sidcup is a local girl, you know."

"So I'd heard," John said.

"Fact," the driver said. "Seems funny to be calling a woman that age a girl. She must be sixty, sixty-five, I guess. But we think of her as a girl. I suppose because she never married."

The taxi pulled up under the white-latticed porte-cochère. John got out and paid the driver. The smile on the driver's face changed, as he pocketed the money, to one of artificial but nonetheless grave concern. His voice dropped to a level of almost pious sympathy. He said, "Hope everything is okay, Mr. McGonnigle."

John, walking up the three wooden steps, hoped so, too. Then, just inside the door of the once elaborate Hewitt family's foyer that was now the Dogwood Lane Rest Home's waiting room, he stopped to wonder what the hope meant. How could everything be okay for someone waiting for death? Or for those waiting with him?

"Yes?"

John came out of his troubled thoughts. He turned toward the woman he assumed was a nurse. It was difficult to tell. All the employees, male and female, in the Dogwood Lane Rest Home resembled one another: elderly, yet not really old; not-very-bright looking, yet not actually stupid; dressed in white, yet not completely in white; obviously making an effort to keep up with more chores than they could take care of, and yet not really trying very hard.

Ellie's father had spent his last years in a sanatorium near

New Rochelle, and she had found the Dogwood Lane Rest Home for John six years ago. She had explained that it was typical of all country sanatoriums. The help, which was local, was also mostly part-time: housewives and retired workmen living on pensions who were willing to trade a few of their hours for a few extra dollars but were unable, since they had no true call, so to speak, for the nursing profession, to bring genuine warmth or enthusiasm to their work.

"Is it all right if I go down to one forty-two for a few minutes?" John said to the elderly, not-very-bright looking woman in the white dress, blue cardigan, and black tennis sneakers who had addressed him.

"Oh, yes, of course," she said politely, even eagerly. She was clearly relieved to learn that what he wanted involved no effort on her part. Then the troubled look came back into her face. She could have been trying to remember if she had turned off the oven before she left the house to go to work. "Ooh, now, wait," she said. "You say one forty-two?"

"Yes," said John. When he and Ellie lived in Stamford, he used to come here once a week. During the past two years, since they had moved to New York, he had made no more than a dozen visits, perhaps fewer.

"I think—" the woman said, but her thoughts either refused to take shape or were unspeakable. She stopped, shook her head worriedly, and said, "You mind waiting while I go look?"

She pushed through the swinging door that led to the long corridor. As the door chunked back and forth in diminishing arcs, John turned to examine the Blue Cross and Blue Shield advertisements thumb-tacked to the bulletin board on the wall over the switchboard. The switchboard began to buzz. After a few moments, during which the attractions of the Blue Cross prose began to pale, John wondered if he should do anything about the buzzing. Suppose he were calling from New York, as he did every now and then, and there was no answer? Remembering that, on a number of occasions, there had been no answer for quite a long time, John turned toward the switchboard. At this moment Miss Sidcup came into the waiting room through the narrow door at the far end.

"Hello," she said pleasantly to John. In a smooth, unhesitating flow of movement that had a coltish grace surprising in a woman her age, she slid onto the chair behind the switchboard, pulled a gold-tipped red cord from a neat little nest behind the double row of black keys, and plunged it into a golden hole under a glowing light. The light went out. The buzzing stopped. Miss Sidcup's crisply efficient, faintly musical voice said, as she lifted the earpiece to the side of her head, "Dogwood Lane Rest Home, good afternoon."

While she listened, John saw that, with her free hand, Miss Sidcup was making an arithmetical calculation with a silver pencil on a pad she had apparently brought into the room with her.

"Any time at all," she said into the switchboard mouthpiece. Her voice sounded friendly and reassuring and gracious in an inoffensive, ladylike way. Her eyes, and John was sure her mind as well, followed the swift movements of the silver pencil. He had noted on a number of previous occasions Miss Sidcup's talent for doing two or more things at once. "No, we don't have what are known as visiting hours," she said. "We like our patients to feel that they are in the equivalent of their own homes, you see, and we like their friends and relatives to feel the same way. Aside from the middle of the night, and even then, for some people and in certain cases, we have no rules about that, visitors are always welcome. By all means. No, she's fine. I've just come from her room. She's watching television and is in a very cheerful frame of mind. Do come by. Please. Not at all. We love our patients to have visitors. You're quite welcome."

Miss Sidcup pulled the plug from the board. She set down the earpiece. She drew a line under the calculation on the pad. She plunged the silver pencil into the pocket of her starched white blouse. She picked up the pad, rose from the chair and, with a smile and a gesture that reminded John of John Barrymore in *Don Juan* holding out a rose to his newest target, Miss Sidcup said, "How nice to see you, Mr. Sayer."

"I hope I'm not getting in anybody's way," John said. "I suddenly found I had the time to come out for a visit, but I didn't have the time to call, or I'd have missed the train, so I ran for it, and took a chance."

"I'm glad you did," Miss Sidcup said. It struck John that what gave Miss Sidcup the look of someone slightly removed from the hurly-burly of daily life was her posture: she looked as though she were standing in a handsome wooden frame. With her tall, slender figure, blue-white hair, wrinkled face devoid of cosmetics, rimless pince-nez, severe white dress, pleasant but totally impersonal smile, and that curious way of holding her hands, one laid into the palm of the other, as though she were caressing a pair of gloves, Miss Sidcup looked the way she undoubtedly wanted the world to see her: a woman who, without a moment's hesitation or preparation, could step onto any stage or before any camera and play with conviction the role of Florence Nightingale. She said, "I've been meaning to call you."

"Oh, no," John said. He knew what Miss Sidcup meant when she said she'd been meaning to call him. "I thought he can't get out of bed without help?"

"He can't," Miss Sidcup said. "I regret to say that he must have bribed someone to buy it somewhere outside for him and sneak it into his room. Just who, I don't know, and I must confess it distresses me. But try as I do to get the best help possible, I am forced to lean heavily, much *too* heavily, on part-time workers. And they, unfortunately, are not reliable."

Lest this confession be construed as a reflection on her institution, Miss Sidcup tipped her head ever so slightly, as though seeking a more attractive arrangement for herself in the invisible frame, and she rearranged her hands, placing the bottom one into the palm of the top one.

"What worries me, really, is not the bottle of whiskey, but where he got the money." She undid her hands and revealed that they contained the small pad on which she had been making her calculations with the silver pencil. "According to my figures, the monthly sum from the trust fund sent by the bank, plus your own check for the difference between the bank's check and our charges here, these balance out correctly except for some laboratory tests Dr. Easthall ordered last week. But they won't show up on the ledger sheet until next month, so the only place he could have obtained the money is from an outside source." Miss Sidcup, lifting her glance from the figures on the pad, might have been Edith Cavell bracing herself to face the German firing squad. "Mr. Sayer," she said gently, "you haven't been sending him any money?"

"Good Lord, no," John said. "But I can guess where he got it. Or rather, he probably didn't use actual money."

Miss Sidcup's eyes spread and her lips parted in the sort of look of gently ironic inquiry much favored by Jane Austen's illustrators.

"I don't understand," she said.

"He was never very good about money, mainly because he never had much, and what little he had always went on liquor. That's why my father set up the trust fund, to make sure he'd have something to keep him out of the gutter in his old age," John said. "As a result, he worked out all sorts of ways to get what he wanted without money. I remember once he hocked his shoes in Wellesville, that was the town near where we lived in Dutchess County. He pawned his shoes to get a quart of sherry, and then walked all the way home in his socks. My guess is he gave something to one of your employees, Miss Sidcup, his watch or whatever he still owns, and the employee either swapped the whiskey for it, or sold it and bought the whiskey for him, and pocketed the difference as a fee. In any case, I don't think you should worry about it."

"I can't help worrying," Miss Sidcup said. She shook her head sadly. "A thing like that, one bottle of that dreadful stuff, and he loses the ground Dr. Easthall managed to bring him along on for several months."

"How's his general condition?" John said.

"Today, not very good, I regret to say, all due to his flurry with the bottle," Miss Sidcup said. "Dr. Easthall is hoping there will be no permanent damage, but it's so difficult to tell. The combination of his age, the liver deterioration, the diabetes, and the effects of the last stroke, keeping him alive is almost like keeping half a dozen balls in the air at one time, if you know what I mean. And then, to do a thing like *that*." Miss Sidcup shook her head sadly and said, "I wonder if you'd talk to him?"

John said, "About the drinking?"

"Yes," the white-haired old nurse said. "If he would just understand the damage he does to himself, I'm sure he'd stop."

Suddenly, before John's eyes, the carefully constructed image of the lady with the lamp fell apart. Behind the façade of the selfless lover of mankind, the wise and dedicated woman who had roamed the world to help the ailing and the needy and then come back, full of experience and honor, to spend her final years in one last effort at service in the town where she had been born, behind this glowing portrait of the useful life magnificently used, John saw now the distressing truth: Miss Sidcup, perhaps like other saints before her, was a stupid woman.

Avoiding that gentle, ladylike glance full of worldly wisdom, through which he could see all too clearly at work the mental processes of the born boob, John said, "I don't know how much I can do. After all, he's been drinking pretty heavily for more than sixty years. But I'll certainly talk to him."

"Oh, thank you," said Miss Sidcup. She sounded as though John had just presented her with a new wing for her rest home. "You're the only one he's got," she said. "He's bound to listen to you."

The almost insane obtuseness out of which this statement came was so unbearable that John turned with relief toward the sound of the swinging doors chunking open. The harassed woman in the blue cardigan and black tennis sneakers came in, scowling worriedly. Then, with obvious relief, she saw that John was not alone.

"Oh, Miz Sidcup," she said. "This genman wahnidda gohn one forty-two, so I wint downa have a look, and—"

"Is he tidied up?" Miss Sidcup said. Not curtly, nor even unkindly, but with that edge of authority in her voice that she had undoubtedly learned long ago was a more than adequate substitute for intelligence.

"Oh, yes," said the woman in the sneakers. "Side fum a little apple juice, I mean, he spilled it downa frunna his pajamas, not much, he's nice n' clean."

The graceful smile swung back toward John. Miss Sidcup said, "I leave him in your hands, Mr. Sayer."

John nodded. For half a dozen years, ever since he had learned about his father's trust fund, he had wondered uneasily if somebody else's hands might not have done a better job. He pushed through the swinging doors and started down the corridor toward room 142. As always, his first thought was what a silly number. The house was admittedly larger than most. Yet it obviously did not have anything like a hundred and forty or more rooms under its roof. His second thought, which also as always followed promptly on the heels of the first, was that the first one was unkind. The passion for pretension, he had discovered in a decade of practicing law, was probably as deeply rooted and basic to the human animal as the passion for power. Mrs. Loring, the old cook in the Deucalion main house, had once derived some gratification essential to the support of her days from insisting on being known as the colony's housekeeper. Miss Sidcup obviously now drew an important part of her emotional sustenance from preceding the identification of the sixteen rooms on the ground floor of her rest home with the numbers one and four.

John reached the closed door of what he would have called 2 but Miss Sidcup called 142. He paused to listen. There was no sound from within. Good, John thought. At least this visit would not be marred, like so many of his others, by the running battle with the television set. John turned the knob, shoved in the door, and saw he was wrong. The television set was on, but Ike Ten Eyck, propped against the pillows on his narrow bed and holding the remote control gadget, had apparently turned off the sound.

"Oh," he said sourly, "I figured it was you."

"Hello," John said. "How could you figure that? Until about an hour ago, when I decided to come on out, I didn't even know myself I was coming. How are you, Ike?"

"How the hell do you expect me to be?" said the voice imbedded in the bundle of skin and bones under the sheets on the bed. With a stab of the shock that struck John whenever he came here, he realized that the eighty-two-year-old man was approximately the same size as, and undoubtedly weighed no more than, his nine-year-old son Sam. "I got about as much liver left as that fool what's-his-name, the one in the White House, has brains," Ike Ten Eyck said. "That mutt Easthall, the one calls himself a doctor, he can't decide whether to give me insulin or Ex-Lax for my diabetes; one whole half of me, right down the middle, from the part in my hair to the athlete's foot between my toes is as dead as Kelcey's nuts since the last stroke, so when I want to take a leak, it takes six or more of these dopey old bitches they got working in this place to lift me onto the pot; and I manage to get my hands on a decent bottle of whiskey, they not only take it away from me, they start reading me Andy Volstead's old speeches, the horse's ass. Aside from that, I'm fine."

"How did you manage it?" John said. He came down the long, narrow room, past the TV set and the bathroom door, to the maple armchair with the red and yellow chintz pillows near the window. "I'll sit here, if you don't mind?"

"What I mind and don't mind is a great big fat joke around here," said the old man on the bed. "If you're going to sit in that God damn thing, turn so I can see your face, and never you mind how I managed it. If I tell you, you'll squeal to Sidcup, and somebody will get fired, and I'll have to start all over again finding a jailer with a character as weak as my own. What she say when she called you?"

Turning as instructed, so that his back was to the window, John said, "She didn't call me. I found I had some time, and I hadn't seen you for a while, so I decided on the spur of the moment to race for the two-ten. I made it, and when I got here, a few minutes ago, Miss Sidcup told me about the booze."

The shriveled figure on the bed moved slightly. John realized that, even when lying down, Ike Ten Eyck leaned to one side.

"She tell you to talk to me about stopping drinking?" Ike Ten Eyck said. "Sidcup?"

John hesitated. He was made uneasy, as always, by the odd combination of gentle sweetness and sardonic savagery in the watery blue eyes.

"Naturally she told me to talk to you about stopping drinking," John said. "She runs a rest home. She's a nurse. She wants you to get well."

"Do you?"

John looked quickly at the man on the bed. He was a part of John's oldest memories. This was the man about whom, not quite two hours ago, in his own office on Lexington Avenue, John had almost said to Vincent Howe, when telling the theatrical producer he reminded him of someone he knew, "You remind me of someone I once loved."

"Now, what the hell kind of question is that?" he said.

"A very simple one," Ike Ten Eyck said. "Sidcup, that old fool, naturally she wants me to get well. Or almost well. So does Easthall, another fool. The longer they keep me alive, the longer their fees keep rolling in. But you. For Christ's sake, Johnny, I'm gone, or most of me is, anyway. But the part that still works, the little piece up here that can still tell fact from bullshit, Johnny, it tells me you're a married man, with kids, and groceries cost like hell. They always did. I hate all this. Don't you see that? I'm like a hole in a bag of flour," Ike Ten Eyck said. "Draining away stuff that could be useful to people who need food."

"Let's not go into that again," John said. "Father left the money for all this. The bank pays the bills."

"Not all the bills," the old man said. "He didn't have enough at the end to leave. You know that."

John, who did know it, said, "Is that why you're sneaking booze? To kill yourself? So I won't have to pay out a few bucks every month when the bills run a little higher than what the bank sends?"

"No, Johnny," Ike Ten Eyck said. The sardonic glint in the watery blue eyes grew brighter. "I drink because I don't know how not to. You can't build your life around alcohol for seventy years, the way I have, then suddenly try to build your life without it, just because some stupid nurse and her stupid pal doctor give it the pitying head shake and the tsk,

tsk, tsk. Suppose I did what they want? Suppose I never took another drink? What the hell would I get? An extra week? Or month? Or year? Can't these boneheads understand I'd rather have another week the way I always had it before they locked me up, rather than another year the way they've got me now? Look at me," Ike Ten Eyck said. "What the hell good am I to anybody, including myself?"

The room was suddenly booming with mighty roaring sounds that seemed to have a physical reality, like invisible giants trying to pummel their way to freedom by breaking through the walls. Then, as abruptly as they had entered the room, the booming roars vanished. Dropping back into the chair, John saw what had happened. Ike's good hand, which had perhaps unintentionally turned up the sound of the remote control gadget, had managed to turn it down. Now the relentlessly jovial man on the TV screen was saying in more normal tones, "Dee ee tee ee, DETE, the detergent with the force, the strength, the power to—" The voice stopped, but the lips continued to move, as Ike Ten Eyck said, "Drop dead, you stupid son of a bitch."

"Don't lose your temper," John said. "All the poor guy is trying to do is sell some soap."

"To hell with him," the old man on the bed said savagely. "To hell with all of them, the bastards. Walking around on their two good feet. No God damn nurses or doctors or rotten liver or diabetes or anything telling them what to do. The healthy fucks, let them drop dead, all of them, the bastards." The narrow, white-haired head moved on the mound of pillow. John's heart lurched. Ike Ten Eyck was crying. "Johnny, don't be mad at me," the old man said wearily. "I can't help living even though I don't want to." A pleading note entered the quivering voice. "Besides, whatever it costs you, Johnny, when I *do* go, the capital in the trust fund, all that, what your father put in, you'll get all that, Johnny. So you'll really be paid back for everything I'm costing you, won't you?"

John said, "We can do better than that, Ike. You and I, we can make ourselves enough money, right in this room, to buy the Dogwood Lane Rest Home and add a swimming pool full of eight-year-old scotch."

The dried-up little head moved again on the pillow. To the ceiling, his voice gruff, Ike Ten Eyck said, "Gimme one of them snot rags, Johnny."

John leaned across to the small table between the maple chair and the bed. He plucked a Kleenex from the box, and placed it in the good hand on the bedsheet. The hand crumpled the tissue, lifted it, and dabbed the white wad up and down around the nose that, like Mr. Vincent Howe's, leaned in the direction of the downward slanted lips.

"Johnny."

"I'm here," John said.

"In the bathoom," Ike Ten Eyck said. His voice was firmer. His glance was still fixed on the ceiling. "Go in the bathroom."

John rose, walked around the bed, and opened the bathroom door. As always, he gulped back his revulsion, not so much at the smell, which was mostly medicinal, but at the sight of the white porcelain bedpans and other paraphernalia with which Miss Sidcup's staff tended to the many wants of the old man who really had only one.

"What do I do now?" John said.

"In the corner, back of the can," Ike Ten Eyck said. "That white tin thing with the brush in it for swabbing the pot. Open it up."

John stepped into the bathroom, leaned down, opened the white tin thing, and said, "Now, look, Ike."

"Shut up and bring it over," the old man said. His voice tightened as he repeated the words. "Shut up and bring it over."

John pulled the flat pint bottle from the white tin thing and brought it to the bed.

"I hope you know what you're doing," he said.

"You're God damned right I do," said Ike Ten Eyck, still addressing the ceiling. "You'll have to put a hand behind my head."

John unscrewed the cap, put a hand behind the old man's head, and held the bottle to the withered, liver-spotted lips. Ike Ten Eyck drank, gulping greedily.

"Listen," John said, pulling the bottle away.

"Shut up," the old man said. "Put it back."

John hesitated, glanced worriedly at the door behind him, then put the bottle back to Ike's lips. Another inch of the liquid disappeared.

"Okay," John said. "That's enough."

"Damn right it is," the old man said. His eyes were closed. His tongue came out and licked the last drops from his lower lip. He said, "Thanks, Johnny. Put it back."

John replaced the bottle and closed the bathroom door. He went back to the maple and chintz chair.

"That's the way to treat an old friend," he said. John was aware that the bitterness in his voice reflected nothing but embarrassment for his own weakness. "Make him an accomplice to murder."

"Nobody's gonna die," Ike Ten Eyck said with a small smile. "Not for a while. Not till the bottle's empty." He moved his head on the pillow and turned the smile on John. "Okay, kid," the old man said. "Tell me how we're gonna get rich."

John told him about his visit to Arnold Zucker that morning, and the proposition Vincent Howe had made to him after lunch.

"What bothers you about it?" Ike said when John finished.

"Who says anything is bothering me?" John said.

"You came out here," Ike said. "In the middle of a business day. And that bitch Sidcup didn't send for you."

John hesitated, trying to recapture the emotion that had brought him out here. He remembered with discomfort that he had known, even as two hours ago in his office he had started to reach for the phone, that it was not from Ellie he would get the reassurance he sought.

"I'm just not sure I should do it," he said.

"Didn't sound like they expected you to do much of anything," Ike said. "Except draw up some papers. You're a lawyer. You do that all the time anyway. Plus answer a few questions for that director woman. Quill you say the name is?"

"Yes," John said. "Gwendolyn Quill."

"Christ," Ike said. "The names people have."

"Look who's talking," John said. "Ike Ten Eyck."

"What else you gonna call a man his stupid parents name him Irvin?" Ike said. "Irvin Ten Eyck. There's a shingle to go through life behind. Could you stop these people from doing this show if you wanted to?"

There was no difference in tone between the casually spoken question and the preceding comment on names. But John could tell, as when he was a boy he had always been able to tell in Ike's presence, that the conversation had turned a corner. The shrewd old drunkard on the bed, who had always been old and had always been drunk—though now obviously older and, at least in the resulting deterioration, far drunker —was still shrewd.

"I haven't looked up the law on it," John said. "But I'm sure there's enough in the books on invasion of privacy to make it possible for me, yes, I'm sure I could stop them from doing the show, if I *wanted* to stop them."

"Maybe that's why they came to you in the first place," Ike said.

John looked at the face that resembled a slightly pink walnut. He wondered if Ike had meant more than his words at first hearing conveyed. John said, "You mean as a sort of bribe not to cause trouble?"

"I don't know if maybe the word bribe ain't too tough," Ike said. "Gimme another one of those things, will you?" John reached over and placed another Kleenex in the good hand resting on the bedsheet. Ike Ten Eyck did not use it. The wrinkled fingers, which looked like shriveled wax beans, toyed with the piece of tissue. The old man, still addressing the ceiling, said, "I'd say what they're doing, it's the sort of thing a smart person would do. Remember how Mrs. Loring, when she wanted me to do something, something she really wanted and she wanted me not to argue but to go ahead and do it, she'd arrange to not be around when I wanted you to steal a bottle of grape tonic for me from the commissary?"

John had forgotten, but was now oddly pleased to remember. He said, "I sure do. She was nice."

"Mrs. Loring?" Ike said, his voice rising.

"Yes," John said, suddenly uncertain. "Wasn't she?"

"She was a bitch," Ike said. "All women are. They can't help it. Nature fixes it for them that way right from the start. A woman that's not a bitch ends up behind the eight ball. Take your mother. Take Dinah Tristram. Remember?"

John couldn't believe it would ever cross Ike's mind, no matter how fogged with drink, that he could possibly have forgotten. He said sharply, "What the hell are you getting at?"

"Women," Ike said. "Only the bitches make it into the home stretch. The decent ones haven't got a prayer. Biology and men can't be out-foxed. They're a couple of tough, hard facts. The bitches face this, and act accordingly. Your mother didn't. Neither did Dinah Tristram. So they paid the bill, the way all us losers do. But these boys you're involved with now, these Zuckers and Howes and that Gwen Quill, they sound tough. Even though one of them is a woman, this Quill woman, they sound like a gang of men. Smart men. Lining up a deal. Figuring all the angles. Deciding you're one of them."

"Me?" John said. He knew he didn't sound very bright.

But he also knew he was in the presence of the one human being before whom it didn't matter how he sounded.

"Sure," Ike Ten Eyck said. "They want to do a show about Sennacherib Sayer and Deucalion. Both are dead. But Sennacherib Sayer's son is alive, and he happens to be a lawyer, so why not go to him and ask him to climb aboard? What have they got to lose? They need a lawyer, anyway. They've got to pay for one. Why not pay for one who happens to be Sennacherib Sayer's son? They'll get just as good legal work for their money as they'd get by hiring another lawyer. That part of it you can bet your ass, Johnny, they've checked on. In addition, for the same price, at no extra charge, they get on their side the only man who could maybe cause them trouble by standing in their way."

The quavering old voice, running down with the unusual effort its owner was demanding of it, disappeared into a heaving sigh.

"In other words, I'm being had," John said slowly, with great care. He wondered why the conclusion, to which the wise old man on the bed had steered him, should seem so disappointing. "You're saying, Ike, I should tell these boys to forget the whole thing?"

The look of astonishment on the pink walnut that rolled toward John on the pillow was startling.

"You crazy or something?" Ike Ten Eyck said.

John shook his head irritably. He said, "I don't understand what you're getting at."

"I'm not surprised," the old man said. "You've forgotten the only thing that matters."

"What's that?" John said.

The good hand on the bedsheet crumpled the piece of face tissue and held it, tight and hard, as though trying to squeeze from it some sustenance for the effort that lay ahead. After a few moments Ike Ten Eyck apparently felt he had it.

"What these monkeys want," he said. "This Zucker and that Howe and the woman, Quill, plus all the others on their team, whoever they are, what they want doesn't matter, because all they want is money. But what you should want, what you can give them, the thing that makes this deal make sense, *that's* the thing that counts."

Baffled, and wishing he were not, John Sayer said again, "What's that?"

The bundle of skin and bones on the bed heaved. John saw

that, God alone knew how, the half-paralyzed body had turned to face him.

"He was a great man," Ike Ten Eyck said. "No matter what happened in the past, that fact can't be changed. Sennacherib Sayer deserves to be remembered. He deserves they should do this show about him. Nobody's ever told the truth about Deucalion and what happened. You remember all that stuff in the papers, the lies, what they said about him. None of it was true, Johnny. You know that. Here's a chance for the world to learn the truth. No matter what happens, Johnny, he's earned that." A flash of anxiety brought the dead blue eyes to momentary life. "Don't you understand that, Johnny? He wasn't only your father. He was also a great man."

John nodded. As always when he came to the only person who had ever called him Johnny, Sennacherib Sayer's son had got what he had come for.

"Yes," John said. "I understand."

Part II

2

WHAT HE DID NOT understand was how he could have forgotten.

The fact of Sennacherib Sayer's greatness had always been an accepted commonplace of his son's life. Like the fact that John's mother had golden yellow hair; and wore rimless octagon-shaped eyeglasses with silver earpieces; and had come to America from Sweden to study nursing shortly before the outbreak of what her husband called Mr. Wilson's War. When he thought about it, John was proud of the fact that his father was a great man. But he did have to think about it before he felt proud, and what he thought was not very concrete.

John was usually reminded of Sennacherib Sayer's greatness by one of the other kids in the Deucalion Children's Guild. These kids were constantly making sarcastic comments about the high-handed manner in which John's father ran the colony, comments that had clearly originated with their parents. At such times John used to get a picture in his mind of a huge, shapeless, fiery glow. This glow was somewhat like

the last of the setting sun when it went down on a summer
day behind the stand of birch trees at the juncture of West
Pasture and Aaron's Brook. This swift stream formed Deucalion's northern boundary and separated the colony from
Godwin's Tract, the wooded land some people said now belonged to the New York Central and ran all the way down to
the Hudson. Except that John, even at ten, knew better. The
Hudson was at least twelve miles away—Ike Ten Eyck said
more than fifteen, in case anybody was interested in his opinion—and nobody owned that much land. Not even the Godwin family which, again according to Ike, who had been born
on Godwin property, owned pretty damn near half of Dutchess County.

In any case, when that fiery glow appeared in John's mind,
he made an effort to remember to concentrate. This was not
always easy because it usually happened in the middle of a
game during recess or after classes when some kid called out
an insult about the Sayer family. But if John did remember,
he could bring an image of his father into the front part of
his mind. He had several images to choose from, but somehow John always selected the one that showed Sennacherib
Sayer on the stage in the Barn Hall, addressing the assembled
Deucalion colonists on some matter of policy or re-organi-
zation or discipline. This image went very well with the fiery
glow in the back of John's mind. The combination showed
the tall, handsome figure, with the thin lips, sharp nose, and
prematurely snow-white hair parted in the middle. This figure
was not unlike the figure of George Washington at Valley
Forge that Mrs. Loring, when she had any free time from her
duties as cook in the Main House, was painting in the Revolutionary War mural that she hoped to have completed on
the walls of the Main Dining Room for Deucalion's tenth an-
niversary.

In the image in John's mind his father was not, of course,
wearing the kind of clothes Mrs. Loring was painting onto
the figure of George Washington in the mural. Sennacherib
Sayer, in the image in his son's mind, was wearing the three-
button pepper-and-salt tweed suit he wore in most of his
newspaper photographs. The clothes, however, did not matter. There was something about that jutting jaw, those thin
lips, the sharp eyes, even the white hair that could almost
have been a colonial wig but wasn't, that made John's heart
beat a little faster. The way it beat when he looked at Mrs.
Loring's unfinished portrait of George Washington. It made

him realize, with an odd little feeling of exultation mixed with fear, that this man was something more than his father.

Just what that something more was, aside from the word "great" which evoked the fiery glow in his mind, John Sayer understood for the first time on the afternoon of his tenth birthday. It did not seem odd that the moment of comprehension should have been the result of something Ike Ten Eyck said. He didn't say it at once, of course, because the handyman detested Mr. Tristram, the chairman of the Children's Guild. If Ike had been dying of thirst, John's father had once said with a laugh, the handyman would have found the energy to insult the schoolmaster before asking him for a drink of water. What Ike said, when he came into the Children's Guild building in mid-afternoon on the day John Sayer was ten years old, was, "I'll take young John, if you don't mind."

Mr. Tristram was diagramming on the blackboard the palindrome "Able was I ere I saw Elba." He turned, holding the piece of chalk upright, the way Poseidon held his trident in the framed picture near the schoolroom door. He said coldly, "I do mind, Mr. Ten Eyck, and I'll thank you to leave this classroom at once."

"You save your thanks for people who do you favors, a group I don't happen to belong to, and don't ever intend to join," Ike said. He raised one of his grease-smeared hands and made a beckoning motion with the forefinger. He said, "Come on, Johnny."

John felt the bench move slightly under him. Alfie Crocker on his right and Charlie Devon on his left had shifted their bodies with anticipation. So did the eighteen other boys and girls in the room. Scenes between Ike Ten Eyck and Mr. Tristram, or for that matter between Mr. Tristram and any one of a dozen or more people at Deucalion, were not very unusual. The schoolmaster was short-tempered and sharp-tongued, and openly hostile to the colony's ruling group. But this was the first time such a scene was taking place in the classroom, during school hours.

"John Sayer, you remain where you are," Mr. Tristram said. He sounded perfectly calm, but John knew the schoolmaster was far from calm. Mr. Tristram, who was very fat, had a small, pointed chin. It receded slightly into the thick rolls of flesh that circled his neck like a badly tied scarf. John had learned long ago that when Mr. Tristram was hopping mad these layers of fat, normally the color of tallow, grew red and quivered, like a plate of Jell-O when the table is jostled.

The schoolmaster's scarf of fat was quivering now as he said, "In this room, during school hours, I am the master, and only I give orders."

"Except on special occasions, when somebody else's orders are more important," Ike said. "Let's go, Johnny. Your mother's orders is I'm to go on over to the Children's Guild and get you right away, and here I am, getting you."

John looked worriedly from Ike in the doorway to Mr. Tristram in front of the blackboard, but he did not move. He did not doubt that Ike was telling the truth. The handyman was too shrewd to leave himself open to an accusation of disrupting colony routine without proper authorization. But he also took so much pleasure in annoying the schoolmaster that John was certain Ike wanted to prolong the scene as long as possible.

"I don't believe Mrs. Sayer would send you on such an errand without written authorization," Mr. Tristram said. "She knows the procedural rules laid down in our charter as well as anybody here knows them, and probably better than most. Until you can provide such authorization, Mr. Ten Eyck, I will ask you again to leave this classroom."

"Come on, Johnny, we're in a hurry," Ike said. This time John responded because, even before the handyman's arm moved, John saw what was about to happen. The crumpled wad of paper, which Ike threw with a fast overhand pitch, caught Mr. Tristram on the chest. He staggered, as though he had been struck by a rock. The back of his head rasped against the blackboard and smeared the chalked word "Elba." The boys and girls in the classroom giggled. Ike said, "There's your authorization, Mr. Chairman of the Children's Guild, sir, if you please, I thank you. What about it, John? Get the lead out, boy. This is a big day in the Sayer family."

"Are there ever any small ones?" Mr. Tristram said sarcastically. He stooped for the wad of paper. He did it too fast, or rather without the deep inhalation that was the necessary prerequisite in a man of his girth to the stooping process. The gasping grunt that resulted sent another wave of giggles across the classroom. Coming erect with the wad of paper, Mr. Tristram swept a glare around the room like a scythe biting into a clump of tall grass. It stilled the giggles. Breathing hard, the schoolmaster smoothed the crumpled wad. Even from the far side of the room, John recognized the piece of his mother's gray note paper. *"Dear Mr. Tristram,"* Mr. Tristram read aloud. He boomed out the words as though he wanted to be heard by the men in the Carpenters' Guild building all the way over at the other side of Center Pasture. *"Would you please be good enough to excuse John from class at once as I want him to accompany Mr. Ten Eyck down to Wellesville to meet the train on which Mr. Sayer is arriving from New York. Thank you. Griselda Sayer Parenthesis Mrs. S. Close Parenthesis."*

The schoolmaster's fat red face came up. His sarcastic voice came up with it.

"Thank you, Mrs. S. Sayer," he said. "Thank you for providing me with a much-needed illustration that will enable me to make clear to my class something that it has seemed to me for a long time needed clarification." Mr. Tristram came forward two steps, toward the boys and girls on the benches. Again he raised the piece of chalk as though it were Poseidon's trident.

"Nine years ago, in the Year of Our Lord Nineteen Hundred and Nineteen, when most of you were as yet unborn, and the Single Tax Colony called Deucalion was founded by one Sennacherib Sayer and a group of like-minded people, they were all under the impression that they were investing their time, their energies, and their emotions, not to mention their good hard cash, in an enterprise that would free them from the inconveniences, the irritations, the frustrations, and the downright horrors of economic regimentation and servitude to which life in the twentieth century has been reduced by the men who run our society. Little did they know, boys and girls, little did those happy pioneers suspect, dear children, that what they were actually doing, what they were in truth building, what in point of fact they were pouring their time and energies and emotions into, not to mention the aforementioned good hard cash, was a personal fief for the Sayer family, and particularly for its self-appointed ruler and emperor, Mr. Sennacherib Sayer."

The fat schoolmaster, not quite so red-faced now but much shorter of breath, turned toward the door. In it Ike stood, holding John's hand.

"May a lowly varlet make so bold as to inquire, Mr. Ten Eyck, what great honors are about to be heaped upon our lord and master to justify the disrupting of the routine of the Children's Guild on an ordinary school day?"

Ike Ten Eyck took a swipe with his free hand at his slanting nose, somewhat like a cocky little boxer clearing the air before tackling a much bigger man. He said, "Sure you might make so bold, and since for once you've remembered your manners and called me mister, I don't mind telling you." Ike reached down and took John's hand and started leading him through the door. Across his shoulder, the handyman tossed a handful of words in the general direction of the schoolmaster. "Mr. Sayer has just been appointed to the Supreme Court by Mr. Hoover."

They were well past the last houses of Northeast Cottage Grove, halfway down the rutted path called East Cottage Lane toward the Main House, before John was able to control his excitement.

"Ike," John said. "Mr. Hoover? You mean Mr. *Herbert* Hoover? The *Pres*ident? In *Wash*ington?"

"Who else?" Ike said. "He's the only one has the right to appoint people to the Supreme Court, ain't he?"

John didn't answer. He trotted along beside the handyman, struggling with this new meaning of his father's greatness. Up to now his father's greatness had been something that made Sennacherib Sayer more important than the fathers of Charlie Devon or Alfie Crocker. Or the fathers of any of the other kids who lived in Deucalion. Or the fathers of the kids who lived down in Wellesville. Now, all at once, as a result of Ike Ten Eyck's announcement, John saw that his father's greatness was not limited to the people John knew. His father's greatness extended beyond Deucalion, beyond Wellesville, all the way to a place like Washington, a place John had never seen but had merely heard about. His next thought, which circled warily around the possibility that his father's greatness might extend even to places John had *not* heard about, was almost frightening.

"Ike?" he said.

The handyman was rubbing his lips with the back of his free hand. John knew this meant they were going to make a stop at the lilac clump near the corner of the vegetable garden. Ike spoke without turning his head or pausing in his hurrying lope.

"Now don't start asking questions," he said. "We gotta get down to that train, and we ain't got too much time."

"I was just thinking about the Supreme Court," John said. "That's pretty big stuff, I guess."

"You *guess?* I thought that Children's Guild was supposed to be a school," Ike said. "Don't that Fat Ass teach you anything? We got a hundred and twenty million people in this country. Only nine of them get appointed to the Supreme Court. You bet it's big stuff."

"I know that," John said. He tried to sound innocent, even dumb. He was working his way by easy stages toward the question he really wanted to ask. "I was just thinking about why they got appointed."

"Now there's the kind of question I'd expect a boob like Fat Ass to ask," Ike said. "You know what a court is?"

"Sure I do," John said. "I was just—"

"Yeah, sure you do," Ike said sarcastically. "It's a place you got trouble, you broke a law, somebody did you dirt, you go there and you make your complaint. The other guy, the one you're complaining about, he answers the complaint. Maybe he calls you a liar, maybe you call him back. Whatever it is, it's two guys in a battle, one on each side, and somebody has to decide which one is right. That someone is a judge, and the place he does his deciding, that's a court. There's all kinds of courts, all over the country. Big ones, little ones, medium ones, all kinds, I don't know how many. But one thing I do know, one thing everybody knows, the biggest one, the champ, that court is the Supreme Court down in Washington, and another thing I know and everybody else knows, to run the champ they use only champs, and that's what those nine men are: champs. Eleven champs out of a hundred and twenty million people, and now your father is one of those eleven, and now here's what I want you to do, Johnny."

John knew what Ike wanted him to do. They had reached the clump of lilacs at the corner of the vegetable garden. He said, "Wait. There's something I want to know."

"There's always something you want to know," Ike said. "If I answered all the questions you want to know, I'd never get my work done around this place, and the Executive Committee would fire me, and then how would I get my groceries?"

"There's one thing," John said. "If you'll just tell me—"

"I'll tell you, I'll tell you," Ike said impatiently. "But first I want you to do something for me." He squinted against the sun at the commissary building on the hill, as though the plan he was putting into words had just occurred to him. "This morning. When I was putting a new hinge on the cupboard near the back door up there in the commissary, I left my bottle of tonic in with the others by mistake. Now I feel my cough coming on, I better get hold of it. But I don't want to go up there myself because Mrs. Loring, all she has to do is clap her eyes on me, and she'll have a dozen jobs for me, so I want you to go up and get it, Johnny." Ike dug into the pocket of his brown overalls and came up with the key. "You see Mrs. Loring or anybody else, you go on right through and skip it," he said. "But you don't see anybody, and nobody sees you, you open that cupboard and you bring me my bottle of tonic. If you're a friend of Ike Ten Eyck's, nobody will see you, and my bottle of tonic looks like all the other bottles in the cupboard, so you just take the first one you see, and get the lead out, because I'll be waiting right here."

Years later, when he started his first groping efforts at working out the meaning of what had happened to him during those early years at Deucalion, John began to understand the agony with which Ike Ten Eyck had done his waiting behind that clump of lilacs. Just as he began to understand why the apparently ageless little handyman with the slanted face and leaning body, no matter how desperate he was for his bottle of tonic, could not send the boy to fetch it without first working his way through the elaborately fabricated lie that neither of them believed.

The commissary was an L-shaped structure, set perhaps twenty feet back of the Main House. Mrs. Loring felt more jealously proprietary about it than Mr. Tristram felt about the Children's Guild. Before the Deucalion Executive Committee had purchased the hundred acres between Aaron's Brook and the Wellesville Road, the L-shaped structure had been a three-sided shed, open on the north to the former owner's cows and horses which had grazed in what had been known even then as Center Pasture. Soon after the establishment of the colony, when Sennacherib Sayer and his family moved into the Main House, and the colonists began to build and settle into the four groups of cabins that formed the corner boundaries of the rectangular Deucalion property—Northwest, Northeast, Southwest, and Southeast Cottage Groves—Mrs. Loring began to agitate at the weekly Full Meetings for the allocation of colony funds. She wanted to convert the partially open shed into a weather-tight structure suitable for storing the raw materials of what she called her craft. This was, of course, cooking.

Her talent in this field had been on view for a number of years, beginning in 1915. At that time Mrs. Loring—even then she had been vague about the existence of Mr. Loring

—had arrived from what she always dismissed impatiently as "Don't ask me, honey, what *part* of the God damn Middle West." Almost immediately she opened The Trencherman on West Eighth Street, between Fifth and Sixth Avenues. Here for almost five years—including the fourteen months of America's involvement in the Great War, when basic commodities like white sugar and butter were in scarce supply— Mrs. Loring had served for twenty-five cents, on pine tables unadorned by tablecloths or napkins, what enough Greenwich Villagers called the best meal available in New York City to make her a small legend. This did not, however, make Mrs. Loring happy.

She was a small woman, from the top of whose head a five-foot-two runt like Ike Ten Eyck could eat grapes without rising on his toes. At war within her tiny body were two passions: Mrs. Loring's lust for cooking was no stronger than her desire to paint. The fact that she was, even by her own admission, a pretty terrible painter, did not alter or even diminish the intensity of her desire. It was her inability to reconcile the two passions that had drawn her, as John was to learn later it had drawn so many other colonists, to Deucalion.

"Serving a full meal, including a fish course and a meat course, for twenty-five cents is a tough job," John had once heard Mrs. Loring explain to his mother. "It can be done, and I did it for almost five years. But it takes every minute of your day, and part of your night. There was plenty of times during those years on Eighth Street when I was up at three in the morning to be down at Washington Market by four because the shad were running in the Hudson. If you got there early enough, especially if you were a woman, they'd let you have a couple of sackfuls cheap enough to make it possible to get it on the tables on Eighth Street and stay inside my twenty-five cent price. But you start at three in the morning to get shad roe on your tables for your customers, and you don't have much time left to get paints on your canvas for yourself. The satisfaction I was getting out of my cooking was being canceled out every day by the dissatisfaction of not getting a lick of painting done. Finally, I went to Klaus Immensee for help. He was just beginning to build that fancy Park Avenue practice of his, and I said I was being torn apart, and asked what should I do. Klaus said he was in the same boat. He was making a fortune stroking and coddling all those well-heeled psyches, but he had absolutely no time to go to his carpentry shop and do what he really wanted to do, namely, cabinet work. My third or fourth session with him, Klaus told me about this Single Tax colony he'd just heard was being organized up in Dutchess County. He said he was seriously considering giving up his practice, taking whatever money he had, and buying a place in this Deucalion to save his sanity. My next session on his couch, Klaus told me he'd had an interview with Mr. Sayer and it looked as though they could find a place for him in the colony's Carpenters' Guild, with the right to call on him for psychiatric help whenever somebody needed it, and I asked him would he introduce me to Mr. Sayer. He did, and when I told Mr. Sayer my problem, he said he was sure that whatever I got for selling The Trencherman on Eighth Street would be enough to buy me a share in Deucalion. I could do all the cooking in the Main House, he said, which would not be much, since the only people who'd be living in the Main House would be Mr. Sayer and his wife and son, plus any new colonists who hadn't yet finished their cabins, and Mr. Sayer himself would be down in New York most of the week, anyway, so I could have all the rest of my time to paint."

John remembered the thoughtful look that had come to Mrs. Loring's face as she had paused to refill her and his mother's tea cups and give him another of her just-baked apricot tarts.

"I didn't realize at the time, of course," she had continued slowly, "that Mr. Sayer was a vegetarian. Not that I would have let that influence me. The state I was in, I would have jumped at the chance to join Deucalion if I'd been told Sennacherib Sayer was a cannibal. It's just that—"

Mrs. Loring had hesitated over her teacup and shot a troubled glance, first at the Revolutionary War mural she was painting around the Main House dining room, and then at Mrs. Sayer.

"What I mean is that cooking for a vegetarian is like pitching for a kindergarten team," Mrs. Loring had said. "You don't really get a chance to throw your fast one. That's why what I was thinking, Mrs. Sayer, if I could get that shed out in back closed off—make it into a regular commissary, I mean—I could do something with mushrooms, for example. They're easy to raise, if you've got the space, and I could get some canning equipment. That sort of thing. It doesn't cost much, and I'm sure whatever it did cost, it would pay for itself soon enough, the money we'd save not having to buy out-of-season vegetables and fruit, using our own canned, I mean. But the first thing, as I say, the first thing is getting that shed closed off, a wall built on the north side, and what I think I'll do, I think I'll bring it up at next week's Full Meeting."

Mrs. Loring had brought it up at next week's Full Meeting, and at the Full Meeting after that, and at John did not know how many succeeding Full Meetings, until finally the funds had been allocated, and the shed had become a commissary. The canning equipment alone had long ago paid not only for itself but also for the construction work. The former shed was now a neat labyrinth of shelves piled with jars of fruit, vegetables, jellies and jams; cupboards full of mushroom caps; counters stacked with crocks of pickles, kegs of sauerkraut, bottles of vinegar, jars of mayonnaise, and receptacles containing so many varieties of homemade foods that John did not wonder Mrs. Loring found it necessary to maintain a complicated card inventory system to keep track of them all. If she herself wondered occasionally at the result of her industry, Mrs. Loring certainly did not comment on it. At any rate, she had never done so in John's presence. He had, however, heard others comment on it, among them his mother.

"That poor woman," she had once said to John's father at the dinner table after Mrs. Loring had served the carrot cutlets. "She came to Deucalion so she could do less cooking and more painting, and while she's certainly doing less cooking up here than she did down on Eighth Street in New York, she's been trapped by that commissary into so much canning, that I don't think she's touched a brush to canvas for over a week."

"She'll get back to her painting as soon as she really wants to paint," Sennacherib Sayer had said. "I mean wants it with her whole being. Right now she doesn't. People who want to avoid doing something always manage to invent their own obstacles and hurdles. If Mrs. Loring had really wanted to paint down on West Eighth Street, she would have managed to serve something to her twenty-five-cent customers other than shad roe, which required her to be in Washington Market at three in the morning. If she really wanted to paint up here at Deucalion, she would not have invented that commissary and started her one-man canning factory. By the way, my dear, these carrot cutlets are quite good. I wonder if you would mind suggesting to Mrs. Loring that next time she makes them she might grind in several walnuts. I saw in the paper this morning that the British Medical Association has discovered the lowly walnut contains linoleic acid, which is extremely useful in keeping down the average individual's blood pressure. It's an experiment worth trying, I think, and might even be beneficial to Mrs. Loring. I'm worried by her color. She's much too flushed most of the time. I don't like all that grape tonic she keeps making and drinking for her digestion."

John, who had tasted it once out of curiosity, didn't like it, either. He wondered why Ike Ten Eyck did. John supposed Ike liked the stuff because it tasted like sherry and Ike liked sherry. But John did not feel he was on very sure ground. Since his father was a strong defender of the Eighteenth Amendment, he would not allow alcohol in the house or on the Deucalion premises. As a result, John had never tasted real sherry. Coming stealthily into the commissary, he made up his mind to taste some as soon as possible and, if it could be arranged out of his allowance, buy some for Ike. John was getting a little tired of this sneaking into the commissary every time Ike ran out of tonic.

Moving swiftly, on his toes, past the counter of open crocks in which the new pickles were steeping in their first brine, John paused to lift one out and take a bite. The crunching of his teeth, which sounded surprisingly loud, reminded him that he was not supposed to advertise his presence. He dropped the pickle back into the crock, looked quickly across his shoulder at the open door, saw that he was unobserved, turned the corner into the shorter arm of the commissary ell, and stopped short. Mrs. Loring was on her knees in front of the open cupboard to which John was holding in his hand the key Ike had just given him.

"Oh, John, good," the tiny woman said. "I was hoping to catch you at the Main House before you drive down to meet the train." Mrs. Loring stood up, holding a bottle of the grape tonic, and slapped with her other hand at the dust on the knees of her blue knickers. "Isn't the news wonderful?" Mrs. Loring said, and she smiled. "How does it feel to be the son of a Supreme Court judge?"

"Pretty good," said John. He had not yet had time to think about that. At the moment he was thinking what Ike would say if he came back empty-handed. "You want me for something?"

"Yes." Mrs. Loring's smile changed slightly. Her small, narrow face pinched to one side. John saw she was making a stab at a conspiratorial wink. "People don't get appointed to the Supreme Court every day in the week, and I want to do something to celebrate." She set the bottle of grape tonic on the cupboard, reached under her apron, and came out with her black snap-top change purse. "When you and Ike are down in Wellesville," Mrs. Loring said, clicking the purse open, "I'd like you to go into Jensen's Drug Store and buy me a bottle of liver extract." She held out a fifty-cent piece. "It costs forty-five cents, and you can get yourself some candy with the nickel change."

"My father says candy is bad for the teeth," John said.

"Not on a day when he gets appointed to the Supreme Court," Mrs. Loring said. "On a day like this your teeth are perfectly safe. Here." John took the coin and Mrs. Loring said, "You don't have to tell your father about the candy." John, who knew that, thought it best not to comment. Mrs. Loring said, "You don't have to tell him about the liver extract, either."

John thought that over, and decided he'd better not act without information. "Why?" he said.

Mrs. Loring hesitated. She looked across her shoulder at the other door, which led out to the strip of lawn that separated the commissary from the rear of the Main House. She turned back to John. "I don't want to do anything wrong," she said. "But I do want to do something to celebrate. Your mother put carrot and walnut cutlets on the menu, with boiled rice and spinach, and I thought—" Mrs. Loring hesitated. She looked worried. She said, "You won't tell if I tell you?"

"Of course not," said John but, just in case, as he said it he crossed the middle and forefinger of his right hand behind his back.

"I know how to do a wonderful sauce that will make those damn cutlets taste like meat," Mrs. Loring said. "But I've got to have some liver extract to do it. If I tell your mother I'm using liver extract, or if your father finds out, they'll both have a fit. If you don't squeal, I can tell them it's crushed dried mushrooms mixed with sage and dill weed and a pinch of ginger. They won't know the difference, and we'll all have something that tastes like food for a change. All right? I mean, will you?"

"Sure," said John. He had on a number of occasions eaten some of Mrs. Loring's bootleg dishes. He could feel his mouth begin to water.

"Oh, that's wonderful," Mrs. Loring said. John turned to go, and she said, "Wait." He turned back. Mrs. Loring took the bottle of grape tonic from the top of the cupboard, twisted her face in the conspiratorial wink, and put the bottle into John's hand. "Give this to Ike," the cook said. "On the day Mr. Sayer gets appointed to the Supreme Court, tell Ike he doesn't have to steal the stuff."

John decided, on his way back down the hill to the clump of lilac, to tell Ike no such thing. It was a shock to realize that all those times during the past couple of years, since Ike had started sending him up the hill to steal bottles of Mrs. Loring's grape tonic, he had not been stealing them at all. Once he was out of the commissary, however, the shock began to change in John's mind to a small feeling of power. All of John's life, Ike Ten Eyck had always known everything. Now, unexpectedly, John knew something Ike didn't know. He decided to hoard the information. John didn't know for what. He merely sensed that knowing something somebody else did not know, even if that somebody else was a close friend, gave him an advantage. John Sayer, at ten, had not yet had a chance to enjoy many advantages over other people. Watching Ike peering out impatiently from behind the lilacs, and knowing what he knew that Ike did not know, the boy for the first time in his life felt superior to, and therefore sorry for, the man.

He said, "Ike, why did the President do it?"

Ike Ten Eyck took a long gulp, then squatted down on the grass, the lilac trunks behind him. He crossed his legs, set the bottle between his shoes, and leaned forward to cup his hands protectingly around the neck. It was an attitude with which John had grown familiar. Ike was waiting for the tonic to take hold.

"Because the President wants only champs on the Supreme Court," he said. "And that's what your father is: a champ."

John had known this for a long time, although not until today had he known how much of a champ. He did not find Ike's answer satisfactory.

"That's not what I mean," John said. "I mean why did it happen today?"

"Why the hell not today?" Ike said. "You can't appoint people to the Supreme Court till there's an opening. Somebody who's on it, they die or they resign. Mostly die, though. That makes an opening, and the President starts looking around for somebody to fill it. All kinds of people want the job, naturally, and all kinds of friends recommend them to the President, but in the end it's the President makes up his own mind himself. I imagine your father got recommended by lots of people, not only his friends, because he's such a famous lawyer."

Ike licked his lips, and an inward look came into his narrowed eyes. This meant, John knew, that the handyman was gauging the extent to which the tonic had taken hold. Then Ike drew the bottle from between his shoes, tipped it up to his mouth, and reduced the contents by almost a third.

"Yeah," he said finally, with a sharp, gasping intake of breath. He shook his head and wiped his mouth with the back of his hand. "That's the stuff to give the troops." He set the bottle back between his toes and tugged the leather shoe lace tied to the brass overall button on his chest. The big gold repeater came free. He squinted at the watch and said, "Four more minutes, maybe five." He slid the watch back into the overalls. "Not only on account of he's a famous lawyer," Ike said. "There's plenty of them that's that. I imagine the President picked your father on account of the *kind* of famous lawyer he is. Not all the time saving the rich from jail or from the other crooked rich. But *battling* the rich. Fighting them to keep the bastards from screwing the poor. That time two years ago, the electric company in New Jersey? The one wanted to jack up their rates? They tried to hire your father? Remember that?"

John, who did, but only vaguely, said, "Yes."

"Any other lawyer would have grabbed the fat fee and done it," Ike said. "But not Sennacherib Sayer. He told them to go screw, and he offered his services free to the consumers' committee, and he not only beat those bastards, the company. They didn't get the higher rates they wanted. Your father also got the consumers a rebate. A rebate? No, a reduction in rates, I think. Whatever it was, it was just the opposite of what the company wanted to pay him for, and he did it for nothing. No fee. Like all those jobs for the government? Those investigating committees he's on? A dollar a year, that's all. One dollar a year, that's all Sennacherib Sayer takes when he works for his country. They want to pay him more? The law says he's got to *take* more? He says give it to charity. That's what Sennacherib Sayer says. All that, and then starting a place like this, this Deucalion, that takes a champ, too, you know. No matter what that Fat Ass Mr. Tristram says. He's just jealous of your father, the way a lot of people around here are jealous of Sennacherib Sayer. All those cracks about how he lives in the Big House while they gotta live in cabins, and he runs the place like he's a king, that's all crap. They're just jealous, that's what it is. They're just plain jealous. But not the President. Down there in Washington, the President knows. He's got people telling him. They tell him a man like Sennacherib Sayer, a great lawyer like that, he's fighting all the time for the people and against the trusts. A man like Sennacherib Sayer, he gives his time to the government for free. A man like Sennacherib Sayer, he starts a place like this Deucalion, it's a dream people have had since maybe way back to the Garden of Eden. A new way for human beings to live together, that's the kind of man the President appoints to the Supreme Court."

The gold repeater came popping out of the overalls again. The slanted face tipped further over so the narrowed eyes could get a better look. Ike Ten Eyck jumped up and shoved the bottle down into his pocket.

"What are you doing, making me waste time with fool questions?" he said. "Your mother will burn my ass."

The notion that his mother would even think such a thing, much less do it, always aroused in John two reactions: first, he thought it was funny; and second, he felt he should be angry with Ike for saying it.

John knew, of course, that much of the language Ike used in his presence he would not have dared utter in the presence of John's parents. Or, for that matter, in the presence of any other Deucalion colonist. Certainly not in the presence of any colonist who was also a parent. On the Deucalion Code which, when he bought his shares and was admitted to membership, every colonist signed and swore to uphold, the things the members had banded together to fight against were just as clearly defined as the things they were determined to strive for. Among the things they were sworn to fight against, which included the use of alcohol and tobacco, was what Sennacherib Sayer, who had composed the first draft of the Code, called "the pointless use of pointed obscenity."

"No sensible, civilized individual can be unaware of the salutary effect on the harassed human spirit of the occasional use of the Anglo-Saxon expletive," he had written in the supporting footnote that was printed in the booklet called *DEUCALION: A Statement of Faith*, which was mailed out all over the world to people who wrote for information about the colony. "No sensible, civilized individual can be equally

unaware of the importance in this connection of the word
'occasional.' To employ such words indiscriminately is not
only to blunt their usefulness, but also to coarsen the spirit of
those who do so."

It never occurred to John, when he was talking to Ike Ten
Eyck, that they were coarsening their spirits. On the other
hand, it always occurred to John, as he climbed the front
steps of the Main House, that he was moving into a world
somewhat different from the one he inhabited when he was
alone with Ike Ten Eyck, and in this other world he had better watch his language. Watching it now, John did not at
once see that his mother was coming down the circular stair-
way in the hall.

"John," she said. He turned and saw she was carrying the
large cardboard box from Siegel Cooper in New York in
which the Christmas ornaments were stored in the attic. And,
as always when he had been away from her for any length of
time—half an hour, half a day—John was momentarily overwhelmed by his own sense of inadequacy. She was in his eyes
so unbelievably beautiful, as a mother should be; and he
loved her so fiercely, as he knew she loved him; and she was
so terribly frightened, as only her son seemed to realize.

Almost everybody else, John was aware, thought of her as
being very much like her husband: arrogant, vain, convinced
always that her way was right, and relentless in her efforts to
see that her way was carried out. John had even heard, or
rather overheard, people say that she looked like a Prussian
officer disguised as a woman. Only John, to whom her erect
carriage and severe features were an integral part of her
beauty, grasped that she was not at all like Sennacherib
Sayer. Only John knew that his mother lived with a secret
terror, and the boy ached with the desire to ease her fears, to
help her and shield her. But he did not know how, because
John did not know what she was afraid of, and he knew he
could not ask, because he sensed it had something to do with
his father. Often, seated on his bench in the Children's Guild,
trying to look attentive while Mr. Tristram up front explained to the class a problem in arithmetic or syntax, John
would rapidly run through in his mind the facts he knew and
the things he had heard. He ticked them off swiftly, almost
without thought, the way he recited the multiplication table
when Mr. Tristram called on him. He hoped that the casual
inventory would unexpectedly turn up some aspect of the

puzzle that more thorough and troubled examinations had not revealed.

John knew that his parents had met during the flu epidemic immediately following the war. His father, who had been on Peyton March's staff, had been stricken on the troop transport that brought him home. As soon as the ship docked at Hoboken, Sennacherib Sayer had been rushed to Bellevue where, from among the hundreds, perhaps thousands, of available nurses, fate had chosen to send to the bedside of the distinguished nearly-fifty-year-old lawyer a girl named Griselda Johannson, age twenty-two, late of Stockholm, Sweden. They had been married six weeks later. Six months after that, Sennacherib Sayer settled his young bride in the Main House of the newly-founded Single Tax colony in Dutchess County to which he had given the name Deucalion.

Because of his work in Washington and his practice in New York, he could not give the colony all of his time. But its place in his thoughts and affections were clear: unless something urgent prevented him, he came up every Friday and remained at Deucalion until Monday; here he paid taxes and voted; his son had been born nearby; and here his wife was raising the boy as Sennacherib Sayer felt a child, in the third decade of the twentieth century, should be raised. His interests were so far-ranging and varied that Woodrow Wilson, who had admired and used Sennacherib Sayer's talents even though he detested his personality, had once called him "this bush league Leonardo da Vinci."

What the boy did not know, what troubled John Sayer so much that at times his distress was almost physical, was the answer to the question that dogged his days: what had changed the laughing, open-faced, twenty-two-year old girl in the newspaper photographs in the scrapbook on the shelf in the Main House library, into the woman of thirty-three who was a thin-lipped martinet to the Deucalion colonists? On the bottom step, reaching John, her mind came back to the hall of the Main House and Mrs. Sayer said, "Did Ike tell you?"

John said, "Yes," but he was drowned out by Ike's petulant, "Now, Mrs. Sayer, that's really rubbing it in I'm some kind of a dope."

Even though the sweet expression on his mother's face did not change, John could tell, from the glint of sunlight that suddenly cut across her rimless octagonal lenses, that she had moved her head for a closer, sharper look at Ike.

"Ike, you know better than that," she said in the voice that

John had heard other kids in the Children's Guild playground deride as a top sergeant's bark, but that always made her son feel she was calling to him in the dark in a whisper for help. He could not forget the one time, a year ago, when he had tried to offer it. John had come awake in the middle of the night, aware that something unusual was happening. He sat up in bed, wondering what it was, and then he heard his mother's sobs. The harsh noises, coming down the hall from his parents' bedroom, seemed to be torn from her throat in spite of her efforts to stifle them. For several terrified moments, John lived with the horror that his mother was being beaten. Then he remembered that it was the middle of the week, and his father was down in New York, and that particular horror vanished. But the terror remained. It dragged the boy out of bed and down the hall. Before he had time to think, John had opened the door. The faint squeak of the hinges had an unusual effect. The sobs stopped abruptly. His mother's face came up out of the pillow. In the moonlight he could see the shock in her eyes change to embarrassment and then anger. "Go to bed," she had said sharply, harshly, and then, as though trying to erase the harshness, she had added, very quietly, "Please go to bed, John. Nothing is wrong." He had gone to bed, carrying the memory of her sobs with him. The memory came alive whenever he heard her voice, even when the words she spoke were casual and unimportant, as it came alive now when she spoke to Ike.

"I'm sorry, ma'am," Ike said. "Just that, *you* know, how could I *not* tell him?"

Mrs. Sayer said, "I don't know, Ike, but there are times when you are under the influence when you manage some remarkable feats. Did Mr. Tristram make a fuss?"

"Not enough to bother," Ike said. "Just shot his face off, as usual."

John's mother frowned and said, "I wish there were something we could do about Francis Tristram's persecution complex."

"Only one thing to do with that type," Ike Ten Eyck said. "Drop-kick him out of the club."

"I wish we could, but we can't, and you know it," Mrs. Sayer said. "Besides, Mr. Sayer won't tolerate that kind of talk, Ike, so I suggest we have no more of it."

"I wouldn't say it in front of Mr. Sayer," Ike said. "Mr. Sayer is the type man that's always turning the other cheek."

"The whole spirit of Deucalion is to turn the other cheek,"

John's mother said. "You've been here from the beginning, Ike. That's long enough to learn what we stand for."

"Mr. Tristram's been here a year now," Ike Ten Eyck said. "How come he hasn't learned what we stand for?"

John's mother poked at the high black comb that always held the two tightly braided knots of golden yellow hair together at the back of her head like twin headlights on a toy automobile.

"I don't know," she said. "It seems simple enough for a schoolmaster to grasp, but perhaps his wife gets in the way of his grasping it."

John, who had wondered about it before, found himself wondering again why his mother, who liked everybody, did not like Mrs. Tristram.

"I'd kick them both out," Ike said. "You heard what he said at the last Full Meeting."

John's mother stomped across the hall, to the wall at the right of the front door. On it, framed in black, hung a copy of the Deucalion Code. She pointed to a paragraph at the left, about halfway down the page.

"I know," Ike said. "But I'll tell you something about all that stuff about free speech and keeping an open mind, Mrs. Sayer. I been doing a lot of thinking about it lately. Mainly, I admit, on account of every Full Meeting I gotta sit there and listen to this Mr. Francis Tristram sound off how the original Single Tax idea Mr. Sayer started with, it's become perverted, and now what we are, Deucalion is nothing but a fancy summer place for a bunch of phoney artists, he says, and intellectuals and that other word he's always throwing around."

"Aesthetes," Mrs. Sayer said. "He's very fond of that, which I can understand since he's married to one."

"Yeah," Ike Ten Eyck said. "Well, I don't know about those words or about the Single Tax, but I'm beginning to know quite a lot about free speech and the open mind. I been watching it around here, Mrs. Sayer, especially that Mr. Tristram, and I'll tell you something about the open mind, Mrs. Sayer. A man that concentrates on keeping an open mind, all he gets is a draft going through his head."

The silver earpieces moved slightly as Mrs. Sayer's pink and white cheeks bunched up in a quick smile.

"Ike, you are outrageous," she said. "You are also right, I think, but the whole purpose of Deucalion is to give people a chance to develop and express their true personalities, and some of them seem to need an open mind to do it, perhaps because what they do can only be done in a draft, such as composing the kind of poetry Mrs. Tristram composes, for example. In any case, you must never let Mr. Sayer hear you say things like that."

"I won't," John said. "But I wish you'd tell him with this Mr. Francis Tristram, turning the other cheek, all it gets you is another sock in the jaw. He's a jealous sorehead, and the only cure for those boys is to send them away from wherever they are, or to go away from there yourself, and you know with this bird which course of action I'd recommend, Mrs. Sayer."

"I do indeed, and I share your feelings, but we are in the minority, so let that be the end of it, Ike, please," John's mother said. "This is a very exciting day, and I would not want it to be spoiled."

"Neither do I," said Ike. "But Mr. Francis Tristram does."

Mrs. Sayer's octagonal lenses glinted again.

"He said something?"

"Nothing special," the handyman said. "But you know the kind of person he is. It's a big day in the Sayer family. Not only for young John—"

"All right, Ike," Mrs. Sayer said. "If you please."

John knew it was his birthday, and he had known for almost a week that they were planning a surprise birthday party for him. He now pretended to be absorbed by the framed Deucalion Code on the wall.

"But also now this great news about the Supreme Court," Ike said. "What's a better chance for a man like that Mr. Tristram to cause trouble than on a day like this for the new justice and his family?"

John's mother's lips came together in a thin line. Then she said, "Mr. Sayer has not yet been confirmed, Ike, so calling him the new justice is a bit premature, but just the same we'll have to disappoint Mr. Tristram on that score. There will be no trouble tonight. Hold this, John." John took the Siegel Cooper box, and his mother reached up to the gold fleur-de-lis pinned to her shirtwaist. She pulled out the little watch on the spring cord, snapped the case open, looked at the face, snapped the case shut, and let the watch wind back into place. "The important thing, John, and you, too, Ike, is when Mr. Sayer gets off the train, you're not to say a word."

There was a moment of silence, and then Ike, puzzled, said, "A word about what, Mrs. Sayer?"

"The Supreme Court," John's mother said. "Mr. Sayer

doesn't know about it yet, and I want to prepare everything before he does."

Astonished, John said, "He doesn't *know* about it?"

"The train he takes every Friday to come up here leaves New York at two-fifteen," Mrs. Sayer said. "And the call from Washington came in at almost two-thirty, half an hour ago."

"But it'll be in all the papers," Ike said. "He'll see it in the papers."

"Not the papers Mr. Sayer will be reading on the train," John's mother said. "He'll have bought those in Grand Central, and they were all printed hours before the President's secretary tried to reach Mr. Sayer in his office in New York. When they were told he'd left to catch the train to Deucalion for the week end, they called here, and the President's secretary said they would not release the news until this evening, so his family will have a chance to be the first to tell him, and that's exactly what I'd like it to be. Family." John's mother reached down and took the Siegel Cooper box from him. "Mrs. Loring thinks we can get a nice table decoration out of these Christmas ornaments, and I suspect she's planning to do something special about dinner, because she's been prowling around out in the commissary, looking mysterious, so you can keep John out from underfoot by taking him down to Wellesville with you. Provided you're all right, Ike."

"I'm fine," Ike said. "Nothing wrong with me."

"We'll see about that," Mrs. Sayer said. She dipped into the pocket of her apron and brought out the two walnuts. "Come on."

"Ah, no!" Ike's voice rose in the wailing shriek of protest that was only partly sincere. He clearly knew what John had for some time suspected: his mother did not really object to the handyman's consumption of Mrs. Loring's grape tonic. However, because Sennacherib Sayer would have objected, it was his wife's duty to act as though she did. "We don't have to go through that, Mrs. Sayer."

"Yes, we do," she said. "Let's not waste time." She walked across to the dining room door and held up the walnuts. "Come on, Ike," John's mother said. "We don't want to be late."

Scowling, the handyman shuffled grudgingly across the foyer and thrust out his arms, palms down. The gesture pulled up the legs of his brown overalls, so that John could see the concealed bottle outlined against the cloth. He was sure his mother saw it, too, because the light glinted across the octagonal lenses as she moved her head, but Mrs. Sayer disregarded the concealed bottle. Carefully, as though she were placing a couple of eggs into a saucepan of boiling water and trying not to crack the shells, John's mother placed a walnut on each of Ike's hands, wedging them into non-rolling position against the knuckles.

"Now, then," she said, stepping back. "Successfully across to the north door, and by successfully, Ike, I mean without dropping them, if you please, or you will have to drive down into Wellesville without the benefit of John's company."

Scowling harder, Ike caught his lower lip in his teeth and with a lurch, started forward. If John had not seen that lurch many times before, it would have made the boy gasp. Now he merely held his breath, as John knew Ike was holding his. That first lurch was always intentional. With luck it should carry Ike—who was traveling along the west wall of the dining room, below the boyhood segment of Mrs. Loring's mural —as far as the point where George Washington stood poised in the act of throwing the silver dollar across the Potomac. When he got that far, Ike always paused under Washington's outstretched arm for a deep, refilling gasp of air. Also, he always managed to keep the crazily shivering walnuts from rolling out of their shallow resting places against his knuckles. He managed it again now. The gasping sound ended and Ike lurched forward on the second lap of his test. It carried him through the north door, below the rearing horse that was being shot out from under George Washington at the battle of Fort Duquesne. From the rear hall the sound of the walnuts hitting the uncarpeted floor could be heard clearly in the dining room. But John knew this did not matter. By some unspoken agreement, his mother always disregarded whatever happened once Ike got through the door. She disregarded it now. Ike reappeared in the doorway with the walnuts. He came across and returned them to Mrs. Sayer with a small, triumphant flourish.

"No need to be cocky," she said, dropping the nuts into her apron pocket. "On your way, both of you, and Ike, please, do drive carefully."

"As if I ever drive any other kind of way," he muttered to John, who was following the handyman down the back steps and out to the Ford truck. It was parked on the barren piece of lawn at the end of East Cottage Lane that served as the garage for the Main House. "The trouble with women," Ike said, "even a woman like your mother, who is less trouble than most, they're always so busy worrying about what they *think* is going to happen, they don't have time to worry or do something about what's happening under their noses." Ike boosted John up into the seat and came around to climb in behind the wheel. "Instead of doing something about that troublemaker Mr. Francis Tristram, the son of a bitch," Ike said, "your mother worries about my driving."

His fussy little stabs, with both hands and feet, at the levers and pedals had their usual result. The truck started with a lurch that would have snapped John's head from his body if he, veteran of hundreds of such starts, had not been braced for it.

"Mr. Tristram paid for his shares like everybody else, and he built his own cabin like everybody else," said John. He had heard both sides of the argument so often that he thought he understood them. "Until he wants to sell his shares and his cabin," John said, "and the Executive Committee says okay and approves the person he wants to sell to, there's nothing my mother or anybody else can do."

"That's how much *you* know," Ike said, guiding the truck around the more treacherous ruts at the turn from East Cottage Lane into the Wellesville Road. "People like Dr. Crocker, he's some kind of big bug in that laboratory over to Poughkeepsie; or Mr. Schwartz, he draws all them pictures for the magazines; or Mr. Fennell, with his paint factory up in Albany, all those people that they make their living somewhere outside, and they just *live* here at Deucalion, those people, sure. Like you say, until they themselves they want to sell and get out, nobody can do anything to them. But a son of a bitch like this Mr. Francis Tristram, he makes his *living* here on Deucalion. The Executive Committee didn't give him the job as chairman of the Children's Guild, he wouldn't have to eat. What your mother could do, she could work on your father to get the Executive Committee they should hire themselves another chairman for the Children's Guild, and you'd see how fast that son of a bitch Mr. Francis Tristram, the troublemaker, you'd see how fast he'd be out on his ass."

The Wellesville Road wound gradually, in long, semicircular scallops, down the mountain from the Godwin plateau. It now took one of its periodic dips. Ike glanced back, across his shoulder, and apparently saw what John saw: the Main House had disappeared from view. He held the shaking steering wheel with one hand. With his other, Ike dug down into

the overalls. He came up with the bottle, which he held out
to John.

"Take the plug out of that," Ike said.

John unscrewed the cap and held it while Ike took a long
swig of the grape tonic. When the handyman held the bottle
out again, John twisted the cap back into place.

"That's the way to handle Mr. Francis Tristram," Ike said.
He shoved the bottle back into his overalls. "Cut off the bastard's income. Starve the son of a bitch out." The road, coming to the end of the scallop, lifted the truck into position for
the next descent, and Ike said, "Kee-rist!"

He hit the brake. Mrs. Tristram, who had been walking on
the wrong side of the road, looked up and smiled. She was
totally unaware, John could see, that, a moment ago, her life
had almost been snuffed out.

"Hello," she said. Then, a moment later, her mind came
back from wherever it went when she was working on a
poem. Mrs. Tristram recognized them. The smile seemed to
come into focus. She said, "Ike. John. Hello."

"Hello," Ike said with that curious, almost halting defer-
ence that always puzzled John. If you hated someone as
much as Ike hated Mr. Tristram, it seemed reasonable to
John to assume you would hate his wife just as much. But
Ike's feeling for Mr. Tristram clearly did not extend to the
schoolmaster's wife. There was another possibility of course.
John had once worked it out in his own mind after listening
to an exchange between Ike and Mrs. Tristram. The handyman had some very strict rules about sportsmanship. Perhaps
he did not feel it was sportsmanlike to hate members of the
opposite sex. Especially if they were under age. Dinah Tristram had married the schoolmaster a year ago on the day before they sailed from their native England to settle at Deucalion. The rumor was that she had been sixteen on her wedding day. Leaning down toward her from the high front seat
of the truck, Ike said sharply, but without anger, as though
speaking to a child, "You shouldn't walk on that side of the
road, Mrs. Tristram. When you're walking you should stay
on the left side of the road, facing the traffic. Coming around
that turn, we almost killed you."

Mrs. Tristram's eyes, which were green, spread wide with
shock. Then, quickly, they crinkled with laughter.

"Oh, Ike, now really, you wouldn't do that," she said.

"*I* wouldn't," he said. "But this damn truck, it comes

around a curve like that, moving blind, *it* might. You want a lift?"

"No, thank you," Mrs. Tristram said. "I'm working on a—" She paused and, with the back of her hand, as she tipped her head to one side, she brushed the long brown hair from her forehead. It was a gesture that had long ago identified her in John's mind with the weeping willows on the bank of Aaron's Brook back of the Children's Guild building. Her whole body, which was very thin, almost reedy, seemed to sway when she did it, as though moved by a breeze. "I was working on an ode," Mrs. Tristram said, smiling shyly. "To your father," she said. With a nervous start, John realized she was addressing him. "Francis just told me the extraordinary news."

"Yes, ma'am," John said. He felt foolish, as he always did in Mrs. Tristram's presence. He didn't understand how anybody so young could be a wife, or how anybody so nice could live in the same cabin with Mr. Tristram.

"Francis says it's a very great honor," Mrs. Tristram said.

"It sure is," Ike said. "Only nine men out of a hundred and twenty million."

"That's why I thought it would be nice to have an ode ready for him," Mrs. Tristram said. The shy smile reappeared on her face. "I've never written an ode before."

"You don't watch where you're going, you'll never write another one," Ike said. "In fact, you may not finish this one. Which way you heading?"

"Nowhere, really. Just walking," Mrs. Tristram said. "Odes are quite long, you know."

"Well, hop in," Ike said. "We'll give you a lift."

"Thank you, no," Mrs. Tristram said. "One can't compose poetry while riding in a truck." Then, apparently afraid she had hurt Ike's feelings, her thin face creased in a troubled look. "I mean *I* can't," she said. "I have to walk to do it."

"I don't like anybody from Deucalion walking these roads alone," Ike said. "Especially women."

Mrs. Tristram laughed and said, "Oh, Ike, it's perfectly safe."

"No, it ain't," Ike said. "Not the way these people up here they hate us. Times I don't feel safe myself, walking around Wellesville."

"Ike, you're exaggerating," Mrs. Tristram said. "There may be a certain amount of antagonism among the local people. There always is to a place like Deucalion because people are always afraid of writers and poets and artists. But they're afraid because they don't understand, not because they think we'll do them any harm."

"People they're afraid, they're dangerous," Ike said. "It's not the harm they think we can do them that worries me. It's the harm I think they can do us. I know these farmers up around here, Mrs. Tristram. I was born and raised with them. When it comes to places like Deucalion, they're a bunch of mean, narrow-minded boobs. You better hop in and we'll give you a lift."

"But Ike, then I won't be able to compose my ode."

"I'm sure Mr. Sayer he'd rather have you safe than have your ode," Ike said. "You really shouldn't be out walking, Mrs. Tristram. These boobs around here, they don't have any idea what goes on at Deucalion, and it doesn't do any good to tell them, because I've tried. They think what we're running up there is a great big—"

Ike's voice stopped, and John did what Mrs. Tristram did: he looked at the handyman sharply.

"A great big what?" she said.

"Oh, they've got these dopey ideas it's a free-love colony and all that stuff," Ike said with obvious discomfort. "You know the kind of lies they tell about us."

"If they're lies," Mrs. Tristram said, "I see no reason to pay any attention to them. Thank you for the offer, but I prefer to walk." She took a step backward, away from the truck, and then, as her hand came up in the swaying motion toward her hair, the thin face broke in the shy smile. "Thank you for worrying about me," Mrs. Tristram said. "I won't walk very far, Ike, and I'll be very careful."

"Well, okay," Ike said. "But I wouldn't go beyond the boundary of Stonecraft Farm." He fumbled and kicked at the levers and pedals. The motor started. John braced himself for the lurch as Ike's slanted face broke in a grin. "Make it a short ode," he said to the schoolmaster's wife, and the truck leaped like a startled rabbit. By the time it reached the crest of the next scallop, from which, looking back, John could see Mrs. Tristram's slender figure vanish, Ike had started to sing the song that always accompanied them on their trips down into Wellesville.

"Will you take it in your hand, Mrs. Murphy," the handyman roared above the erratic sputtering of the motor. *"Oh, it only weighs a quarter of a pound!"*

There were twenty-four verses, according to John's count.

Part of the fun of driving down into Wellesville with Ike on Friday afternoons was singing all twenty-four before they reached the station. Sometimes they didn't make it, usually because Ike, who punctuated his singing with nips at the grape tonic bottle, would insist on repeating favorite verses. As a result, there would be a wild dash at the end to reach the station on time. But at that stage of the trip, as a rule, Ike had to concentrate so completely on handling the truck that there was no energy left for singing. That was what happened this time, although Ike kept muttering, as he guided the truck around the long, tricky curve from the Wellesville Road into Main Street, that the trouble was the time they had lost in stopping to talk with Mrs. Tristram.

"That son of a bitch," he said. His hands, gripping the steering wheel, shivered up and down with the jumping of the truck on the badly paved piece of road. "The bastard is a pain in the ass even when he's not around," Ike said. "Why the hell does his wife have to be out walking when we're late to meet your father's train?"

John didn't answer. Not because he knew an answer was not called for, or would not have been heard by Ike. But because he was suddenly in the grip of the strange feeling that always came over him when he entered Wellesville. Perry Schwartz, who lived at Northeast Cottage Grove and made his living as a magazine illustrator, was fond of saying Wellesville was the only small town he knew that Norman Rockwell would have had trouble converting into a *Saturday Evening Post* cover.

"The trouble is Wellesville isn't really a town," Perry Schwartz said. "It's a few public conveniences that came into existence because some damn fool decided this was a good place for the New York Central to stop."

It did not stop very often. In fact, only twice a day: at 9:30 in the morning, for people going south, toward New York; and at 6:10 in the evening, for people who had come up from New York or points in between. But, because the town sat in the center of one of the richest dairy and cattle farming areas in the East, the railroad station, which handled a great deal of freight, was the largest single structure in Wellesville. The rest of the town did indeed look as though it had been designed, or rather thrown together, to fit Perry Schwartz's definition.

Scattered around the station, on both sides of the poorly paved section of the Wellesville Road called Main Street, were a one-story bank; a two-story frame building called The Wellesville House; a garage and filling station; Jensen's Drug Store; a livery stable; a grocery store; a butcher shop, and perhaps a dozen other structures in which, so far as John could see, people met to talk and smoke and buy and sell odds and ends of clothing, farm equipment, and hardware. None of these buildings, including the railroad station, had been touched by paint since the day it had been completed. And Milton Fennell, the paint manufacturer from Albany who lived at Southwest Cottage Grove and was Perry Schwartz's rival for the unofficial title of Deucalion's clown, said the last building in Wellesville had been completed in time to hide Major André on his way up the river to buy the plans of West Point from Benedict Arnold.

As a result, no matter how inventively varied the color schemes of the original builders may have been, time and the weather had reduced all their efforts to the same lifeless gray. It aroused, at least in John, the odd feeling that, no matter how brilliantly sunny the weather, he was entering, when he came into Wellesville, a place where it was raining. This specific feeling was appropriate to his general feeling about the town: it frightened him.

Not so much because of the hostility of the local people to Deucalion, about which Ike had talked to Mrs. Tristram on the Wellesville Road. John knew about that hostility. Everybody at Deucalion knew about it and talked about it. As long as he was up on the mountain, however, at Deucalion, John knew this hostility was merely talk. And when he was down in Wellesville, he was always accompanied by Ike, with whom John felt safe anywhere. What frightened him about the town was the way it made him feel about himself: it made John feel different.

Up at Deucalion, for example, all the women, including his mother, wore knickers, and all the kids in the Children's Guild wore the short khaki pants—copied from the *lederhosen* Sennacherib Sayer had brought back from Austria— which the Executive Council had adopted as the official Deucalion school garb. Up at Deucalion John never thought about what he was wearing. The moment he entered Wellesville, however, he found it difficult to think of anything else. Everybody, it seemed to John as the truck bumped down Main Street, was staring at him. And in the stares was the reminder that he was not like other boys; that he lived in a strange place; was being educated in a curious way; among people who had worked out a form of existence that made them all, in the eyes of the rest of the world, freaks. It frightened John to realize that, to all those staring eyes on Main Street, he was a freak.

"Friggem," Ike said.

John pulled his glance from the group of men lounging on the porch of The Wellesville House and said, "What?"

"Lettem stare their eyeballs out," Ike said. "They're nothing but a bunch of small-town cow flop shovelers. You're the son of a justice of the United States Supreme Court. Here we are. Made it again, and with time to spare."

The spare time was not much. The train was already rumbling into the station. Ike took a long, final swig of grape tonic. Final, that is, until they got back to Deucalion and Ike could set in motion a new scheme for sneaking another bottle out of Mrs. Loring's commissary. In the presence of Sennacherib Sayer, however, the handyman wouldn't dare take a nip. He took his last one fast and managed, as the train stopped, to drop the empty bottle out of the truck into the clump of sumac at the end of the platform.

"Now remember what your mother said," Ike said. "Not a word about the Supreme Court."

"You must think I haven't got any brains," John said. "How can I forget a thing like that?"

"I don't know about your brains," Ike said, climbing down to the ground. "But your tongue is getting good and long. Let's see about your legs."

John climbed out to the piece of floppy tin over the front right wheel and jumped down. Straightening up, he saw the eyes of the loungers on the platform staring at him.

"Remember what I said," Ike said in a loud voice. "Friggem all. Big and small. Let's go."

They went up the platform, past the line of men leaning against the walls and the freight carts. The men watched the handyman and the boy with insolent grins. John knew, as long as he was with Ike, they would do no more than grin. The handyman had a reputation as a quick man with a knife. Aside from some intricate whittling, John had never seen Ike do anything with a knife to justify this reputation. It was possible that Milton Fennell, who said the reputation had been deliberately invented by Ike himself, was right. Just the same, it worked. Only the grins followed them to the end of the platform, where Sennacherib Sayer always came out of the last car, swinging his fat briefcase and struggling with the hastily pulled together armful of newspapers, magazines, and books he had been going through on the way up from New York. The fact that his father had not come out this time did not cross John's mind as an observed fact until Ike stopped moving and turned. John turned with him. Looking up, he saw that Ike was scowling.

"What's the matter?" John said.

"We miss him?" Ike said in a puzzled voice. He took a step back down the platform, toward the parked truck, then turned again, toward the conductor who had just stepped from the train.

"Joe, you seen Mr. Sayer?"

"Hello, Ike," the conductor said. "Mr. Sayer? He got off the other end. How's it going?"

"Pretty good," Ike said, taking John's hand. "Thanks, Joe. Come on, Johnny."

They went back down the platform. The insolent grins followed them. When they reached the truck, Ike said irritably, "Now what the hell?"

On the front seat, dumped in an untidy heap, were the fat briefcase and the pile of newspapers, magazines, and books.

"He probably went across the street to get something in Casey's," John said. Casey's was the general store next to The Wellesville House that sold a little bit of everything, including newspapers and tobacco. "You wait for him," John said. "I gotta go over to Jensen's."

"What for?" Ike said.

"Liver extract," John said. "Mrs. Loring's cooking up some sort of surprise for tonight."

"Better not let your father catch you," Ike said. "A boy your age fooling around with liver extract."

"Aah, shut up," John said and laughed as he ducked Ike's poke at his head. "Be right back."

He trotted down Main Street, keeping close to the edge of the cracked sidewalk, hurrying toward the only spot of color in Wellesville. In the window of Jensen's Drug Store, flanking the dusty display of Castoria bottles, were two glass jars almost as tall as John. They were shaped somewhat like the huge urns in the illustration for *Ali Baba and the Forty Thieves* that hung on the Children's Guild wall. The jar on the left was full of a red liquid. The one on the right, blue. Both were transparent. Neither was marked. Both gave the boy, who had no idea why the jars were there or what they contained, a sense of excitement so intense that it made him forget his fear of walking down Main Street by himself. John stood there for a while, staring at the big jars and enjoying the excitement. Then he fished Mrs. Loring's half dollar from his pocket, went in, and bought the bottle of liver extract from Mr. Jensen.

"Forty-five," the druggist said, "and a nickel change."

"I'll take candy for the nickel," John said. He dipped down, to peer into the glass case next to the drug counter, and said, "A Sixteen-to-One, please."

Mr. Jensen brought out the cigar-shaped bar of peanut-studded chocolate, and said, "Four cents to go."

"A Mary Jane," John said. "No, two, please."

Mr. Jensen brought out the flat yellow slabs, and said, "Two cents to go."

"A pack of Three-X," John said.

Mr. Jensen brought out the chewing gum, and said, "One cent to go."

John hesitated, torn between a Strawberry Lip Cutter and a strip of pink and white Polka Dots. He moved around to the side of the glass case for a better view of the Lip Cutter. Sometimes the bright red cream did not quite fill the crimped tin plate. If this were so now, the Polka Dots would be a better buy.

"Anything wrong?"

John heard Mr. Jensen's voice, somewhere above him, and he knew he should reply, but he couldn't. He kept staring into the candy case, or rather at the distorted images on the glass of the candy case. The images were a man and a woman, two people behind him, in the far corner of the drug store, and all at once John was afraid to straighten up. He didn't know why. He knew only, from the way his father and Mrs. Tristram were standing together, that he should not have seen them. It made him think of that terrible night a year ago when he had been awakened by his mother's sobs. Then he heard Mr. Jensen's voice again. Guessing that the druggist had repeated his question, John did straighten up and said, "The Lip Cutter, please."

"Thought you fell asleep down there," Mr. Jensen said. He pulled the Lip Cutter from the glass case and dropped it on top of the other candies in the small paper sack. "There's your change."

"Thanks," John said, taking the sack. He turned and headed for the door, keeping his eyes fixed straight ahead. He managed to get safely out into the street, but as he turned right, up toward the railroad station, he couldn't resist a quick glance in through the window, past the tall jar of red liquid, and then John was sorry he had taken the risk. It was his father, all right. The tall, slender, white-haired figure was standing beside the weighing machine. One hand was resting on the slot out of which, after you dropped in your penny, came the small card with your fortune printed on it. The shoulders in the pepper and salt tweed jacket were tipped forward slightly because the schoolmaster's wife, to whom John's father was talking, was so tiny. John had time to see the faint, troubled scowl with which Mrs. Tristram was looking up into the face of his father. He had time to be struck by a curious image: his father looked like a long, thin, white-topped question mark bent protectingly over a fragile little exclamation point. And he had time to note that his father was also scowling as he talked rapidly and earnestly. Then John was beyond Jensen's window. He kept right on going, forcing himself to think about which piece of candy he would start on first. By the time he reached The Wellesville House, it was all right. He had stopped thinking about what he had just seen in the drug store. When he reached the truck, he had finished the Sixteen-to-One bar and started on one of the Mary Janes.

"He's not in Casey's," Ike said.

"Who?" John said.

"Who do you think?" Ike said irritably. "You said he probably went across to Casey's, so I went over, but he wasn't there. You get the liver extract?"

"Yeah," John said. "Want a bite?"

"What is it?"

"Mary Jane."

"I hate peanut butter," Ike said. "You know that."

John did know it. That was why he had eaten the Sixteen-to-One bar first, so he would not have to share it. Now that it was gone, he felt guilty.

"I've got a Lip Cutter and some gum," he said. "You want them?"

"I want your father," Ike said, peering up Main Street. "If we're late, your mother will say it's because I stopped in the Wellesville House for a freshener." He shook his head and said, "The ideas women have, boy. They think all you do, you just walk into a place, the way you did before Prohibition, and say gimme a shot. Now where the hell would he have gone?"

"What's bothering you, Ike?"

"Oh, hello, Mr. Sayer," Ike said. "Didn't know you were in the station."

John's father said, "Hello, John. Why so solemn?"

"He's got his jaws cemented together with a Mary Jane," Ike said.

"Well, a Mary Jane today means a visit to the dentist tomorrow," John's father said. He reached down, seized John, and hoisted him up to the front seat of the truck. "Let's go, Ike," Sennacherib Sayer said. "I'm hungry."

Perhaps it was the hunger that made him silent.

Ike, guiding the truck up the scallops of the Wellesville Road, finally said, "You all right, Mr. Sayer?"

John's father, who had been staring out at the road, drew a deep breath. He smiled, and said, "Yes, I'm fine, Ike. Just a little tired, but otherwise fine. Been a good week?"

"Pretty good," Ike said. "The Farmers' Guild got the last of the strawberries in, and the Actors' Guild, you listen to Peter Midden, they're ready to give us *The Pirates of Penzance* anytime the Executive Committee drops a hat. You, sir?"

"Like yours up here, pretty good," John's father said. "I wish I didn't have to spend so much time in Washington, or rather on the train to and from Washington."

"You could fly," John said. "There's airplanes going to all kinds of places now."

"Yes, I know I could, but I'm not going to," Sennacherib Sayer said. He smiled down at his son. "That's for you and the members of your generation, who I imagine will probably forget how to walk. My generation, we older birds, we have too much respect for the law of gravity."

"I'm not so sure I like that we older birds, sir," Ike said. "You and I, Mr. Sayer, we're exactly the same age, sir, fifty-seven my last birthday, and I wouldn't mind doing a little flying."

"Perhaps you will, some day, if things go as well as I hope they will, and we put in our own airfield at Deucalion," Sennacherib Sayer said. "And if we're exactly the same age, Ike, then you were fifty-eight your last birthday, but I won't tell anybody."

"Oh, well, sir," Ike said, "what's a year more or less."

"At our age, a fleeting moment," John's father said. "Why, I can remember when a year was an eternity, when a single day would stretch ahead, limitless, waiting to be—" He paused, and the sad look slid away. John was glad. He hated to see that look. It involved only his father's eyes. They would narrow and seem to turn inward, as though they were examining something their owner kept hidden from the rest of the world. What happened to the eyes at such times was enough to turn his father's face into the face of a stranger. "And your week?" he said to John. "Better than merely pretty good, I hope?"

"Yes, sir," John said. Then, made suddenly bold by the desire to keep that look from coming back to his father's face, he said, "Would you like a Mary Jane, sir?"

As soon as the words were uttered, the boldness vanished. John, who knew how his father felt about candy, knew he had made a mistake. Sennacherib Sayer was staring sternly down into the paper sack his son was holding out.

"Johnny," Ike said, his eyes leaving the road to shoot an annoyed glance at the boy on the seat beside him, "I think, if I was you, I'd chuck that bag of junk outa the truck and—"

His voice stopped, clearly on a note of surprise. John didn't blame him. A surprising thing had just happened: the stern look went the way the other look had gone, and his father was smiling.

"Yes, I think I would very much like a Mary Jane, thank you," Sennacherib Sayer said. He pulled the candy bar from the sack and peeled away the wrapper. He took a cautious bite, and nibbled carefully, using only his front teeth. Then he said, "Why, it tastes like peanut butter." He took a larger bite. "I feel I've earned this moment of debauched celebration," John's father said. "Yesterday, in Washington, I told the President I was getting too old to take any more assignments. I told him from now on whatever free time I had from my law practice I wanted to spend here at Deucalion. While I said it with my heart in my mouth, because I was afraid he would say what he's said before, just this one more job and then I'll let you alone, this time I must have been more persuasive than usual. The President said if I was determined to go and sit on a bench, why, he would see what he could do to arrange it."

John could feel rather than see Ike shooting him another glance. Even though he was afraid to turn, because his father might guess he and Ike knew something they were concealing from him, John could not resist the temptation. He turned, and Ike winked at him, and John's father said, "What are you two up to?"

"Coming down the mountain, on the way to meet the train," Ike said smoothly, "I told Johnny if you went to Washington this week, you'd probably come back with the President of the United States our next shareholder in Deucalion."

"If it would help spread the Deucalion idea," Sennacherib Sayer said, "I'd urge the Executive Committee to give him his shares for nothing. But somehow I don't feel, although I wish I could, that the future of the race lies with presidents and kings and prime ministers. They don't seem to grasp the human equation. I tried to tell the President, for example, I tried to explain why Deucalion was important, why I could do more up here than down in Washington or any other place he wanted to send me, but I couldn't make him understand. He couldn't grasp it. Which is puzzling, since he was a poor boy himself, and poverty is the one element that—" John's father paused. The boy's heart tightened, as though the muscles inside his chest had been pulled in like reins. Sennacherib Sayer's eyes had narrowed. The turned-in look had reappeared on the handsome face. "Perhaps he wasn't poor enough," John's father said quietly, as though speaking to himself. "It makes a difference."

The truck lumbered up the tip of the rutted road, hung for a moment at the top of the bend, then rolled down into the next scallop. Ike cleared his throat as he shifted gears for the climb. John knew he was doing it to shake his father out of the mood into which his own words had pushed him. But the small trick, which John had seen work many times, did not work now. He looked up at his father, saw the white-haired head was turned away, and John looked at Ike. The handyman seemed troubled. He was chewing his lower lip as he held the shaking steering wheel. Then the truck came to the top of the scallop, and they were at Stonecraft Cut.

"Shall I stop, sir?" Ike said quietly.

"Yes, please," Sennacherib Sayer said. He was looking out at the valley for which John knew, from so many previous rides, his father had been watching. "Just for a moment, Ike."

The handyman cut the ignition, pulled the brake, and rested his elbows on the steering wheel. John opened his mouth, so his breathing would make less noise. There was something about the view from Stonecraft Cut that belonged with the turned-in look on his father's face. John had learned the importance of complete self-effacement when the two came together. The view was, of course, spectacular. From this point on the Wellesville Road the whole world seemed cupped in a frame that consisted of three mountain ranges. For Sennacherib Sayer, however, the view obviously meant something more. Ike said John's father liked to stop here on his way to and from the train because this part of Dutchess County reminded him of Wales, where Sennacherib Sayer's parents had been born. John had heard his father say there was a resemblance. But the boy suspected it was more than the resemblance that drew his father and held him. It was holding him now, his long, thin body slack on the seat of the truck, his eyes fixed dreamily on the mountains.

"It's so peaceful," John's father said. "You'd never think it could kill you."

John, surprised, turned toward Ike. Obviously just as surprised, Ike had turned toward John. The two movements brought Sennacherib Sayer's head around.

"That's what I should have told the President," he said. "I should have told him why my father left Wales, and came to this land of great promise, and how the land killed him before the promise was kept, and then maybe even a President would have understood why Deucalion is important."

He turned back, toward the valley, and stared out in brooding silence at the mountains.

"We go on now, sir?" Ike said finally, in a low, hesitant voice. "Mrs. Sayer said not to be late, sir."

The white head dipped in a nod. Ike kicked and poked at the pedals and levers. The truck lurched back into life.

"They didn't shoot him, of course," Sennacherib Sayer said quietly. His narrowed eyes came away reluctantly from the mountains to the road ahead. "They didn't stab him with a knife, or bludgeon him with a sashweight, or slip poison into his food, but they killed him just the same. A poor Welsh coal miner who wanted only one thing. The chance to walk upright, as God had intended him to walk, and not like one of those blind pit ponies with which every day of his life he had to crawl down into the hell of the mines. But there was no walking upright in those days for a Welsh coal miner. Or even today, for that matter. But it was much worse then. I remember hearing him tell, when I was a boy in Chicago, what life was like when he was a boy in Wales. I remember thinking he was exaggerating. But he wasn't. Not one bit, and he finally decided there was only one way out: to leave Wales and come to America. But that required fifty dollars for a steerage passage, and the only way a Welsh coal miner got fifty dollars in those days was by dying, and even then he didn't get it. The insurance company gave it to his wife."

John's father drew a long, slow breath, as though it were a refreshing swallow of cool water on a hot day, and he shook his head.

"He got the money," Sennacherib Sayer said to the cracked windshield of the Ford truck. "By selling a piece of his life. Fifty dollars for five years. That was the going rate in Wales at the time. He didn't actually get the fifty dollars, of course, but that was all right, because what my father got was what he wanted to spend the fifty dollars on: a steerage passage to Canada. And when he got there—to Richard MacIntosh's wheat farm in Manitoba, to be precise—he started paying off the debt. The way hundreds of other young immigrants from Wales and Lancashire were paying off their debts to Richard MacIntosh and a dozen other big wheat farmers in Manitoba in those days."

Sennacherib Sayer laughed. It was a laugh John had heard before, from the platform of the Barn Hall, when his father, presiding at a Full Meeting, after being badgered from the floor by someone like Mr. Francis Tristram, finally rose to reply. Before you heard a word you knew, from the laugh, that the reply would put an end to the badgering. It was a laugh of triumph.

"About fifteen years ago, just before the war," Sennacherib Sayer said, "when Mr. Wilson asked me to arbitrate the labor dispute at Standard Steel, I remember late one night in the Wardman Park Hotel, when we were deadlocked and it looked hopeless, as it always does at regular intervals during an arbitration, I remember saying to the men at both sides of the table that things were not as hopeless as they looked, because men did make progress, things did get better, even for the common laborer, and one of the union men said bitterly he had never found it so. Well, I said, here we are, in nineteen fourteen, fighting over a clause that calls on the management of Standard Steel to pay its laborers time and a half when they are asked, during very busy periods, to work on Sundays. But thirty years ago, in eighteen eighty-four, when my father was paying off his fifty-dollar debt on Richard MacIntosh's wheat farm in Manitoba, he had to work later on Sunday nights if, in the morning, he had gone to church. I remember the look on the face of that union official. You mean to say, he said, your father worked seven days a week for five years to pay off a fifty-dollar debt, and if he took a couple of hours off on Sunday to worship his God, he had to repay the time with night work? I not only mean to say it, I said, but I do say it, I said, and the union official said why, that's slavery!"

Sennacherib Sayer paused. That small laugh, the odd little sound of victory, again filled the front seat of the Ford truck.

"That's right," he said. "That's what I would have also called it: slavery. But Richard MacIntosh and the other Manitoba wheat farmers who were growing rich on pieces of my father's life and the lives of other men, they didn't call it slavery. They called it a business arrangement. My father and these other men had wanted something. Richard MacIntosh and his friends provided it. My father and these other men were merely paying for what they had received. If we heard about such an arrangement today, in the enlightened year of nineteen fourteen, I said to the men at the arbitration table in the Wardman Park Hotel, all of us would be outraged, not only the union representatives on this side of the table, but, I feel sure, the Standard Steel representatives on this other side of the table, and they all agreed that was so. It was all I needed to break the deadlock."

This time, when John's father paused, he didn't laugh. He ran his thin, strong hand down the side of his thin, strong jaw. He might have been feeling his way back into a past in which he found it difficult to believe.

"What my father broke was his heart," Sennacherib Sayer said quietly. "Although at the time I don't think he knew that. People who live with a dream never think of the price they are paying to achieve it. Most of the time they don't even know they're paying it. My father didn't, although he did know, I remember his saying once that he sensed it, that Canada was not the place. It had seemed the place back in Wales, where any place *outside* of Wales would have seemed the place. But once he got to Canada, those five brutal years of paying back his steerage passage, they took the shine off Canada. The minute those years were over, the minute the debt was paid, my father put on his clean shirt and headed for the border. Getting across in those days was no problem. Immigration quotas were just a thought in those days in the backs of some legislative heads. The problem was what it had been in Wales, in Manitoba, in I suppose every place since the Garden of Eden: how to eat. My father solved it finally in the kitchen of a restaurant on Chicago's South Side that specialized in sea food. It had never occurred to him that his youth in the Welsh coal mines, and the later years on Richard MacIntosh's wheat farm in Manitoba, were the ideal preparation for shucking oysters, but that's how it worked out. Opening oysters and clams."

Sennacherib Sayer shook his head. This time, when he laughed, there was a touch of wonder in it.

"Opening oysters and clams," he said to the cracked windshield of Deucalion's only piece of automotive transport. "What a way to spend one's life! Opening oysters and clams for *other* people! Yet that's what my father did. Spent his life opening oysters and clams for other people to eat. Oh, he didn't intend to spend his life at it. When he took the job in the Dolphin Restaurant in eighteen eighty-nine, it was a temporary thing. He was hungry, and he'd been hungry ever since he'd left Manitoba, and this was just a way to get fed until he gathered his strength. What he didn't know," Sennacherib Sayer said. He paused again. He seemed to shiver slightly. John could feel his father's body shake on the seat beside him.

"What he didn't know," Sennacherib Sayer said in a low voice, "my father didn't know his heart was broken. I don't think he ever found out. I think all the things that happened to him from then on, meeting my mother, getting married, having a son, all those things happened to a different man. Different in my father's mind, I mean. Or a part of his mind. The part where the dream lived on. In that part of his mind he was still young, and strong, and he had just settled in a great new country, where young and strong people were welcome and needed and could, by working hard, make their fortunes. No, not *their* fortunes. That was already an old-fashioned notion even in 1890. Their *family's* fortunes. That was the American dream in those days. As the immigrant dreamed it, at any rate. Without the dream, he couldn't have carried on. Without the dream he couldn't have got out of bed at five every morning, made a coal fire in the kitchen stove, cooked himself some coffee and fried bread, walked five miles in the dark to the Dolphin Restaurant and, at night, walked five miles back to the two-room flat in which he sheltered the people for whom he kept the dream alive: his wife and his son. By the time I got old enough to grasp what was happening, that his life was really over, that the dream was no more than that, I was walking five miles every morning, too. But I wasn't walking to a sea food restaurant kitchen to open oysters. I was walking to the Huron Law School on La-

Salle Street, in which my father had enrolled me as soon as I got out of high school. I don't know where he got the idea that the law was the way out of the dream. Or rather into it. Maybe it was that his great hero, Lincoln, had been a lawyer. Maybe it was nothing more than an instinctive feeling for justice. I have often thought it was something shrewder, perhaps. Something his Welsh nose for the heart of the matter had led him to see: to become a Richard MacIntosh, you had to have some capital to start with; to become a Lincoln, you needed only the desire, and the brains, and the education. He implanted the desire in me so early that I never questioned its existence. He assumed I had the brains. And he paid for my education."

Sennacherib Sayer drew in another long, slow breath. He blew it out even more slowly.

"He paid for it with another piece of his life," John's father said. "It wasn't much bigger than the piece he gave to Richard MacIntosh for his steerage passage from Cardiff. But it was worth more. It came harder. It was no longer part of the life of a young man, but of an old one. Old before his time, perhaps. But old just the same. It was the last piece he had to sell. He was dead two weeks before I graduated from Huron. That's when I found out where my tuition had come from."

The truck, swinging into the next upward-curving scallop, swung John with it, against his father. He was surprised by how hard his father's arm felt against his shoulder. Looking up, John saw that the hardness was also in his father's face. Sennacherib Sayer's whole body was knotted with the tension evoked by his bitter memories. John had the feeling that the memories had overwhelmed him, that his father was talking not to his son and to Ike, but to the world that had fashioned him, to the sun and the sky that now surrounded him.

"From a money lender," he said. "And to pay it back, since there was never anything left from what my father earned shucking oysters, he started bringing home part-time work from a necktie factory. The factory specialized in those already-knotted bow ties that were once so popular, the kind that fastened around the neck with an elastic. The work was called 'turning.' The bits of silk were stitched by machine at the factory into long strips of little sacks. Every night, on his way home from his long day's work at the Dolphin, my father would stop at the factory for a bundle of these strips. Then, at home, he and my mother would sit at the kitchen table, tearing the little silk sacks free from the strips, turning them inside out, and stuffing them with small squares of canvas filler. Every morning, on his way to the Dolphin, my father would stop at the factory to deliver his bundle of 'turning,' the little silk sacks stuffed with canvas which the operators would complete by hand, with needle and thread, into finished bow ties. I don't know how much my parents earned by this work, but it was enough to get me through law school. Or rather to repay the loan that got me through law school. When he died two weeks, as I said, before I graduated, my father left nothing, but among that nothing there were no debts. He was a proud man. I'm sure he was proud of that. My mother was certainly proud of it. And grateful, too. She couldn't have carried on as long as she did, which wasn't very long, if she'd had to continue working to pay off a debt. As it was, she lived long enough to see her son actually practicing law. But not long enough for the son to prove to her how grateful he was to her and to her husband for what they had done for him."

In the sudden silence, as the truck bumped along, John watched his father's hand go up again to stroke the edge of the long jaw.

"Youth is, of course, a time of taking, not giving," Sennacherib Sayer said. "Nature probably knew what she was doing when she made selfishness a normal part of that time. If she hadn't, if young people had to waste time on gratitude during the period when they are best able to absorb the lessons that help preserve the race, the race might not get preserved. Just the same, it has its advantages. By the time you're old enough to think about how you got to be what you are, and you want to thank the people who helped make you what you are, those people are no longer around. When my time came, not only were my mother and father no longer around. They were no longer even people. I mean in my memory. What I remembered was not a couple of human beings who had given me life, and an education, and whatever in the way of character or ability I might possess. No. What I remembered was two bowed heads, both white, bent over a kitchen table late at night, picking away with calloused fingers at little sacks of silk and poking into them little squares of canvas. The horror of it was that nothing remained of them that I could love. They had become a couple of machines."

John became aware of an unexpected new noise. He

turned and saw that it was his father's fist, pounding gently against the door of the truck, as though he were keeping time to a piece of slow, sad music.

"I remember thinking," Sennacherib Sayer said, "with a feeling of shock, I remember thinking: *is that all?* Is that why my father came out of the coal pits, I asked myself, and worked off his debt to Richard MacIntosh, and walked five miles twice a day to shuck oysters for other people's lunches and dinners? The answer was, of course, no. He had done all that, and my mother had helped him, they had done all that to keep their son out of the coal pits, to keep him from having to sell pieces of his life to people like Richard MacIntosh and the money lenders. It came to me that I was what I was because my parents had become what they had become, and that's when I knew where the battle was. That's when I knew that so long as a single person was in danger of becoming what my mother and father had become to me, as long as a single human being could still become something of which nothing remained that another human being could love, the battle was not over. That's when the idea for Deucalion came to me."

The truck crested the last scallop. Almost with an audible sigh of relief, it came out on the flat stretch of road that ran from the boundary of Stonecraft Farm to the colony.

"We're told that man does not live by bread alone," Sennacherib Sayer said. "And most of us believe it, because most human beings believe what they're told. But the fact remains that most of us live our entire lives in the pursuit of our bread, the way my mother and father did. I find that wrong. We're not like the other animals. We have the power to think. We have the power to consider the future. We have the power to control our environment. We have the power to govern ourselves. We have the power to know right from wrong. Why shouldn't we use that power to reduce the earning of our bread to the smallest instead of the largest of our activities? Why shouldn't we use that power to turn ourselves into human beings other human beings will never forget and always love? Why shouldn't we use that power to live, not for the Richard MacIntoshes and the money lenders, but for ourselves and each other? In short, why shouldn't we use that power not to destroy ourselves but to give ourselves more life?"

Sennacherib Sayer shook his head.

"If I'd used my brains," he said, "that's what I would have

told the President yesterday in Washington when he made his little joke about my wanting to sit on a bench and his being willing to help me to do it. Look." He pointed toward the Main House, which had just come into view. "It's not much," Sennacherib Sayer said. "But it's a beginning. If we can make it work here, other people will be encouraged to make it work in other places. The proof is in the fact that there were so many people willing to try the Deucalion idea as soon as I announced it. Rich people as well as poor. Businessmen as well as artists. I tell you, Ike, it's got to work and it's going to work. We've had our rough spots these last few years, but now that I'm going to be able to spend more time up here, we'll smooth them out." John's father suddenly laughed. He said, "You may think you're just a handyman driving a somewhat decrepit Ford truck, Ike, but you know what you're really doing?"

"What?" Ike said.

"You're helping to change the world," Sennacherib Sayer said. Then, his voice rising, "Good Lord, what's that?"

"Looks like a crowd," Ike said. He winked at John. "I hope it ain't a fire."

"If it is," John's father said, "it's the first one I've ever seen accompanied by a brass band."

"It's Mr. Duhart," John said. "With the Music Masters' Guild."

"At this hour of the day?" his father said. "What's been going on up here this week,"

"Don't know," Ike said. "Everything was pretty quiet when Johnny and I left about an hour ago."

"Well, it's not quiet now," Sennacherib Sayer said. "Step on it, Ike. Let's see what's happening."

The first thing John saw, or rather heard, as the truck pulled into the parking area at the Main House, was Mr. Duhart and the members of his Music Masters' Guild. They were lined up in front of the porch, wearing their green tam-o'-shanters, playing "Hail to the Chief." They were making a good deal of noise but, as the truck stopped, Mr. Duhart jerked his baton upward, in the familiar signal, and the song came roaring out louder. John was aware of a great many other people, grouped on both sides of the porch, but he didn't really see them. His eyes were on his mother. She stood on the porch, looking out across the heads of Mr. Duhart's musicians toward the truck. She stood up very straight, her shoulders squared, her hands clasped lightly against her

shirtwaist, her lips parted in a small smile. John couldn't see
her eyes, because the setting sun, coming in from Aaron's
Brook across West Pasture, glinted on the octagonal lenses of
her glasses. But he knew she was watching his father. John's
heart, which had been thumping with the excitement of their
arrival, began to hammer in a different way. He turned to
look at his father. Sennacherib Sayer was still sitting in the
truck beside him. John saw that his father was staring out,
with a small smile, across the heads of Mr. Duhart's musicians, at his wife on the porch. They seemed so pleased to see
each other, they were so clearly caught up in a moment of
shared privacy, that John wondered uneasily why his heart
should have begun to hammer in that different way, the way
that was always for him a reminder of the secret fear with
which his mother lived. Then, as though he were totally unaware that other people were near, John's father jumped down
from the truck. He nodded and waved his hand as he moved
through the men and women who called to him from both
sides. He stepped around Mr. Duhart and climbed the porch
steps. He put his arms around his wife, and kissed her. He
didn't have to lean down to do it, the way he had leaned
down over Mrs. Tristram when he was talking to the schoolmaster's wife in Jensen's Drug Store. Sennacherib Sayer and
his wife were almost exactly the same height.

"She's telling him now," Ike said quietly.

John's mother, still leaning close to her husband in the posture of this kiss, was saying something into his ear. There was
no start of surprise. No movement of elation. No gesture of
disbelief. The tall figure in the pepper-and-salt tweed suit remained motionless, listening. Then, slowly, the white head
moved again. Sennacherib Sayer placed a kiss on his wife's
other cheek. He moved his arm up, around her shoulders,
and turned her with him to face the people spread out below
the porch. There was something about the two tall people
standing side by side, perfectly calm, smiling slightly, like pictures John had seen of George V and Queen Mary greeting
their subjects from a Buckingham Palace balcony, that made
them seem total strangers. John had a moment of fear, as
though he had suddenly discovered he was alone in a hostile
crowd. He remembered his father's voice, on the front seat of
the truck, describing his youthful memory of the two bowed
heads, both white, bent over a Chicago kitchen table late at
night, picking away with calloused fingers at little sacks of
silk and poking into them little squares of canvas. John's mo-

ment of fear became a stab of panic. The image of his own father and mother had begun to slip away from him. Then Ike, perhaps sensing what was happening, put his hand on the boy's shoulder, and the panic began to ease away. Sennacherib Sayer raised a hand and said, "My dear friends." He became John's father again.

"My dear friends and fellow colonists," John's father said. "The pattern of comment a man makes on an occasion like this has been laid down by other and better men, on other and greater occasions. If I seem to slight that pattern now, it is not because of disrespect for tradition. It is because I cannot believe any man before me has ever been granted the gift of being able to say what I am about to say now." Sennacherib Sayer paused. He turned the smile briefly on his wife, then turned back to the Deucalion colonists. "There is no place in all the world where I would rather have learned of this great honor the President has bestowed on me than right here, at Deucalion, among the friends who have cast their lot with me in our efforts to refashion a corner of God's earth into something worthy of Him; at the side of the woman I love; on a day that had already been set aside as a time of joy and celebration because it is my son's birthday."

The colonists below the porch burst into applause. Dr. Duhart's baton flashed in an imperious arc. The green tam-o'-shanters broke into "Happy Birthday to You." John's face grew hot as the colonists turned toward the truck.

"Surprised?" Ike said.

"Uh-huh," John said.

Ike laughed and said, "That's the way to do it. Lie with the best of them. It makes people happy."

Mrs. Loring's small, narrow face appeared at the side of the truck.

"You get it?" she shouted above the music.

"Get what?" Ike shouted back.

"Pipe down," John said. "She's talking to me." He pulled the bottle of liver extract from his pocket and handed it to the cook. "I spent the nickel on candy, like you said."

"It's my birthday present to you," Mrs. Loring said. "Happy birthday." She shoved the bottle into the pocket of her apron, sent a quick glance toward the porch, and said, "Wait till you taste those carrot cutlets."

"Wait till Mr. Sayer hauls you up on charges at a Full Meeting for corrupting the morals of the young," Ike said.

"You shut up," Mrs. Loring said. "This is a secret."

She moved off, around the crowd of colonists, toward the kitchen door at the side of the Main House. Ike said, "While she's cooking them carrot cutlets, I better see what I can do about getting me a bottle of grape tonic for my cough out of that commissary." He dug into his pocket for the key to the cupboard and said, "Now, here's what I'd like you to do, Johnny."

But Johnny didn't do it because, just then, Mr. Duhart's men brought the song to a snappy finish. Sennacherib Sayer, coming down from the porch, said: "Thank you, one and all, my dear friends. Now let us repair to our various tables for the evening meal, as we have a long and excellent program prepared for tonight. We will gather in the Barn Hall at eight." He reached into the truck, lifted John from the front seat, swung him up on the pepper-and-salt shoulders, and marched back up to the porch, singing "Happy Birthday." The colonists and Mr. Duhart's men, dispersing toward their cabins, laughed and applauded and shouted, "Happy birthday, John!" On the porch John's mother took him down from his father's shoulders, held him close for a moment or two, then whispered in his ear, "Happy birthday, darling."

He didn't exactly feel happy, the way he felt when he and Ike were rolling down the mountain in the Ford, bellowing "Mrs. Murphy," and John knew it had something to do with his mother's secret fear and his inability to help her, but he didn't worry too much about that. John knew he would get to feel happy at the table, when he was opening his presents. He was right. The good feeling started with the sight of the table decoration which, as his mother had said, was made from the Christmas ornaments. It did not, however, look like a Christmas decoration because of the way his mother and Mrs. Loring had mixed the glass balls with the flowers and acorns. The feeling got better when Mrs. Loring brought in the cake. The pink and white frosting brought Sennacherib Sayer's eyebrows up. Mrs. Loring, who was watching him, laughed.

"No, sir," she said. "Not a drop of sugar, Your Honor. Egg white, strawberry syrup for coloring, and whole wheat flour."

"My congratulations," Sennacherib Sayer said. "Yours is truly the spirit of Deucalion, and I suggest we refrain from Your Honor until the appointment is confirmed by the Senate. The most exclusive club in the world can be pretty sticky about the President's appointments on occasion. Up here I am Sennacherib Sayer, colonist."

"Yes, sir," Mrs. Loring said. "I put two extra candles to grow on. One for John, and one for Deucalion."

"Let us hope they both grow up to be fine, healthy adults," John's father said. "Ready?" John nodded and his father said, "Blow!"

John pulled in his breath, held it while his father and his mother and Mrs. Loring smiled, then hurled it out with all his strength. A funny thing happened. The blast reduced the ten tiny flames to a small mass of writhing smoke in which were imbedded ten glowing dots. But the blast seemed to flow on and on, across the cake, down the table, and out into the hall, where it apparently rattled the front door. Then John, who had made himself dizzy with the effort, felt his strength coming back. His eyes began to focus again. He saw that something had indeed happened to the front door: Dr. Crocker had come through it.

"Excuse me, Sen," he said. "I know this is an intrusion, but something urgent has come up."

John's father was obviously just as surprised as the other people in the dining room. He said, "Max, you sound upset."

Dr. Crocker was a research physicist in the General Electric laboratories in Poughkeepsie. He did not upset easily. John had heard his father say many times it was the mild-mannered little man's scientific mind that made him the most valuable member of Deucalion's Executive Committee.

"I'm sorry," he said. "But I'm very upset. Could I have a few moments with you in private, Sen?"

He got, instead, a few moments of silence. John became acutely aware of a number of things: the unpleasant smell from the snuffed-out candles on the cake; the way, even though the expression on her face did not change, his mother's hand moved apprehensively to the gold fleur-de-lis that held her watch pinned to her shirtwaist; Mrs. Loring's sudden absorption in the condition of the cake knife, the edge of which she kept testing with the back of her thumb nail. Only John's father did not seem, like their visitor, upset.

"Why, Max, you've been with us from the beginning," Sennacherib Sayer said. "You know there's no such thing as privacy here at Deucalion. Within the limits of decency, everything that concerns one member of Deucalion concerns all its members. What's on your mind, Max?"

Dr. Crocker sent his troubled glance toward John's mother before he said, "Francis Tristram has called a Full Meeting."

"I don't see any reason in that for being upset," John's father said. "The charter states clearly that any member of the colony, by making the request to a member of the Executive Committee, can call a Full Meeting of all the colonists at any time. I assume Francis has made such a request to you."

"Yes, Sen, he has," Dr. Crocker said.

"Very well," Sennacherib Sayer said. "Schedule the meeting."

"He wants it tonight," Dr. Crocker said.

"You mean *now?*" Sennacherib Sayer said.

"Yes," Dr. Crocker said. "Right after dinner."

"But we have a celebration scheduled," John's mother said. She talked English, which had been taught her at high school in Stockholm, with the slight accent and faintly mannered precision of someone to whom it would always be a second language. Only in moments of stress, however, did her choice of words take on a touch of formality, as though she were reading a proclamation. She now said, "Not only is it John's birthday. It is the day on which a great honor has been bestowed upon his father."

"That's what I told Francis Tristram," Dr. Crocker said. "I said I was sure the Full Meeting could wait, but he said no. He insisted, Griselda. I'm sorry."

"But you are not the one to be sorry," John's mother said. "It is Mr. Tristram who is being outrageous." She turned to her husband. "Sennacherib," she said, and at once John could feel the tension in the room increase. Nobody, not even his mother, ever pronounced his father's strange name in full except on formal occasions. "Surely, Sennacherib," John's mother said, "you will not permit this?"

"I will try to prevent it," John's father said. "But that's really all I can do, Griselda. Try. I can't prevent the meeting, or even postpone it, by ordering it postponed. The charter is quite specific about that." He turned back to Dr. Crocker. "Did Tristram give you an agenda?"

Dr. Crocker shook his neat, round, bald head. He said, "Merely that some information had just come to his attention and he felt all the colonists should be apprised of it at once."

"What information?"

Everybody turned toward the little woman holding the cake knife. Anger had reddened Mrs. Loring's face. Dr. Crocker took a step backward, as though he didn't quite trust her next movement with that knife.

John's mother gave the cook a nod of approval before she turned back to Dr. Crocker. "What information can Mr.

Francis Tristram have discovered, and about what, to justify this revolting display of boorishness?"

Dr. Crocker changed his clothes every evening as soon as he got home to Deucalion from his job in Poughkeepsie. Now he nervously twisted in both hands the coonskin cap which, when he had it on his head outdoors, made him look, Ike Ten Eyck had once told John, like Daniel Boone on his way to take an arithmetic test that he was pretty sure he didn't have a chance of passing.

"Griselda, I'm sorry," Dr. Crocker said. "Tristram refused to elaborate or explain. All he told me was he'd discovered this information. It was shocking, he said, and the colonists were entitled to hear it and act on it immediately. Therefore, he was exercising his right under the charter to call a Full Meeting at once."

"His right!" John's mother said contemptuously. "Did not that pompous man avail himself of the opportunity to call it his duty?"

The coonskin cap took another beating from Dr. Crocker's nervous fingers.

"As a matter of fact," he said awkwardly, "that's the word Tristram did use. I thought—" Dr. Crocker paused. He looked at John's father, then down at the racoon tail he was mangling. He said, "I thought, in view of all the bad feeling there's been around lately, Sen, I thought I'd edit out that part of what Tristram said."

"The bad feeling around here has all been caused by Mr. Francis Tristram and nobody else," Mrs. Loring said angrily. Holding the cake knife as though it were a tennis racket and she was getting into position for a backhand chop shot, she advanced on the research physicist. "Am I right or am I wrong?"

Backing away, Dr. Crocker said, "Mrs. Loring, all I'm doing is reporting what Tristram told me. Don't act as though I have anything to do with it."

"How else am I supposed to act?" Mrs. Loring demanded. "Klaus Immensee says the worst thing for me is to keep things bottled up inside me. You feel somebody is a louse but you're afraid to say so, or even to feel it. So you don't say so, and you pretend you don't feel it. Next thing you know, you've got a rash, or you think people are following you down the street, or you wake up in the middle of the night bathed in sweat and afraid someone is coming up the rainpipe to cut your throat or rape you."

"Mrs. Loring," John's mother said sharply. "There are children present."

"You bet there are," Mrs. Loring said. "And I'm one of them. Sixty-two years old, and inside, my emotional life, no more grown up than John here." The cake knife came down in a vicious swipe at the imaginary tennis ball. John, by moving his head just in time, managed to keep it attached to his neck. "I gave up my restaurant in Greenwich Village," Mrs. Loring said. "I came up here to Deucalion because Klaus Immensee said unless I got away from the tensions that were killing me, unless I got to a place and among people where I could paint and express myself, and *be* myself, I'd be dead in five years. Well, I'm not dead," Mrs. Loring said. "And I've been here nine years, practically from the beginning, and I'm not only alive, but I'm functioning, and if I'm not completely happy, I've got the hope that up here I'll somehow work it out and reach that, too. And I'm not going to have that taken away from me by a loudmouth son-of-a-bitch troublemaker like Francis Tristram."

She stood there, under the figure she had not quite finished in her mural, the figure of George Washington meeting Cornwallis, apparently surprised not by the sobs that were suddenly shaking her but by the fact that she had run out of words. Nobody seemed to know what to do. Nobody except Sennacherib Sayer. John's father rose and came around the table. He did something John had seen him do many times to many people at Deucalion. He put his hand on Mrs. Loring's shoulder, and it was as though she had been placed gently into a relaxing bath. The tension eased out of her like water draining from a tub. The knotted creases in her face smoothed away as she turned with a look of devotion to the tall, white-haired, handsome figure.

"Nobody is going to take it away from you," Sennacherib Sayer said quietly. "We started Deucalion, people like you and me, Mrs. Loring, we started this place to drag from the harsh indifference of a mercenary civilization the moments of peace and beauty that make men and women worthy of being men and women. You're a better and happier human being than you were when you joined us, Mrs. Loring, and nothing and nobody is going to stop us from making you, as well as all the rest of us, still better and still happier." He paused, touched her wrinkled cheek gently, and said, "That's a promise, Mrs. Loring."

Across the cook's head he signaled with his glance to

John's mother. Mrs. Sayer rose and came to Mrs. Loring. She put her arm around the cook, and led the now clearly exhausted woman out of the room.

"Max," John's father said to Dr. Crocker. "Did you edit anything else out of what Francis Tristram said to you?"

The bald head moved twice, once left, once right.

"You know better than that, Sen."

John's father said, "Of course I do. But we all have our moments of doubt."

"I've never had mine," Dr. Crocker said.

John's father gave him a quick glance.

"You won't have any, either," Sennacherib Sayer said. "Not as a result of anything I do or say, Max. Is that clear?"

"It was never anything else, Sen."

John's father nodded.

"Good," he said. "Now you go back to your dinner. I'll see what I can do to get Tristram to postpone the Full Meeting. If he refuses, very well, he has that right. We'll join him at the Barn Hall at eight and hear his important information."

John's father waited until Dr. Crocker left the room. Then he sat down at the table and pulled the small black leather notebook and the black and gold Waterman from his pocket. He didn't seem to have to think about what he wanted to write. Sending the pen swiftly back and forth across the page, he worked for several minutes. He re-read what he had written, tore the sheet from the notebook, folded it, and stood up. He went to the secretary that Lester La Croix and the members of his Carpenters' Guild had made the year before as a Christmas present for the Main House. John's father rummaged among the pigeonholes and found an envelope. He sealed the note into it, and turned back to the table.

"John," he said. "You know Mr. Tristram's cabin?"

"Yes, sir," John said. "Northwest Cottage Grove. Last on the right facing the Carpenters' Guild."

"Take this to him, and wait for an answer."

"Yes, sir," John said.

He took the envelope, started for the door, and heard his father say, "John."

He stopped and turned back.

"Yes, sir?"

"I'm sorry about your birthday party," Sennacherib Sayer said. "We'll finish it when you get back. Meantime." He put his hand in his pocket and pulled out a small package. "Happy birthday, John."

"Thank you," John said, taking the package. "May I open it on the way?"

"Of course," his father said. "And John."

"Yes, sir?"

"Keep that envelope in your pocket until you get there and hand it to Mr. Tristram."

This seemed simple enough, especially since John's excited interest in the schoolmaster's unusual demand for an immediate Full Meeting had been diverted by his father's present. To examine it in privacy, without delaying the delivery of the envelope to Mr. Tristram, John decided to cut across Center Pasture. This way he would avoid running into Alfie Crocker or Charlie Devon or any of the other kids who lived off West Cottage Lane. At this time of day, between supper and bedtime, they would have a ball game going in West Pasture. Even if they had not yet heard about Mr. Tristram's demand for the Full Meeting, which would provide the raw material for quite a circus, they would have plenty of cracks to make about John's birthday. Ordinarily, this would not bother him. Ike had taught him how to give as good, and better, than he received. And John enjoyed seeing the faces of some of those smart alecks when he uncorked a few variations of "Mrs. Murphy" as reworked by Ike from song to epithet. But tonight John didn't care about that. Tonight he cared about his father's present.

Cutting across West Pasture, in which he could hear the cows chomping, John tore the paper from the small package, revealing a small cardboard box. He opened it, and stopped walking. The box contained a beautiful silver Ingersoll. On the white face of the watch, under the name of the maker, somebody had scrawled a signature in black ink. The letters were very tiny, and the handwriting was not very legible, so John could not read the name. But this did not stop his heart from suddenly jumping with excitement. He had never seen an autographed watch, but knowing his father was a great man, John knew the signature had to belong to somebody who was also great. Already, in his mind, he could see the faces of the other kids when they saw his treasure. Then he saw the face of a cow, staring directly at him, and John came out of his happy trance.

"Beat it," he said to the cow. Clutching the Ingersoll, he broke into a trot to make up for lost time. Between the Carpenters' Guild Building and The Dairy Farmers' Guild barn, he swung left, toward West Cottage Lane. Here he had the satisfaction of learning his tactics had been sound: beyond the cabins of Northwest Cottage Grove, which screened him from West Pasture, John could hear the shouts and screams of the ball players. He trotted up the lane, toward the last cabin on the right of the Northwest Cottage Grove group. Then he slowed down, as he always did when he came near the home of the Deucalion schoolmaster.

The colony's charter stated clearly that no member could exercise any control over another member's taste in the design of his dwelling place. "Self-expression," Sennacherib Sayer had written in the original prospectus, "begins at home." Nevertheless, two controls had entered the consideration of the colonists almost at once: the nature of the terrain they had purchased, and the raw material available on it.

The land between Aaron's Brook and the Wellesville Road was very flat. The problem of drainage, therefore, was a constant worry. To solve it, no matter how they may have felt the solution affected their desires for self-expression, the colonists were forced to heed the advice of their scientifically-trained fellows. People like Max Crocker and Milton Fennell pointed out that the most sensible, meaning the cheapest, procedure was to group the cabins in four clusters, at the corners of the rectangular tract, where the land was just sufficiently higher to allow rain water and sewage to run off naturally.

The second consideration was actually a pleasant one, at least for Deucalion colonists. Godwin's Tract, out of which the colony's hundred and fifty acres had been cut, was almost exclusively white birch land. Some of the colonists had, of course, in their dreams of the good life, seen themselves living in homes hewn from forests of oak and maple. Some of them even tried, after they bought their shares in Deucalion and arrived to begin carving new lives for themselves, to give flesh to their dreams. But oak and maple had to be purchased and trucked in from Poughkeepsie and Albany, which was expensive, whereas anybody with an axe could obtain all the birch he wanted by spending no more than his own energy. As a result, the log cabin became as typical of the Deucalion landscape as it was of illustrations in books dealing with the life of Abraham Lincoln.

There were two exceptions to this uniform picture: the Main House, a New England salt box that had come with the property and was, by charter, reserved for the use of the

Chairman of the Executive Committee and his family; and the home of the Chairman of the Children's Guild.

The latter was the newest structure on the Deucalion tract. It had been started almost a year ago, soon after Francis Tristram and his bride arrived from England, and finished shortly before Easter. There had been a certain amount of criticism. None of it was official, of course, since the charter made the schoolmaster's position and rights unassailably clear. In the interests of harmony, however, without which, he could not stress too often, the Deucalion idea was doomed to failure, Sennacherib Sayer made it a point to have a series of private talks with small groups of colonists.

"It seems to me the way for us to look at it is to try to look at it the way Tristram looks at it," John's father had said to one such group. "Tristram is a Cockney. You may not appreciate precisely what that means, being Americans, but I do, because my parents come from Wales. Being a Cockney means more than being poor, the way being born on New York's Lower East Side means being poor. This is because Cockneys are more than products of a slum, the way I am the product of a slum because of the section of Chicago where I was born. Being a Cockney is at least in part a state of mind, and under the British class system, it is not a very pleasant state of mind. Oh, there are Cockneys who rise above this state of mind, and are even proud of their origins. But Francis Tristram is not one of these. He is actually more typical, at least of Cockneys who have intelligence and talent and manage to acquire some education. Francis Tristram is bitter about his origins. He felt that in England, as a Cockney, he didn't have a chance to exploit his full potential, and he may be right. I would think, for example, it was much easier for me to grow up and make my way in the world undamaged, at least not permanently damaged, by my Chicago slum origins, than it would be for Francis Tristram if he had remained in England, teaching at their equivalent of our grade schools. It was the desire to escape his fate, a fate he considers unfair, that attracted Francis Tristram first to emigration, and then to Deucalion."

John remembered the way his father's face, when he paused for breath, took on that turned-in look, concentrated around the eyes. It was the look with which he seemed to be staring back into a fragment of the unpleasant past, the look that always made John uneasy.

"But we all know, of course, how close love is to hate,"

Sennacherib Sayer went on. "I remember, shortly after the war, when I was in London on a mission for Mr. Wilson. I remember being taken by a couple of junior officials to see one of the places in the East End where a zeppelin had dropped a bomb. All at once, without warning, in a distinctly Cockney accent, one of the young men said bitterly: *The Hun 'it it, but 'e didn't 'it it 'ard enough.* My surprise must have been clear on my face, because the other young man laughed and said: *Don't mind Bert; 'e's just talking about a place 'e loves.* I think Francis Tristram suffers from the same double feelings, as it were. He hates England for its class society and the fact that he was born into one of its lower classes. But he can't help loving that society, including some of its upper classes. I think that's one of the reasons, in addition, I'm sure, to loving her, why Tristram married the daughter of a clergyman with one of the more desirable livings in Kent. I know nothing about what went on, but I do know that the vicar in a Kentish town is socially a number of cuts above most of his parishioners. Mrs. Tristram's father could not have viewed with favor the attentions to his very young daughter, no more than fifteen at the time, I would guess, of a Cockney schoolmaster. I'm sure that's why they had to elope. It's even possible that the necessity for eloping helped form their desire to join us here at Deucalion. Or perhaps it was only Tristram's desire, because his wife naturally does not have his resentment against the British class system, except perhaps in an intellectual way. But it's not an intellectual thing to her husband. Francis Tristram, born a Cockney, has this hatred in his guts, and I suppose he'll always have it, or at least some part of it. That's why I say if, to make some sort of peace with his private demon, Francis Tristram had to marry an upper-class girl who writes poetry, perhaps to help give that peace some permanence he must live in the sort of house that Cockneys rarely live in, and are almost never born in. In short, gentlemen, if Francis Tristram wants it, and by charter we can't stop him from building it, I say let him have in Dutchess County what more properly belongs in the Cotswolds, namely, his Tudor cottage complete with thatched roof."

He had it. But the permanent peace it was supposed to bring him had not come with it.

House-to-house visiting was not very common at Deucalion. The colonists saw each other so often at the group activities arranged by the various Guilds that there was very little

time for dropping in on individual friends or whipping up
small dinner parties. While almost all the cabins were, as a
result, used most of the time as bedrooms and studios, there
was a steady flow of informal traffic between them, especially
those inhabited by families with children. Tools and toys
were constantly being borrowed and returned. The Dairy
Farmers' and the Farmers' Guild delivered their products almost daily. Members of the other Guilds, such as the Carpenters', for example, were always stopping by to check the
measurements of the space where a table or a bunk bed was
going to be built. The only colonist's home on the Deucalion
tract at which nobody stopped by, except by invitation, was
the Tudor cottage built by Francis Tristram for himself and
his wife. And the invitation, which always involved the
schoolmaster's official duties, was always very specific about
time. In short, nobody ever actually visited the schoolmaster,
but many people had appointments with him.

Nobody was anxious to change this, either. Sunny disposi-
tions were not the rule at Deucalion. Most of the colonists,
while pleasant enough, had been brought to the place by the
sort of inner turmoil that, every now and then, drove affable
Mrs. Loring to an outburst of hysterical sobs. Solitude was
sought after, and respected. The solitude of the Tristrams,
however, was respected for a different reason. Soon after
their cottage was finished, and they moved out of one of the
bedrooms in the Main House that were provided by charter
for the use of new colonists while they were building their
cabins, something happened to the relationship between Tristram and his wife.

For months after they arrived from England, while they
lived in the Main House with John and his parents, the English couple had seemed an attractive and almost embarrass-
ingly typical pair of honeymooners. Nobody, certainly not
John, ever heard the schoolmaster raise his voice to his wife.
And Mrs. Tristram, of course, was generally believed to be
incapable of speaking above a shy whisper to anybody, especially her husband. Once they disappeared behind their own
front door, however, this changed. Their neighbors in Northwest Cottage Grove began to hear and gossip about the
Tristrams' quarrels. Cornelius Hill, the head of the Shoemak-
ers' Guild, whose cabin was twenty feet south of the Tudor
cottage, reported worriedly to Sennacherib Sayer one night
that he thought the schoolmaster was beating his wife. Hill
said he had heard Mrs. Tristram screaming.

There were some who said Sennacherib Sayer should have done a bit of investigating before he undertook to speak to the schoolmaster about this, because everybody knew Corny Hill's hearing was deteriorating and his imagination was as active as a child's. Others said Sennacherib Sayer had done precisely what the situation called for. As Chairman of the Executive Committee it was one of his duties to speak out against, if not to prevent, violence. While that particular argument was never settled, this much was clear to all: from that moment, the night Sennacherib Sayer spoke to Francis Tristram about Cornelius Hill's report, the breach between the schoolmaster and the rest of the colonists, which had appeared for the first time when Tristram and his wife moved from their temporary quarters in the Main House into their own home, began to grow wider. It did not affect Tristram's work. But it did affect the way his pupils felt about him.

John, for instance, would never, if he could help it, walk up or down the northern end of West Cottage Lane. If he couldn't help it, he always slowed down and edged over to the far side of the rutted path, so that he would have as much distance between himself and the Tudor cottage as the narrow lane permitted. He did this now, even though slowing down seemed pointless, since John knew he had to go into the cottage, or at least knock on the door, to deliver his father's envelope. Yet it wasn't completely pointless, because only by slowing down could he make certain he would hear, if there was anything to hear, what Cornelius Hill had reported to John's father *he* had heard. All John heard now was the sizzling rasp of the crickets, and the first evening honks of the frogs from Aaron's Brook. He stepped across the path and knocked on the door.

"Yes?"

"It's me," he said. "John Sayer. I have a message from my father."

There was a series of rustling movements and the door opened.

"Hello," Mrs. Tristram said. She looked tense and worried, the way she had looked when she was standing near the penny scale in Jensen's Drug Store, talking to his father. "May I have it, please?"

For a couple of moments, as he stared at her outstretched hand, John did not grasp what she meant. When he did, he started to worry.

"My father said I should give it to Mr. Tristram," he said.

"Oh, really, now, don't be silly," Mrs. Tristram said. John looked at her in astonishment. He had never heard the schoolmaster's wife sound like that. The look on his face may have reminded her of this fact. Mrs. Tristram smiled quickly. With the swaying motion that always did such a funny thing to his heart, she brushed away the brown hair from her forehead.

"Mr. Tristram is not at home," she said. "If you'll give the message to me, I'll give it to him when he comes in."

What she said sounded sensible, but it made John worry more.

"My father said I should wait for an answer," he said.

"Oh," Mrs. Tristram said. She looked thoughtful. "Well, John, do come in and we'll work this out." She held the door wide. He stepped in. She closed the door and said, "May I see the message?"

The envelope was out of his pocket, and he had handed it over, before John realized this was not right.

Helplessly, he said again, "My father said to give it to Mr. Tristram."

She smiled as she poked her finger under the pasted down flap and flipped it open.

"But you can't do that if Mr. Tristram is not here, can you?" she said gently. Her green eyes swung downward, toward the sheet from his father's notebook. "You mustn't worry, John. I'm sure your father would approve. And if you'll just wait—"

Her voice trailed off. She had caught her lower lip in her teeth and she was reading the note. She took a long time about it, John thought. Almost as long as his father had taken to write it. When she looked up, finally, he had the feeling she had forgotten he was in the room. Her eyes, meeting his, reflected surprise. She might have been wondering how she happened to be here. Or perhaps even who he was. Then she seemed to remember, and she smiled.

"It's difficult," she said. For another few moments that was all she did say. Suddenly, unexpectedly, she said, "How nice it must be to be ten years old." She reached out and touched John's cheek. Her hand was so cold that he winced. The hand fell away quickly. A flush rose in the small, shadowed hollows under her cheekbones. "I'm sorry," Mrs. Tristram said. "Happy birthday, John."

"Thank you," he said, feeling terrible. "I didn't mean—" But the words wouldn't come. How did you tell someone you had not shrunk away out of distaste? Because you didn't like her? John held out his hand and said, "Look what my father gave me."

Her eyes spread wide and her lips formed a circle.

"But how lovely," the schoolmaster's wife said. "May I?"

"Sure," John said. "Look what's written here."

She took the watch in both hands, as though she were cupping a flower.

"Aitch, ee, are, bee, ee, are, tee," she read slowly. Then her voice quickened. "Herbert Hoover!" she said. "The President of the United States! He had the President of the United States write his name on the face of your watch!"

"Yes," John said. He wondered if he hadn't been misjudging her all during the year he had known her. He had been unable to make out the name on the watch, but she had made it out at once. It had never occurred to him before that Mrs. Tristram, who was beautiful, was also smart.

"How like him!" Mrs. Tristram said. "To think of something fresh and original for a present. Something nobody else would think of. And to take the time and trouble to get it done. I don't suppose there's another boy in all the world who has a watch with the name of the President of the United States written on the face."

"No, ma'am," John said. He was now convinced he had misjudged her. This woman was smart. She had thought right away of exactly the same thing he had thought of.

"Or, for that matter, an adult, either," the schoolmaster's wife said. "Without any doubt you are the only person in the whole wide world who owns a watch with the name of the President of the United States written on the face." She handed back the watch. "What a wonderful thing to know on one's tenth birthday. He must have had the President do it yesterday, when he was in Washington."

"Yes, ma'am," John said. He wondered how Mrs. Tristram knew his father had been in Washington yesterday.

"Yes, how very like him," she said. Her glance darted around the room, across John's head, as though she had heard a sound that disturbed her. "Not many famous men are as kind and thoughtful as your father," Mrs. Tristram said. Then, quickly, "Wait."

She ran to the fireplace. From a narrow shelf above the mantel she took down a small silver object and brought it back to John.

"Here," she said. "It's your birthday present. I've been saving it for you."

This was a lie, of course. But John didn't mind. It was the sort of lie he himself would have told if he had forgotten somebody's birthday, say Ike's, and didn't want to make him feel bad. Besides, the thing she had given him was very pretty.

"Thank you," John said. "What is it?"

"A pair of grape scissors," Mrs. Tristram said. "Georgian. My mother gave them to me. I thought you might like them. Not that one does much grape cutting here at Deucalion, but I thought you might like them because they're so pretty."

"Yes, thank you," John said. "What about the answer to my father's message? He said I should give it to Mr. Tristram and wait for an answer."

"Well, you gave it to Mr. Tristram's wife, so I suppose Mr. Tristram's wife had jolly well better come up with an answer." She looked at him in silence for several moments. John could feel his face grow hot. It was as though she were trying to read the answer in his mind. "It's quite astonishing, really," the schoolmaster's wife said at last. "Do you know how long ago I was ten years old, and people were giving me presents on my birthday?"

"No, ma'am," John said.

"Seven years ago," Mrs. Tristram said quietly. "How odd, how unbelievable to think that seven years ago I was your age."

John did think about it for a few moments. But he didn't get very far. Seven from ten left three, which was the age of Charlie Devon's kid sister, Michelle, and John could not imagine himself as ever having looked or sounded like Michelle Devon. Seven plus ten was seventeen, the age of the schoolmaster's wife today, but John could not imagine himself looking and sounding like Mrs. Tristram, either. It was all too complicated, and not very interesting. What he had to get was that answer to his father's message.

"I better get back," John said. "My father is waiting for an answer to this message."

"Yes, of course," Mrs. Tristram said. She looked again at the page from Sennacherib Sayer's notebook, then looked up. "Would you tell him all I know is it has something to do with our financial picture."

"Sure," John said. "All you know is it has something to do with our financial picture."

"That's right," Mrs. Tristram said. "Now I think you'd better hurry back."

"Yes, ma'am."

"Happy birthday, John."

"Thank you."

Cutting back across Center Pasture, John stopped only once: to wind the watch. He wasn't sure about the exact time, so he left the hands as they were, showing twenty minutes after eight, but the ticking was very satisfactory. He kept the silver ball against his ear as he trotted. Perhaps that was why he did not hear Ike calling him until the handyman, coming across from the back of the commissary, was practically on top of him.

"What the hell's the matter?" Ike said. "You deaf?"

"I was listening to this."

"Where'd you get it?"

"My father," John said. "For my birthday. That's President Hoover's name here. He signed it himself. With a pen."

Ike took the watch and, in the twilight, held it close to his face.

"Well, I'll be damned," he said. "I never saw anything like that before."

"Damn right, you didn't," John said. "Mrs. Tristram says I'm the only person in the whole wide world who owns a watch with the name of the President of the United States written on the face."

"Be better if you owned one that showed the right time." Ike took out the large gold watch with the snap front that wound with a tiny gold key kept in a slot behind the stem. Ike claimed he had inherited the watch from his father, who had been a conductor on the New York Central. Mrs. Loring, who had done some research on the area and its people when she was planning her mural, said the Ten Eycks had been riffraff from the day the first one showed up in Wellesville before the Civil War, and Ike didn't even know who his father had been. She said he had probably stolen the watch or picked it up in a pawn shop. In any case, it was the one possession Ike treated with care. He was proud of the fact that he was the only person at Deucalion who could always be counted on to know the correct time. He set John's new Ingersoll at eight minutes to eight, handed it back, returned his own watch to the pocket in his overalls, then said, "Mrs. Tristram? That where you been?"

"My father sent me over with a message," John said.

Ike gave him a sharp look and said, "Message for who?"

"Mr. Tristram."

"You just gave a message to Mr. Tristram?"

"He wasn't there," John said. "I gave it to Mrs. Tristram."

Ike turned to look behind him. John thought this was pretty silly, since they were standing practically in the middle of Center Pasture, and the only living things within hearing distance were a couple of cows.

"What was the message?" Ike said.

"I don't know."

"Oh, a written message?"

"In an envelope," John said. "Pasted. I gotta get to the Main House. My father is waiting for the answer."

He started toward the commissary, but Ike stopped him.

"Lemme see the answer."

"I can't," John said. "It's not written."

"Something she told you?" Ike said. "Mrs. Tristram?"

"Yeah."

"What she tell you?"

"All she knows is it has something to do with our financial picture."

"That's the message?" Ike said. "All she knows is it has something to do with our financial picture?"

"That's right, and cut it out, Ike. I gotta get the message to my father."

"Well, you ain't gonna get it to him at the Main House," Ike said. "He's over at the Barn Hall."

John hesitated. When his father said he would be at a certain place, he always was.

"I don't know," John said. "He told me to bring the message back to the Main House."

"When he told you that, he probably figured he could talk Fat Ass out of calling that Full Meeting for tonight, but he didn't, and I just saw him heading up East Cottage Lane with Dr. Crocker. If that message is going to do your father any good, you better get it to him where he is, not where he was. Come on."

It did occur to John as he trotted along beside Ike that, if his father said anything later about not getting the message where he had told John to deliver it, John could say Ike had talked him out of going to the Main House. But as soon as this occurred to him, John was so ashamed of himself that he pretended the thought had occurred to somebody else. While he was trying to choose the somebody else on whom he could hang this piece of cowardice, Ike said, "Oh, Jesus."

"What's the matter?"

"They started."

"They couldn't," John said. "It's not eight o'clock." He looked at his new Ingersoll. "It's only—" He paused. A terrible thought had crossed his mind. "Unless your watch is wrong?"

"My watch is never wrong," Ike said angrily. "I'm the only one on this place always has the right time."

"Well, I don't know," John said. "Dr. Crocker said the meeting was called for eight o'clock, and if they already started, then it's now eight o'clock or after."

"Maybe the President shoulda put *you* on the Supreme Court, not your father," Ike said. "You're not arguing a case. You're delivering a message. Come on."

Halfway across the cleared space in front of the Barn Hall front door, Ike stopped. John stopped beside him. John didn't ask why. He sensed what Ike had apparently sensed. Something was wrong. Certainly something unusual was happening. The front door, which was always open, except in the winter or during a storm, was shut.

"I wonder—" Ike started to say, then looked down at John. It was the sort of look his mother occasionally gave him when, about to say something in John's presence to Mrs. Loring or his father or another adult, she realized a child, *her* child, was present. Ike said, "Let's go see what this is about."

They walked up to the door. Ike took the big iron ring and pulled. The door came open, but not very far. Frank Poynter, the chief of the Dairymen's Guild, poked his head out. He looked annoyed until, in the fading light, he recognized the handyman.

"Oh, okay, Ike," he said. He started to shove the door open wider, then saw John, and stopped. "I'm sorry," he said. "No kids tonight."

"He's got a message for his father," Ike said.

"I can't help that," Frank Poynter said. "My orders from the Executive Committee were no kids. You want to come in, Ike, okay. Not you, John, I'm sorry."

Ike hesitated, then said, "I'll read about it in the funny papers. Good night, Frank."

"Suit yourself," Mr. Poynter said.

His head disappeared and the door was pulled shut from the inside.

"Why'd you do that?" John said.

"I don't take orders from no butter-churning cheese-maker," Ike said. "Come on."

He moved around to the west side of the barn and John followed. The building, which backed up on Aaron's Brook at the northern end of the Deucalion property, had been in very bad condition when the colony took over the land. The Carpenters' Guild had done a great deal of work on it, but most of this work had been done in fits and starts, between other and more important jobs, and almost all of it had been done for utilitarian reasons: to keep out the rain; to convert the old cow stalls into benches for spectators; to shore up the floor so that it would support a hundred or more people gathered for a meeting. Almost nothing had been done to the old barn for cosmetic reasons. As a result, it was the one structure at Deucalion that still looked from the outside as it had looked for years before the colonists arrived: a weather-beaten old barn that could stand several coats of paint.

It was this appearance that had provided the people of Wellesville with their first opportunity to do something concrete about their hostility to what they called the nuts from New York: the First Selectman, who also happened to be the Fire Commissioner, arrived one day with an order. Until the colonists equipped the barn with fire extinguishers, he said, and a fire escape, they were forbidden to hold meetings in the place. The news of the order, which was issued on a Wednesday, had been telephoned down to New York by Mrs. Sayer. On Friday, when Sennacherib Sayer came up on the train for the week end, he brought the fire extinguishers with him. And Lester La Croix, by working his entire Carpenters' Guild through the night of Thursday, had constructed a fire escape, complete with two sets of ladders, on the north side of the barn, facing Aaron's Brook. It was to this fire escape that Ike now led John.

"Try not to make any noise," the handyman said. "Not that anybody'll notice. The noise those cheesemakers make themselves once they open their yaps to say a few words beginning with fellow colonists, it's enough to bust your eardrums."

John took hold of the ladder, then turned.

"How about what Mr. Poynter said? No kids?"

"You're not a kid any more," Ike said. "You're ten years old today. Now stop bellyaching and get going."

John got up to the first level and stepped aside to wait for

Ike. The handyman came up beside him and pulled a bottle of grape tonic from his pocket. He took a swig, replaced the bottle, and belched.

"How about the noise *you* make?" John said.

"Natural sounds get lost in the night," Ike said. "Hold my pants."

John seized the crossed shoulder straps of Ike's overalls. The handyman crawled through the high, narrow window, dragging John in after him. Even though John had never before entered the Barn Hall in this way, he knew where he was: on the wide ledge that had once been the hayloft. It hung over the rear of the barn, and was now used as a storage area, mostly by the Carpenters' Guild because it was a good place for drying lumber. Crawling along behind Ike, who kept his skinny body below the level of the lumber stacks, John had to hold his nose with his free hand. The resinous smell made him want to sneeze. When Ike stopped crawling, John did sneeze, but he managed to get his other hand up in time. What emerged, as a result, was a muffled thump caused by the fact that the smothered eruption lifted John's body slightly from the floor.

"Breathe through your mouth," Ike hissed. He edged forward, on his knees, to a gap between the stacks. Breathing through his mouth, John edged up beside the handyman and lay down flat. He rested his chin on the backs of his crossed hands, as Ike was doing. Thus, their bodies side by side, they could peer down into the Barn Hall, where the meeting had indeed started. Dr. Crocker was on the platform, talking to the colonists spread out on the benches.

Behind Dr. Crocker, on the wall to which were fastened a huge reproduction of the Deucalion shield and a framed copy of the Deucalion Code, hung the Seth Thomas clock H. G. Wells had presented to the colony when the British novelist had been Mr. and Mrs. Sayer's guest at the Main House for a long week end a number of years ago. The visit had taken place when John was not quite three, and so he remembered very little about it. But he knew what everybody else at Deucalion knew, namely, why the Englishman had chosen a clock as his present to the colony.

The colonists had numbered fewer than forty at the time. When he addressed them at a Full Meeting in the Barn Hall, Wells had devoted most of his speech not to complimenting them, although he did tell them of his admiration for their efforts, but to warning them. The story of civilization, he had pointed out, was not a story of triumphs but a story of defeats. Touching briefly on the Sumerians, the Mesopotamians, and the Egyptians, Wells pointed out that, while each had achieved a culture that had seemed to its people indestructible, destruction was nonetheless the fate of each. And the thing that had destroyed them, just as it had later destroyed the Persians and the Greeks and the Romans, was not an armed enemy with superior weapons, but an invisible enemy that could neither be seen nor felt. The enemy was time.

Nobody had yet figured out how to deal with this enemy, Wells had pointed out, and until this *was* figured out, every civilization, including ours, was doomed to the destruction time had visited upon its predecessors. The Englishman had drawn a parallel between the invisible enemy and something very visible indeed: the jungle. Men cleared large pieces of it, he said, built homes, planted fields, reaped harvests, went on to invent alphabets and calendars, and then one day, when nobody was looking, the insidiously patient jungle crept up, silent, unnoticed, and obliterated everything that man had built with so much care. Until somebody found a way to deal with this enemy, Wells said, there was only one thing man could do: remain on constant guard. Not a moment must be allowed to go by unnoticed. Every fragment of time had to be watched and accounted for. Perhaps the constant surveillance would lead to the chink in the enemy's armor. Perhaps. For this reason, Wells had concluded, as a symbol of his appreciation for what Sennacherib Sayer and his colleagues were trying to do, he hoped they would accept, with his gratitude for their hospitality and his high hopes for their success, something that all people looked at, but very few people saw: the enemy's mocking sentry—a clock.

As it turned out, it was not a very good clock. According to Ike—who had admired Wells because, while the handyman drove him around the countryside, the Englishman had told him some very good dirty stories—the novelist had seen the clock on the lawn of an antique shop on the Wellesville Road, had asked Ike to stop the Ford truck, and had bought the clock a couple of hours before he made his speech to the Deucalion colonists in the Barn Hall. It was, in fact, Ike Ten Eyck's sardonic theory that the idea for the speech had come to Wells when he saw the old clock on the antique shop lawn, a fact that raised the Englishman in Ike's estimation. Among the other facts that Ike happened to know was, John thought, an odd one: the clock had cost Wells five dollars. Among the facts that everybody at Deucalion knew was, John learned, an embarrassing one: the clock, soon after its donor's departure, had stopped working.

Nonetheless, as a sort of salute to the great man who had briefly been in their midst, it was an unwritten rule at Deucalion that, before a Full Meeting started, some member of the Executive Committee, usually Max Crocker, would move the hands of the clock to the time at which the meeting began. When the meeting was over, he would move the hands to the time at which the meeting ended. The previous Full Meeting, which had taken place the preceding Friday, had ended at eleven minutes after nine. John, who had been present at that meeting, as were most members of the Children's Guild, remembered seeing Dr. Crocker, after banging his gavel, move the hands of the clock to 9:11.

Peering down into the Barn Hall now, as he lay flat beside Ike on the floor of the former hayloft, John could see the Seth Thomas clearly. The hands were still fixed at 9:11. The fact that Max Crocker, as meticulous about ritual as he was about scientific data, could have forgotten to move the hands of the clock to the moment when the meeting had begun, indicated to John that this was no ordinary meeting. The whole feel, indeed the smell, of the crowded chamber below him indicated that he was present at something extraordinary.

"Ike," he whispered.

"Shut up," Ike said. "Here comes Fat Ass."

Mr. Tristram, seated in the front row to the right of the platform, was lifting his large bulk into standing position.

"With the chair's permission," the schoolmaster said. From this, John, who had been attending Full Meetings since he was six, knew that Mr. Tristram had been recognized by Dr. Crocker. "I would like to register a protest against the censorious tone with which the chair informed the assembled colonists that it was I who had asked for this Full Meeting."

Dr. Crocker's bald head flushed pink.

"Since Mr. Tristram has called specific attention to what I had hoped would be noted only by implication," he said, "I might as well add to my censorious tone a few frankly censorious words. The Chairman of the Children's Guild is, of course, within his rights when he calls this meeting. But it seems to me, since Mr. Tristram knows as well as we all do, that other plans had been made for this evening, plans to which we have all been looking forward, it would have been a matter of simple good manners to postpone this meeting, at least until tomorrow."

The rolls of flesh around the schoolmaster's neck grew red and started to quiver.

"There are things more important than good manners," he said. "Survival happens to be one of them."

From his perch on the former hayloft, John could see the sudden stirring on the benches behind Mr. Tristram. The schoolmaster turned. John could see Mr. Tristram's pointed chin digging into the fat of his neck.

"Yes, survival," Mr. Tristram said to the people on the benches behind him. "Survival of this colony." He turned back to the platform and said sarcastically, "Since I assume the chair is equally interested in the survival of Deucalion, I am certain I will be granted permission to ask Mr. Sennacherib Sayer a few questions."

"Son of a bitch," Ike muttered.

"What's happening?" John said.

"How the hell do I know?"

"Then what do you mean son of a bitch?"

"I mean Fat Ass," Ike said. "He's a son of a bitch. Now shut up. I'm missing this."

What they had missed, John guessed as he turned back to the meeting, was some sort of argument about whether or not the schoolmaster had the right to ask Mr. Sayer any questions from the floor. John's father, who had been seated in the front row to the left of the platform, was standing up, facing Mr. Tristram across the aisle.

"It wouldn't be, Mr. Sayer," the schoolmaster was saying, "that you are afraid to answer my questions, would it?"

"Not while the sun rises in the east and sets in the west," John's father said with a short bow. He turned toward the platform and said, "It's quite all right, Mr. Chairman."

"I'm sure the chair is greatly relieved to have received Mr. Sayer's permission to discharge the function granted to it by our charter," Mr. Tristram said. The elaborately sarcastic manner, with which John had long ago become familiar in the classroom, somehow did not convey quite as much sarcasm as the schoolmaster obviously intended.

"The chair would be even more relieved, Mr. Tristram, if you would get on with the business for which you called this meeting," Dr. Crocker said.

The schoolmaster's fat figure dipped in a bow.

"With pleasure," he said. He turned toward John's father.

"Mr. Sayer, I would like to ask why, after nine years of what everybody agrees has been a successful operation, Deucalion is on the verge of bankruptcy?"

A murmur rose from, and seemed to shroud, the benches below like a physical cloud. It caused John's body to grow tense.

"Are we on the verge of bankruptcy?" John's father said in surprise. John could feel the tension increase.

"You are the head of this colony," the schoolmaster said to Sennacherib Sayer. "Surely if anybody knows whether or not Deucalion is on the verge of bankruptcy, it should be you, Mr. Sayer?"

"The head of any organization or enterprise, whether it be a colony like Deucalion or a grocery store, is not always able to carry all its details in his head," John's father said sharply.

"Am I to understand, Mr. Sayer," the schoolmaster said, "that in your mind the imminent bankruptcy of Deucalion is a detail?"

"Where did you get this idiotic idea about imminent bankruptcy?" Sennacherib Sayer said.

"Is it idiotic?" Mr. Tristram said.

"So far as I am concerned," John's father said, "it is worse than that."

"Well, then, let us see what it is to someone who is in a position to know." The schoolmaster turned to Dr. Crocker on the platform. "With the chair's permission, may I ask Rudolph Weer to rise?"

"Why?" Dr. Crocker snapped.

"Because Mr. Weer is the Chairman of our Finance Guild," Mr. Tristram said. "Need I say more?"

"Yes," Dr. Crocker said. "A great deal."

"I will be glad to say all of it," the schoolmaster said. "As soon as I ask Mr. Weer a question or two."

The bald man on the platform sent a confused glance toward Sennacherib Sayer. Even John could see that this was a mistake.

"Must you obtain permission from Mr. Sayer for your every act?" Mr. Tristram said. "I'm not asking you to do anything illegal, expensive, or detrimental to the honor of our colony. All I am asking, Dr. Crocker, is permission to ask a fellow colonist a couple of questions in the presence of *his* fellow colonists."

Dr. Crocker put a hand to his pink scalp, as though to

press back the rising flush of rage and embarrassment, and he said, "Mr. Weer, do you mind?"

The accountant rose from his seat on the bench immediately behind John's father. Rudy Weer, who had sold his lucrative practice in New York to study higher mathematics at Deucalion, was taller than John's father. This was tall indeed, since Sennacherib Sayer stood six feet two in his bare feet. Nevertheless, looking down on him from the hayloft, Rudy Weer looked small. John supposed this was due to the way the accountant held his body, hunched forward and over, as though he was constantly trying, without success, to read through his thick glasses a smudged number in the telephone book.

"No, of course not," Rudy Weer said to Max Crocker on the platform. "I don't mind at all."

"Thank you," Dr. Crocker said. "Proceed, Mr. Tristram!"

"Thank *you*," the schoolmaster said with one of his mock bows to the platform. He turned to the accountant. "Mr. Weer, is Deucalion on the verge of bankruptcy?"

The accountant scratched his head. He pushed the glasses up on his nose. He peered at the floor. He blew out his breath in a sigh that was clearly audible up in the hayloft.

"Oh, God," he said. "These large type questions."

"Is this one too large for you?" Mr. Tristram said.

"It's not it's too large," Rudy Weer said. "It's, well—"

His hand, which John noticed for the first time was so large that it looked like a pitcher's glove, ended the sentence in a short, choppy, downward gesture.

"Well, what?" the schoolmaster said.

"It's, well—" Again the large hand made the same gesture. "I mean, Mr. Tristram, you ask is Deucalion on the verge of bankruptcy, it's like asking is the country on the verge of war."

"I fail to see the similarity," Mr. Tristram said.

"Well, every country is always on the verge of war," Rudy Weer said. "In the sense that any minute, without warning, some other country might do something. I don't know what. Sink one of our ships on its way to supply our marines in Nicaragua, say. Shoot our ambassador, somewhere in, oh, China, maybe. Or the other way around. An agitator here shoot somebody *else's* ambassador. I don't know. What they call an international incident is what I mean. One of those things. It could happen at any minute, and it could lead to war. So in that sense, you ask me are we on the verge of war, the answer is yes, we are. But in another sense, of course we're not on the verge of war. I mean there are no immediate signs we're on the verge of war. You get me?"

"Not quite," Mr. Tristram said. "You mean that at any moment Deucalion might be plunged into bankruptcy by some unforseen incident?"

Rudy Weer's unhappy face became more unhappy.

"I didn't say that," he said.

"I didn't say you did," Mr. Tristram said. "You drew a parallel between the country's safety and Deucalion's solvency. From the parallel I tried to draw an inference."

"I thought we were dealing in facts," Sennacherib Sayer said. "Not inferences."

The schoolmaster's portly body turned toward John's father.

"It seems to me more accurate to say we are dealing in evasions," Mr. Tristram said. The round body turned back to the accountant. "Let me try again, Mr. Weer. Is Deucalion at the moment in a healthy financial position?"

The accountant worked his way through the head scratch, the glasses push, the floor peer, and the long, audible sigh. John had the feeling he was watching an uneasy runner tag all the bases, while the umpires were huddled in an effort to decide whether or not the ball he had just hit across the fence was to be scored as an out or a home run.

"Put it this way," Rudy Weer said. "We've got a going concern here called Deucalion. Like any other going concern, we got income and we got expenses. Right?"

"You tell me," Mr. Tristram said. "I hope it leads to an answer to my question."

"I'm doing my best," Rudy Weer said. "Our income, first it's when a new member joins the colony. He pays for his shares. Then later, running along from day to day, we have a lot of things. The Dairy Guild, say. Whatever milk and butter and so on we don't use up ourselves, we sell. And what we get, the money, *that's* income. Right?"

"I am aware that money coming in is called income, yes," Mr. Tristram said.

"Then the other side," Rudy Weer said. "Expenses. The colony has to pay real estate taxes. We have to pay for things that are the responsibility of the entire colony, not just one person. Ike Ten Eyck's salary, for example. The price of the Ford truck he drives, another example. The gasoline he needs to keep it running. Seed and fertilizer for the Farmers' Guild.

Lumber and tools for the Carpenters' Guild. Fiddles and sax-ophones for the Musicians' Guild. Textbooks and chalk and what not for the Children's Guild. You get me?"

"I got you," Mr. Tristram said dryly. "A long time ago."

The accountant looked hurt.

"Well, gee whiz, Mr. Tristram," he said. "All I'm trying to do is answer your question."

"I hope you will not think me unreasonable if I hope you try a little harder," the schoolmaster said. "Is Deucalion on the verge of bankruptcy? That's the question."

"I'm trying to tell you," Rudy Weer said.

"Couldn't you do it with a yes or a no?"

"One of the kids in the Children's Guild, they ask you is Ramsay MacDonald a good prime minister of England," the accountant said. "Could you answer it with a yes or no?"

"Certainly," Mr. Tristram said. "The answer is no. Ramsay MacDonald is a turncoat. Stemming from the people, he used them to achieve power, playing on their fears and hopes to obtain their votes. Having obtained them, having achieved power, he has found it sweet and, I have no doubt, profitable. Dining at the tables of the rich. Lining his pockets and the pockets of his friends while the Welsh coal miner who voted for him wastes his life away in starved idleness, living on a miserable dole, and his children die of rickets and worse. No, I say, Ramsay MacDonald is not a good prime minister."

The schoolmaster paused, breathless and red-faced. John wondered what the fat man was so angry about. He noted that Mr. Tristram had sounded not unlike his own father on the seat of the Ford truck a couple of hours ago.

"But you don't say it in one word," Rudy Weer said. "Some questions can't be answered in one word. Your ques-tion is Deucalion on the verge of bankruptcy is like that. I'm trying to answer it. I tell you we have income. On the other side we have expenses. When the income is bigger than the expenses, we're in good shape. When the expenses are bigger than the income, we're not in such good shape. It's like Dickens in *David Copperfield*. You remember what Mi-cawber says?"

"Certainly," Mr. Tristram said. He turned slightly. His chin came up and out of the folds of flesh around his neck. "Income one pound, expenses nineteen shillings and sixpence, result: happiness. Income one pound, expenses twenty shill-ings and sixpence, result: tragedy." The schoolmaster turned back to the accountant. It occurred to John that Mr. Tristram had just put on a small, proud performance for the assembled colonists. To Rudy Weer, he said, "I think that's a close enough quotation, give or take a word."

"Sure," the accountant said. "And it's what I mean about Deucalion."

"Are we at the moment happy?" Mr. Tristram said. "Or are we at the moment tragic?"

The head scratch, the glasses push, the floor peer, and the long, audible sigh did not refresh Rudy Weer.

"Well," he said wearily, "we're a little in the red."

"How little?" Mr. Tristram said.

"I don't know. I'd have to go over to the Finance Guild Building to take a look at the books."

"When did you take a look at the books last, Mr. Weer?"

"Today, of course," the accountant said with a touch of anger. "It's my job. I work at it every day, like everybody else up here works at their jobs every day."

"Since I am one of those everybody elses," the schoolmaster said, "I can tell you I had thirty-six boys and girls in my Children's Guild classroom today. I am sure Mr. Hill can tell us how many pairs of shoes he repaired today at his Shoemaker's Guild bench. I am sure Mr. Midden can tell us how many hours he rehearsed today for his Actors' Guild presentation of *The Pirates of Penzance*. Why are you the only Guild head at Deucalion who cannot tell us something that pertains to the work he did today?"

"I didn't say I couldn't," Rudy Weer said. He seemed to become more interested in the invisible phone number, apparently printed somewhere on the floor of the barn, at which he was constantly peering. "Exact figures are hard to remember," he said. "Without going over to look at the books, all I can give you is an approximation."

"An approximation will do," Mr. Tristram said. "How deeply, Mr. Weer, is this colony in the red?"

"As of this morning, we're behind about eight thousand dollars."

"When you say behind, Mr. Weer, you mean we, this colony, Deucalion, in our relations with the outside world, we owe eight thousand dollars that we cannot at the moment pay?"

"Oh, we'll pay it, all right," Rudy Weer said. "When money comes in. It's just a temporary situation."

"Created by what?"

"I just told you," Rudy Weer said. "We have expenses. We

have income. When one is bigger, we get one situation. When the other is bigger, we get another. It seesaws back and forth."

"Has it always done that?" Mr. Tristram said. "Seesawed?"

"Certainly."

"More so now than usual?"

"Well, I don't know," Rudy Weer said. "We're bigger now than we were when we started nine years ago. A hundred and sixty-four colonists run up bigger expenses than forty colonists. That's only natural."

"It certainly is," the schoolmaster said. "And it is equally natural, Mr. Weer, is it not, for a hundred and sixty-four colonists to run up bigger income than forty colonists?"

"Yes, I suppose so."

"You suppose?" Mr. Tristram said. "Don't you know?"

"Of course I know," Rudy Weer said. "You've got a very funny way, Mr. Tristram, a very funny way, I call it, of making the simplest little innocent fact sound suspicious."

"Do you know why that is, Mr. Weer?"

"No, but I can see you are going to tell me."

"I will indeed," the schoolmaster said. "It is because I *am* suspicious."

"Just a moment!"

John moved his head. It was Dr. Crocker on the platform. He jumped up.

"Yes?" Mr. Tristram said.

"You're going to have to explain that, young man," Dr. Crocker said. John had a moment of surprise. It had never before occurred to him that anybody considered Fat Ass a young man. "Suspicion is a dirty word here at Deucalion," Dr. Crocker said.

"I can think of a dirtier one," Mr Tristram said coolly. "Peculation."

The almost visible murmur rose again from the benches. This time, however, it did not strike John with the impact of a gust of perfume.

"Son of a bitch," Ike Ten Eyck muttered.

John did not turn toward the handyman or ask questions. He could not take his eyes from Mr. Tristram. The schoolmaster's fat body looked as though it was swelling.

"We are waiting for an explanation," Dr. Crocker said severely.

"I shall give it to you," Mr Tristram said, and the thin lips in his fleshy face did something John had never before actually seen but had read about in books: they curled. "The sooner you stop these interruptions, Dr. Crocker, the sooner you will get it." The schoolmaster turned back to Rudy Weer. "Tell me, please. Who is in charge of our colony's funds?"

"Who is in charge—?" Rudy Weer's voice, automatically repeating the schoolmaster's question, stopped. It occurred to John up in the hayloft that the accountant looked startled and confused, like a man jolted awake rudely from a deep sleep. "You mean who controls our money?"

"That is precisely what I mean," Mr. Tristram said.

"Why, our Executive Committee," the accountant said. "Everybody knows that."

"And our Executive Committee," the schoolmaster continued relentlessly, "consists, of course, of Mr. Sayer, the Chairman; Dr. Max Crocker; Mr. Perry Schwartz; Mr. Milton Fennell; and Dr. Klaus Immensee. Correct, Mr. Weer?"

"Yes," the accountant said. He gave it two syllables, as though suddenly unsure of the pronunciation of the simple word. He's being cautious, John thought worriedly. Why? What was there to be cautious about? Everybody knew who was on the Executive Committee.

"Now, Mr. Weer, as head of our Finance Guild, we all know that you are authorized to draw and sign checks on the Deucalion bank account." The schoolmaster paused and jerked his head slightly to one side, as though the collar of flesh had grown constricting and he wanted to free his vocal cords for their next effort. "What I would like to know now, Mr. Weer, is this: is there anybody else in this colony, presumably a member of the Executive Committee, who has the authority to draw and sign checks on the Deucalion bank account?"

Even John, who had never before known the answer because he had never before heard the question, knew it now from the way Rudy Weer's long, bowed body turned so the accountant could send his nearsighted, troubled glance directly at Sennacherib Sayer. Because he turned with him, or rather moved his head to follow Rudy Weer's glance, John saw his father's face tighten.

"Just a moment, Rudy," Sennacherib Sayer said. "I'll answer that." The lean, white-haired head turned toward the schoolmaster. "According to our charter, Mr. Tristram," John's father said, "I am authorized, as Chairman of our Executive Committee, to draw checks on Deucalion's bank account. You know that, Mr. Tristram. Everybody in this room knows that. Since you have, however, elected to profess igno-

rance, and you seek information in open session at a Full
Meeting by quizzing your fellow colonists, information that
you and everybody else already possess, it seem obvious that
you have something else in mind. I demand that you stop this
nonsense at once, and tell us what this something else is."

"Yes," Dr. Crocker shouted from the platform. "I agree!
We *all* demand—!"

"Max," Sennacherib Sayer said.

"No, I'm sorry, Sen," the flushed, bald-headed man in the
buckskin shirt said from the platform. "The head of the Children's Guild has been throwing around words like 'suspicion'
and 'peculation.' Words that I thought we'd all left behind us
nine years ago when we came here to Deucalion to work out
a new and better way of life. I demand that he explain those
words."

"I will try to," Mr. Tristram said.

"Without further questions," Max Crocker said. "I want an
explanation."

"Max," John's father said.

The bald head shook stubbornly.

"No, Sen, I'm sorry," Dr. Crocker said. "I'm in the chair,
and I'm demanding that the head of the Children's Guild
stop this embarrassing exhibition—"

"Embarrassing to whom?" the schoolmaster said. His voice
slid in under the anger from the platform the way, John
thought, his mother's cake knife slid in under a slice of Mrs.
Loring's apple pie.

"To all of us!" Dr. Crocker shouted. His own voice obviously took the physicist by surprise. He looked startled,
then ashamed, as the echoes came bouncing back from the
rear of the barn toward the platform. The bald man seemed
to cringe slightly, as though trying to avoid the chain of noise
he had himself set in motion. "I mean," Dr. Crocker said in
what now, by comparison, sounded like a whisper, "I want
you to get on with a statement of your intentions, Mr. Tristram."

The plump body, which it suddenly occurred to John made
the schoolmaster look like a sweet potato mounted by a child
on two cloves to simulate feet, dipping forward in the mocking bow.

"My intentions are the saving of Deucalion from disaster,"
Mr. Tristram said.

The murmur rose from the benches. John decided this time

it sounded like a swarm of bees he had once inadvertently kicked into angry life on the far side of Aaron's Brook.

"For a long time," the schoolmaster said, "in fact since several months after I arrived at Deucalion a little more than a year ago, during all this time I have been turning over in my mind a truly puzzling fact. For nine years Deucalion has been functioning with what the outside world assumes is success. More and more people have been attracted to our colony. Meaning that more and more money has come into our exchequer as more and more shares have been purchased. Also, still more and more money has come in as more shoulders have been put to the wheel, so to speak, placing more of our land under cultivation and producing more products that have been sold with profit to the world outside our boundaries. In spite of this rising income, however, I soon discovered that, in the financial sense, our colony has never achieved success. On the contrary. We always seem to be on the thin edge. Mr. Weer objects to my characterizing this thin edge as the verge of bankruptcy. Very well. I will resort to his own phraseology. He says we constantly seesaw from being in the red, as he put it, to coming back into the black. But we never come back far enough into the black, I noticed, to build up a reserve. A reserve out of which, next time we start seesawing, we will not saw, or see, into the red again. This puzzled me, as I say. I am not an accountant. I am a lowly schoolmaster. But my equipment as a schoolmaster includes a working knowledge of simple arithmetic. Not to mention a mind trained to respect curiosity as a healthy attribute. Arithmetic and curiosity led me, during the past months, to do more than wonder about Deucalion's financial state."

The schoolmaster paused, perhaps for breath, which he certainly seemed to need. But John sensed up in the hayloft that Mr. Tristram had enough breath. What he had paused for, John could see, was a quick glance at Dr. Crocker on the platform, at John's father and Rudy Weer, both of whom were on their feet, and at the rows of benched colonists around them, who were on what Mrs. Loring would have called tenterhooks. John didn't know what tenterhooks were. But he knew the picture on the wall of the Children's Guild that showed General Wolfe, standing with his staff on the Plains of Abraham, surveying the troops of General Montcalm gathered in the distance. It seemed to John that Mr. Tristram, surveying his fellow colonists, had that same look of controlled but not concealed confidence: a general who knows he is going to win the imminent battle but feels it would be wise—since God, who is on his side, is also a sardonic practical joker—to act as though he believes the issue is in doubt.

"Several days ago," Mr. Tristram said, turning back to the platforms, "I decided to ask for an investigation."

"Of what?" Dr. Crocker rapped out.

"Why, my dear doctor," Mr. Tristram said. "An investigation of the manner in which the great Sennacherib Sayer had been handling the financial affairs of this colony."

The small, strangled sounds from the small, buckskin-clad figure on the platform cut through the rising murmur from the benches.

"Son of a bitch," Ike said.

"What does he—?"

John got no further.

"Shut up!" Ike said, and punctuated the words with his elbow.

"Are you—? Are you—?" the strangled sounds settled down into a squeak of incredulity. "Are you accusing the Chairman of our Executive Committee of—?" Dr. Crocker could not utter the word, whatever the word was. "Are you —?" he said again. "I mean, Mr. Tristram, I am asking if—"

"I am making no accusations," Mr. Tristram said with an elegant wave of his hand. "That will come later. At the moment I am merely calling for an investigation."

"An investigation of what?" Dr. Crocker said.

"An investigation of the financial affairs of this colony," Mr. Tristram said.

"But why is that necessary?" the bald man said, "I don't understand what is happening here." He turned and said helplessly, "Sen, perhaps you can explain what all this—?"

"Mr. Sayer will have his chance to explain," the schoolmaster said. His voice seemed to be tightening. "That is why I am calling for an investigation."

"To do what?" Dr. Crocker said, his voice rising with impatience.

"To save us from bankruptcy," Mr. Tristram said.

Rudy Weer called, "But I just told you, Mr. Tristram, that we are not—"

The last word seemed to cause the schoolmaster physical pain. All his flesh started to quiver.

"And I tell you," Mr. Tristram suddenly shouted, "that

these attempts on your part and the part of Dr. Crocker to conceal the culprit will no longer work. It's out in the open now, my friends. Out in the open. For all the world to see!"

Sennacherib Sayer's voice, quiet but steely, came through the rising murmurs.

"What is out in the open?"

"The hypocrisy of our leadership," the schoolmaster roared. The rolls of flesh around his neck were now almost purple. "The world knows Sennacherib Sayer as a figure larger than life," he bellowed at Sennacherib Sayer. "Savior of the poor. Healer of the mentally sick. Preacher of the good life. A bush league Leonardo da Vinci, according to your own President Wilson. Ha!" The pointed chin dug into the layers of purple flesh. "Bush league Leonardo da Vinci my bleeding arse!" The schoolmaster's hand shot out. The fat forefinger trembled. "Cheat!" he screamed. "Embezzler! Liar! Hypocrite!" The round body gathered itself for a special effort. *"Whoremaster!"* Francis Tristram screamed. "I demand an investigation! I call upon all my fellow colonists—!"

John never found out precisely what Mr. Tristram was calling on his fellow colonists for. The schoolmaster's sharp shrieks were suddenly blunted and buried under the explosion of voices and scraping noises from the surrounding benches. And Ike Ten Eyck, apparently no longer concerned about concealment, was on his feet. He dragged John around the stacked lumber to the narrow window through which they had entered the hayloft. He squeezed through and turned. He reached back in, to help John crawl through, then started down the ladder. John followed. Before he could reach the ground, Ike reached up and swung him off the ladder. He grabbed John's hand and hauled him at a trot across Center Pasture, past the dark windows of the Children's Guild, toward East Cottage Lane. Behind them John could hear the excited voices of the colonists coming out the front doors of the Barn Meeting Hall. Their words were, of course, indistinguishable, but John didn't mind that. What he minded was not being able to see their faces. It seemed important to see them, but he couldn't. The night sky had clouded over while he and Ike had been lying face down in the hayloft. Besides, Ike was hauling him along too fast for successful backward glances. In a few moments these were useless. Even the roof of the Barn Meeting Hall, which was the tallest building on the Deucalion property, was concealed by the fences of the chicken runs along which Ike was trotting. Not until they reached the back door of the Main House did John grasp why the handyman had been in such a hurry.

"Up to bed," he said, glancing back toward the now very faint sounds of the disturbance they had left behind. "Quick."

John saw that Ike did not want John's mother to know the boy had seen and heard what had happened.

"Okay," John said.

He wondered where his mother had been sitting. Then, as he ran up the back steps, he had a stab of guilt. Why had he not looked for her? Why had it not even occurred to him that she was sitting on one of the benches spread out below him? The old feeling, the feeling that he had somehow failed her, began to claw at his insides.

"Johnny."

He stopped and turned, feeling slightly sick. Ike's face, tipped up so that the glow from the kerosene lamp in the kitchen window fell directly on it, looked curiously shrivelled. It was as though some inner suction was deepening all the old wrinkles and slowly making new ones.

"Close your door," Ike said. "No lights. When they get home, I want them to think you're asleep and you've been asleep."

"Okay," John said.

"And Johnny."

"What?"

"Don't you think about what you heard until I get a chance to talk to you in the morning. That clear?"

"Yes," John said.

But it wasn't. For one thing, John couldn't stop thinking. For another, it was long past morning before Ike got a chance to talk to him. By that time John had had a restless night and a worse half-day. He heard his mother and father come in, minutes after Ike had hustled him up to bed. It was clear from the number of voices rising and falling downstairs in the front room that they had not come in alone. John did not know when he fell asleep, but he did know, when he woke up, that it was important to get to Ike. When he got downstairs, he asked Mrs. Loring, "You got any idea where Ike might be?"

"With your mother," Mrs. Loring said. "I've got oatmeal and cracked wheat. Which would you like?"

John didn't want either. The thought of food made his stomach knot. Nor did it seem to cheer Mrs. Loring. Or even interest her. She kept looking worriedly across John's head, out the window that faced West Cottage Lane.

"I don't care," John said. "Oatmeal. Where's my mother?"

"She went out for a walk with Ike and your father," Mrs. Loring said. Then, much too casually, she added, "You know. One of their walks."

This was, or rather should have been, perfectly natural. All the colonists did a great deal of walking, and nobody did more than the Chairman of the Executive Committee and his wife. They had laid out long ago a series of favorites. Most of these involved crossing Aaron's Brook into the birch forests of Godwin's Tract. What struck John as far from natural was that his mother and father should have gone off on one of their leisurely rambles on the morning after what had happened in the Barn Hall the night before.

"Which way?" John asked.

"I don't know," Mrs. Loring said. She frowned at the saucepan in her hand, then said, "Sit down and I'll get your oatmeal."

When she came back, John said, "They say anything about where they were going?"

"Who?"

"My mother and father and Ike."

"Not to me," the cook said. "Would you like a little sugar? I won't tell your father."

"No, just milk is fine," John said. "Who went out first? My mother and father? Then Ike? Or together?"

"You trying to pump me?"

John's face grew warm.

"John," Mrs. Loring said, "did you hear what happened last night?"

His first reaction was relief: she did not know he had been present at the meeting. John's second reaction was disappointment: Mrs. Loring thought he was a sap, like Charlie Devon or Alfie Crocker, from whom large events could be concealed by telling him to go to bed early.

"Sure I heard," he said. "Mr. Tristram called a Full Meeting. You were here, you just brought in my birthday cake when Dr. Crocker came and told us."

"I mean what happened *at* the meeting?" Mrs. Loring said. John said, "What happened?"

"He set a trap," the cook said with sudden passion. "That son of a bitch, he set a trap," she said. "For your father." The deepened wrinkles of her face became moving rivulets as her body started to shake. "He wants to destroy us," Mrs. Loring said, her voice rising. "He wants to destroy Deucalion, that's what he wants to do, and he knows the only way, the *best* way is to destroy your father."

"Not really," said Sennacherib Sayer.

Mrs. Loring's shaking body whipped around. John's spoon, clattering into the plate of oatmeal, caused him to jump in his chair. His father was standing in the doorway.

"Not really," Sennacherib Sayer said again. "It is neither the best way, Mrs. Loring, nor the only way. The best way, indeed the only way, to destroy Deucalion is to succumb to the fears aroused by unhappy and fearful people like Francis Tristram." John's father came into the room, toward the cook, moving slowly, talking as he moved. "We must not read our own fears into Mr. Tristram's," Sennacherib Sayer said gently. "He has asked for an investigation of our financial affairs, and such an investigation he shall have. Rudolph Weer is preparing the books and records at this very moment in the Finance Guild cabin. By tomorrow afternoon, when the investigation takes place, in full view of every colonist, this unpleasantness aroused by Francis Tristram will have vanished. It may be, as you put it, Mrs. Loring, a trap in his mind. It is not that in mine. I want it to cease being that in yours." He placed his hand on the cook's elbow and said, "John, a spoon submerged in oatmeal is useless to a hungry boy."

"Yes, sir," John said. He fished the spoon from the plate, started to lick the handle clean, thought better of that, and used his nakpkin. "Good morning," he said.

"It has almost ceased to be that," Sennacherib Sayer said, glancing at his watch. "The walk has awakened my dozing appetite. Mrs. Loring, would there be another bowl of that delicious-looking oatmeal in your kitchen?"

"There certainly would," the cook said, and she turned toward the door, in which John's mother had appeared. "You, Mrs. Sayer?"

"I think not," John's mother said. "Thank you."

The motor of the Ford truck exploded outside the window. John pushed back his chair, ran across, and saw Ike backing the truck around to face the Wellesville Road.

"Hey, Ike!" The handyman turned and poked his head out the front window. John yelled, "Wait for me!"

"Ask your father!" Ike yelled back.

John turned. Sennacherib Sayer said, "No, I think not. Not this morning, John."

"Why not?" his mother said.

John's father, turning with obvious astonishment, could not have been more astonished than his son.

"I beg your pardon?" Sennacherib Sayer said.

"I said why not?" his wife said. She seemed to be aware that she was making history. Her voice shook. "John always drives down into Wellesville with Ike."

Sennacherib Sayer's eyes crinkled at the corners.

"The frequency with which John drives down into Wellesville with Ike, my dear Griselda, does not change the fact that I don't want John to do it today."

"Nor does your reply actually answer my question," Mrs. Sayer said. Now, in addition to her voice, her hands were shaking. "I ask why not?"

John never knew whether his father intended to answer the question because, at that moment, the phone rang. Mrs. Loring, who looked frightened, jumped.

"Ooh!" she said. "That's long distance. The *New York Times*. They called while you were out walking. They want to ask you about the Supreme Court thing. I told them to call back."

For another moment or two Sennacherib Sayer's puzzled glance remained on his wife. Then he turned and walked around the dining-room table. He went out into the hall, where the phone hung on the wall under the stairs. Ike beeped the Ford truck horn. John's mother leaned down to the half-open window.

"He'll be right out," she said, and then, straightening up, "Go ahead, John."

He turned, aware that what he was doing was preposterous, and exchanged a glance with Mrs. Loring. The cook seemed to realize it was preposterous. She shrugged. The movement of her narrow shoulders seemed to say, "Don't look at me. I don't know what this means any more than you do." Ike beeped the horn again.

"I said go ahead," John's mother said. The edge in her voice was almost a physical stab. "Ike is *waiting*."

John ran. Out the back door of the dining room, across the kitchen, down the steps, and along the grass to the truck. Ike reached down, hauled him up into the front seat, and went to work on the levers and pedals. Perhaps he was aware of what had just happened. The handyman certainly acted as though

he realized it was important to be under way before Sennacherib Sayer got off the phone. The truck lumbered out onto
the Wellesville Road and Ike gave it the gas. He didn't ease
up until they were beyond the boundary wall of Stonecraft
Farm. By that time the radiator had begun to steam.

"What are you trying to do?" John said. "Blow us up?"

Ike gave him one of those sideswiping glances that seemed
to be less a conscious movement than a part of the way his
leaning body worked.

"You feel all right," he said.

It was not a question.

"I'm all right," John said.

"Because there's nothing not to be all right about," Ike
said. For the next few moments his concentration on the road
ahead was so intense that the words he spoke might have
been uttered without his knowledge, by some invisible third
person on the front seat of the truck who had, for the time
being, appropriated the driver's vocal cords. "There was no
time to explain certain things to you last night," Ike said.
"Your father and mother, if they found out I took you to
that meeting, you and everybody else at Deucalion could say
good-bye to Ike Ten Eyck. The dumb bastard would be out
looking for a new job this morning."

"Why didn't you go over to the Children's Guild this
morning?" John said. "You were supposed to fix the fireplace.
All week you've been saying Saturday morning I gotta fix
that God damn Fat Ass' fireplace."

"I didn't get to doing it because your father asked me to
take a walk with him."

"Mrs. Loring says my mother went along."

"You don't have to go to law school and when you grow
up become a lawyer like your father," Ike said. "You got a
career all picked out and ready and waiting. You could practically join this William J. Burns Detective Agency right
now."

"I'm just telling you what Mrs. Loring said," John said.

"It was a council of war," Ike said. "That son of a bitch
Tristram, what he did last night, what you saw him do at that
meeting, he came out in the open. We knew for a long time
he's had it in for your father, but last night he finally came
out in the open. Because last night he figured the time was
ripe. It's the day your father gets appointed to the Supreme
Court. A son of a bitch like Tristram, he figures that's the
day to hit your father with a bucket full of mud. On a day

like that, no matter what you say about a man, no matter now many lies you tell about him, it's bound to sound terrible."

"What Mr. Tristram said last night," John said. "Were they lies?"

"There's lies and there's lies," Ike said to the scallops of Wellesville Road that ground up toward them and kept disappearing beneath their feet. "That stuff how we're almost in bankruptcy and your father has the power to write checks. Everybody, when they're short of money, you could say they're almost in bankruptcy. A place like Deucalion, we raise milk and butter and vegetables, we sell some furniture, some paintings, statues, the stuff turned out by the different guilds that sell their stuff, until the money comes in every month for that stuff, naturally the treasury is short. Then you say well, here we have a man who has the power to write checks, so maybe we now know why the treasury is short. Or like the way that son of a bitch puts it, why we're almost in bankruptcy. It all sounds fine, everything clean and neat and logical, except it's a God damn lie. A man attacks you like that, hits you with a coal scuttle full of lies on a day when the President he's picked you out for a great honor, you have any brains, you figure out a way to fight the son of a bitch, and Sennacherib Sayer one thing he's got plenty of, he's got brains. This morning, when he was using them, he asked me to come along, and your mother, naturally she's worried by the attacks from this bastard, she asked could she come along, too. That's how we all happened to be out, all three of us walking, and that's how it all got straightened out."

"All what got straightened out?"

"Day before yesterday, when you were still only nine years old, you were a polite boy," Ike said. "Today, now that you're ten, you're beginning to sound like a little snot. What got straightened out is how to handle Fat Ass. We went over first, me and your mother and father, we went to the Finance Guild, and Rudy Weer said he could get all his books and records ready for an investigation by tomorrow afternoon. Your mother said tomorrow is Sunday, and it wouldn't look good to do a thing like that on Sunday, but your father said frig that."

"Oh, sure," John said.

"Of course he didn't," Ike said. "I'm just saying. What are you so touchy about this morning? He said Tristram wants an investigation, he's going to get it the first opportunity, and if the first opportunity is a Sunday, that's too bad, it'll have to be done on a Sunday. Besides, by Monday, when your father has to go back to New York and all those reporters jump on him for interviews about the Supreme Court appointment, your father doesn't want any of Mr. Francis Tristram's crap laying around on the floor. Once we got settled, your mother left us. You satisfied?"

"He didn't want me to go into Wellesville with you," John said.

"Who didn't?" Ike said, and John knew as a fact something he had merely suspected when he had made the statement: his father's refusal had not been a mere whim. When Ike was not rattled, he had no trouble thinking up a more adroit way to stall a question than by repeating it.

"My father didn't want me to go into Wellesville with you this morning," John said.

"Then how come you did?"

"He went to answer the phone, and my mother said I could."

The most surprising thing was the fact that Ike forgot to act surprised.

"Probably about the entertainment," he said, and then Ike apparently realized he had forgotten something. "The other thing your father did," Ike said, "I mean after he settled with Rudy Weer about tomorrow, the investigation, he said we'll schedule for tonight, that's Saturday, we'll schedule for tonight the program we had scheduled for last night, the entertainment that got knocked out of the box last night because Fat Ass called the Full Meeting. So naturally, it's your birthday party got knocked out of the box last night, and most of the kids in the Children's Guild they're in on the entertainment, naturally your father figured you'd better stick around, not go cruising down into Wellesville with Ike." The handyman paused and dropped another of his slanting looks down on John. Then he said, "What you're probably thinking, here's a funny one, my father says don't go with Ike, then your mother says do go with Ike, it's not really funny at all. It's just your mother didn't have time to explain to your father it was okay for you to go with me, because you're not in on any of the entertainment. She didn't have time because he went to answer the telephone and me, the truck was already rolling."

"I'm one of the policemen in *The Pirates of Penzance*," John said.

"But Mr. Midden is not ready to give that yet," Ike said. "*The Pirates of Penzance* was not scheduled for last night, and it's not going to be done tonight, so there's absolutely no reason you couldn't go with me now. You got that clear?"

"Sure," John said.

"It's absolutely not funny at all your father said don't go and then your mother said do go," Ike said. "What's bothering you?"

The answer was that this was the first time his mother had ever argued with his father. It was also the first time she had allowed him to accompany Ike into Wellesville without first making the handyman carry the walnuts across the dining room on the backs of his hands. But John decided to hide behind another answer.

"I'm trying to think if there's anything about the meeting last night you didn't explain to me," John said. "All those words Mr. Tristram was screaming."

"Let me see," Ike said. All the slanting lines of his face moved visibly with the exaggerated effort at deep concentration. "Cheat. Embezzler. Liar. Hypocrite. What else? Cheat. Embezzler. Liar. Hypocrite. No, I guess that's the works. Any of those words you don't understand?"

"No," John said.

"Then let's quit the post-mortem and get the dust out of the old sound box." Ike cleared his throat and began to roar. "*Oh, will you take it in your hand, Mrs. Murphy.*"

John joined him. They sang all the way down the mountain into Wellesville, but it was not one of their best performances. John knew that Ike knew they were both aware they had both avoided mentioning the only puzzling word Francis Tristram had hurled at Sennacherib Sayer: *whoremaster.*

"Hey," John said. "You passed the station."

"Good boy," Ike said, guiding the car up Main Street. "At least your eyes are still as sharp as they used to be when you were only nine. I passed the station on purpose. Because today I don't want to park there. Those smart alecks always hanging around, if they heard anything what happened at Deucalion last night, I don't want to hear them with their smart remarks on this particular morning."

He swung the truck into the alley on the north side of the Wellesville House and pulled the emergency brake. He did it with a slow, careful tug. Not at all like the savage yank to which John had grown accustomed as the final punctuation of a drive with Ike Ten Eyck.

"Aah, hell," the handyman said.

"What's the matter?"

"Mrs. Loring asked me this morning to bring her another bottle of that crap you got her yesterday. Liver extract, and I gotta go up to Casey's for your mother's wool. Here, wait." Ike dug into his overalls and came up with a half-dollar. "Go down to Jensen's, and *you* get the liver extract. Okay?"

"Sure," John said. He took the coin, jumped down from the truck, and said, "Meet you back here?"

"In a few minutes," Ike said. "I won't be long."

John had not gone very far down Main Street when a startling sight stopped him in his tracks: Mrs. Tristram tooling down Main Street on a bicycle.

At first John thought it was startling because he had not known the schoolmaster's wife owned a bicycle. A couple of moments later, as Mrs. Tristram turned the corner beyond the railroad station and disappeared, John realized that was not the reason. He had found the sight startling because it answered a question that had been walloping around uneasily in his mind since the day before, when he saw his father talking to Mrs. Tristram near the weighing machine in Jensen's Drug Store: How the hell had she got there?

A quarter of an hour, maybe twenty minutes, earlier John and Ike had left Mrs. Tristram behind on the Wellesville Road, walking her way into the ode she was composing in honor of John's father. Now that he understood how she had got there, why had John and Ike not seen her pass them on the road to town? The obvious answer, that she had not used the road but had cut across the smoothly terraced fields of Stonecraft Farm, led to the most disturbing conclusion of all: the reason why neither John nor, to his knowledge, anybody else at Deucalion had known that Mrs. Tristram owned a bicycle was that the schoolmaster's wife kept it concealed somewhere beyond the boundaries of the colony.

Suddenly excited by the impact of this discovery, John decided he had to convey it to Ike. He turned, hurried back up Main Street, toward The Wellesville House, and ran into the handyman coming out of the police station.

They stood there, on the sidewalk, facing each other in a way that John found disturbing. He couldn't understand why, but he felt as though he had caught Ike doing something dirty. Ike seemed to feel the same way. Or perhaps John merely imagined that. He didn't know. He had no such doubts, however, about the feeling. It was like the day before, which had been charged with a special meaning because it was his birthday: John felt that his relationship to Ike was changing, right then and there, before his eyes. Ike must have felt it, too, because a funny little expression rearranged all the creases in his face as the slender, slanting body moved forward, one hand upraised in a pleading gesture. He seemed to be warning John against thinking the thought that had invaded his mind. Then the handyman stopped moving, and the funny little expression disappeared.

"Where's the liver extract?" Ike said.

There was something in his voice John had never heard before. He was accustomed to Ike's sardonic gruffness. When the handyman told John that the day before yesterday he had been a polite boy but now that he was ten he was beginning to sound like a little snot, the boy knew Ike was kidding. He knew also that Ike was not kidding now. Ike was sore and, because Ike's anger frightened John, it made the boy sore, too.

"I'll go and get it," he said, turning away.

"Why the hell haven't you already got it?"

Turning back, regretting his words before they were uttered, John said, "The same reason you haven't got my mother's wool. I've been doing something else."

"Doing what?" Ike rapped out. But the question came too late. The boy had already decided not to convey to the handyman the exciting discovery that Mrs. Tristram kept a bicycle hidden secretly somewhere off the Deucalion property. This was a secret he wouldn't share. Not with anybody. Not even with Ike.

"Just walking around," John said.

The handyman gave him a suspicious look. John felt better. The remark had not been thought out. It was a mere evasion. Yet Ike had obviously assumed it was more than that. The assumption, even more obviously, had brought him to the brink of another question. John wished Ike would ask it. The boy was suddenly so anxious to retort angrily "None of your damn business!" that he almost said the words before Ike asked the question. Perhaps that was why the handyman decided not to ask it.

"Well, get the lead out," he said instead. "If you're not back in the truck with that liver extract by the time I'm back with the wool, you're walking home, sonny boy."

"No, I'm not," John said. "You wouldn't dare leave me behind."

"Try me and see," Ike said. He strode away, toward Casey's General Store. Walking down to Jensen's, John wished he had not laid it on the line like that. He knew Ike well enough to be sure the handyman would make good on his threat. John also knew that, if he didn't force Ike to make good on the threat, he would lose whatever it was he had gained yesterday by crossing the line from being nine to being ten.

He dragged his feet on the way to Jensen's, fighting a compulsion to run. He circled the drug store aisles several times before he approached Mr. Jensen for the bottle of liver extract, wishing he could make the purchase hastily. He moved back up Main Street in a foolish amble, praying his feet would disregard the instructions of his mind. And when he turned into the alley beside the Wellesville House, the truck was there.

The victory brought a lump to John's throat. The fact that Ike had allowed him to win showed that Ike was not sore at him any more. John was grateful for that. The least he could do to show his gratitude was share with Ike the discovery about Mrs. Tristram and her hidden bicycle. Then Ike was waving to him from the front seat of the truck, beckoning him to hurry, and as John trotted down the alley, he began to have some second thoughts.

He remembered the sense of power that had come to him the day before with the decision to conceal from Ike the discovery that, during all these months of sneaking bottles of grape tonic for Ike from the commissary, Mrs. Loring had been aware of the thefts. Adding to that knowledge the secret about Mrs. Tristram's bicycle made the sense of power grow stronger. John liked that. He began to feel what his mother and father and Ike had said he would feel when he passed his tenth birthday: grown up.

"I'm sorry," he said to Ike as he climbed into the truck. Apologies were cheap. Cheap? They cost nothing. A couple of easy words, casually spoken, and he could keep his two treasured secrets for himself. The worthless words had relieved him of the sense of obligation he felt to Ike for no longer being sore at him. Part of the growing-up process, John sensed, was acquiring the skill of casual hypocrisy. "I came as fast as I could," he said casually. "Jensen's was crowded. You get the wool?"

Ike patted the paper sack on the seat beside him. He kicked and poked at the levers and pedals that set the truck in motion. And he said just as casually, "That George Jarvis is a pain."

John did not know Mr. Jarvis. But he had seen Wellesville's First Selectman, Fire Commissioner, and outspoken enemy of Deucalion often enough on the street to ask with interest, "What he do now?"

"Oh, nothing much," Ike said. "It's just he's such a gabby old woman, you see him coming, unless you got the whole day to kill, you better run." He guided the truck up Main Street, into the first of the ascending scallops of the Wellesville Road. "Reason I was late getting your mother's wool," Ike said to the windshield, "I was walking up to Casey's little while ago. I pass the police station, someone taps on the window, and it's George Jarvis. We went to school together, George and I, so I can't exactly tell him to drop dead, and I popped in. Guess what he wants?"

"What?" John said.

"He wants to know was it true up at Deucalion we're planning to build a zeppelin mooring mast. Y'imagine the crap you have to listen to? I told George he wants fairy tales, go to the library and borrow a book. That's how I met you on the street back there. I was coming out from George."

John knew Ike was lying, but he didn't mind. On the contrary. Ike's lie made John feel better. No matter what the handyman had been doing in the police station, the fact that Ike felt it was necessary to explain it away evened up whatever discomfort John might still have felt about keeping to himself the secret of Mrs. Tristram's hidden bicycle. After all, Ike had been grown up for a long time. Casual hypocrisy was old stuff to him. He said, "What's on the program this afternoon?"

"I don't know," John said. "Mr. Poynter's supposed to take the Upper Half of the Children's Guild across to Camp Cody for bivouac drill. But maybe what happened last night and all, maybe that's all changed."

It wasn't. Shortly after John got back to the Main House, the head of the Dairymen's Guild showed up with Charlie Devon and Alfie Crocker and half a dozen other kids lugging knapsacks and cooking utensils and sections of pup tent. John joined them, carrying his blanket roll and mess kit. The group moved up East Cottage Lane, stopping at the cabins of Southeast Cottage Grove and then Northeast Cottage Grove to gather the rest of the members of the Upper Half of the Children's Guild. By the time they reached Willow Walk, which ran along the Deucalion side of Aaron's Brook, and paused for the tricky crossing, John had gathered that none of the kids knew what had happened the night before. He found this puzzling.

They all knew there had been a Full Meeting, and they all knew children had been barred. John had taken it for granted they would be curious about why they had been barred. He had been looking forward to the small sensation he knew he could cause—behind Mr. Poynter's back, of course—by letting it be known he had been present. Since this pleasure was denied him, John chose a substitute. He decided it was more fun to know something the others didn't know and keep it to himself. Especially since, by doing so, he could have the additional pleasure of telling himself he was doing it out of loyalty to his father.

"Come on, John," Mr. Poynter called. "Snap out of it."

John edged out onto the first rock of the chain that formed a crude bridge across Aaron's Brook. Mr. Poynter always helped the boys across, one at a time. This was pretty silly, since there was not a boy in the group who had not crossed the brook dozens of times without help, but Mr. Poynter didn't know that. Godwin's Tract, at the other side of Aaron's Brook, was out of bounds for members of the Children's Guild unless accompanied by an adult. Most adults at Deucalion were too busy with their private and guild activities to find time for their children. For this reason the Children's Guild had been one of the first to be organized when the colony was founded. Mr. Poynter, as head of the Dairy Farmers' Guild, was probably the busiest member of the colony, since the largest part of Deucalion's income came from the sale of its excess milk to outside bottlers. But Mr. Poynter had served in the Army Engineers during the war and, for several years before he settled his problems by coming to Deucalion, he had tried to work them out by pouring his free time into community service as a scoutmaster in Brooklyn. Busy as he now was, Mr. Poynter could not resist demonstrating to young people how to tie a sheepshank, make a fire with wet matches, or find the right terrain for pitching a pup tent.

He had found the clearing in the birch forest at the far side of Aaron's Brook, known as Camp Cody, before John Sayer could walk. By the time John crossed the line, at the age of eight, into the Upper Half of the Children's Guild, and was allowed to join Mr. Poynter's Saturday afternoon bivouacs, Camp Cody had begun to look like an illustration in the Boy Scout Handbook. It was as pretty as a brand new pair of ice skates. Perhaps for that reason John had begun, after his first year, to find the place a bit dull. Everything was so neat and orderly that going there was not unlike pitching camp in the dining room at the Main House. Mr. Poynter, however, did not find it dull. Even though the routine was precisely the same every Saturday afternoon, he threw himself into it as though he was going through it for the first time. John had long ago started to go through it without thinking. While his hands drove the tent pegs and his legs carried him to the stacks of firewood, his mind moved about on entirely different business. For this reason he did not realize, until some minutes after Mr. Poynter gave the order, than an unusual thing had happened.

"Hey, stupid," Charlie Devon said.

John had been thinking about Ike's explanation of why he had gone into the police station. He looked up from the canvas bucket of water he had just filled at the brook, and automatically, without thought, made the traditional reply.

"Look who's calling who stupid." Then he saw that Charlie had wrapped himself in his blankets and was lying under his shelter half. John said, "You going to sleep or something?"

"So are you, stupid," Charlie said.

John started to swing the bucket. But Mr. Poynter called sharply, "None of that!" John turned and saw that the head of the Dairymen's Guild, also wrapped in blankets, was lying in his own tent. "Get going," Mr. Poynter said. "Lights out in three minutes."

It sounded nuts. Even through the massed leaves, the bright sun could be seen. John pulled out his father's birthday present. The Ingersoll showed six minutes to three.

"We going to *sleep?*" he said.

"That's right," Mr. Poynter said. "Naps for everybody. Come on, John."

John got his blankets. He noted that all the other members of the group were already tucked away. He wrapped himself in the manner Mr. Poynter had long ago established as correct—shoulders covered, feet free—and crawled into his pup tent.

"When I say 'Lights Out,'" Mr. Poynter called, "everybody close their eyes. This is not an exercise. This is for real. Anybody doesn't get some sleep this afternoon, he won't be

allowed to stay up for the entertainment tonight. Ready?
Here, we, go! One! Two! Three! Lights! *Out!*"

John closed his eyes. When he opened them, Mr. Poynter
was tramping around the stone fireplace in the center of the
camp site, laying out the potatoes and ears of corn that
would be baked for supper, and John realized that his long
discussion with Mr. Jarvis about where to place the zeppelin
mooring mast had been part of a dream. It was a pleasant
subject, however, and John's mind kept going back to it all
through supper; while they broke camp; and during the hike
back to the Main House.

"Your mother and father went over to the Barn Hall,"
Mrs. Loring said when he came in. "I'm to go over with you
after you clean up."

"You go on," John said. "I don't need anybody to go over
with me."

"Your father thinks different," Mrs. Loring said. "He told
me to wait for you, so stop arguing and start scrubbing. I
want to get there before Miss Gilchrist lights the fire."

John didn't blame her. It was the most spectacular moment
at any Deucalion entertainment. Vallee Gilchrist, who had
been the highest paid sob sister in the world of New York
tabloid journalism, had come to Deucalion at fifty to write a
life of St. Francis of Assassi. Somewhere in her researches
she had come across a description of the bonfires used by the
Inquisition for torturing its victims. Kip Hauser, who lived in
the cabin next to Miss Gilchrist's, told the kids in the Children's Guild that she had once sketched for him on paper the
plan for such a fire. Kip was, of course, a notorious liar, so
John was not the only one who doubted that Miss Gilchrist
had given away her secret. Like most of the kids, however,
John didn't really care to know the secret, if indeed there was
a secret. What mattered was that Vallee Gilchrist seemed to
know how to get an astonishing and almost instantaneous
blaze from a comparatively modest arrangement of birch
logs. And the reason why Deucalion entertainments always
started so promptly was that nobody cared to miss the moment when the tall, haggard woman, wearing around her
neck apparently endless ropes of amber beads, touched the
flame of her red candle to the arrangement of logs and tinder
on which she had worked for a couple of hours. John and
Mrs. Loring did not miss it now.

They had come across Center Pasture, through the scythed
lane between the chicken runs and the vegetable garden, to

the open space at the south side of the Barn Hall. Here all the outdoor aspects of a Deucalion entertainment were always held. The fire had been laid, and the colonists were seated around it in a series of semicircles, all facing toward the Barn Hall. Some sat cross-legged on the grass. Others had brought small pillows or stools. Most of the kids, John noticed, were sitting, as usual, on the prompt books that Wade Duhart always passed out when they arrived. The head of the Music Masters' Guild never knew what hymns or other songs would be chosen by the colonists—the choices were always spontaneous—for the "sings" that interspersed the rest of the entertainment. But he liked to make sure that the children had the words right. He came hurrying up to John and Mrs. Loring with one of the black oilcloth-covered books just as Miss Gilchrist, looking almost terrifyingly regal, made her entrance. It was always the same, and it never failed to make John's heart jump.

Vallee Gilchrist, who was now about sixty, suffered from a slowly crippling form of arthritis. It had changed her once brisk walk to a slight, uneven limp. As a result, when she moved out from behind the half-closed Barn Hall door, and started across the lawn, holding the red candle in one hand and shielding the small flame with her other, all the amber beads around her neck, and the heavy Mexican silver bracelets on her arms, bounced and clanked against her bony body, creating a delicate, ominous sound. It was like the distant rattle of horse's hooves made by the piano in the pit at a Tom Mix movie. Then Miss Gilchrist dipped down, touched the candle flame to the carefully arranged, kerosene-saturated logs, and the column of flame shot up into the evening sky with a huge, sighing *whoosh*. In the explosion of light, John saw his father and mother, sitting cross-legged on the grass side by side in the first row of colonists. Then, as though to remind him that the problems set in motion the night before had not yet been settled, he saw, at the other side of the fire, also sitting on the grass, the heavy, lumpish figure of Francis Tristram and the delicate, tiny figure of his wife.

"Take this and go sit with your friends," Mr. Duhart said. He poked the prompt book into John's hands. "You want one, Mrs. Loring?"

John didn't hear the cook's reply. He had moved off, down the lane on the left, toward the group that included Kip Hauser, Alfie Crocker, and Charlie Devon. John slid down among them, poking the prompt book under the seat of his *lederho-*

sen, as his father rose. Sennacherib Sayer turned to face the colonists. He raised his hand to signal the start of the song that opened every Deucalion entertainment.

"Here we halt our march, and pitch our tent," John bellowed along with the others to the music Wade Duhart and his green tam-o'-shantered men were suddenly sending out across the flames. *"On the rugged forest ground, and light our fire with the branches rent, By winds from the beeches round."* The words thundered out in a rousing flood of sound that John did not bother to try to understand. He had grasped long ago that poetry was not meant to be understood. What counted was the noise it made. If the noise was pleasant, then the poetry was good. This noise was very pleasant indeed. *"Build high the fire, till the panther leap,"* John roared happily, *"From his lofty perch in fright, And we'll strengthen our weary arms with sleep, For the deeds of tomorrow night."*

After the opening song Max Crocker came down front, into the glow of the fire, and made a short speech about how proud he and all the rest of his fellow colonists were because of the great honor the President of the United States had the day before conferred on their beloved leader. He supposed they were all wondering how this great honor was going to affect Sennacherib Sayer's relationship to the colony he had founded, and Dr. Crocker, having taken his courage into his trembling hands and asked Sennacherib Sayer directly, was now happily able to tell them what the founder and leader of Deucalion had told him that very afternoon in so many specific words: being a member of the Supreme Court would mean he could spend more time at the colony. He had long wanted to arrange his life in such a way that this would be possible, but outside pressures which he had been unable to resist had always stood in the way. Now, at long last, his many outside duties would be reduced to one large responsibility; his seat on the bench in Washington. This would mean he could not only come to Deucalion, as he always had, on Fridays and remain until Mondays, when the court was in session, but in addition, he could spend the months of recess working uninterruptedly, side by side with his fellow colonists, on the many projects that had thus far, in spite of their nine years of active existence, been merely sketched.

The applause that greeted this speech by Dr. Crocker was interrupted by Lester La Croix. The head of the Carpenters' Guild leaped to his feet and called for three cheers and a tiger for the one, the only, the great Sennacherib Sayer. The response was overwhelming but it did not, apparently, satisfy Lester La Crois.

"Now, how's about a good rousing dose of 'Little Lamb'?" he shouted. The dying cheers rose again into the evening sky. John slid the prompt book out from under his pants. So did all the kids in his group. The words of "Little Lamb" were tricky. The green tam-o'-shanters went to work. Lester La Croix, his face suddenly streaked with sweat in the firelight, cried: "Let's go!" A hundred voices, including John's, went lustily with him into: *"Little lamb, who made thee? Dost thou know who made thee, Gave thee life, and bade thee feed, By the stream and o'er the mead?"* Out of the corner of his eye, as he swung along with all the others into the closing words, *"Little Lamb, God bless thee,"* John saw the trick mule. Milton Fennell and Perry Schwartz had been working on it for a week. It came edging out the Barn Hall doors. It was made of canvas and several of Mr. Poynter's army blankets. John was wondering who had the head and who had the tail, when Mr. Fennell's unmistakable hoarse voice emerged from the region of the tail with the first line of the vaudeville routine he and Perry Schwartz had worked out long ago: "It's a great day for the race."

The head of the mule, speaking with the voice of Perry Schwartz, asked: "What race?"

"The human race," the tail said, and then exploded in a choking roar of laughter. Whereupon the head, enunciating with cold clarity, demanded of the tail, "What are *you* laughing at? *You* don't belong to it."

This brought down the house, or rather the colony, including the trick mule. When it rose, the head moved in one direction, and the tail in another. The result, a ripping noise as canvas separated from blanket, reduced everybody, including John, to helpless whimpers of ecstasy. Everybody, that is, except Klaus Immensee, who jumped up and, in his heavy German accent, demanded, "So now 'A Sunny Shaft Did I Behold.' Ja?"

Kip Hauser, next to John, uttered one of Ike Ten Eyck's favorite words. John didn't blame him. "A Sunny Shaft Did I Behold" was lousy poetry. It did not make a pleasant noise. Nonetheless, the rules of a Deucalion entertainment being firm and clear, John thumbed the pages of his prompt book. To the music provided by Wade Duhart's men, he sang along loudly if not enthusiastically, *"A sunny shaft did I behold,*

From sky to earth it slanted: And poised therein a bird so bold—Sweet bird, thou wert enchanted!"

Dr. Immensee's taste in songs may not have coincided with that of the members of the Children's Guild. He had, however, other talents. With one of these he now proceeded, as he always did at these entertainments, to redeem himself: Dr. Immensee held the entire audience almost literally spellbound for a full hour with his magic tricks. Everybody was so grateful for this most professional section of the entertainment, that not even John begrudged the doctor his request, with which he always closed these performances, that he be allowed to sing a solo. One thing about Dr. Immensee's solos, John felt: you didn't have to join him in the dopey words. All you had to do was listen. A few minutes later, it began to come over John that you didn't even have to do that.

"So soon may I follow, when friendships decay, And from Love's shining circle, the gems drop away," were the heavily accented words John was hearing when he became aware of a commotion to the left of the performer. *"When true hearts lie withered, and fond ones are flown,"* Dr. Immensee sang throbbingly to the starry night sky, *"O who would inhabit this bleak world alone?"*

Through the quavering sounds, dribbling away toward the silence that always found the singer spent but happy, came the voice of Peter Midden.

"Oh, yes, we're thoroughly rehearsed," the head of the Actors' Guild was saying to someone. "But the policemen are all played by children, and it's almost midnight now."

Somebody answered him, but the reply was lost in the applause for Dr. Immensee. He bowed, picked up the suitcase in which he carried his magician's equipment, and moved happily into the shadows. Dr. Crocker, taking his place in front of the fire, raised his hand for silence and got it.

"And now, as a special treat," he said, "Peter Midden will present a long-awaited event: the Deucalion Actors' Guild presentation of *The Pirates of Penzance*."

Kip Hauser again uttered Ike's favorite word. Then, his voice rising in surprise, he said, "Hey! That's us!" It was also Francis Tristram, who played the part on the police captain, and a dozen or more other members of various guilds. John was not sure of the number of people in the cast because Mr. Midden had not had enough copies of the script to go around. As a result, the boys who played the policemen had never seen anything but the smudged purple and white mimeographed sheets that contained only the words of the few songs in which they were involved. Also, they had never attended a full rehearsal. Mr. Midden's prime concern had been with his principals. He had rehearsed the boys only in his spare time, most of which he never knew was available until it was on him. Whenever Mr. Midden had found he was ready for them, Mr. Tristram had led John, and the other seven boys who played policemen, across from the Children's Guild building to the Barn Hall. Mr. Midden would supervise the rehearsal of their scenes until some of the adult actors arrived, then send the boys and Mr. Tristram back to their classes. Thus, while John knew his part, he knew very little else about the play. He was surprised, for example, as the cast came into the Barn Hall from their places around the fire, to discover that Ike Ten Eyck was among them.

"What part have *you* got?" John said.

"I'm not in the damn thing," Ike muttered. "Mr. Midden asked me to help with the frigging sets."

Mr. Midden, looking harassed, came along and said, "Standing around shooting off your mouth is not my idea of help."

Ike, who clearly had a reply to this, never made it. Not in John's presence, at any rate. Before the handyman could open his mouth, Mr. Midden had dragged him away. Mr. Tristram took his place, appearing among the excited boys as though he had risen from a trap door at their feet. He was carrying the blue coats with brass buttons that Shana Genover and the members of her Seamstress' Guild had been working on for weeks.

"Here, now, lend a hand, somebody," the schoolmaster said, breathing hard. John took half the bundle, and Charlie Devon took half of John's half. Mr. Tristram distributed the rest of the coats as he talked and hustled the boys up the Barn Hall to the stage. "Mr. Poynter says you've all had a nap this afternoon during your bivouac exercise, so there's no excuse for any nodding on post, as it were. Here, this looks like a good spot."

There were no dressing rooms in what passed for the Barn Hall's backstage area, and it had been established long ago by Mr. Midden that he didn't give a rap where his actors dressed and made up, so long as they remained back of the sight lines. These, John saw by peering around Mr. Tristram's struggles with his blue cop's uniform, were being chalked by Ike while the frantic director of the Actors Guild barked instructions. John could understand Mr. Midden's frenzy. He had been pleading for more than a week with the Executive Committee to set a date for the *Pirates* performance. His cast was ready, he had insisted, and unless a date was set they would, he feared, go stale. It seemed odd that the Committee, after refusing for so long to give Mr. Midden a date, should have decided to call for the performance tonight, without warning, at the end of an entertainment that had already gone on somewhat longer than usual, at an hour that was long past Deucalion's official curfew.

"Ready, everybody!"

Mr. Midden may have been frantic, but John could see that he was also pleased. The annoyance of the unexpected was clearly giving way to the excitement of imminent fulfillment. John, standing back of the slanting chalk line and buttoning his blue tunic, did what he guessed Mr. Midden was probably doing: he watched the benches out in front fill slowly with colonists coming in from Miss Gilchrist's dying fire; and he counted Mr. Duhart's musicians as they took their places on the chairs immediately below the platform; and he tried not to worry about whether or not he would remember his part.

This consisted of singing three songs and performing one piece of business. The singing was easy. John did it in chorus with the seven other boys who played policemen, and with Mr. Tristram, who played their leader. When he forgot a line, all he had to do was hum along with the others until he came to the part he knew. The piece of business was more difficult, mainly because John had to do it alone. Or rather, he had to do it alone in response to growled orders from Mr. Tristram. It had gone very well at the last rehearsal. Mr. Midden had complimented both the schoolmaster and John. But John was suddenly in the grip of an emotion he had no way of knowing was fairly common: the terror that came with the sudden awareness that there was a great difference between rehearsal and performance.

To conceal the terror from others seemed as important as fighting it off. Working at both, John heard himself saying a great many things to the other boys in blue tunics, who all at once could have been total strangers, and to Mr. Tristram, who seemed to have lost his face. John did not hear any of the words he uttered, or know in response to what he was uttering them. Neither did he care. The trick was to remain afloat. He must have managed it because, all at once, he could hear the orchestra playing; and he knew the curtain was up because, from where he stood in line with the other policemen, waiting for their cue, he could see, beyond the white glare of the stage, a great shapeless mass of darkness. In it, occasionally, when somebody moved on a bench, a streaking glint of light darted from an earring or a string of beads or a pair of eyeglasses. Then the sounds on stage changed and, through the barely controlled terror, came a stab of warning.

"Ready, chaps!" Mr. Tristram hissed. He raised his policeman's club to the position beside his ear. As Mr. Midden had directed, he sang along with the music, very softly, *"Though in body and in mind, tarantara, tarantara, we are timidly inclined, tarantara."* Then, sharply, the schoolmaster said, "Go!"

They went, stiff-legged, swinging their arms up shoulder high, eyes fixed straight ahead, following Mr. Tristram's portly figure. As soon as they came out into the white glare, John knew it was going to be all right.

"When they see you like that," Mr. Midden had said, "all seven boys in a regularly graduated line, from the smallest in front to the tallest at the back, except for John being out of place, it'll get a big laugh."

It did. And John, who was the cause of it by being out of place, forgot his terror. He began to glow with pleasure. He could scarcely wait for the next laugh. It came with Mr. Tristram's first order.

"Grrr!" he growled, as Mr. Midden had directed. Stiff-legged, like a mechanical soldier, John took a step forward, as Mr. Midden had directed. The audience roared, as Mr. Midden had predicted.

"Grrr!" Mr. Tristram growled again. Stiffly, John turned left. Once more the audience roared. Or did they? They certainly responded. But this time, to John's anxious ears, the response was not quite a roar.

"Grrr!" Mr. Tristram growled a third time. A trifle uneasily, tensing himself for the laughter, John started marching up the row of policemen, as Mr. Midden had taught him, toward his proper place at the end of the line, and at that moment it seemed to him the Barn Hall fell apart.

Concentrating on his own movements, his ears straining for the sounds he hoped would come pouring toward him across the slight barrier of Mr. Duhart's soft music, John was totally unprepared for the kind of sounds that suddenly ex-

ploded down in front. It was neither laughter nor applause. It
could have been hammering. There was no doubt that it was
mixed with female screams. And it stopped the music dead.
In the island of unexpected silence, a voice that sounded familiar to John roared six preposterous words.

"This is a raid! Nobody move!"

But of course everybody did. Especially, John's confused
eyes noted, Mr. Francis Tristram. The schoolmaster, who all
at once looked not funny but foolish in his policeman's tunic,
was screaming something and rushing forward, toward the
footlights, as though he intended to hurl himself into Mr. Duhart's musicians. The fact that he didn't was due to something even more preposterous than the six roared words. Up
onto the platform, as though using the backs and shoulders
and necks of Mr. Duhart's musicians as stepping stones, came
Mr. George Jarvis and several men John had seen many
times in the streets of Wellesville. They were policemen. Indeed, like the First Selectman, they were wearing uniforms.
This, in John's mind, made the crazy sight even more crazy.
The uniformed men, led by Mr. Jarvis, fell on the uniformed
figure of Mr. Tristram. They did not grab the schoolmaster.
They did not hit him. They fell on him. Literally. As though
they were parts of an enormous manhole cover. The result
was frightening. They might have driven Mr. Tristram into
the ground. The schoolmaster vanished. It was the last John
saw of him that night.

"Come on, shake a leg!"

John turned toward the voice barking in his ear and saw it
belonged to Ike. As the handyman started dragging him off
stage, through the crowd of crazily yelling and suddenly unrecognizable colonists, two images popped up in John's mind,
like lantern slides on a screen. The first showed him facing
Ike on the sidewalk in front of the police station that morning. The second showed Ike, on the seat of the Ford truck,
explaining to the windshield that he had been called into the
police station by George Jarvis, who had wanted to check on
a rumor that the Deucalion colonists were planning to build a
zeppelin mooring mast. Then the lantern slides winked out,
the images vanished, and it was very much the way it had
been before.

Again Ike was hauling him at a trot across Center Pasture,
past the dark windows of the Children's Guild, toward East
Cottage Lane. Again John could hear behind them the excited voices of the colonists. And again Ike was dragging him

along too fast for backward glances. There was, however, one difference. When they reached the Main House, Ike did not lead John to the back steps and order him up to bed. Ike led him up the front steps. When they came into the dining room, where his mother and father were seated at the table, John had the feeling that they had been waiting for him. So, apparently, had Mrs. Loring. She came in a moment after John and Ike entered the room. She was carrying a pitcher of milk and a platter of her sugar-free oat cookies. She set them in the center of the table and looked at John's mother.

"Glasses," Mrs. Sayer said gently.

Mrs. Loring's face twisted irritably. She said, "Really, I think my mind is going," and went out.

"Will you join us?" John's father said.

For a confused moment John did not realize his father had addressed Ike.

"No, sir," the handyman said. "I'll just stand."

"You don't have to," Sennacherib Sayer said. He gestured to the chair beside him. "Cookies and milk taste better when consumed sitting down."

"Thank you, sir," Ike said. "I think I'd rather stand, Mr. Sayer."

"As you like," John's father said, and then to John, "But you'd better sit, I think. It's been quite an experience."

John sat down beside his father, who gave him a reassuring smile. Then, as though it had occurred to him that more was needed, he touched John's shoulder. John looked at his mother. She was scowling down at the table. The boy's heart lurched with the old feeling of helplessness. Mrs. Loring came in with the glasses.

"Ike says he prefers to stand," Sennacherib Sayer said. "But I wish you would sit with us, Mrs. Loring."

"Thank you, but I think I'll just stand, too," Mrs. Loring said. "I'm sort of jumpy, Mr. Sayer."

"There's no need to be," John's father said. "That's why I wanted to gather you all in a group at once. To reassure you about what just happened." He smiled down at John. "Upsetting, I know, but in a way not without a bit of thrill and excitement, eh, John?"

"Yes, sir," said John. He thought it was a funny way to look at it. But he had grown accustomed long ago to the fact that his father did not always look at things the way most people did. It was part of being a great man, John supposed.

"In order for us to cope *with* what has happened," Sen-

nacherib Sayer said, "I feel it is important for us to understand *what* has happened. By us, I mean the entire colony.
But before I go on to explain it to others, I want to make it
clear here in my own household. If all of you here understand, I will be easier in my mind about explaining to the
others." He pulled out his watch, studied it with a small
scowl, then slid the watch back into his pocket. "It is a few
minutes after one in the morning. I think I can accomplish
both before the night is out, and I feel it is important to do it
before the night is out. Very well." He reached for the milk
pitcher, but Mrs. Loring beat him to it. "Thank you," Sennacherib Sayer said as she filled his glass. He picked it up
and said, "Griselda?"

"Thank you," John's mother said. She took the glass of
milk from her husband and was passing to him the empty
glass in front of her, when Mrs. Loring exploded.

"What's happening, Mr. Sayer?" she almost screamed.
"What are they doing to us?"

John's father scowled at her. He put out his hand and
touched her arm.

"What we have just witnessed," he said, "is a demonstration of something Henry James pointed out long ago. There
exists in this country a definite hostility to art. An *active* hostility. Not just a dislike. I mean quite precisely what I say
when I say an *active* hostility. We here at Deucalion have
been aware for years, ever since the colony was founded nine
years ago, that our neighbors dislike us. Tonight we have at
last seen what up to now we have merely felt: a demonstration of that hostility. The fact that Deucalion is only inciden-
tally an artists' colony does not change the feelings of our enemies. The fact that we actually subsist as farmers and arti-
sans is beside the point. *Their* point. The point of people like
George Jarvis. For a long time, I have been told, he has plot-
ted to destroy us, and for a long time I dismissed the rumors
as no more than that. But I see now that I was wrong. Do
you understand what I am saying, Mrs. Loring?"

She nodded, very quickly, and put both hands to her
flushed cheeks. Then she swallowed hard and said, "Try some
of these." She pushed the platter of cookies toward him. "If
you're going out at this hour, you'll want something in your
stomach to carry you."

"Thank you," Sennacherib Sayer said. "I'm afraid I must
go out. No. Correction. I withdraw the word afraid. I *feel* I

must go out. I *know* I must go out. It is the only way to cope with the George Jarvises of this world."

He took a cookie and bit into it. He scowled at the broken edge as he chewed.

"But what can he do to us?" Mrs. Loring said, and she began to lose control again. "What can Jarvis do? What *has* he done?"

"What Mr. Jarvis has done is so devilish that it demonstrates he has been planning it for a long time," Sennacherib Sayer said. "Planning and waiting his chance." John's father popped the remainder of the cookie into his mouth and talked around it as he chewed. "Under a form of local option," he said, "which is a legal phrase meaning that the citizens of an area are free to make certain laws affecting themselves but not interfering with the rights of their neighboring citizens, the citizens of Wellesville long ago enacted a series of blue laws."

"Blue laws?" Mrs. Loring said.

"I think I heard talk of it when I was a boy," Ike said. "But I don't remember hearing anything about it since then."

"Well, George Jarvis must be about your age," Sennacherib Sayer said. "Because he remembered."

"George and I went to school together," Ike said.

"I could wish Mr. Jarvis had carried away from the classroom the same liberal view of the world that you did," John's father said. "Unfortunately, he did not. These blue laws are at least half a century old. Nobody has paid any attention to them for years. For a man not only to remember them, but to act on them as George Jarvis did tonight, indicates a narrow-minded, vindictive view of life that must be fought. I intend to fight it."

"Sennacherib," his wife said.

"Yes, my dear?"

From the sound of their voices, from the way they turned toward each other to direct their voices, John had the uneasy feeling that he was watching not his parents but a couple of actors in a play.

"What are blue laws?" his mother said.

"And what have they got to do with us?" Mrs. Loring said.

"Puritanical enactments designed to restrict the pleasures of the people," Sennacherib Sayer said. "They were originally thought up by the narrow-minded bigots of our early colonial times who also thought up the notions about punishments for witchcraft. I have not yet had a chance to look into the actual local statutes, but from the bellowing noises George Jarvis and his men were making when they broke into our Barn Hall, I gather there is a statute on the local books which forbids any form of public entertainment on the Sabbath."

"Mr. Midden's Guild giving *The Pirates of Penzance* for us?" Mrs. Loring said. "Since when is that a public entertainment?"

"Since Mr. Jarvis so chose to interpret it," John's father said. "It is now my duty to disabuse him of that notion, and I intend to do my duty."

"Pardon me, sir," Mrs. Loring said. "Did you say Sabbath?"

"I did," Sennacherib Sayer said.

Mrs. Loring shook her head desperately.

"But this is Saturday night, sir."

"It was," John's father said patiently. "As soon as we went past midnight, however, we were technically giving a performance on the Sabbath." Again he pulled out his watch and glanced at it. "It seems to me a clear indication of the vindictiveness of Mr. George Jarvis and his cohorts, a clear sign that this has been in the backs of their minds for some time, that they should have burst into our Barn Hall when the Sabbath was less than half an hour old."

"The dirty rats," Mrs. Loring said. "They must have been watching us every Saturday night for there's no telling how long. Just waiting for us to go over the line, past midnight, into Sunday."

"The hypothesis seems reasonable," John's father said. He touched her arm again. She was shaking. Sennacherib Sayer said, "And we must be reasonable in everything we do from now on. We cannot counter violence with violence. To do so would be to descend to the level of our enemies. I believe they have made a mistake in seizing Francis Tristram. It is my duty to make them pay for it."

The uneasy feeling came back at John, like a swinging shutter, but from another direction. He was seeing again the moment when Mr. Jarvis and his men fell on the schoolmaster like an enormous manhole cover. Mrs. Loring, making an effort to speak calmly, asked the question John did not dare ask.

"Why did they grab him?" she said.

"Quite obviously because he was the only adult who actually was on stage and performing at the moment of the raid," Sennacherib Sayer said. "To have seized John, or any of the other boys, would not have suited Mr. Jarvis' purpose. They are minors. Arresting children is not very popular, even with people who support blue laws. It was Mr. Tristram's bad luck to be caught. I shall now see what I can do to change his luck." John's father finished the milk in his glass and stood up. "Assuming, that is, that here, in my own household, all is clear?"

The handsome, white-haired head moved in a slow circle, like a searchlight sending its probing beam through the night. One by one, as though actually touched by a shaft of light, the heads nodded. First Ike's, then Mrs. Loring's, and even though John did not really find it all clear, he knew what his father wanted, and he also nodded. The handsome, white-haired head moved on.

"I do not understand it," John's mother said. "That this should happen, right now, to Mr. Tristram, after what happened last night. It is very disturbing."

"It's what he deserves," Mrs. Loring said, her voice suddenly tense and uneven. "The rotten troublemaker. It's what he deserves."

"That is not the point," John's mother said.

"Precisely," Sennacherib Sayer said. He put his hand on Mrs. Loring's shoulder. John could see the tension begin to ease out of the cook's body as his father spoke to his mother. "If you are referring to Francis Tristram's hostility toward me, I ask you to put it out of your mind. Personal feelings must always be subordinated to larger issues. I do not like Francis Tristram, but I like even less the notion that any man, even if he is my sworn enemy, should be denied his rights."

"That is not what I mean," Mrs. Sayer said. She touched a forefinger to the nose piece of her glasses, as though tapping the octagon-shaped lenses into better position, so that she could see her husband clearly, as she spoke to him. "I mean that what has happened, where it may lead—" She paused and then, in a voice that sounded more like Mrs. Loring's than her own, John's mother said tensely, "Sennacherib, be careful."

John's father smiled.

"It is a piece of advice I would urge on all of us," he said. "Now I must be off. Ike, I'd like you to come with me. As for the rest of you, please go to bed and get a good night's rest. I will see you in the morning."

He didn't. That is, he did not see John, who was told by

Mrs. Loring, when he came down for breakfast, that his father had driven into Wellesville with Ike.

"What for?" John asked.

"To see if he can get that damn Francis Tristram out of jail," the cook said. "I got some pancake batter."

"Okay," John said. He sat down at the table. He did it with a thump that took him by surprise. The word jail had come as a shock. He had seen Mr. Jarvis and the other policemen fall on Mr. Tristram. Later, in this room, he had heard all the talk about the schoolmaster being arrested. And John had dreamed a good deal about what he had seen and heard. But somehow he had not pictured Mr. Tristram in an actual jail. Partly, John supposed, because he didn't really know what the Wellesville jail looked like. He guessed it was part of the police station, probably somewhere out in back, but that didn't help. John had never been in the Wellesville police station. His mother came into the dining room as Mrs. Loring brought in the pancakes.

"Good," Mrs. Sayer said. "I wanted you to make a good breakfast."

"How can anybody get anybody out of jail today?" John said. "It's Sunday."

The light bounced sharply from his mother's glasses, the way it always did when she moved her head rapidly to take a more precise look at someone.

"Your father felt he had to make the effort," she said.

"Just like him," the cook said. "Ruining his one day of rest to help a terrible man like that, a man who is his enemy."

"He felt he must make the effort," Mrs. Sayer said again.

Mrs. Loring seemed to have something to say to that. But her glance was fixed on John's mother's face. Apparently what she saw there made the cook change her mind.

"I have some more batter," she said instead.

John's mother didn't seem to realize the cook had spoken to her. She was staring across John's head, out the window, as though watching for something. Then Mrs. Loring's words apparently caught up with her. John's mother smiled quickly, not a good smile, a sort of automatic crinkling of her face in the direction of a smile. She said, "Thank you, Mrs. Loring, no. But John will have some more, won't you, John?"

She sounded funny saying even that. John didn't have to handle it, however, because at that moment the front door opened and Rudy Weer appeared in the foyer. John's mother stood up and went to meet him.

"Sorry to bother you," the head of the Finance Guild said. "I was just wondering what about that investigation, Mrs. Sayer?"

"Yes," she said, and that was all John's mother did say. She stood there, just outside the dining-room door, hands folded in front of her, staring down with a small scowl at the foyer floor, as though Rudy Weer had brought in a couple of rug samples and asked her to make a choice.

"Mr. Sayer said yesterday it was to take place at two o'clock today in the Finance Guild cabin," Rudy Weer said. He glanced uneasily at his watch. "It's almost one o'clock now?"

"Yes," John's mother said, still staring down at the invisible rug samples.

Mr. Weer drew a deep breath and said helpfully, "I could do it, if Mr. Sayer wanted me to? I mean I've got all my records ready? But it seems sort of silly without Mr. Tristram? I mean, him being the one called for the investigation, without him present it sort of, well—"

His voice trailed away. As though she had finally made up her mind about which rug she wanted, John's mother said, "It does seem a trifle pointless, doesn't it?"

"*I* think so," Rudy Weer said. "But of course it's up to Mr. Sayer?"

"Well, he's down in Wellesville trying to get Mr. Tristram out of jail, so we can't ask him, can we?"

The tone of her voice seemed to take Mr. Weer by surprise. He took a half step backward, away from her.

"No, ma'am, I guess we can't," he said.

"Guessing is hardly necessary," John's mother said. "Since we're dealing with a hard fact. If Mr. Sayer is not here, we can't ask him, can we?"

"No, ma'am," Rudy Weer said uncomfortably.

"The conclusion, then, seems clear," John's mother said. "Until Mr. Sayer does come back, and we *can* ask him, the most sensible thing to do is to postpone the investigation, isn't it?"

"Yes, I guess—no, I mean, yes, it does," Rudy Weer said.

"I wouldn't worry about it," John's mother said. "It is *my* guess, and this *must* be a guess, since I have not conducted a poll on the subject, it is *my* guess that after what happened last night, everybody at Deucalion has forgotten about this afternoon's investigation."

"Yes, that's probably true," Rudy Weer said. He sounded relieved. "Then you think it's all right just to—?"

"I certainly do," John's mother said. "Unless Mr. Sayer comes back within the next hour, of course, and says otherwise."

"Well, if he does and he wants to go ahead with the investigation," Rudy Weer said, "I'll be right there, waiting."

"Good," Mrs. Sayer said.

Rudy Weer left. John's mother came back into the dining room. She stood just inside the door for several moments, her hands folded, her lips pursed, her eyes fixed on John's plate. He wondered if he should say something about the pancakes. His mother had told him several times that, when he liked something Mrs. Loring had prepared, he should speak up and say so because praise made people feel good. John didn't know what to say about these particular pancakes. They were probably good. But he didn't really know. Even though he had eaten most of what was on his plate, he suddenly could not remember the flavor. Then his mother solved that particular problem by eliminating it. She turned abruptly and went to the secretary. There was something familiar about the way she rummaged among the pigeonholes. When she found what she wanted, John knew why it was familiar. His father had done that on Friday night. Now his mother did another thing his father had done Friday night. She sat down at the table and wrote several lines on a sheet of her gray note paper. She sealed it in one of the matching envelopes, and turned to John. Even her gesture, as she held out the envelope, was so much like his father's gesture, that John was not surprised, not at first, anyway, to hear his mother say almost exactly what his father had said Friday night.

"John," she said. "You know Mr. Tristram's cabin?"

"Sure," he said.

"Would you go over, please, and give this note to Mrs. Tristram?"

"Sure," John said again. He came around the table, noting to himself, for no reason at all, that this was the difference between his father's statement Friday night and his mother's statement now: his father had asked him to deliver his note to *Mr.* Tristram.

When he reached the Tudor cottage John stopped and put his hand into his pocket. Touching the little silver scissors seemed to make him feel better. He knocked on the door. No answer. He knocked again. Still no answer. John looked down at the gray envelope his mother had given him. On it she had written "Mrs. F. Tristram" and, in the lower-left-hand corner, "By hand." The sight of the strong letters, clear and angular, leaning slightly to the left, resembling print rather than script, brought into his head the image of the beloved face. To escape the image, John shoved the door open and stepped into the cottage.

"Mrs. Tristram?" he said, and knew there would be no answer. It did not occur to him to know how he knew until the knowledge was solidly imbedded. Then he knew that, too. If she had been in the cottage, he would have smelled her.

Until now, this moment, his knowledge of her had been confined to an image: the slender body swaying as the delicate hand brushed backward, against the long brown hair that hung forward, over the beautiful forehead. No, the beautiful face. Now he knew his knowledge was deeper than that. In addition to the image there was the smell. Faint, as delicate as the gesture, but much more clear: it was the smell of Mrs. Loring's bread when it came out of the oven. No wonder he had never noticed it before. It was so commonplace, and so wonderfully exciting. John felt hungry as he moved into the cottage. When Mrs. Loring was baking, the whole Main House knew it. John realized now that, when he was near Mrs. Tristram, the whole house knew it, too. Even when he didn't see her, he knew she was there. And since there was no smell of fresh bread, hot from Mrs. Loring's oven, he knew Mrs. Tristram was not in the cottage.

He didn't mind. In fact, John was pleased. He had not realized until this moment that he was hungry to know how she lived.

He moved across the room in which she had taken the silver grape scissors down from the mantelpiece. His breath came faster as he pushed open the door to the right of the mantelpiece. It was, as he had suspected, a bedroom. Even Tudor cottages—which, like all other homes at Deucalion, had been built by hand by the people who planned to live in them—were bound to be almost primitively functional. This one certainly was. The manner in which it was functional sent John's spirits soaring. The only furniture in the room was totally different from the furniture in his parents' bedroom. Mr. and Mrs. Sayer slept in a double bed. Aside from a chair and a stool, on both of which crumpled clothes were piled, there were only two pieces of furniture in this bedroom: canvas army cots.

John spent a few moments wondering how a body as large and shapeless as Mr. Tristram's could get any sleep on an object so narrow, but it was the most casual sort of wondering. John didn't really care. What counted was the sense of relief, the feeling of gratitude for the fact that there was no double bed. This feeling was so strong that he felt a trifle giddy. Feeling foolish but grateful, embarrassed but excited, he walked into the room. He moved without hesitation, led on by the smell of Mrs. Loring's freshly baked bread, to the corner near the window. Then the door out in the living room crashed open and Ike's voice cut through John's complicated feelings.

"Mrs. Tristram?" Ike called.

John ran to the bedroom door. Ike was coming across the living room toward the door. He stopped short.

"For Christ's sake," he said.

Before Ike could say the rest, John held up the gray envelope.

"My mother sent me over with this message," he said. "She said give this to Mrs. Tristram."

Ike took the envelope and tore it open.

"Hey!" John said.

Ike didn't seem to hear him. The thin, lined face knotted in a scowl as the handyman's slanted body bent over the note.

"Oh, Jesus," he murmured. Then, sharply, as he looked up: "How long ago? When did your mother write this?"

"I don't know. A few minutes ago. She wrote it and told me to take it over and I came over. That's how long. Walking from the Main House to here."

"How long have you been here?"

"I don't know," John said. He realized with a stab of shock that he was telling the truth. He pulled out his father's birthday present, and had another shock. Rudy Weer, just before John's mother wrote the note, had looked at *his* watch and said it was almost one o'clock. John's Ingersoll showed a quarter to three. Almost two hours had gone by. Had he been lost all that time, or nearly all that time, in the smell of fresh bread in the bedroom? John said slowly, "I came in because nobody answered when I knocked. I thought maybe—"

His voice stopped. Ike had turned and was hurrying to the front door. John ran after him.

"Hey, Ike!"

The handyman neither turned nor answered. He was moving toward the Ford truck. It was parked to the right of the cottage. Running after Ike, John was struck by another thought: he had been so absorbed in the smell of fresh baked bread that he had not heard the truck pull up to the cottage. He caught Ike as the handyman swung up onto the front seat.

"What should I tell my mother?"

The handyman looked down on him with an irritated frown. John had the weird feeling Ike did not remember who he was.

"The note," John said. "You want me to tell my mother Mrs. Tristram wasn't home?"

"No, don't say anything," Ike said. Then, fumbling and kicking at the levers and pedals, he seemed to realize his reply was no solution. John would have to tell his mother something. "Here," Ike said. He reached down. John grabbed his hand. Ike swung him up into the truck. "Don't say nothing to nobody."

As a piece of advice, it made no sense. So long as he was in the moving truck, the only person to whom John could say anything was Ike. Grasping that, John grasped the result: whatever it was that his mother and Ike were upset about, Ike obviously felt it could be helped by keeping John away from his mother. This was clear as soon as the truck came bumping out of West Cottage Lane into the Wellesville Road. Ike tramped on the gas. The truck went roaring past the Main House. The obvious question, the question that loomed up in John's mind, could not be asked. If Ike had wanted to tell him where they were going, he would have told him. A few minutes later, John did not have to ask. As they approached the stone wall that served as the eastern boundary of Stonecraft Farm, Ike slowed the truck, then pulled it up onto the grassy shoulder between the wall and the road.

"Stay here," Ike said, and jumped out of the truck.

"Ike, wait."

The handyman turned back.

"I got no time, Johnny," he said irritably.

The sound of his own name, spoken by the only person who had ever called him Johnny, was reassuring. It told John what he didn't really have to know but was glad to hear. He was doing the right thing. Giving up one of his precious secrets was the proper way to say good-bye.

"Look," he said. He pointed to the bicycle. It lay in the tall grass beyond the wall. Somebody had tried to hide it by pulling a pile of dry branches up in a sort of lean-to against the wall. But the job had been done in haste, and whoever had done it had not bothered to check the work. Besides, John had seen the bicycle the day before in Wellesville. He was not likely to forget those colors. "It belongs to Mrs. Tristram," he said to Ike. He spoke with great care. After all, he was handing over something precious. "Nobody knows she has a bike," John said. "She keeps it hidden. But I saw her yesterday—"

"Oh, for Christ's sake," Ike said, and turned away. Before John could say anything, the handyman had disappeared on the run around the bend of the stone wall. His voice, however, lingered. After Ike's body disappeared, the tone in which his words had been uttered remained behind. They told John that, to the only man who had ever called him Johnny, his farewell present was not a present at all. Mrs. Tristram's secret was not a secret to Ike.

"Mister Sayer!"

His father's name came at John like a blow. There was something desperate in Ike's voice as he repeated it. John jumped down from the truck. He followed Ike's desperate voice around the bend of the stone wall, and stopped.

For a moment, for an hour, perhaps for an eternity, he stood motionless and stared. It was like the exercise in observation at Mr. Poynter's bivouac drills. Each boy was led up to a cleared space on which several dozen items of camping equipment had been tumbled in an untidy heap; the boy was given sixty seconds to examine the pile. Then, he turned his back and rattled off for Mr. Poynter as many items as he could remember. John had always done very well in this exercise. He did very well now.

He saw the small tent pitched against the stone wall in such a way that it was completely concealed from the road. He saw Ike, his voice calling John's father's name over and over again, as though it were a litany, standing in a curiously discreet way at the other side of the wall. John saw the tent flap open. He saw his father come out. He saw Mrs. Tristram come out after him. He saw them both come to the wall. He saw Ike move toward them on his side of the wall. Then John saw, behind them, something none of the others saw. John saw Mr. Tristram, coming across the field.

Of all the things his mind recorded, this was the first one John found surprising. The schoolmaster had been arrested the night before. He was supposed to be in jail down in

Wellesville. What was he doing here, in this hidden corner of Stonecraft Farm? Then John saw Mr. Tristram's face, which was scratched and streaked with blood, as though he had been in a fight, and John saw what Mr. Tristram had in his hand, and John knew what Mr. Tristram was doing here. A moment after that John even knew how Mr. Tristram had got here. Behind him, yelling as they ran, came Mr. Jarvis and two of his policemen. John could not hear what they were yelling, but that was not important. The noise was enough. It caused John's father and Mrs. Tristram and Ike to turn. John turned, too. But in the opposite direction. The exercise was over. Nobody must know he had been there.

Nobody did. He was out on the Wellesville Road, running hard toward home, when he heard the gun. John remembered wondering if it was the gun Mr. Tristram had been holding, or one of the guns Mr. Jarvis and his policemen had been holding, and that was the last thing John remembered.

Except for the metallic wailing scream. It came at the moment when John knew he was finished. He could run no further. His heart was hammering its way out of his chest. His throat burned with the pain of breathing. Then he heard the wailing scream, and he fell to his knees. Mr. Poynter's training in observation came thrusting up through the horror to help him: John saw the smoke pouring from the windows of the Main House.

It was an important piece of information. Without it John would not have known that the wailing scream was the siren of the Deucalion fire engine.

3

TWENTY-FIVE YEARS LATER, driving down the Turnpike from New Haven toward Edesboro, John Sayer could still hear that metallic, wailing scream.

He could hear it so clearly that, involuntarily, John turned to the man in the soiled raincoat on the seat beside him. Could Mr. Mancini hear it, too? John wondered.

"Yes," the policeman said with a nod. "Clearly." He pulled down the brim of his Swiss mountaineer's hat and poked out his lower lip in a thoughtful pout. "That's the way you remember it?" he said. "All the things that happened up at Deucalion on your tenth birthday?"

John hesitated, then said slowly, "That's how I remembered it a year ago. On the day I met Arnold Zucker for the first time, and then went out to Stamford in the afternoon to see Ike Ten Eyck in the Dogwood Lane Rest Home."

Mr. Mancini's pouting lower lip came forward a fraction of an inch.

"What's wrong with it?" he said. "The way you remember it?"

John shook his head slowly. The weight inside, the decision sitting heavily on his brain while the clock of his life ticked away the remaining minutes, suddenly seemed unbearable.

"What difference does it make?" he said wearily. "Why don't we stop this? Nothing is going to change."

"How do you know?" Mancini said. "You're not even sure about what you remember. How can you be sure about what's going to happen?"

"Because you just told me," John said. He said it to the windshield. He wished his was not the only car on the Turnpike. If there had been traffic, anything to distract his eye, he might have been able to move his thoughts from the weight of the decision. "You said in fifty minutes I'm scheduled to die in an accident at Edesboro," John said. "What good does it do to go back over all this stuff that led to my decision, if the decision is already made?"

Mr. Mancini glanced at his watch.

"Thirty-eight minutes left," he said. "Going back to Deucalion took twelve of your fifty."

"Why don't you speed up the car?" John said. "Why don't we reach Edesboro now, this minute, and get it over with?"

"Because you're entitled to think it over," the policeman said. "It's my job to see that you *do* think it over. If I see to it that you use the time properly, you might change your mind. Just because you decided to commit suicide doesn't mean you have to go through with it. It isn't as though you've been sentenced in a court. It's your own decision. I can't repeat often enough—you don't have to go through with it."

John shook his head again. He was tired of the argument. The policeman obviously thought he was offering John something valuable. He couldn't seem to grasp that John wanted nothing but oblivion.

"I *want* to go through with it," he said, "I didn't make the decision on the spur of the moment. I thought about it. I thought it out very carefully. I didn't *want* to make the decision. My thinking led me to it. When I thought it all out, I *had* to make the decision. I couldn't see any other way out for me. Don't you understand that? I don't want to live through the next thirty-eight minutes."

"You don't have any right to say that," Mr. Mancini said. "The next thirty-eight minutes are not so much offered to you, as they're forced on you. You must use them. You have no idea what you might remember."

Desperately, John said, "That's not true. I know what I'll remember, and I don't want to remember it."

It was the policeman's turn to shake his head.

"Everybody thinks that," he said. "But they're wrong. Look at you, just now. All those things you remembered about your tenth birthday. You're not sure about any of it."

"I didn't say that," John said. "I said—"

"You're not sure about any of it," Mr. Mancini repeated quietly. "You don't really know what happened that day at Deucalion. You have a vague idea, but you don't know what really happened. For example, that girl, the schoolmaster's wife. Was your father sleeping with her? Was that why the schoolmaster asked for the investigation of the colony's financial affairs? Because he was jealous? And he hoped to uncover something that would destroy your father? And did your father fight back by framing the schoolmaster? Getting him arrested for violating the blue laws? So that the investigation couldn't take place?"

"I don't know," John said. "I don't want to know. All I want now—"

"Were you in love with that girl?" The policeman pressed on as though he had not been interrupted. "That Dinah Tristram? You were only ten, sure. But she was only seventeen. Were all of you caught up in something that was too complicated for a ten-year-old to understand? Did you want—?"

"I don't know," John said. He found himself holding onto his voice as though it were an overloaded paper sack about to come apart in his arms. He did not want to cry. Not in front of a stranger. Even with only thirty-eight minutes of life left to him. "I don't know," he repeated. "I don't know. Why don't you leave me alone?"

"Because it's my job to make you look back," Mr. Mancini said. "Learning what you don't know could change your decision. Finding out what really happened could save your life.

You've got the thirty-eight minutes." He looked at his watch. "No, thirty-six. Why not use them?" he said. "What have you got to lose?"

John could feel his hands go tight on the steering wheel. Through the mixture of confusion and weariness and fear, his attention had been caught. He gave the man in the soiled raincoat a quick glance.

"That's what my wife said," John said slowly.

"When?" the policeman said.

"That night a year ago," John said. "When I came home from seeing Ike Ten Eyck in Stamford. I told her what had happened during the day. My visit to Arnold Zucker and then to Ike out in Stamford. All that. And when she asked what I was going to do about it, I said I didn't know. I said I was still undecided about going to see this Miss Gwen Quill the next day, even though I'd promised Vincent Howe I would, and that's when my wife said it."

"What have you got to lose?" Ellie had said. "You're never going to make up your mind about should you or should you not let them do this show about your father until you go see this director what's-her-name. Quill?"

"Gwen Quill," John said.

"It's perfectly obvious that your two meetings this morning seem to have left some doubt in your mind about the project," Ellie said. "This may be because all they can do, really, is talk about it as entrepreneurs. Naturally they assure you it's all going to be on a very high artistic level, and your father's memory won't be tarnished or libeled and all that. But they don't really know. Miss Quill is really the only one who does know, or should know. I mean she's the only one who can talk about it artistically. She's the one who's going to write and direct it. In fact, she's already written an outline, didn't Mr. Howe say?"

"Yes, he did, and that's why I'm undecided about going to see Miss Quill tomorrow," John said. "Why don't I ask Mr. Howe to let me read Miss Quill's outline before I go to see her, is what I mean. Sort of do my homework before the session takes place?"

Vincent Howe did not agree.

"Aah, now, look, fella, no," he said on the phone the next morning when John called and asked if he could see the outline before he met Miss Quill. "Gwen doesn't like to do it that way. She wants to *read* it to you."

"But that's not necessary," John said. "I know how to read."

Mr. Howe laughed, not very enthusiastically.

"Like Arnie Zucker said, you're a boy with the jokes, Mr. Sayer. But really, no kidding, that's not the point. What's on paper, the outline, it's in Gwen's special sort of shorthand. Not those chicken track squiggles. Pitman or Gregg or whatever. I mean it's in Gwen's special lingo. The way she talks to herself as a director. Unless you're inside her mind, the written outline won't mean much to you. It's Gwen the director and Gwen the writer, the combination, *that's* who did the outline, and to really get it, you've got to get it from Gwen, face to face, fella. She always works like this. It's how she writes."

"Well," John said. He was annoyed by the small defeat. For it had to be that. He could hardly make of Miss Quill's purely mechanical writing habits an issue affecting the life of the project. "It seemed to me a sensible thing to do," he said into the phone. "I like to do my homework before I go to a meeting."

"You don't have to do any homework for a meeting with Gwen, fella," Mr. Howe said. "All you have to do is listen. How about doing it right now?"

"Isn't it a little early?"

"Not for Gwen," Vincent Howe said. "This girl never sleeps. Could you meet me in front of her house in ten minutes?"

"Make it fifteen," said John, and then wished he hadn't. The small defeat would not be wiped away by a small display of childishness. "I just want to sign some papers, before I leave the office. What's Miss Quill's address on Fifty-fifth Street?"

Mr. Howe gave him the number and said, "It's a gray house. I'll be standing in front."

Actually he was sitting on the stoop, reading a newspaper, a fact that pleased John. He had never actually seen a man sitting on a New York stoop, except in movies and TV plays about life in slum areas. There was something innocent and disarming about the sight. It made John think that perhaps what he had assumed to be Mr. Howe's carefully constructed portrait of himself as a homespun type was not a construction at all. Perhaps the tan suit and the tan hat and the boldly

striped tan tie and the pointed tan shoes, all somehow giving
the impression that they had been assembled to match their
owner's thinning tan hair, were Mr. Howe's notions of sarto-
rial elegance? They would probably have been Ike Ten
Eyck's notion of how he should dress on a visit to the big
city. And Mr. Howe, from the moment John heard his voice
on the phone yesterday, had reminded him of Ike. Then Mr.
Howe looked up from his newspaper, saw John approaching,
and leaped to his feet with a cheery "Hi, fella!" John had a
stab of loyalty for his old and once beloved friend. Ike Ten
Eyck would never have called anybody "fella" and still
wouldn't.

"Good morning," John said. "I see you don't believe in
wasting time just staring at the passing scene."

"If I don't find out what Winnie Winkle is up to, my day
just doesn't jell," Mr. Howe said. He slapped dust from the
seat of his pants. "Funny thing about comic strips. The ones
you read when you're a kid, you read the rest of your life.
Habit, I guess. Like smoking. Some dump, hey, fella?"

"Must have been a beautiful private home in the days before taxes," John said, staring up at the gargoyles over the
front door.

"Some railroad tycoon, I think Gwen said. Supposed to be
the last job Stanford White did before he got shot by Harry
Thaw. Shall we go up, fella?"

Mr. Howe pulled open a door heavy and ornate enough to
have graced the entrance of St. Patrick's. In the vestibule he
pressed a black button on a brass panel that had sixteen
names on it.

"I hate these damned automatic elevators," Mr. Howe said
as he pushed the 4 button. The tiny car started swaying upward. "I'm always afraid I'm going to get stuck between
floors." John released an amiable grunt. The space was too
confined for anything but the most intimate kind of conversation. The same thought must have crossed Mr. Howe's mind
because the pleasantly crooked grin suddenly lighted up his
face and he said, "Of course I wouldn't mind getting stuck if
the other passenger was a cute babe, hey, fella?"

John smiled noncommittally. He had learned long ago that
there was no sensible reply to these small self-serving declara-
tions about their sexual powers with which some men felt it
necessary to fill the gaps in almost any conversation. Besides,
John was suddenly wondering why Mr. Howe, whose face
was no more than eight inches from John's, was chewing

Sen-Sen so vigorously. It was a habit, John had noticed, with heavy drinkers. Was it possible that Mr. Howe, who looked so much like Ike Ten Eyck, shared the handyman's weakness for alcohol? It would certainly have to be pretty close to a weakness if Mr. Howe was camouflaging his breath at ten in the morning.

"Here we are, fella," he said.

Mr. Howe pushed open the elevator door. John followed him out into a small hall, and saw that there were four apartments on the top floor. He followed Mr. Howe to the door marked "A." A voice behind the door called, "It's open!" The room into which John followed Mr. Howe looked like a store.

"Lemme take your hat, fella," the producer said.

John handed over his hat. While Mr. Howe fussed with the door of a closet, John looked around. He wondered why the room gave him the feeling that he had stepped into a store. At the same time, he wondered why he didn't seem to know what kind of store it was. He could have been in the fancy delicatessen on Madison where Ellie bought the cheese he liked. Or he might have stepped into one of the better Fifth Avenue department stores. There was that same feeling of totally impersonal elegance. Also, the same knowledge that whatever you got here would be good, but you wouldn't get it cheap, and you certainly wouldn't get it free. John supposed part of the reason for this impression was the huge picture window that formed the entire street side of the room. On a ledge under it stood a number of pieces of highly polished driftwood. Looking across their silhouettes into Fifty-fifth Street was not unlike looking into a display window at Bonwit's. Another reason, John felt, was that all the furniture was low and blond and Scandinavian. This gave him the impression he was surrounded by showcases. Then he forced himself to concentrate, the way he used to concentrate for Mr. Poynter's observation exercise during Saturday afternoon bivouac drill at Deucalion, and John had it. Two things were responsible for the impression that he had wandered into a store.

One was the wall to the right of the picture window, facing the door. It consisted of floor-to-ceiling bookcases. On them sat a brand new, complete set of the Modern Library. The set had obviously not been touched since it had been unpacked. The books were arranged, John saw, by number, as identified in the publisher's catalogue, and they were the only books in the room. The long, symmetrical rows of glistening dust jackets, every book exactly the same size, each row exactly the same length, every section of bookcase completely and neatly filled from end to end, like square sausage casings, these were an invitation not to read, or even to browse, but to order from these samples for shipment to readers in other places.

The second thing that helped create this impression that he had stepped into a store, John saw, was the display of silver cigarette boxes and ash trays. There must have been a couple of dozen in the room. All were engraved in various ways with names and dates and expressions of affectionate admiration. All were beautifully polished.

"You seem to like my living room, Mr. Sayer."

John turned toward the voice, and was startled. He saw only Vincent Howe, who was closing the closet door. John had assumed when they were outside and the voice had called "It's open!" that Miss Quill was in her bathroom or bedroom and had not wanted to keep them waiting in the hall while she finished dressing. He saw now that there was a door set at right angles to the closet in which Mr. Howe had just disposed of John's hat, and that it did open into a bedroom. In fact, this door *was* open. But the bedroom beyond it, John could see, was empty. Then he heard an odd, sharp little laugh. He turned again, toward the picture window.

"Do you really like it?" said the creature in the low blond chair. John's mind had started to form the word "thing." But the instinct toward precision, which had brought him to the study of law more than a dozen years ago, moved him now toward the more accurate word "creature." The thing curled like a cat in the blond chair was, after all, alive.

"I certainly do," John said. "I've never been in a room like this before."

"There aren't many like it," the creature said.

"Here, hey, you two," Mr. Howe said. He came forward fast. "Gwen, this is John Sayer, and this, fella, is the one and only Gwen Quill."

"How do you do?" John said.

Miss Quill said nothing. She did it aggressively. She did not merely remain silent. She made of her silence a positive act. Positive and, with obvious intent, insulting. Screw you, Miss Quill's manner was saying. John found himself wondering what *that* would be like. Because the thing—no, the creature! —curled in the chair was neither male nor female. Thin, small, and probably short—although that might not prove to be so when it stood up—the creature had neither breasts nor hips. The black bolero pants and the striped blue and white Basque shirt were plastered to the coiled body like a rubber glove to the hand of a surgeon. No bumps. No bulges. No hint as to how, if you should want to screw Miss Quill, you would go about it.

The dull red hair did not help. It was cut like a man's, with a part on the left side, and slicked back neatly over the ears. These were fascinating: coming to points at the top; splayed out at the bottom in thick lobes. To these were clipped silver discs almost as large as some of the smaller inscribed ash trays that dotted the room like chicken pox. It was the eyes, however, that made John want to get behind something solid to separate him from Miss Quill. They were watery and, at the centers, not very sharply defined. The brownish irises might have been a couple of fried egg yolks that had broken when the eggs had been dropped into the pan and had spread out onto, and discolored, the whites. As a result, Miss Quill seemed to have trouble focussing. Her lids blinked and her eyeballs rolled. The impression of shiftiness reminded John of something Winston Churchill had said about the Germans: they were always either at your feet, or at your throat. Miss Quill couldn't seem to make up her mind, John thought, whether to burst into tears and throw herself on the mercy of the court, or leap from her chair and sink her teeth into his jugular vein.

John had no such difficulty. The sight of Miss Quill had made up *his* mind. All the uncertainties of the last twenty-four hours had fallen away. He was not going to allow Mr. Howe to produce a play about Sennacherib Sayer and Deucalion. Not while creatures like Miss Quill were associated with the project.

She was so clearly something venomous and evil that John knew instinctively nothing good could come of knowing her. He recognized Miss Quill for what she was: the incarnation of all the reasons why men and women call upon lawyers to help them fight the savage battles in which have ended relationships begun in love. John was trying to decide why the sight of Miss Quill, who couldn't have weighed more than ninety pounds, should be so frightening, when the various details of her appearance, which his neat mind had carefully catalogued, suddenly came together in a single image: Miss Quill looked like a demented jockey.

"I've told Mr. Sayer all about the project and about you,"

Mr. Howe said. "Maybe you'd like to say a few words yourself, Gwen?"

"I certainly would," Miss Quill said. "My research, which was extensive, included a careful study of newspaper and magazine photographs as well as newsreel shots. They indicate that Sennacherib Sayer was one of the handsomest men of his day. I didn't realize his son was just as handsome."

"I'll tell my wife you said that," John said. "It should please her."

"Oh, then you're married?"

"Didn't Mr. Howe tell you that?"

"Mr. Howe is a producer," Miss Quill said. "This means he doesn't know his ass from a hot rock about anything except money."

Vincent Howe put his entire slanting body beside a cackling laugh. It flung him into a chair facing Miss Quill.

"Didn't I tell you this girl makes with the jokes, fella?" he said. "Sit down and take a load off. Gwen's got a lot to say."

"The first thing I want to say is a question," she said. The watery, shifty eyes crinkled. John realized with a twinge not unlike the beginnings of nausea that Miss Quill was trying to look arch. She said, "Why were you so eager to ram it right down my throat at the start, Mr. Sayer, that you're married? You scared I'll try to rape you?"

"Not in front of Mr. Howe," John said.

Miss Quill laughed. She said, "You don't know my sexual habits, buster."

"I didn't come here to hear about your sexual habits, Miss Quill," John said. "And I do have to get back to my office, so could we get down to business?"

Miss Quill shifted her sexless, coiled body in the blond chair. She said dryly, "Vinnie, I don't think Mr. Sayer likes me."

"Nobody likes you at the beginning," Mr. Howe said. He turned to John. "She gets better, fella. In fact, she gets great." He turned back to Miss Quill. "Tell him what you said to Prince Bernhard." The sandy-haired little head swivelled toward John again. "That's the guy he's married to the Queen of Holland. He was here a few months ago, some sort of trade mission, or maybe a UN thing, and he went to see *Fig Leaf*, then said he'd like to meet the director." Another twist of Mr. Howe's head. "Tell him, Gwen."

"I told the prince most men, when they first meet me, they

want to vomit," she said. "Ten minutes later they're trying to get their hands between my legs."

"I suppose it's a lucky thing for the moral tone of the city that you don't meet many of them in Macy's window," John said.

"Didn't I tell you?" Mr. Howe said. "He makes with the jokes."

"I'd like to see him make with something else," Miss Quill said. "Especially in Macy's widow."

"If you have any influence with Miss Quill," John said to Mr. Howe, "I suggest you use it and get her to get down to business. I'm not staying for much more of this."

Miss Quill's watery eyes narrowed. She said, "Make coffee, Vinnie."

The sandy-haired little man rose. He sloped off through a door that John supposed led to a kitchen.

"He doesn't mind, apparently, being used as a doormat," John said.

"Very few men do," Miss Quill said. "Have you seen *Fig Leaf?*"

"No."

"You're missing something. Take your wife. It'll give you both a new slant on screwing. My first title for it was *Venus Envy.* You get the joke?"

"I do," John said.

"I'm glad you're not one of these jerks who think the pun is the lowest form of humor. It's only low to people who can't make good puns. I'll bet Sennacherib Sayer could tear off some good ones."

"I don't know," John said. "I don't remember."

"It's just about the only thing didn't show up in the research," Miss Quill said. She poked a hand behind her back and pulled out a stenographer's notebook. "He was quite a guy, your old man," she said. "You know that, don't you?"

"Yes," John said. "I know that."

"You really know it?" Miss Quill said. "Or you just saying you know it?"

"What difference does that make to you?"

"It'll help me see you in the clear. Right now I can't. Not quite. You're sort of fuzzy at the edges. What do I see? A big, tall, handsome son of a gun. Brooks Brothers type. Sort of stuffy. Neat in his habits, including his thinking habits. Embarrassed by a dame like me talking dirty. Probably embarrassed by any woman talking about sex. Good legal practice. Married. Two kids. Both in a good school. Lives in a good, old-fashioned apartment house like The Nebraska, which means he doesn't give a damn about status, living on the East Side, that crap. Which in turns means a solid citizen who knows who he is and lives in peace with the world around him, so he doesn't need all that gook about status. That's the picture I get looking at you," Miss Quill said. She paused. One of the enormous silver earrings swung out like a Ubangi's lower lip as she tipped her strange head to one side. "You know what's wrong with the picture?" she said. "Why it's fuzzy at the edges?"

John hesitated, annoyed with himself for feeling a sudden quickening of the pulse. Trying not to sound eager, he said, "Why?"

"It's not real," Miss Quill said. "It's too good to be true. For the son of a famous man like Sennacherib Sayer."

"What should the son of a famous man be like?" John said.

"In revolt," Miss Quill said. "Your famous father was a lawyer? You should be anything *but* a lawyer. A ditch digger, maybe. Or a pickpocket. He was interested in improving the lot of the common man? An early socialist? You should be a reactionary prick. And so on. All opposites. Defying your father on every count. That would be the average situation. But you, no. You've *copied* your father on every count. Become a lawyer. Wear his kind of stuffy clothes. There's only one thing I'm not sure about. You're prissy about sex."

"I don't think you can say a man is prissy about sex merely because he feels having intercourse with a total stranger in Macy's window might be considered a questionable pleasure."

"How do you know till you've tried?"

"Have *you* tried?"

"No, but very often I do it with other people watching."

John was aware of a slight prickling at the base of his scalp. He said, "I thought you're a director, not an actor."

Miss Quill's snake-narrow, boneless body shifted slightly in the blond chair.

"Go ahead, run us into the ground," she said. "Mr. Sayer, are you aware what the problems are that a director faces? Making a musical out of the life of Sennacherib Sayer?"

"Mr. Howe implied that you've licked them," John said.

"I don't know," Miss Quill said. "I won't know until you tell me, Mr. Sayer. That's why you're so important to this project." She set the notebook on her knees and flipped back the cover. "A show must have unity," Miss Quill said. "Especially a musical show. A single, central core that holds it together. Usually that central core is a love story. The life of Sennacherib Sayer doesn't have such a central core. Or rather, Mr. Sayer, it has two of them. Our hero married late in life, when he was almost fifty. He lived happily with his wife for almost eleven years, and then she died tragically. Less than a year later, when he was pushing sixty, our hero married again, a woman more than forty years his junior, a young girl. Fun and games, huh, Mr. Sayer? I mean, kiddo, go make a musical comedy out of *that!*"

"Yet that's what you propose to do," John said. "Isn't it?"

Miss Quill's slicked back dull red hair caught the sunlight from Fifty-fifth Street as she nodded slowly.

"If I've licked the story," she said. "Yes." She flipped a page of the notebook. "Here, follow me, please," Miss Quill said. "The most interesting thing my research dug up about Sennacherib Sayer was something that's never quite explained. Not by the mountains of press clippings and so on that I've read, anyway. His career up to nineteen twenty-nine is one long record of public service. Court battles for the underdog. War service for Woodrow Wilson. Founding the colony up in Dutchess County. Trust-busting, and so on. All very noble, and all dull as piss. Then in nineteen twenty-nine, when he's fifty-eight years old, one hell of an interesting thing happens. President Hoover appoints him to the Supreme Court. Three days later, before the confirmation hearings can even begin in the Senate down in Washington, the nomination is withdrawn. Why?"

The prickling at the back of John's scalp started to move down his spine. The feeling of impatience with, even revulsion for, this grotesque creature had been slowly eroded. Miss Quill had begun by trying to shock him. She had ended by interesting him. John didn't have time to figure out why. He felt vaguely that it was because Miss Quill had abandoned her childish mannerisms and got down to business. There was something impressive about the way she was discussing her problem. It was the talk of a professional. Someone who knew her—his?— business and was going about it without waste motion. Without even, it occurred to John, much interest in the person to whom she was talking. The intensity of her concentration, he realized with a sense of shock, made

Miss Quill almost attractive. It was the attraction of a piece of functioning machinery.

"The newspapers you researched must have explained why the Supreme Court nomination was withdrawn," John said. "I was only ten at the time, and they kept most of the papers away from me. But the ones I did manage to see—"

"Yes, I know," Miss Quill said. "I've seen them, too. But they don't satisfy me, Mr. Sayer."

"I'm afraid I don't understand," John said.

Again Miss Quill's eyes narrowed.

"Are you making with the jokes, like Vinnie said? Or are you serious?"

"Jokes about what?" John said. "That I don't understand what doesn't satisfy you?"

"You really don't?" Miss Quill said.

"No, of course I don't," John said. "How the hell should I know what doesn't satisfy you?"

"Steady, buster," Miss Quill said. "Don't forget that Brooks Brothers suit. All right, listen. What do the old newspapers say? The papers that reported what happened at the time? The papers I've just read? The way I put it together, they say on a Friday in June of nineteen twenty-nine, the day President Hoover appointed Sennacherib Sayer to the Supreme Court, he was accused by the Deucalion schoolmaster of misusing the colony's funds. An investigation was set up for Sunday. Before it could take place, however, your father, according to the tabloids, arranged to have the schoolmaster arrested for violating the local blue laws. The papers say your father got the schoolmaster to give a performance of *The Pirates of Penzance* that lasted past midnight on Saturday, into Sunday. This violated the Sabbath, and the schoolmaster was arrested. While the schoolmaster was in jail on Sunday, Sennacherib Sayer, and I'm just quoting the tabloids, Mr. Sayer, they report that your father shacked up with the schoolmaster's wife. Instead of shacked up, maybe I should say tented up. The tabloids say this little love nest was a tent in the woods. The schoolmaster, according to the tabloids, had suspected hanky-panky between his wife and Sennacherib Sayer for some time. In fact, according to the *New York Graphic*, I think it was—" Miss Quill paused. The head of boyishly-cut dull red hair dipped over the notebook. "Yes," she said. "According to the *Graphic*, the schoolmaster's accusation against Sennacherib Sayer, the accusation about misusing colony funds, that was done as an act of revenge by the schoolmaster against your father. When the revenge didn't work, because Sennacherib Sayer outsmarted him by getting the investigation postponed by getting him arrested, the schoolmaster blew his cork. He escaped from the jail down in Wellesville, and tried to kill your father. Luckily, the cops were right behind him, and they managed to kill the schoolmaster before he could take another shot at Sennacherib Sayer. In the meantime, while all this was happening, and again please note that I am merely quoting the newspapers of the time, they report that Sennacherib Sayer's wife knew about her husband carrying on with the schoolmaster's wife. In fact, she had tried to stop it. She had accused Sennacherib Sayer to his face. He had denied it. There was, the papers say, a long series of ugly scenes between husband and wife. These culminated in an attempt by Mrs. Sayer to get the truth out of the schoolmaster's wife. She sent a note to the schoolmaster's wife and asked for a showdown. When it was not forthcoming, when Mrs. Sayer found out that, at the moment she expected the schoolmaster's wife to come to her and deny what Mrs. Sayer believed had been happening, at that moment the schoolmaster's wife was actually in that tent with Sennacherib Sayer, when Sayer's wife discovered this, the tabloids report, she set fire to the colony's main house, then committed suicide among the flames. When all this broke in the papers on Monday, President Hoover withdrew the nomination of Sennacherib Sayer to the Supreme Court." Miss Quill flipped shut the notebook on her knees with a small, sharp slap of finality. "Those are the facts as revealed by my research," she said. "Reading what was published by the press at the time."

"And it doesn't satisfy you?" John said.

"Does it satisfy you?" Miss Quill said.

"I don't know," John said slowly. "If that's what happened—"

"*Is* that what happened?"

John felt his face tighten in a scowl of puzzled surprise.

"You just said yourself, Miss Quill, that it's what the papers reported."

"Screw the papers," she said. "They don't care about the truth. They care about facts."

"What's the difference?"

"Art, buster," Miss Quill said. "Ay, are, tee. Art."

"Huh?" John said. Miss Quill laughed. He was surprised.

Her laugh sounded pleasant. "I'm sorry," he said. "I guess I'm out of my depth."

She gave him a long, calculating look. She might have been trying to guess his weight.

"Are you trying to throw me a curve?" Miss Quill said finally.

She said it with such a total lack of artifice, her voice was so genuinely troubled, that John felt impelled to say with complete sincerity, "Miss Quill, I don't know what in Christ's name you are talking about."

The lack of artifice in his own voice seemed to have some sort of effect on her. John didn't know what it was, since most of it was obviously internal. But it also caused Miss Quill to shift her body in the chair. Now she was partly in profile to him, with the light from Fifty-fifth Street behind her. John saw that, in at least one respect, he had misjudged Miss Gwendolyn Quill. She did have breasts. They were not very large. It occurred to John, with an irrelevance that disturbed him and made his face flush, that her breasts were no larger than his own. But they were breasts. And they were bound together under the blue and white Basque jersey by some contraption of the lingerie manufacturer's art that did not cover the nipples. These stuck out, sharply, like cloves on a baked ham. Staring at them, John couldn't believe what was happening in his loins. This is, he told himself sharply, an ugly woman who is not even a woman. This is a sexless embodiment of evil.

It said, "Mr. Sayer, why do you think I want to do this play?"

He said, "I wish you would tell me. All I've been able to gather from Arnold Zucker and Vincent Howe is that they think it will make a lot of money. I'm not against that. I simply do not see *how* the money will be made. To put it bluntly, Miss Quill, why the devil should anybody pay money for a ticket to see the story you have just outlined?"

"They shouldn't, and they wouldn't," Miss Quill said. "I have no intention of putting that story on the stage."

"How can you do anything else?" John said. "If you were writing a play about John Doe, an invented character, okay. You can make up anything you want. Something attractive. Something beguiling. Something the public will—"

"Might, Mr. Sayer."

"All right, *might* be willing to pay to see. But you're telling the story of a real man. How can you disregard the true facts about the life of Sennacherib Sayer?"

Miss Quill said, "Are you telling me, Mr. Sayer, that the facts I have just repeated to you, the facts I have dredged up out of the newspapers that reported the end of Deucalion, are you telling me those facts are true?"

John said, "But of course they are." Then, seeing the look on Miss Quill's face, he heard his voice say, "Aren't they?"

Miss Quill's shrug brought the cloves sharply against the tight Basque shirt. John thought they would cut through the fabric.

"A play is not a newspaper," she said. "A play is a work of art. In a work of art you take the so-called facts and you get to the essential basic, deeply rooted truths buried in the facts. The writer for a newspaper is a reporter. The writer for the stage is an artist. When we read the reporters who wrote the newspaper accounts of that strange week end, when you were a boy of what, Mr. Sayer?"

"Ten," John said.

Miss Quill's watery eyes flicked. John was reminded of his mother when she used to move her head to take a sharper look at something.

"That means you're only thirty-five."

"Why *only?*"

"You look older," Miss Quill said. "Must be the long family jaw or something. I've studied photographs of Sennacherib Sayer taken at the time he was appointed to the Supreme Court, when he was fifty-eight. He looks older. Was his hair really all white?"

"Pretty much," John said.

"Well, as I said, or started to say, when we read the reporters who wrote the newspaper accounts of that strange week end when you were a boy of ten, what emerges? A picture of a pretty terrible man, and not really a credible picture. We get the public figure. The do-gooder. The selfless citizen of the world. The international bleeding heart. A sort of boy scout on a grand scale. A fighter for the underdog. Behind this pious façade of the good white knight in shining armor, however, we are led by the leering tabloid reporters to believe, there lurked the true man. A man who was financially irresponsible, stealing money from the Deucalion treasury to pay personal debts, a man without a sense of decency or honor, an insatiable lecher who would scheme to have an innocent schoolmaster arrested so he would be free to bang his teen-age wife. Do I exaggerate, Mr. Sayer?"

John was thinking of the smoke pouring out of the Main House on that terrible Sunday.

"Not about what the reporters wrote," he said. "No."

Miss Quill said, "Do you believe they wrote the truth?"

Behind that smoke, in the bedroom she had for ten years shared with Sennacherib Sayer, John's mother lay on the floor, her wrists cut with the razor Sennacherib Sayer's father had brought with him from Wales.

"Mr. Sayer."

John came up out of his thoughts. Miss Quill had shifted her position on the blond chair. Now she sat cross-legged, her toes tucked under her. She was no longer in profile to him. The sharp little cloves, straining at the blue and white fabric, had vanished. But John could now see the line of silver zipper that stretched up the front of Miss Quill's bolero pants from the crotch to the place where normal human beings had their navels.

"Sorry," John said. "I was thinking of something else."

"I said do you believe the reporters wrote the truth about your father and what happened at Deucalion that week end?"

John realized that Miss Quill believed they had not. He could tell not only from the fact that she had asked the question, but from the way she had asked it. She wanted him to say no.

"I was only ten," he said. "And they kept the newspapers away from me."

"Ten is a hell of a lot brighter than people who are no longer ten think," Miss Quill said. "And you were right there on the spot. Besides, you loved your father, so people saying and writing those things about him, you must have had some reaction."

"I loved my mother, too," John said.

"I see," Miss Quill said, and she frowned down at her notebook.

"Why do you say it that way, *I see?*" John said. He wished he could stop staring at the zipper in Miss Quill's crotch. All his reactions suddenly felt wrong. He didn't want to be thinking what he was thinking about Miss Quill's body at the same time that he was trying to hold onto a feeling about his father and mother that was as old as the wailing, metallic scream of the Deucalion fire engine.

"I think I see why you became a lawyer," Miss Quill said.

"It's a profession that deals with facts. Not unlike the way a newspaper reporter deals with them. There's nothing of the artist in the lawyer. The artist would see at once, as I see, and as you don't, Mr. Sayer, that what the reporters wrote about your father is as far from the truth as Poughkeepsie is from Pago-Pago."

"How far is that?" John said.

"As the crow flies, I'd guess about six or seven thousand miles," Miss Quill said.

"Then there must be another truth," John said. "Is that what you mean?"

"Not *another*," Miss Quill said. "There is *the* truth. Just one. And that's what I propose to tell in our play."

"You'd better tell it to me first," John said.

"Don't get truculent," Miss Quill said. "I'm well aware that we can't do this show without your permission, and if you're not aware by now that I'd give my entire sexual apparatus to do this show, you're not very bright. I want your permission. But I don't want to get it by peddling my ass or performing any of the other tricks some writers might use. I want your permission because, and only because, when you hear my version of the truth you'll start to cream right in your Brooks Brothers pants."

"To judge by your language," John said, "I would say, Miss Quill, that you are not interested in having your version of the truth serialized in the *Saturday Evening Post.*"

"You are but so right, buster," Miss Quill said. "I use the language of James Joyce, who happens to be my literary hero. And since I know damn well that my version of the truth about your father would have pleased old Jim, I will not go ahead with this play unless it also pleases Sennacherib Sayer's son. Why? Because Sennacherib Sayer's son, meaning you, because of your legal position, even though you may be a literary boob, you are for me at this moment a tougher and more important critic than Jim Joyce, and that's the mark I'm shooting at with this play. What do you think of that?"

"I think you're a very ambitious woman," John said. "As well as a surprising one. I never thought of my father in the same category with James Joyce."

"Neither do I," Miss Quill said. "It's me, Gwendolyn Quill, *I'm* the one thinks of herself in the same category with Joyce."

He looked at her sharply, to see if she was kidding. He

saw that she was looking at *him* sharply, to see how he reacted to her insolence.

"Okay, Miss Joyce," John said. "Tell me the truth about my father."

She laughed, and shifted her body in the blond chair. She flipped open the notebook. John wished she hadn't moved. She was back in partial profile to him. The cloves were again straining to tear through the blue and white fabric.

"For the sake of dramatic unity," Miss Quill said, "I have decided to build the entire first act around the week end we have just discussed. To set a time bomb, so to speak, ticking over the story from the very start, I propose to begin with the arrival of the news at Deucalion that Sennacherib Sayer has just been appointed to the Supreme Court. He doesn't know this. When the play opens, your father is on the train from New York on his way up to Deucalion for the week end. His wife receives the news by phone. We now go through, during the first act, all the actions we have just discussed. The excitement of the appointment. The schoolmaster throwing a bomb into the excitement by accusing Sayer of defalcation of funds. The investigation that is thwarted by the arrest of the schoolmaster. The shooting of the schoolmaster by the pursuing police. The destruction of Deucalion by fire and the suicide of Sennacherib Sayer's wife. Curtain." Miss Quill paused and looked up from her notebook. "Basically the same story the newspaper reporters told. Right?"

"It certainly sounds so," John said.

"Except for one thing," Miss Quill said. "Artistic interpretation. As follows. Using the same trolley tracks the reporters used, the facts just outlined, I asked myself is there some other way of looking at them? Many months ago, almost a year ago, Mr. Sayer, when I first got the idea for this play, I asked myself that. And the answer was: there *must* be. It did not make sense that a man of Sennacherib Sayer's dimensions, a man who looms up even after all these years that have gone by as a man of stature, a great man, a man whose record of achievement to this day is staggering, it did not make sense to me that such a man should in fact have been nothing more than a hypocrite, an embezzler, and a whoremaster. What's the matter?"

John had not realized how much the word had jolted him. He picked up the silver ash tray toward which his startled hand had leaped.

"Nothing," he said. "I just happened to notice this." He

read aloud the words engraved in the bottom of the ash tray: "To Gwen with love from her grateful cast U.S. Foundry Hour production *The Eleventh Minute of the Eleventh Hour of the Eleventh Day* November 11, 1953 NBC-TV."

"Yes, well, what about it" Miss Quill said irritably. "My casts always give me a souvenir of the shows they appear in." She gestured toward the dozens of gleaming silver cigarette boxes and ash trays dotted around the room. "Why should this one throw you?"

"It didn't," John said. "It's merely that—" His voice simply stopped. The capacity to invent a covering lie had deserted him. He could not explain why he should be so upset by hearing again the word Francis Tristram had hurled at John's father across the Barn Hall at the Full Meeting a quarter of a century ago. "It's very nice," he said, setting down the silver ash tray. "I'm sorry, Miss Quill. I didn't mean to interrupt."

"Well," she said. She flounced slightly in the chair. John was glad she did. At least those infuriatingly distracting nipples were no longer staring him in the face. "I was saying what the papers reported about a man like Sennacherib Sayer just didn't seem to me could be true," Miss Quill said. "All that stuff about calling the cops, getting the schoolmaster arrested, anybody could have done that, anybody who loved him." Into John's mind came the sudden sharp image of Ike Ten Eyck slipping out of the police station on that awful morning. "I did some more research and some more thinking," Miss Quill said. "Not only about Sennacherib Sayer, but about the people who came to join him at the colony, giving up their former ways of life to live up at Deucalion. Klaus Immensee, for example, one of Freud's early students. What the hell was he doing on what the world outside considered a free-love nut farm? A Mrs. Loring, who had given up her Greenwich Village restaurant to join the colony. I discovered she had a curious background of religious hysteria out in the Midwest. I looked into about a dozen of these so-called nuts. The more I looked, the more an interesting pattern appeared. A pattern about Sennacherib Sayer. In addition to his many talents as a lawyer, a negotiator, a brilliant analyst of complicated political situations and so on, he seems to have had a talent that we usually associate with men of medicine and wearers of the cloth. You've heard the phrase *laying-on-of-hands?*"

"I think so, yes," John said. His mind leaped back to a scene at Deucalion that, until that moment, he had completely forgotten: his father stopping the mounting hysteria of the cook in the Main House merely by placing his hand on Mrs. Loring's elbow.

"Freud's early discoveries, as we know," Miss Quill said, "were the result of his interest in hypnotism. There seems to be no doubt that all through the ages there have been people who were able to accomplish much the same result by the force of their personalities, sometimes merely by touching other people. You might say they had something in them, a kind of an emotional charge or vibration, a sort of psychic electric current, maybe, that could be communicated to others by touch, and that had a soothing effect on those others. A lot of these healers, for that's what they are, many of these people are unaware of the fact that they possess this gift. I believe, Mr. Sayer, that your father was one of those people."

John nodded slowly.

"You agree?" Miss Quill said. She sounded surprised and annoyed, as though she had been counting on creating a more spectacular effect.

"I don't know," John said. "I was nodding merely to indicate I am following you. I didn't mean to interrupt."

"I think your father didn't know he possessed this gift," Miss Quill said. "No, let me put it another way. He was unaware that he was doing anything of a medical nature. He naturally knew he had a soothing effect on disturbed people. He would have been a fool if he didn't recognize the effect he had on such people, and Sennacherib Sayer was no fool. He knew the effect he had all right, but I believe he didn't think it was anything more than the effect of his own quiet, reflective nature on people who were unquiet. I mean that in my opinion he didn't think this set him apart, and I'm sure he didn't feel he had the right to deny whatever help he could give to people who needed it. He was that kind of guy. It comes through even in the newspaper accounts. Except they see it one way, I see it another. So now for our play. Mr. Sayer, are you awake?"

"Certainly I'm awake," John said.

"You don't look it," Miss Quill said.

"Keep talking, Miss Quill, I'm listening."

"Our play," she said. "The truth about Sennacherib Sayer. I don't believe he was screwing that schoolmaster's wife. I don't believe that for one minute. I think the truth behind what the literal-minded newspaper reporters saw is that the schoolmaster's wife was a very upset young woman. 'Disturbed' is the word doctors use. She'd married the schoolmaster when she was sixteen. He met her when she was fifteen. What happened between them in England, the thing that resulted in their running away to America, that's material for Act Two, where I may want to flash back, although I'm not sure yet. Sticking to Act One, I think when the schoolmaster and his bride came from England to Deucalion, all the girl's terrors came to the surface. To put it bluntly, she was at the end of her rope, about to go off her rocker. Instinctively, she turned for help to the white-haired father image of the colony, Sennacherib Sayer. Knowing he could help her, as he had helped others, Sennacherib Sayer went right ahead and helped her. By talking to her, taking walks with her, being alone with her. Being completely innocent in his own mind, naturally he was outraged by the suspicions aroused in his wife's mind and the schoolmaster's mind. Being a strong and fearless man, as well as a proud son of a bitch and a stubborn one, he refused to be deflected from his duty by suspicions. Result: tragedy. How's that for a first act?"

Before John could reply, Vincent Howe came in from the kitchen with a tray.

"Coffee, folks," he said.

Miss Quill gave him a look that, coming from any other face, would have merely reflected its owner's annoyance with an interruption. Coming from the face that had brought to John Sayer's mind the image of a demented jockey, the look could have been a fire hose turned on full. It made Mr. Howe stagger. John jumped up and caught the other side of the tray just in time.

"Vinnie," Miss Quill said. "Go get some crullers."

She might have announced to the slanting little man that the play he hoped to produce, which had not yet been written, had just been awarded the Pulitzer Prize.

"Sure thing," Mr. Howe said happily. Then, as he started jauntily toward the door, he gave John's arm a happy pat. "Sure thing, fella," Mr. Howe said. He winked broadly. He went out, but the puzzling triumphant words came back again through the closed door. "Sure thing, fella."

"What's he so cheery about?" John said.

Miss Quill slid out of the blond chair and came up beside him. She did it without moving her feet, or so it seemed, as though she were a toy rolling along noiselessly on concealed casters. John's original guess that she was probably short had been correct. The boyishly cut red hair came to his shoulder.

"Vinnie's cheery because he sees the project is going well," Miss Quill said.

"Is it going well?" John said.

"What do *you* think?"

"Hey, wait, *hey!* I'll drop this God damn tray!"

"Good idea," Miss Quill purred. "It's in the way."

John made one last effort to set it down. But her hands did not ease up, and he could no longer control that particular set of muscles. The best he could do was give the tray a hard, outward shove. So that, as he fell to the couch with Miss Quill on top of him, the tray fell clear, beyond the coffee table, in a smashing clatter of cups and saucers and tinkling spoons.

"He'll be back," John said. He was ashamed of the fear in his voice as he mumbled the words against the blue and white cloth. It felt warm and damp to his face, as though the Basque shirt had just come off an ironing board. "Mr. Howe. He'll be back with the crullers," John said.

"Vinnie never comes back with the crullers," Miss Quill said. "It's his exit line."

4

A YEAR LATER, on the front seat of the car in which he was conducting John Sayer to his death in Edesboro, Mr. Mancini said, "Did he come back? Mr. Howe?"

"No," John said.

The policeman hesitated, as though he wanted to make sure his next observation was properly phrased.

"You felt guilty, of course," he said finally. He paused. John felt he should say something, anything, if only out of politeness, but he couldn't. The effort was beyond him. He stared stupidly at the road ahead, wishing Mr. Mancini would not ask any more questions. "I'm afraid I must," the policeman said. "Unless I ask questions, I can't steer you toward a complete re-examination of the events leading up to your decision to commit suicide. You understand that, don't you?"

John nodded. It was as much politeness as he was capable of.

"This next question will embarrass you," Mr. Mancini said. "It's not asked for that purpose. Please don't be sore."

John nodded again. A curious feeling of unreality seemed to be inching through him. Why wasn't he more frightened? He was on his way to an accident in which he was going to die. The fact that he wanted to die, because there was no other solution for him, did not change the fact that his death was going to be painful. Automobile accidents always were. Why wasn't he scared?

"Because deep down you're accepting these fifty minutes that were given to you," the policeman said. "At first you didn't want them, but now that you have them you're beginning to grasp their value. You realize they might save your life. So don't get sore at my question. It's part of what those fifty minutes are for." Mr. Mancini touched the brim of his Swiss mountaineer's hat, as though for reassurance. "When did you first discover you are impotent?" he said.

"I am not impotent," John rapped out.

"It's all right," the policeman said gently. "I'm not one of the boys. You can talk to me the way you'd talk to a doctor. We both know you're impotent. I merely—"

"I don't know anything of the kind," John said sharply. "You seem to know everything else. You sit there and read my mind, answering my questions before I get a chance to speak them aloud. If you can do that, you ought to know something as simple as I'm not impotent."

"It's not simple," Mr. Mancini said. "That's the problem."

"I was not impotent with Miss Quill," John said angrily. "Knowing everything else, you ought to know that."

"I'm not talking about Miss Quill," the policeman said. "I'm talking about your wife."

"Leave her out of this!"

"How can we?" Mr. Mancini said. "She's the one you're impotent with. Oh, not all the time. I know that. But enough of the time to make it a problem."

"It's no problem," John said. "It—"

His voice stopped. In a little while, when they reached Edesboro, it would cease to be a problem. So would everything else.

"When did it start?" the policeman asked quietly.

"During the war," John said, just as quietly. "In England, with other girls. Before I met Ellie."

"How about at Harvard?"

"No," John said.

"At Harvard Law School?"

John hesitated, scowling at the deserted road.

"Wait," he said slowly. "I think, yes, it started in nineteen forty, soon after I entered Harvard Law School. But it was only partial. Once in a while. It wasn't a total—"

"And when you met Ellie?" Mr. Mancini said patiently. "In England? During the war?" John didn't answer. He couldn't. The policeman said, "Your wife has been very sympathetic. When you refused to see a doctor about it, she didn't press you. She figured you preferred to work it out for yourself."

"The way I worked it out," John said bitterly, "I went right from Miss Quill's apartment to a phone booth, called my wife, and asked her to meet me at Tony's for lunch."

"That was a year ago," Mr. Mancini said. "That can't be the reason you decided tonight to take your life."

"No," John said impatiently. "Of course not."

The car rolled along for a while, moving down the deserted Turnpike without sound. John was suddenly reminded of a ghost ship in a painting.

"Do you remember that lunch with your wife?" the policeman said finally.

John nodded.

"Clearly," he said.

"Don't you think it odd that you should have completely forgotten what had just happened in Miss Quill's apartment?"

"Of course it was odd," John said. "But I didn't know that at the time. All I knew then was that we'd been going to Tony's for years, so he always manages to have a table for us, even if we drop in without warning, which was what happened that day. As soon as we were settled at the small table between the two rubber plants, I told Ellie what I was going to do about Mr. Howe's project."

"You know," Ellie said, "it's almost like being married to two different men."

"In what way?" John said.

"Last night at dinner, you were all full of doubts," Ellie said. "This morning, while you were shaving, you were still telling me that this whole thing made you uncomfortable, and unless Mr. Howe allowed you to read Miss Quill's outline for the play, you wouldn't even go to see her. So what happens? First, Mr. Howe does *not* allow you to see the outline, but you do go to see Miss Quill anyway. Second, she doesn't even have a complete outline, just a sketch for the first act, but a half-hour after you leave her, you are buying your wife an expensive lunch in the middle of a business day, and announcing in a voice quivering with enthusiasm that you are going to allow Miss Quill to go ahead with the play. Am I lunching with the same man for whom I made coffee this morning?"

"If you're not, I've got a suit against someone for alienation of affections," John said. "Hello, Tony. How are you?"

"Fine, Mr. Sayer. You?"

"Fine, thank you."

"Mrs. Sayer?"

"Fine," Ellie said. "It's Tuesday, so I suppose no eggplant?"

"For you, Mrs. Sayer, I have eggplant any day in the week including Sunday, if I was open on Sunday."

"You are a darling," Ellie said. "Then to follow, the broiled shrimp, I think. *Let* me think. Yes, the broiled shrimp."

"One eggplant," Tony said, writing on his pad. "One broiled shrimp. And you, Mr. Sayer?"

"The same," John said. "Except I want a vodka martini on the rocks first, very dry."

"My word," Ellie said. "You *are* celebrating."

"I just have a feeling about this thing," John said. "I don't know why. Come on, join me."

"I've got a Parents' League tea at the Porte School at five," Ellie said. "How are Sam and Jim going to feel if their mother comes in reeling?"

"It's not quite one," John said. "You've got four hours to sober up. Two vodka martinis, Tony."

He smiled at Ellie, who shrugged and said, "What can I do? It's a man's world."

"Two vodka martinis," Tony said, and went across to the bar.

Ellie smiled and said, "You're really excited, aren't you?"

"Yes, I am," John said. "And not only about the money or that this could be for the firm a toe in the door to a lucrative practice in theatrical law. I'm excited about Miss Quill."

"She must be quite a dish."

Startled, John looked sharply at his wife. He saw that Ellie was smiling. He shook his head.

"Good Christ, no," he said. "She's one of the ugliest damn things I've ever seen. About this big. Built like a skinny boy

who probably had rickets or something as a kid. Some bone
disease. With the eyes of a madman. I'm only guessing, of
course, but I'm willing to bet she's a Lesbian, and I'm damned
if I know where the image came from, but all the time I was
with her, I kept thinking she reminded me of a demented
jockey."

"She sounds positively repulsive," Ellie said.

"She is, believe me," John said. "And she doesn't improve
matters with her language, which she obviously picked up in
the gutter. But all that is beside the point, and the point is
that Miss Quill has stuff."

"You mean talent?" Ellie said.

"I mean talent," John said.

"How could you tell? You've never seen any of her work,
except perhaps a couple of her TV shows, which I don't remember either of us ever thinking were particularly memora-
ble, and all she did this morning at your session with her and
Mr. Howe, I gather all she did was talk."

"That's right," John said. "Thank you, Tony. Hold the
eggplant until we finish these, will you?"

"Certainly, Mr. Sayer."

"No, bring mine now," Ellie said. "My husband quite
clearly is warming up for a second drink, but I'll have just
one, Tony."

"Certainly, Mrs. Sayer," Tony said, and went away.

"What I'm excited about," John said, "and what makes me
feel Miss Quill has talent, is her approach to the material.
You know how I've always felt about the whole Deucalion
episode. It's one of those things you want to forget about.
That's why, when I went to see Arnold Zucker yesterday and
he told me what Vincent Howe had in mind, my first instinct
was to say no. To hell with it. What's past is past. Why rake
up old scandal? Especially to make money. I don't want to
sound like a stuffy old fool, but I did think about Sam and Jim
and how it would make them feel if all their chums and
classmates at the Porte School knew there was a musical play
on Broadway, even if it was a flop it would be on long
enough for the reviews to get around, a play that painted
their dead grandfather as a, well, the way the newspapers
painted him when my mother died and Deucalion went up in
smoke."

"Miss Quill doesn't see Sam and Jim's grandfather as a
what you can't bring yourself to say?" Ellie said. "Miss Quill
sees Sam and Jim's grandfather as the victim of malicious

tongues? A wronged man? A great man about whom she is setting the record straight?"

John looked at his wife the way he had looked at her when they spoke for the first time at that officers' club dance in London during the war: with a feeling of surprise. He had not then been accustomed, and after ten years of marriage he was still not completely accustomed, to discovering that behind so attractive a façade there dwelt a first-rate intelligence.

"How do you know that?" he said.

"I've been going to the theatre all my life," Ellie said. "I'm hardly what you'd call an expert. But even the most casual observer must notice that plays about villains are usually less successful than plays about heroes. Here is Miss Gwen Quill, a successful television director with a drive to move onward and upward in what she clearly considers to be a higher art form. She chooses for her vehicle what I gather from what you've told me over the years was an exciting experiment, conducted by an extraordinary man, that ended in an ugly scandal in which the experiment was revealed to have been no more than a cover for the shameful activities of not an extraordinary, but a detestable, man. Obviously, at least to this theatregoer, what Miss Quill has in mind is to show the other side of the coin. To turn the tables. To prove in her play that the central figure in this controversial episode was not a villain but a hero. Am I right?"

"Pretty much," John said. "Oh, thank you, Tony. Yes, I will have another."

"You, Mrs. Sayer?"

"No, thanks, Tony, I'm fine," Ellie said. As Tony moved across to the bar she added, "I think that's fine, John. I'm all for Miss Quill telling her version of the story."

"Her version?" John said. "You mean you don't think it's the truth?"

"Do you?"

"Well—"

"Say no more," Ellie said. "All right. It's the truth. If for nobody else's sake, I'm happy for Sam and Jim. My sons, who up to now have displayed no interest whatsoever in their grandfather, will now learn he was a hero."

"What's wrong with that?" John said.

"What's wrong with it is that he's a hero only until the first act curtain," Ellie said. "What does Miss Quill plan to say about Sennacherib Sayer in her second act?"

"I don't know," John said, and added, "yet."

"Does Miss Quill know?" Ellie said, and added, "yet?"

"Ellie, what the hell are you getting at?"

"The truth," she said. "I'd rather know that, if it was about *my* father, than have a hit on Broadway or get my toe in the door to a lucrative theatrical law practice."

"You mean you think Miss Quill won't tell the truth in her second act?"

"I mean I don't know that she will," Ellie said. "What she plans to tell in her first act apparently pleases you, and I don't blame you. Something you've worried about and been ashamed of all your life, ever since you were a boy of ten, suddenly appears through Miss Quill's interpretation to be far from shameful. It appears to be admirable. Well and good. I'm all for that. But your father lived another ten years after Deucalion went up in smoke. With another wife. How is Miss Quill going to interpret that?"

"Interpret?" John said. "Those ten years were not like the ten years at Deucalion. There was never any controversy about that part of my father's life. It's all simple and straight-forward. Why should it have to be interpreted?"

"Because Miss Quill is writing a play," Ellie said. "The facts are just so much brick and mortar to her. If she can refashion or reinterpret the events that give her the first act, she will most certainly do the same with the material that goes into her second act. I want you to be just as excited about the Miss Quill of the second act as you are now about the Miss Quill of the first act."

"But how can I be?" John said. "Until she writes the second act?"

"She hasn't written the first act yet," Ellie said. "But already you're having two vodka martinis in the middle of a business day."

"I've only had one."

"Two," Tony said, setting it down.

John took a pull at his second drink and set down the glass. He said, "Ellie, what should I do?"

"Well, let's look at what we know," his wife said. "You've now met three people connected with this project. Miss Quill, the Lesbian with the madman's eyes, reminds you of a demented jockey. Mr. Howe, the producer of smash hit musicals who doesn't feel his day has jelled until he learns what's new with Winnie Winkle, reminds you of a Norman Rockwell scoutmaster with a taste for the bottle. Mr. Arnold Zucker, a bald-headed maker of evasive telephone calls, reminds you of a Bronx Scarlet Pimpernel holed up in a Park Avenue hotel. To your troubled consort, who adores you, John Sayer, the last of these three characters seems the most reliable. Before you go any further, meaning before this gets out of the talk stage and you sign any papers, I think you'd better have another chat with Mr. Arnold Zucker."

This proved to be difficult. After John returned to his office and asked Miss Faille to get Mr. Zucker, she reported that the switchboard operator at the Hotel Stanton said Mr. Zucker was out but was expected back in twenty minutes and she had left Mr. Sayer's name and number. An hour later, when Mr. Zucker had not called back, John told Miss Faille to try the Hotel Stanton again. Mr. Zucker's line was busy, she reported, but she was holding on. A half-hour after that, she came into John's office. Looking a trifle baffled, Miss Faille said she had been cut off three times and, after she managed to get the Stanton switchboard back, the operator said Mr. Zucker had gone out again.

"Did you leave a message?" John said.

"Oh, yes."

"Well, then, we'll wait for Mr. Zucker to call back," John said. Miss Faille turned to go, and he said, "No, wait. You remember that Mr. Howe who was in here yesterday?"

"Certainly."

"Call his office and ask if he knows where I can locate Mr. Zucker."

A few minutes later Miss Faille, looking more baffled, came back.

"Mr. Howe said Mr. Zucker is in his hotel suite. He knew Mr. Zucker was there because he had just talked to him on the phone, and if I called him right now he was sure I'd get him."

"All right, call him," John said.

"I did," Miss Faille said. "The switchboard operator says he's out."

"I see."

"Doesn't it—?" Miss Faille hesitated. "I don't mean to pry, but, well, Mr. Sayer, it does seem a little odd, doesn't it?"

John thought of the round, bald man in the red silk robe, sitting on the couch in his Park Avenue living room, surrounded by his wife's elaborately framed paintings of bright green sea water, dropping British accented murmurs into the several phones laced to his head like ivy to a brick wall.

"Well," John said, "Mr. Zucker is an odd man. Let's just forget it until he calls back."

He had not called back by six, when Miss Faille asked if there would be anything else.

"No thank you," John said. "I'll just finish these notes on the Arnold trust before I go home. Good night, Miss Faille."

"Your phone is plugged in to the outside," she said. "Good night, Mr. Sayer."

John waited until he heard the outer office door close behind her before he dialed the Hotel Stanton, and asked for Mr. Zucker.

"I'm sorry, sir," the operator said. "Mr. Zucker just went out. Any message?"

"No," John said irritably and slammed down the receiver. What kind of people had he got himself involved with? Why should the simple process of reaching a man by telephone take on all the devious complexity of a general staff planning how to conceal from the enemy the place names of the D-Day landings? In the taxi that carried him home, John alternated between wishing he had never met Mr. Zucker and wondering what the round, bald man thought he could gain by making it so difficult for John to get him on the phone. When he came into the apartment, John could hear Ellie on the phone in the study.

"Just a minute," she said, "I hear the door." She came out into the living room and said, "It's Mr. Zucker."

John dropped his hat and evening paper, went into the study, and took the phone.

"Mr. Zucker?"

"Oh, hello, Mr. Sayer," the low, rolling voice said. "I have a message asking me to call you?"

John's irritation darted off in several directions. All took the form of questions. Was it possible that Miss Faille, calling from the office, had made the strange request that Mr. Zucker call her boss back not at the office but at his home? And what did Mr. Zucker mean by "a message" when Miss Faille had left at least three? And what had happened to John's anger with the foolish complications of the normally simple process of reaching a man by telephone? Why, in short, was he so damned glad to be hearing Mr. Zucker's voice at last?

"Yes," John said. "I saw Mr. Howe yesterday afternoon, and we both saw Miss Quill this morning, and I promised to get back to you after I did."

Where, as long as he was asking himself questions, had he picked up that annoying phrase "get back to you"?

"I took it for granted that the son of Sennacherib Sayer would keep whatever promise he made," Mr. Zucker said. John wished the round man would stop sounding as though he were reading aloud to a slightly deaf child a news bulletin moving in slowly spelled out electric lights around the Times Building. "I beg your pardon, Mr. Sayer? I didn't catch that."

"I was saying something to my wife," John said. "Excuse me a moment." He put the mouthpiece to his shoulder and said to Ellie in the doorway, "Unless Sam and Jim can be induced to stop breaking up that Greyhound bus with sledge hammers in their room, I'd better have the door shut."

"Remember what we decided at lunch," Ellie whispered. "Be firm."

She went out and pulled the door shut.

John took the phone from his shoulders and said, "Sorry, Mr. Zucker. As I was saying, I've now seen both Mr. Howe and Miss Quill." He paused, waiting for Mr. Zucker to make some sort of comment. Nothing came across the wire. Not even the sort of encouraging grunts with which, when he wanted to urge someone on into saying more, John had had a good deal of success in the past. He said, "Mr. Zucker?"

"I'm here."

"I said I've seen both Mr. Howe and Miss Quill."

"I heard you, Mr. Sayer. What I'm waiting to hear is how seeing them has affected your feelings about our project."

"Well, to be perfectly frank—"

"Are you ever less than that?"

John said, "I beg your pardon?"

"When a man with whom I have been conversing begins a sentence with the phrase 'to be perfectly frank' or its interesting variation 'frankly speaking,'" Mr. Zucker's voice said, "I wonder at once whether the man has been *not* frank with me up to now."

"Well, let me think," John said. For a few moments he did. Then he said, "Mr. Zucker?"

"At your service, sir."

"No, I think I can honestly say I have not been not frank with you up to now," John said.

"Then we can, can we not, dispense with prefatory phrases that might lead one to think the contrary."

John laughed. The fact that it had been so difficult to get Mr. Zucker on the phone no longer mattered. The irritation and the effort had been worth it. Everything was going to be all right. John could tell. He said, "Seeing Mr. Howe and Miss Quill has made me look favorably on the project, Mr. Zucker."

"Good," the throaty voice said. "I felt sure you would. They are both admirable people."

John laughed again.

"Mr. Zucker," he said, "isn't this highly uncharacteristic of you? Committing yourself to an unqualified opinion?"

"I was not referring to their characters, which is no concern of mine," Mr. Zucker said with schoolmasterly severity. "I was referring to Mr. Howe's and Miss Quill's capacities to get a show on the boards. To move a project from the talk phase to the active phase. The phase where coin of the realm is moving from the hands of the public to the pockets of the people involved in the project. This is a very strong concern of mine, Mr. Sayer. Indeed, sir, I might say my only concern."

"Well, I hope you won't think me rude for saying this, but I'm afraid my feelings are a trifle more complicated than yours," John said. "I've got a concern beyond the mere money."

"Name it, sir."

"Miss Quill has only a first act," John said. "Not even that. She has an outline for a first act. Since I know what's in it, and I accept your opinion of her ability, I'm sure it will be a good first act when she gets around to writing it. I certainly like her approach to the material and the way she plans to handle it. But what about the second act?"

"What about it, Mr. Sayer?"

"It seems to me it's the most difficult part of the play," John said. "The first part of the play, the first act, is colorful and dramatic. It's moving and exciting because it deals with the period of my father's life that was all of those things. I could see, once I heard Miss Quill's outline and her approach to the material, I could see why she saw an exciting musical play in Deucalion. But the second part of my father's life, or rather the last ten years of it, that part of my father's life was dull. Not from his standpoint, perhaps. I mean, he was perfectly happy living abroad with his new wife, and she was happy with him. But happiness, I'm beginning to gather, doesn't make for drama. To make her play work, Miss Quill is going to have to make those last ten years, or her second act, at least as dramatic and probably more so than her first act. The fact that I don't see how she's going to do it would not bother me, since I'm not a dramatist, if it were not for the fact that I gathered from our meeting that Miss Quill doesn't see it, either. Not yet, anyway. She as much as said so, which is, of course, admirable. Honesty always is. But my concern, if I may get back to that word, Mr. Zucker, is not Miss Quill's honesty. What concerns me is the image of my father. His memory with the public. Mr. Zucker?"

"I am all ears, Mr. Sayer."

"My father's memory with the public is, as of now, exactly where for years I've wanted it to be," John said. "They've forgotten him. If the public memory is going to be jogged, if the world is going to be pushed into remembering Sennacherib Sayer, I want the world to remember him as Miss Quill plans to portray him in her first act."

"Because Miss Quill's first act tells the truth about your father?" Mr. Zucker said.

"Precisely," John said, aware that until this morning, for a quarter of a centry, he had not known the truth.

"And you want the second act also to tell the truth?" Mr. Zucker said.

"Again precisely," John said. "Which is what causes my concern. If Miss Quill tells the truth, she has no second act. If she comes up with a second act, it will not be the truth. It can't possibly be. Do I make myself clear, Mr. Zucker?"

"If I may borrow one of your favorite words," the English-accented voice murmured, "precisely." There was a pause. During it John had the feeling Mr. Zucker, imbedded in the middle of his couch, was peering across his shoulder to make sure there were no eavesdroppers in his Park Avenue living room. The pause ended with eleven words that came rolling in across the wire from the Hotel Stanton with all the solemn majesty of an encyclical issuing from the Vatican. "What you need, Mr. Sayer," said Mr. Arnold Zucker, "is someone to represent your interests."

Feeling somewhat like the patient in one of those paintings of Charcot's early experiments with hypnotism, John said, "You mean an agent?"

With an obvious effort to rise above its annoyance with a moment of gaucherie, the voice at the other end of the wire said, "I mean someone who is ready and willing to devote all his considerable abilities and energies to seeing to it that what you and only you want in this project, Mr. Sayer, emerges on the stage."

"Can you do that?" John said.

"If I could not," Mr. Zucker said, "I would not make the offer."

"You mean you're making me an offer?" John said. "Right now?"

"I am," Mr. Zucker said.

"I accept," John said. Then, somewhat surprised but not displeased by his eagerness, he added, "I mean, I'd *like* to accept, if you'd tell me how you can do this?"

"Where will you be for the next half-hour?" Mr. Zucker said.

"Right here," John said. "Having a drink with my wife."

"Have two," Mr. Zucker murmured. "When I get back to you, I'd like you to be in a relaxed mood."

John never knew whether he was or was not in a relaxed mood because, when Mr. Zucker got back to him, Ellie had just gone to the bar to mix their first drink.

"It is all settled," Mr. Zucker announced at the other end of the wire. "There will be a clause in the contract that says if, at any time before the play arrives in New York, John Sayer decides he does not want the play to open on Broadway, all John Sayer has to do is serve written notice on the management, meaning Vincent Howe, in the form of a registered letter, and the whole project will be abandoned."

John sat motionless in his study, staring out at the lights of Fifth Avenue on the other side of Central Park, listening to Ellie dropping ice cubes into his glass, thinking about what Mr. Zucker had said and then, in a surprised voice, he said into the phone, "You mean I can stop the thing dead anywhere along the line?"

"Anywhere along the line," Mr. Zucker said.

"When they're in rehearsal?" John said. "When they're on the road?"

"Anywhere along the line, Mr. Sayer, means anywhere along the line."

"But by that time, if they're in rehearsal, if they're on the road trying out the show, large sums of money will have been spent," John said. "Not to mention the time and effort everybody will have poured into it."

"All true, Mr. Sayer," the low voice murmured. "And all, if you choose to exercise your contractual right, all their tough luck."

"Are they crazy?"

"No more so than most people who function in the arts," Mr. Zucker said. "Your astonishment is caused by the fact that you are looking at it from the standpoint of management. This is a mistake, Mr. Sayer. In the theatre, to survive, one must learn to look at things from only one standpoint. Your own. Mr. Howe and Miss Quill want your approval. They must have it, or they cannot go ahead with their project. To get that approval, they must pay. I have extracted the payment. It may be crazy, as you say. But you've got it if you want it. Do you want it, Mr. Sayer?"

John hesitated, then said, "What will it cost me?"

"The usual ten per cent," said Mr. Zucker.

He started earning it within a matter of hours. The next morning, while John was shaving, Ellie came into the bathroom with the news that Mr. Zucker was on the phone.

"Now?" John said. "It's a quarter after seven, for God's sake."

"Ten after," Ellie said, glancing at her watch. "Shall I tell him you'll call back?"

"Yes, please," John said, then remembered his and Miss Faille's efforts the day before. "Maybe I'd better take the call, though."

"Well, make up your mind," Ellie said. "Your son James just told me it says on TV I must not send him off to school without a good hot breakfast in his stomach, so let's just forget the corn flakes bit, Ma, and he's ordered farina. But your son Samuel says now that he's been elected the Fifth Grade's representative on the Student-Faculty Council, he doesn't have to eat any old slop that's shoved in front of him, and besides, he hates farina, so it's either oatmeal or nothing, Ma, which should indicate to you that there is no room in my next half-hour for carrying messages between you and your brand new agent."

"Representative, please, representative," John said, reaching for a towel. "Mr. Zucker hears you calling him an agent, he'll drop me from his list. Which phone is he on?"

"Take it in the bedroom," Ellie said. "I'll hang up in the kitchen."

John swabbed the lather from his face and tossed the towel toward the bathtub. He went out into the bedroom, picked up the phone, and said, "I see you are an early riser."

"I assumed the son of Sennacherib Sayer would not be a late one," Mr. Zucker said. "Are you doing anything important during the next hour?"

"Well," John said, "I usually have breakfast, then go down to my office."

"If it would not inconvenience you to delay the latter," Mr. Zucker said, "I'm sure Miss Quill will be happy to supply you with the former, at least to the extent of a cup of coffee."

"She wants to see me?"

"No, it is *I* who want *you* to see *her*," Mr. Zucker said. "After I talked with you last night, I had a talk with Vinnie Howe, and he said perhaps it would make things simpler all the way around if, while the contracts are being drawn, which is always a lengthy process, if Miss Quill gave you some inkling of what she planned to put into her second act. I agreed this would be desirable, and a few minutes ago Miss Quill called me to say she had it worked out."

"Between the time Mr. Howe talked to her last night and now?" John said. "A quarter after seven in the morning?"

"Yes, obviously," Mr. Zucker said. "Why do you sound so surprised?"

"Well, for one thing, she couldn't have got much sleep."

"That is Miss Quill's problem."

"For another, working out a whole second act in a few hours, even if she spent the whole night on it, that seems pretty fast."

"Television, where Miss Quill got her training, is a speedy medium," Mr. Zucker said. "Also, just as slowness is not necessarily synonymous with excellence, swiftness does not necessarily mean shoddiness. Besides, as to the quality of what Miss Quill has done, you can judge for yourself. That's why she asked us to this meeting."

"Us?"

"You, me, Vinnie Howe, and Irving Ireland."

"Who is he?"

"The composer and lyricist of *Fig Leaf*. Miss Quill feels they worked so well together on that show, he might be ideal for this one. If you approve, that is."

"Mr. Zucker, I know absolutely nothing about music."

"You don't have to know anything about music," Mr. Zucker said. "All you have to do is approve or disapprove of Mr. Ireland."

"But how can I do that if I don't know whether his music is good or bad?"

"I will tell you," Mr. Zucker said. "Can you be at Miss Quill's apartment by eight o'clock?"

"Yes," John said. "I think so."

When he got there, his first impression was that something

had happened to the store since he had visited it last. It was as though the counters had been shifted, so that the aisles, along which he was accustomed to move as he did his shopping, now led to different destinations. He wondered, as he was introduced to Mr. Ireland and said hello to Vinnie Howe and Gwen Quill, what had caused the change. John's agent came up out of his deep chair to shake hands, and John knew what the change was. In his living room at the Hotel Stanton, holding three phones to his head, wrapped in a red silk robe, facing the forest of silver-framed photographs on his Steinway, surrounded by the paintings of angry waves, and flanked by the huge table covered with stacks of play scripts, Mr. Arnold Zucker was a strikingly unique figure. Here in Miss Quill's store, he was just another customer in a sack suit.

He said, "Sit over there." John sat down beside Mr. Ireland, facing a silver clam shell abut the size of a discus in the hollow of which were engraved the words: "To Gwen Quill with love and admiration from the cast of *The Magnificent Journey* NBC-TV October 12, 1954."

"Arnold, stop ordering people around," Miss Quill said. "This is my apartment."

"But Mr. Sayer is my client," said Mr. Zucker. He dropped like a bowling ball back into the deep chair facing John across the silver clam shell. For several moments the pudgy hands moved about uneasily, as though hunting for something without which they did not feel complete, and John was sure he knew what it was. Mr. Zucker missed his telephones. He said, "We're ready, Gwen."

"Just let me give Mr. Sayer a cup of this," Vincent Howe said. The little man winked at John as he came slanting across with the coffee tray. "Cream and sugar, fella?"

"No, this is fine," John said. "Thank you."

Mr. Howe winked again and whispered, "Wait till you hear this, fella." He turned with the silver pot toward Mr. Ireland. "How about you, Irving?"

"None for me, thanks," Mr. Ireland said.

Mr. Howe said, "No coffee?"

"Doctor told me to lay off for a while."

"The old constipation again?"

"Worse this time," Mr. Ireland said. "The doctor thinks my acid condition may have something to do with it, so no coffee."

From her chair near the picture window, Miss Quill said,

"Couldn't we postpone this discussion about the condition of Irving's bowels?"

Mr. Howe laughed, gave John a third wink, and said, "She makes with the jokes."

Noting that Mr. Ireland had not laughed, it occurred to John that perhaps the composer did not know how. He was a long, thin man in a navy blue blazer with gold buttons, a green bow tie dotted with tiny yellow scimitars, and gray suede shoes with thick gum soles. Aside from his clothes, Mr. Ireland reminded John of those men who conduct people to their seats at funeral services.

"You're all familiar with the contents of the first act," Miss Quill said. "I will now tell you what I have planned for the second act."

She brought the notebook out from somewhere behind her back and flipped up the cover. As she read, the men in the room gave her the sort of attention that, John could see, all of them wanted to be identified as undivided. Giving her his own, John noted that, since he had seen Miss Quill the day before, her appearance had changed in only one respect. The skintight Basque jersey had been replaced, or perhaps covered by, a pink version of one of those shapeless, fluffy Italian sweaters that look as though they are made of steel wool or cotton candy. This added nothing feminine to the impression Miss Quill made on John. It was merely as though the demented jockey, in a fit of restlessness, had started and then abandoned an experiment in costuming. The notebook cover dropped back into place with a slap of finality.

"Slow curtain," Miss Quill said, and raised her hand. "What do you think?"

Mr. Howe jumped up and said, "Boy, oh, boy!" He started around the room with the coffee pot.

Mr. Ireland uncrossed his legs slowly, as though with a screwdriver he were separating the two halves of an expensive pair of scissors, then recrossed them in the opposite direction, just as slowly, and said, "None for me, Vinnie."

Mr. Zucker's hands started probing the air for his absent telephones, moved on to smooth his absent hair across his bald scalp, and came to rest in his plump lap as he managed to release a murmured, "Hmmm."

"Thank you, gentlemen," Miss Quill said. "I'm glad you like it. Now for the only one who counts."

The mad, red-rimmed, watery eyes moved toward John. He said, "I'm afraid I don't, Miss Quill."

Mr. Howe, turning toward John with the coffee pot, might have been Herod coming toward Salome with the head of John the Baptist, as he uttered a strangled, *"You don't like it?"*

"Shut up, Vinnie, and go make some more coffee," Miss Quill said.

"I'll go help," Mr. Ireland said.

"Watch your bowels," Miss Quill called. The composer and the producer disappeared into the kitchen. Turning back, she said, "You want to help, too, Arnold?"

"I never abandon a client in time of stress," Mr. Zucker said. "What is it you don't like about Miss Quill's outline for the second act, Mr. Sayer?"

"It's not true," John said. "It never happened. It's a complete and total fabrication."

"In what way?" Miss Quill said.

"In every way," John said.

"That doesn't seem possible," Mr. Zucker said. "You told me, Gwen, you said you were working from the true facts as turned up by your research, did you not?"

"I told it to you, and I'm telling it to Mr. Sayer," Miss Quill said. The skinny legs curled under her rearranged themselves, causing the pink cotton candy sweater to tip slightly. It was as though a toy statue in a window display had been moved on its plinth. A feeling of menace, John felt, had entered the room. "I used the facts as I dug them up," Miss Quill said. "Let me check a few, Mr. Sayer." The cover of the notebook flipped up again. "After Deucalion burned down and your mother died, Mr. Sayer, your father moved abroad. Is that true?"

"Yes," John said.

"He married another woman and settled down in England to write his memoirs," Miss Quill said. "Is that true, Mr. Sayer?"

"Yes," John said.

"Okay, then," Miss Quill said. "First, I am using the memoirs as the frame for the whole story, starting with a prologue before the first act, and adding an epilogue after the second act. This makes the writing of the memoirs the sort of you might say book ends for the play. Second, I am building the second act around the hero finding his true love, the end of the quest through which he lived in Act One, and I am having him find her in his own back yard. These are the two main facts on which I am basing the second half of my play.

You admit both these facts are true. Yet you sit there, Mr. Sayer, and call my outline a complete and total fabrication."

Mr. Zucker's hands rose, like those of a conductor calling in the strings, and John responded.

"Maybe complete and total are exaggerations," he said.

"How do you mean, maybe?" Miss Quill said. "Is my plan for Act Two a complete fabrication or is it not?"

"Well, no," John said. "Not complete."

"Is it a total fabrication?"

"No, I didn't quite mean that."

Mr. Zucker said, "Perhaps it would help, Mr. Sayer, if you told Miss Quill to what *extent,* if any, her outline is a fabrication?"

"What's wrong is the lover," John said. "The man who gets between Sennacherib Sayer and his second wife. There was no such person. My father's second marriage was a completely happy one."

"Oh, for Christ's sake," Miss Quill said.

"What does *that* mean?" Mr. Zucker said.

Miss Quill disregarded him.

"Don't you think I know that?" she said to John. "But I'm writing a play. Since it's a biographical play, I must stick to my basic facts. It would be much easier for me, for example, to do this play if Sennacherib Sayer had been married only once. But he was married twice. I can't disregard that. In the theatre, when you can't disregard something, you must face up to it. You make a virtue of a necessity. That's why I made the central story line Sennacherib Sayer's quest for the ideal mate. This allows me to inject both women into the story from the beginning, gives me a triangle that runs through both acts, and after the first wife dies in the fire, it takes the hero, who is grieving, it takes him some time to wake up to the fact that his true love, his ideal mate, was right there under his nose all the time. A touch of irony, but *nice* irony. It makes you feel warm. It sends you out of the theatre with a good feeling. The two people who should have got together from the beginning, but couldn't, finally make it. Don't you see how nice that is?"

"The lover makes it not nice," John said. "Putting in a lover makes it ugly."

The watery, red-rimmed eyes spread. It was as though the windows on Miss Quill's private inferno had been opened wider. Looking through them, John understood the menace that had entered the room moments ago. One thing, he grasped, that Miss Quill could not stand, one thing that would cause her to kill if necessary, was being criticized or contradicted or accused of being wrong. She had to be right. Always. To live she had to be right.

"Mr. Sayer," she said. Her voice was so tight and hard that John felt the effort to speak must have been painful for her. "You can't make bricks without straw. You can't make a play without drama. In real life nothing happened to Sennacherib Sayer after Deucalion burned down. He merely vegetated for ten years. It was a happy vegetation for him. It's a pain in the ass to someone trying to make a play of his life. Don't you understand that?"

"Yes, and that's why I want you to understand this," John said. "I will not have my father's memory besmirched. I will not have the memory of my mother or the memory of my stepmother dirtied. They were both wonderful women. Neither one was capable of infidelity. What I liked about your first act, Miss Quill, is that it made this point about my father. He was an honorable man. He respected my mother. The accusations in the press that he had been unfaithful to her are proved untrue by your first act. Now you want me to accept a second act in which my stepmother is proved to be capable of adultery. I know what you're going to say. It's never actually committed, you're going to tell me. But you've got two scenes in that second act outline in which she *almost* commits adultery. I won't have that. She was a woman with a great sense of honor. She loved my father. She was a decent human being."

There was a pause, during which the pink ball of cotton candy rearranged itself once more on the invisible plinth. John, glad all at once that Miss Quill was not holding a gun, wondered uneasily if she might be concealing a knife. The deranged eyes were incapable of concealing the truth: his life was in danger.

"Mr. Sayer," Miss Quill said finally. "Are you trying to tell me that decent human beings are incapable of adultery?"

"I don't know about all human beings," John said. "I am speaking about the decent human beings I have known."

"May the voice of reason be injected into this colloquy?"

John turned toward Mr. Zucker.

"It would be welcome," he said.

"As I understand it," Mr. Zucker said, "your only real objection to Miss Quill's plan for the second act is the invented lover. Is that correct, Mr. Sayer?"

"Yes," John said.

Mr. Zucker's bald head moved.

"Gwen," he said. "Do you think there's a way of doing the second act without the invented lover?"

Miss Quill looked down into her lap and ran both hands along the sides of her head. She might have been smoothing her boyishly cut red hair into place, but John knew better. It was the disturbed mind catching itself up, warning itself back from the abyss, whispering; *Be careful, tread easy, hold onto yourself, or they'll find out you're crazy*. The red head came up.

"There might be," Miss Quill said quietly. "It would depend on one thing."

"What's that?" Mr. Zucker said.

"I'd have to know more about the second Mrs. Sayer. The research turned up very little on her."

Mr. Zucker turned to John.

"Can you supply Miss Quill with what she wants to know?"

"That depends on what she wants to know," John said.

Mr. Zucker did something extraordinary. For a moment John did not know what it was. Then he saw that the round, bland, almost Oriental expanse of totally expressionless face had contracted in a small, very small, grimace of annoyance.

"If she asks questions," Mr. Zucker said icily, "will you answer them?"

"If I have the answers," John said. "Yes."

"I think you've got the answers to these," Miss Quill said even more icily.

The door from the kitchen opened. Mr. Howe came in with the coffee pot. Mr. Ireland, behind him, carried a tray of cups.

"How we doing?" the producer said cheerfully.

"Vinnie," Miss Quill said, "go get some crullers."

Mr. Howe looked startled. John did not blame him. It was like one of those machines at the Danbury Fair to which Ike Ten Eyck had once taken him. You put one hand on a metal knob and with your other hand you dropped a penny in the slot. There was a click and a buzz and a charge of electricity shot through you. It was frightening, but also delicious. Mr. Howe looked quickly at John, as though expecting him to say something. John didn't know what to say. He was trying to remember something. Mr. Howe gave him up and turned to look at Miss Quill. He didn't seem to get much help from her. Finally, with a puzzled frown, Mr. Howe turned to look at Mr. Ireland and Mr. Zucker. It was as though he couldn't quite believe he had heard Miss Quill correctly and wanted someone to confirm her statement.

"You—uh—you want crullers?" Mr. Howe said to Miss Quill.

"Yes," she said. "Go get them." The plinth moved again as Miss Quill waved her hand toward Mr. Ireland and Mr. Zucker. "All of you go get some crullers," she said. "Mr. Sayer and I have work to do."

5

A YEAR LATER, on the front seat of the car rolling toward Edesboro, Mr. Mancini said, "By work, Miss Quill didn't mean work, did she?"

The weight inside John's head had suddenly become painful. He was reminded of the foot of a sofa that has been sitting too long in one place on a rug. It should be moved, so the piece of furniture will not make a hole in the rug. But John couldn't move the weight inside his head.

"Of course not," he said in a tired voice, closing his eyes to ease the pain. "You know what she meant."

"Did *you* know?" the policeman said. John opened his eyes and gave Mr. Mancini a puzzled glance. "Did you know when she told the others to leave the apartment," the policeman said, "that she meant you and she were going to bed together?"

"Of course I knew," John said impatiently. "Do you think I'm a—?"

His voice stopped.

"Do I think you're a what?" Mr. Mancini said.

John shook his head slowly. Staring out at the deserted Turnpike, he wished he did not have to make the effort of answering the policeman's question. And yet John did not see how he could avoid it. There was something gentle about Mr. Mancini. Something friendly. John realized he had begun to like Mr. Mancini.

"That's the problem," John said. "When I was with her, in her apartment, I knew what she was up to."

"By getting into bed with you," Mancini said, "Miss Quill believed she could overcome your objections to the way she wanted to write the second act?"

John nodded.

"That's the part I didn't understand," he said. "She was so ugly. She was revolting. She was not at all the kind of girl who had ever aroused me sexually. She looked like—like—"

His voice seemed to drain away.

"A boy?" the policeman suggested. "A man?"

John nodded again.

"And yet, once she put her hands on me, it was—" He paused, hesitated, gave Mr. Mancini a troubled glance, and said quietly, "It was great."

"With Miss Quill you were not impotent," the policeman said. John shook his head. "And that's what worried you," Mr. Mancini said. John nodded once more. "It was as though you were achieving normality in an abnormal way," the policeman said. "By performing the sexual act with a man."

"That's why," John said dully to the road ahead, and he paused to haul in a deep, tired breath. "That *must* be why, after it was over, when I left her, my mind blocked it out. That I'd been with her. That I'd had anything to do with her."

"So there really was nothing wrong about your calling your wife after the first time," the policeman said.

"Nothing wrong?" John said angrily. "I left that horrible woman's bed, and I went into a phone booth, and I invited my wife to come have lunch with me, and you say there's nothing wrong?"

"If you blocked it out of your mind," Mr. Mancini said. "If, when you were having lunch with your wife, you were totally unaware you had just slept with Miss Quill—" The policeman paused and shrugged. "You realize, of course," he said casually, "that hundreds and thousands of men do that every day. They drop in on their mistresses, then go on home to have dinner with the wife and kiddies. It never occurs to them they're doing anything wrong. Certainly not that they're doing anything so terrible that they decide to commit suicide."

"That's not why I decided," John said.

"I know," Mr. Mancini said.

"Then why put me through all this?" John said with sudden fury. "If you know—"

"It's important for *you* to know," the policeman said.

"But I *do* know."

The policeman shook his head.

"You know the beginning, and you know the end," he said. "In the next twenty—" He paused and glanced at his wrist watch. "No, seventeen. In the next seventeen minutes you must get to know the things in between. The things that led to the end."

John's fist began to pound the rim of the steering wheel, noiselessly, gently, as though he were keeping time to a piece of music.

"I know everything," he said through his teeth. "Every God damn step along the way. I learned the last part in New Haven an hour ago. That's why I made my decision. That's why I know it's the only thing left for me to do. Why can't you see that? And if you can't, why don't you leave me alone? I'm tired. My head hurts. I'm going to die in seventeen minutes. Let me live those last minutes in peace."

"There is no peace as long as your mind continues to function," Mr. Mancini said. "You can block out certain things, but not everything. Suppose in the next seventeen minutes you came to the conclusion that you were really in love with Miss Quill? Maybe even that you still are? How would you like to go through those rails at Edesboro with *that* on your mind?"

"You're crazy," John said savagely. "I couldn't love that —that—a thing like that—" He paused. He examined the idea. It made his stomach knot with revulsion. "Why," he said, "she *lied* to me!"

The stupidity of this reply as a refutation of Mr. Mancini's statement hung between them like a physically visible snicker.

"It's true," John said in a sullen voice. "She *did* lie to me."

"As I understand these things," Mr. Mancini said dryly, "in the theatre you have to expect that."

But John had not expected it. He had taken Vincent Howe at his word when, a year ago, following John's second meeting with Gwen Quill in her apartment, the producer had come to see John in his office late in the afternoon.

"I understand, fella," Mr. Howe said, "you and Gwen you worked it out."

"Well, we got that ridiculous lover out of the second act," John said.

"I think that's a big step upward," Mr. Howe said. "I mean, fella, Gwen admits you're right. It was a mistake having that guy in there. He was from left field. She brought him in because she was trying to make the story work, and he stuck out like a sore thumb. Gwen's very pleased. She thinks you've got quite a head on your shoulders, story-wise."

"Nonsense," said John. He didn't think it was nonsense at all, and was annoyed by the fact that he didn't. It was shameful to be pleased by a foolish compliment, conveyed at secondhand, by a slightly preposterous man, from a dubious source. "I don't know anything about story," John said. "I merely know the facts with which Miss Quill is dealing, and that lover simply is not one of the facts. So he had to go."

"And damn glad we all are now, fella, that he did," Mr. Howe said. "It's all a matter of perspective. When you're close to material, the way Gwen's been on this project for months, you get so you lose your perspective. Gwen says that's what happened with her in the second act. She says if it wasn't for you, your coming in like that, cold, with a fresh eye, she never would have seen how wrong it was to have that lover in the second act. And what she'd like, Gwen says she'd like to keep your sense of perspective like that all through the project. Fresh, she means."

"Well, I'll certainly try," John said. "But I don't know that I can guarantee it. As we work along on it, I'm bound to lose my fresh eye, too."

"That would be pretty terrible," Mr. Howe said. "The project, I mean, fella, it would suffer."

"I don't see how it can be prevented," John said.

"Well, let me ask you something," Mr. Howe said. "How close do you want to work along on the project?"

"I don't really know," John said. "I've never been involved in anything like this before."

"Let me ask you something else, fella," Mr. Howe said. "How much time do you have to *give* to the project?" John thought about that for a few moments. Mr. Howe seemed to know the direction John's thoughts were taking because the jaunty little man swept his hand out in an arc, from the Bahooli burial figure Ellie's aunt had brought back from Tangier, to the unframed blue grapefruit that had come off the fence of a Washington Square outdoor exhibit. He said, "Mr. Sayer, you've got an office here. A business. I mean, you're a part of the law firm. You've got clients. Clients have to be serviced. How much time do you figure you could take from your law practice and devote to this project?"

"Since I'm the lawyer for the project," John said, "I suppose I have to think of the project the way I would think of any client, and give it as much time as it requires."

"Most of your other clients, they're what, fella?"

"Corporations, individuals, mainly involving trusts, which is my specialty," John said.

"This play, then, *Deucalion,* it's the first thing of its kind you've tangled with?"

"Certainly," John said. "You know that."

"Don't be impatient with me, fella, please," Mr. Howe said, slanting his entire body into the engaging, crooked grin. "I'm trying to paint a picture for you. Now that you've given us the okay, now that you've approved Gwen's outline and she can go to work, here's what's involved. From now on Irving Ireland and her, they'll be meeting every day. Which means, the way Gwen works, every night. Till all hours. Five, six in the morning, fella, nothing unusual. Just another working day for Gwen."

"How about Mr. Ireland?" John said.

"It nearly killed him on *Fig Leaf,* but he came up with a great score," Mr. Howe said. "So he's got an acid condition and he's got trouble with his bowels, so what? He's also got a hit. And if Irving wants another one with *Deucalion,* he'll have to do it again. Because that's the only way it *can* be done. To find the musical areas, the places where songs and production numbers grow, it's back-breaking work, fella. You can't do it and, the same time, run an office like this."

"You mean," John said slowly, "I'd have to attend all these sessions between Miss Quill and Mr. Ireland?"

"*Have to* is one of those exceptions," Mr. Howe said. "It's entirely up to you. But that's only for openers, fella. All the time Gwen and Irving are hammering out the score and the book, the project is moving ahead on all the other fronts, too. Casting, to take a for instance. Finding someone to play Sennacherib Sayer alone, for instance, never mind the two important women parts, just finding the guy to play your father, Mr. Sayer, that's going to mean interviewing and auditioning dozens, maybe hundreds of actors. Then the sets. Meetings with the designer. Going over sketches. The choreographer. The costume designer. The arranger."

"The what?" John said.

"The guy makes the music arrangements," Mr. Howe said. "For the orchestra. Then the dance arrangements. Another guy to have meetings with. What else? Auditions for dancers *and* singers. Next? Trips to the factory where they're building the scenery, which it's always, don't ask me why, fella, it's always New Jersey. I could go on like this for quite a while, Mr. Sayer, but I think you begin to get the picture. Am I right?"

"Miss Quill and Mr. Ireland," John said. "In addition to their work on the book and the score, will they have to attend all these sessions and meetings and auditions?"

"Again it's that expression *have* to," Mr. Howe said. "They don't but they do, fella. When Gwen is on a project, she's on every single inch of it. She won't leave anything to somebody else. Not even me. She's on everything, including the dates of the out-of-town bookings, and the copy for the souvenir program, and the seating arrangement for opening night. Now, if you want to work that close on the project, and once you start with Gwen there's no stopping. She's a man-eater. If you want to work that close on the project, you're welcome, fella, but you know what will happen?"

"I will resign from my firm," John said. "And perhaps the human race as well."

"That's the least," Mr. Howe said. "I mean if *Deucalion* is a hit, the deal Arnie Zucker has worked out for you, there will be so much dough in it for your firm, I'm sure your partners won't mind carrying the load for the firm while you're tied up working on the play. No, that's nothing. The worst thing, fella, if you get this deeply involved, the worst thing is you'd lose your sense of perspective about the play. Like this thing you saw right away today? That it was a mistake to have that lover in the second act? Things like that you'd never see again. Not so fast, anyway. And if you don't see them, if you lose your sense of perspective, Mr. Sayer, the play is not only bound to suffer. It could maybe suffer so badly it might be a flop, God forbid. Which means all the time you put in, all the work your partners did, carrying a double load for the firm while you were on the play, all that would be wasted, because nobody would make a nickel."

"That would not be good," John said. "Would it?"

"If that happened, fella," Mr. Howe said, "I would cut my throat."

"We can't allow that," John said. "What do you recommend we do to prevent it?"

"I recommend you stay out of all this spadework," Mr. Howe said. "I recommend you save yourself for the big moments. Like today, when you came in and put your finger on what was wrong with the second act. Take casting. Don't come to all the auditions while we weed out the dead wood. When we finally find two or three people we think are right for the part, say, of Sennacherib Sayer, we'll call you, and you come in to give your thumbs down or your okay. Irving gets down on paper four or five songs we all like? You come in and hear them and tell us yes or no. The same with the sets, the minor roles, the costumes, everything. In this way, fella, not only *you* don't break your balls. But *we,* the project, we keep the advantages of your perspective. You don't lose your fresh eye. What do you think, fella?"

"I think it makes sense," John said. "Why don't we give it a try and see what happens?"

What happened was a series of phone calls. The first one, which came three days later, was exciting. Mr. Howe's voice, pumping words into a telephone at the other side of town, was a small, unseen victory parade marching into John's ear.

"Fella," the producer said, "we got the Chelsea."

John hesitated. There were people whose regard he valued. The opinion of others meant nothing to him. He had not yet made up his mind into which category Mr. Howe fitted. Even so, John did not want to appear stupid.

"Is that good?" he said.

"Is that *good?*" Mr. Howe squealed. "The Chelsea is the best musical comedy house in America. Every producer in town is angling for it twenty-four hours a day. Getting *that* one out of the Shuberts, fella, that takes a bit of doing."

"How did you do it?"

"Walked in on them. Told them what the play is about. Told them I had the *Fig Leaf* team, Gwen Quill and Irving Ireland. Walked out with a letter says dear Mr. Howe you got the Chelsea."

"Congratulations," John said.

"Nothing, fella," Mr. Howe said with an engaging touch of mock arrogance. "Just wanted you to know the kind of talent you've signed up with."

Long after the producer had hung up, John could still feel the excitement. He could feel it, but he couldn't quite understand it. What had happened? Mr. Howe had announced that a theatre which other producers wanted had been made available for *Deucalion.* It was, of course, good news, and good news was always exciting. But surely the degree of excitement should bear some proportionate relationship to the goodness of the news? Why should Mr. Howe's announcement of a small—all right, a *large!*—commercial coup make John feel the way he had felt a couple of days ago when Miss Faille had told him his son Sam had been elected Fifth Grade representative to the Porte School's Student Council? He began to look forward to the next call. It came two days later.

"Fella," Mr. Howe said, "we got Mannie De Leon for the sets."

"The sets?" John said. "Oh, he's a designer."

"No, fella," Mr. Howe said. "He's *the* designer. Every producer in town is angling for him twenty-four hours a day. Getting Mannie out from under all that money people keep throwing at him, fella, it takes a bit of doing, that does."

"How did you do it?"

"Walked in on him. Told him what the play is about. Told him I had the *Fig Leaf* team, Gwen Quill and Irving Ireland. Told him I had the Chelsea. Walked out with a letter says dear Mr. Howe I will design your sets signed Emanuel De Leon."

"Congratulations," John said.

"Nothing," Mr. Howe said with a boyish touch of burlesqued conceit. "Just wanted you to know the kind of talent you've signed up with."

Long after the producer had hung up, John was still trying to figure out why this phone call, pleasant as it had been, lacked the excitement of the first. He was aware, of course, that the law of diminishing returns applies to the emotions as well as to the economy. Still, the acquisition of Mr. De Leon brought the project one step further along the road to reality. It seemed to John he should be feeling what Mr. Howe clearly had felt while making this second announcement: a sense of *mounting* excitement. The fact that he didn't made him look forward to the next phone call with a certain amount of clinical interest. It came a week later.

"Fella," Mr. Howe said, "we got Angie Kurtz for the costumes."

John decided to try an experiment.

"Do you think she's right?" he said.

The silence at the other end was more than that. John had a mental picture of the little slanting man rearing back from his telephone as though the instrument had snapped at his lip.

"How's that again, fella?" Mr. Howe said finally.

"I asked do you think Angie Kurtz is right for *Deucalion?*" John said.

"Well, now, look," Mr. Howe said. He sounded like a man on a park bench who feels that, because he has been coming here every day for years with his bag of bread crumbs, he should have been immune from what an ungrateful pigeon had just done to his hat. "Angie Kurtz was good enough for *Fig Leaf*. She was good enough for *True North*. She was good enough for *Near the Wind*. She was good enough for *A Lick and a Promise*. Every one of those shows ran two years or more, and *Fig Leaf* is *still* running. Maybe I don't know how to figure, fella, but I figure if a person is good enough to do the costumes for all those hits, she's good enough to do the costumes for *Deucalion*."

"Then I guess she is," John said.

"What?" Mr. Howe said.

"I said if you think Miss Kurtz is good enough for *Deucalion*, then I think so, too. Because I don't know a damn thing about costume designing, and so I have to go along with the experts, and all of them, in this case, Mr. Howe, add up to you."

Mr. Howe's reply was not exactly unexpected.

"Fella," he said, "I think it's about time you called me Vinnie, don't you?"

"I'll do that on one condition," John said.

"What's that?"

"You don't call me Johnny."

Again the silence at the other end was more than silence.

"All right," Mr. Howe said finally, "I won't. John be all right?"

"John is fine," John said.

"Names are funny," Mr. Howe said. "I hate people to call me Vincent. Vinnie, yes. Not Vincent. You, the opposite. John, yes. Not Johnny. I suppose you got your reasons."

John had. Only one person had ever called him Johnny. It seemed sensible to keep it that way.

"What else do we need," he said, and added, "Vinnie?"

Mr. Howe laughed.

"I like that," he said, and added, "John."

"We've got a theatre," John said. "We've got someone for the sets. We've got a costume designer. What else do we need, Vinnie?"

"I'm working on a choreographer," Mr. Howe said. "I'll call you in a couple of days."

When he did, it was not about a choreographer.

"John," he said. "How would you like to hear some music?"

"Are you offering me tickets to a concert?"

"No, fella, I'm offering you to hear the first three songs by Irving Ireland for a new smasheroo-in-the-making called *Deucalion*."

John could feel something of the excitement that had gripped him during Mr. Howe's first phone call.

"I accept your offer," he said. "Where?"

"My office," Mr. Howard said. "It's got a piano."

It also had, John found when he got there, a sexy blonde with large teeth who sat behind a switchboard just inside the door. She was sealing and stamping a batch of envelopes as though she were exterminating a colony of ants one at a time. From this work she lifted and directed at John the sort of glance with which he imagined a Hatfield might greet a McCoy on a lonely mountain road.

"What do you want?"

"My name is Sayer," John said. "Mr. Howe asked me to drop in."

"About what?"

"Mr. Ireland is going to play some songs for me."

She flipped a switch and pulled back another. Into the mouthpiece that hung around her neck and nestled in her impressive cleavage, she said, "Man out here named Sayer? Says you asked him to come hear Irving play some songs?" There was a pause. Then she said, "You bet." She flipped the switch back into place, and pressed a button under the switchboard ledge. There was a nasty, buzzing roar, like a dentist's drill striking metal. The gate in a heavy wooden fence jumped open. John stepped through. The blonde reached over and pulled the gate shut behind him. She said, "Left, and then first on your right."

Moving left, John had a glimpse of two elderly women, wearing green eye shades, bent over ledgers. The first door on the right was open.

"Come in, fella," Mr. Howe called. John came in and the producer came out from behind his desk. "You remember Irving Ireland?"

"Of course," John said.

The long, sad man set down a glass of milk and rose from a deep chair. He took John's hand gingerly, as though he expected an electric shock on contact.

"Nice to see you again," he said.

"Same here," John said. He noticed, as Mr. Howe closed the door, that Mr. Ireland was wearing the same blue blazer with gold buttons, the same green bow tie with tiny yellow scimitars, and the same gray suede shoes with gum soles he had been wearing when John first met him in Gwen Quill's apartment. John wondered if Mr. Ireland, knowing he was going to see John a second time, had put on the clothes he had worn at the first meeting to make sure John would remember him. The door, as soon as Mr. Howe took his hand from the knob, was pushed open. The blonde poked her huge teeth into the room, and said, "Coffee?"

Mr. Howe said, "John?"

"No, thanks," John said.

"Irving?"

Mr. Ireland put both hands on the buckle of his belt and whimpered softly. He said, "Oh, God, no. No coffee."

"No coffee," Mr. Howe said to the blonde. "And no calls."

"You bet," she said, and removed her teeth from the room.

Mr. Howe said, "Wait till you hear these, fella. Okay, Irving?"

Mr. Ireland nodded. He went to a black upright piano against the far wall, and began to fuss with the contents of an open attaché case on top of the piano. John had the impression that the room was papered with sheets of postage stamps. After a moment or two, he saw why. Almost every inch of wall space was covered with framed posters and playbills. Mr. Ireland sat down on the piano bench and spread some ruled sheets on the rack. He crossed his legs, and began to pluck at the knot at his bow tie as though he had suddenly discovered he was strangling.

"John, you sit here, fella," Mr. Howe said. John took the chair from which he could see Mr. Ireland in profile. Mr. Howe went back to his seat behind the desk. "Which one first, Irving?"

With a tug that seemed to release his voice as well as undo the bow tie, Mr. Ireland said, "Gwen thinks in sequence is best."

"She's right," Mr. Howe said. "You may fire when ready, Gridley." Mr. Ireland looked startled and Mr. Howe laughed. "It's a joke, fella."

"Oh," Mr. Ireland said. Then, to his crossed knees, at which he scowled worriedly, he said, "This first song we're calling 'Great News.' Gwen thinks it'll probably be the opening number, although she's kicking around an idea for maybe musicalizing the prologue, the part about the hero dictating his memoirs in England and then flashing back for the opening. In that case this song, 'Great News,' it would be the second number in the show. But it would still be the first number in the story, if you follow?"

John nodded and said, "I follow."

"Well, then, it's a song for a little boy," Mr. Ireland said. "A boy of ten. He's in school, this thing Gwen says they called the Children's Guild up there at Deucalion, and word comes that his father has just been appointed to the Supreme Court. The class stops, the other kids look at him, and the boy begins to sing. The song tells how he feels to learn that this great thing has happened to his father. It starts slow. Sort of he's feeling his way into the realization his father is a great man. As he begins to understand that, the song gets faster, the other kids in the class join in, and it ends full stage, on an exultant note, with maybe dancing, too. But that will depend on what the choreographer comes up with."

"And if Gwen *likes* what he comes up with," Mr. Howe said.

"And if Gwen likes what he comes up with," Mr. Ireland said to his crossed knees. He lifted his glance to the music on the rack. "All right, then," he said gloomily. "Great News."

He ran his fingers along the keys, coughed lightly, and started to play and sing. At once an extraordinary thing happened. Mr. Ireland, who did not have much of a voice, became transformed by his own croaking sounds. The sadness fled from him. His sallow complexion grew healthily pink. His gaunt cheeks filled and became plump. He seemed to glow, suffused in a joy that was almost painful to watch. But John did watch. He could not take his eyes from the man at the piano. When the last note died away, Mr. Ireland's joy went with it. The plumpness vanished. The healthy glow faded. The troubled scowl reappeared. The sorrowful glance dropped to his knees.

"What do you think, fella?"

With a slight start, John realized Mr. Howe was talking to him. He turned to the producer and said, "I don't know what to say."

It was true enough. Until this moment John thought what had held him was the transformation of Mr. Ireland. John now grasped that something more had happened, and it had happened to him.

"You mean," Mr. Howe said in tones of almost strangled incredulity, and paused. His slanted face fought its own creases to prevent the descent into a totally uncharacteristic frown. "You mean you don't—you don't *like* it?"

"Good God, no," John said. "It's one of the most beautiful things I ever heard.

Mr. Howe beamed. Mr. Ireland nodded sadly. John tried to think of what he had really wanted to say. Beautiful was not the right word. Or rather, it was not the *only* right word. While Mr. Ireland had been playing and singing, a curious thing had been happening to John. He had been feeling again the emotions that had assailed him a quarter of a century ago, on his tenth birthday, when Ike Ten Eyck brought into Francis Tristram's schoolroom the news that John's father had been appointed to the Supreme Court. Mr. Ireland's song had not caused John to *remember* how he had felt. It had caused him to feel that way again. A piece of time that had died long ago had been recreated and made to live again. John looked at the sad man who had done this incredible thing, and he was aware of a very special feeling. He had never admired anybody in quite this way before. Nor had he ever envied anybody in quite this way.

"I'm almost afraid to hear the next two songs," John said. "They can't be as good as that one."

"They can't be, fella," Mr. Howe said happily. "But they are."

"And they were," John said to Ellie that night when, across a drink before dinner, he reported to her the events of his day. "I can't wait for you to hear them."

"When will I?" Ellie said.

"I don't know," John said. "I suppose I could ask Howe if it's all right for you to come down to his office and I could meet you there. Or we might invite Ireland to dinner?"

"No, I don't think so," Ellie said. "I'd rather not get involved with these people. Not at this stage."

John could feel his forehead crease.

"You don't like them?" he said.

"It's not that," Ellie said. "I can't not like them, since I haven't met them. But from what you've told me about them up to now, especially what happened to Mr. Ireland today when he sang his songs, I'm beginning to suspect these are not just new people you're meeting the way we might meet a new couple at a friend's house. No. I think this is a whole new world you're meeting. Every one of them you've told me about so far, Mr. Zucker, Mr. Howe, Miss Quill, Mr. Ireland, every one of them sounds different in a different way. Am I confusing you?"

"A little," John said.

"Well, people are different in different ways," Ellie said. "They're different as individuals, and they're different as groups. For example, say you're traveling. In England, the various English people you meet are different from each other. Yet to you, a visitor, seeing a lot of them for the first time in a group, all of them will have, or seem to have, certain common or national characteristics. The English, for another example, are supposed to be phlegmatic. Then you cross to France. The various Frenchmen you meet will also be different one from the other, but again you'll notice certain common or national characteristics. The French will, as a group, seem to you to be not phlegmatic but volatile. Now about you and these theatre people you've been meeting. I feel from your description of them that, while they're different from one another, they all have certain common or national characteristics. I guess what I'm really saying is that since this project got under way, or rather since you became involved with it, you've not only been meeting some different people. You've gone to another country, so to speak."

John rattled the ice in his glass. The small sounds helped him phrase the question.

"Ellie," he said. "Are you saying that since I became involved in this thing, I've begun to change?"

Ellie rattled the ice in her own glass. The sounds did not seem to help her. Not immediately, anyway. She took a few moments.

"It's not that," she said finally. "Not change. It's just that every now and then you surprise me. You didn't used to do that."

"How do I surprise you?" John said.

"Well, like that day you met Miss Quill for the first time and you called me to meet you at Tony's for lunch. I was sure, from your description of her and the fact she had an outline for only the first half of the play, I was sure you'd say no to the project. Or you'd say to them you'd have to wait and see until she did the second act. But I was wrong. You were enthusiastic about the project. You said you were going to let them go ahead. That surprised me."

"I don't blame you," John said. "I was surprised myself."

"I know you were," Ellie said. "I could tell. The same for a lot of other things these past few weeks. Remember the day you told me Mr. Howe called you to say he'd got that woman to design the costumes?"

"Angie Kurtz, yes."

"Well, what you said you did," Ellie said. "Upsetting Mr. Howe by questioning whether Miss Kurtz was good enough?"

"But that was just a joke," John said. "I wanted to see how he'd react."

"I know," Ellie said. "But when you were telling me about it, it surprised me. Your doing it as a joke, I mean. Knowing you the way I do, while you were telling it, I was automatically assuming you questioned his choice of that woman because you were beginning to worry about Mr. Howe choosing all the people for the project without consulting you. I assumed that's how your thinking would go. But when you said you'd done it as a joke, I realized my thinking was not your thinking. On that point, I mean, and it surprised me." Ellie laughed suddenly and said, "For God's sake, don't look so solemn about it."

"Well, hell," John said. "A man is having a drink with his wife, the way he does every night, and has been doing for ten years, and he suddenly gets told by the bride of his bosom that he's turning into a regular Dr. Jekyll and Mr. Hyde."

Ellie laughed again and came across the study to take his glass.

"I'd better get you another drink," she said. "You've earned it."

"Listen," John said. "You want me to quit this thing?"

Ellie turned from the small marble-topped French table that served as their bar.

"Yes," she said. "But I'm going to argue against your quitting it."

"Who's taking who by surprise now?" John said.

"I know that sounds paradoxical and even stupid," Ellie said. "But it makes sense. To me, anyway. I do want you to quit. I've wanted it for several days. But I don't know *why* I want it."

"Look," John said. "This is beginning to worry me. You sound like you've been brooding about this for some time."

"Well, if four or five days is some time, yes, I have," Ellie said. "But brooding is the wrong word. Thinking is more accurate. I've been thinking about it for several days, and I refuse to believe that thinking is bad for anyone. On the contrary. So few people do it, that it should be encouraged. I've certainly been encouraging myself these last four or five days. People who live together for a long time get to take each

other for granted. There are no more surprises, in the bedroom or anywhere else."

"Ellie," John said, "I don't think that's fair."

"Oh, John, no," she said quickly. "That's not what I mean.
I'm merely pointing out a truth. I've known all about you,
and about me, too, for so long that I've never even thought
about it. Then, these last months, ever since you got involved
with this theatre project, it's dawned on me I *don't* know
everything. As I said, you've been surprising me. At first it
upset me. It was as though part of you had become a
stranger. Or part of you I'd never seen had suddenly started
showing its face. But being upset seemed the wrong reaction.
What was there to be afraid of? Your enthusiasm for an unwritten script? Your upsetting Mr. Howe on the telephone
just for a joke? As I examined the details that had surprised
me, they upset me because they surprised me. I realized that
what was wrong was probably me. The details were silly. My
reaction was not. That's why I don't want you to quit this
project. If you did, it would be because I'm afraid of my
reaction, and I don't like to be afraid. So I have a suggestion.
You stay with the project. But me, I'll keep out."

"You haven't been in it," John said. "Aside from my reporting to you what's been happening, I mean. You haven't
really been involved."

"No, but I almost was," Ellie said. "When I asked you a
few minutes ago when I could hear Mr. Ireland's three songs.
What I'm saying is you're visiting this new country called the
theatre and you're building a house there with a group of
strangers. Good. Me, I'll stay home until the house you're
building in this new country is finished. Then I'll come take a
look at the complete job."

"You mean you don't want to hear or see anything about
the show until it opens?"

"Don't sound so outraged," Ellie said. "That's *not* what I
mean. You've got months and months of work ahead of you.
Every new song Mr. Ireland writes is going to be an event.
The day Miss Quill reads you her script, or even the first part
of it, *that* will be an event. The day you see the actor who
will play your father, another event. The day you see the first
costume sketches will be an event. And so on, and so on, and
so on. During the next months you are going to have more
events than Madison Square Garden. They're all going to be
exciting. Go ahead and enjoy them, then come home at night

and tell me about them. That will do me fine until the run-through."

"Until the what?"

"It's a sort of dress rehearsal without the dresses," Ellie said. "The show gets planned and written and rehearsed, all in private. Only for people in the project, I mean. Then, the day before the company goes out of town for the tryout tour, the producer rents or borrows a theatre for the afternoon. A theatre here in New York, that is, and naturally not on a matinée day, and he invites a couple of hundred people, mostly professionals. Friends of the cast. Friends of the author, the producer, the composer, and so on. Plus friends of the friends, also and so on. Anyway, for this group, the play is run through from beginning to end, exactly as though it were a regular performance, except it's on a bare stage, without costumes, and it's called, surprise, surprise, a run-through. When *this* event takes place," Ellie said, "I'll come." She paused, gave him an odd little look, then said, "If I'm invited."

John stood up and went across to take the glass she was bringing toward him. He kissed his wife, and said, "You're invited."

Part III

6

"**H**OW DOES IT LOOK?" Ellie said.

"I have no idea," John said. "I've heard the Quill woman read it in her apartment, that was the day she finished the script. Then the first day of rehearsals, I heard the entire cast sit around a table and read it. And since then I've seen bits and pieces of it in rehearsal, but I have no overall impression. Seeing it all put together should be quite an experience."

It began at twenty minutes after two, when John met Ellie in front of the Carnegie Theatre on West Forty-fifth Street.

"I've been wondering why here?" Ellie said. "I thought you told me months ago you had the Chelsea?"

"We have, but not until November nineteenth when we come back from our week in New Haven and our three weeks in Boston," John said. "We get to use the Carnegie for free this afternoon for this run-through because Vinnie Howe is also the producer of *Fig Leaf,* which is running here, as you can see from these provocative posters."

"I can see something else," Ellie said. "That man in the skull cap who is waving to you."

John turned, then said, "That's Norman Saul, our press agent, and that's no skull cap. That's his hair. Excuse me a moment."

He moved into the lobby. It was full of people John had never seen before, standing about in chatting groups. He met the press agent near the box office window.

"Gwen told me to find you," Norman Saul said. "She wants to say hello to your wife, but she's busy giving the cast some last minute stuff backstage, so she said could you meet her next door in Willie's for a drink at the intermission?"

"Be glad to," John said. "What do you hear?"

"The word of mouth is great," the press agent said. "All the shows I've done with Vinnie, I've never known him to be this high at this stage. Listen. New Haven. You want a suite at the Taft? Or a double room be okay?"

"A single will do me fine," John said. "This part of the services you get paid for? Or you doing it because you admire lawyers?"

"Don't ask me why, but the press agent always makes the out-of-town hotel reservations for the brass," Norman Saul said. "I also happen to like a few lawyers. You're one of them. Where's your party? I could slip you in ahead of the gang."

He did that, but not ahead of the entire gang. John was surprised, when he and Ellie were finally settled and looking around, by how many people were already seated.

"Who's that at the piano?" Ellie said.

"Irving Ireland," John said.

"Who are you hunting?" Ellie said.

"Our agent," John said. "Arnold Zucker."

"Isn't that him?" Ellie said. "The next aisle? Folding his coat?"

"That's him, all right," John said. "How did you know?"

"From your descriptions," Ellie said, "I knew it had to be. Here comes something."

It was Vinnie Howe, coming out of the wings. The audience applauded as the little man made his slanting way across the brightly lighted stage to the footlights. He grinned happily and held up his hand for silence.

"Good afternoon, folks, and welcome," Vincent Howe said. "The ad agency hasn't finished the poster for this show yet. But when it's ready you'll see that it reads quote, in small type, Vincent Howe Presents. Then in big type, The Gwendolyn Quill Production of *Deucalion*. And that's exactly how it should read. Because this is Gwen Quill's show from start to finish. She conceived the idea. She wrote the script. She worked with Irving Ireland, here, on integrating his music with her book. And these last five weeks she's been rehearsing the pants off a cast of thirty-eight people. What I'm trying to say is that if anybody has the *right* to say anything about this show, it's Gwen Quill and nobody else. Being only the producer, therefore, I'm hereby going to shut up. And now folks, I want you to meet the one and only Gwen Quill."

His slender body, slanting with his gesture toward the wings, touched off a round of applause. The girl who came out toward Vincent Howe took John by surprise. Miss Quill was wearing a smartly-tailored, and clearly expensive, bright green suit made of some sort of tweedy material trimmed with mink; spike-heeled shoes of alligator; and her red hair, cut like a man's and usually slicked back, had been fluffed out in a sort of halo that had a rakishly feminine effect.

"Hey!" Ellie whispered. "She's *pretty!*"

Someone behind them hissed a "Ssssshhh!" and Ellie did.

On the stage Gwen Quill said, "Thank you, Vinnie." He bowed happily, backed away, blew her a kiss, and disappeared into the wings. Miss Quill turned back to the audience. "There goes one of the sweetest guys who ever walked the face of this earth," she said. "What a business this would be if all producers were like Vincent Howe." She shook her head and sighed in a neat little burlesque of hopeless desire. The audience laughed. Gwen Quill smiled and said, "Now, to work. I do not believe in making introductory remarks about a play before a run-through, because I feel such remarks wipe out a very important test. If the run-through audience can grasp what the play is about, if people like you here today, seeing it cold, can get the emotional reaction the playwright and the actors and the director are striving for, if all that can come through on an empty stage, without lights or scenery or costumes, then the production is headed in the right direction. So, as I say, no introductory remarks. I'm going to let the play speak for itself. I would, however, like to say a few words on two points. First, the main role. The part of Sennacherib Sayer is a difficult one. It is very long, and in its emotional range it is very taxing. The man who plays the part is called upon at different times to make you laugh; to tear your heart out; to make you believe he was one of the handsomest men of his day and that he has in him the stuff of greatness; to sing six songs; to lead the chorus in a complicated dance at an American political rally; and later do a soft shoe number with his wife at a church bazaar in the English countryside. As you can see, a role tailored perfectly to the talents of Edmund Kean, Enrico Caruso, and Waslaw Nijinsky."

Miss Quill paused for her laugh, got a titter instead, and said, "Unfortunately these three gentlemen are no longer with us." The laugh came, and she smiled her thanks. "We have been forced, therefore, to settle for a living human being," she said. "A number of stars were available, and several of them were eager to play the part. I suppose it would have been considered good insurance by some producers to hire one of these stars, since their pull at the box office has been established. *Deucalion*, however, is not the kind of play about which you can think of insurance. It breaks new ground in the American musical theatre. It shoots for a mark nobody has tried before. It is, in short, Joycean in its concept. You don't reach for what James Joyce reached for, and at the same time try to play it safe. We decided not to even try. We went out to hunt for an actor who could reach the dimensions the script and the music and Roger Benjamin's choreography call for. We found him, after an eight-month hunt, we found him just around the corner."

Miss Quill paused again. The brief silence reminded John of that moment in the broadcast of a national political convention when the nominating orator, after outlining the staggering qualifications of The Man Who, pauses at last before uttering the magic name.

"Fred Thirkell will be thirty-eight on his next birthday," Gwen Quill said. "When we found him, he was selling orangeade and souvenir programs at the Chelsea Theatre at night, and studying at the Studio during the day. Fred Thirkell has never appeared on Broadway. He's done summer stock, had several small parts in off-Broadway things that didn't do too well, and he's done some TV work of a minor nature. But his parents came from Wales, as did the father of Sennacherib Sayer, and Fred Thirkell was raised in Chicago, as Sennacherib Sayer was, and in our opinion he has in him what this play will, we hope, convince you Sennacherib Sayer had: the aforementioned stuff of greatness. I mention all this only because, the part being as demanding as it is, and Fred's experience being as limited as it is, he may seem a trifle nervous this afternoon. If so, I ask you merely to remember what I've said, and bear in mind that it is temporary. You are about to have, in my humble opinion, the rare privilege of being in at the birth of a great, a *very* great, star."

Miss Quill paused again. There was a spatter of applause but, by quickly raising her hand, she stopped even that. John felt at once the effectiveness of what she had done: Ellie on his right, like the people in front of them, dipped forward in a slight crouch of anticipation.

"Now the second thing I want to say a few words about, and I promise they *will* be few," Gwen Quill said. *"Deucalion* is a play set within the framework of a prologue and an epilogue. When the play opens we would like you to imagine that this bare stage is a small cottage in the English countryside in Kent just before the Second World War. The man you will see seated at his desk is in his late sixties." Miss Quill turned and, as she started off the stage, she said, "Okay, Jess."

Jess Wilentz, the stage manager, came out of the wings. He was chewing a pencil, carrying a chair, and dragging a small table. He set them at one side, took the pencil out of his mouth and raised it above his head. Fred Thirkell, wearing blue jeans and a sweatshirt, walked on from the left. He sat down in the chair, and leaned his elbows on the table. His handsome face assumed a pensive expression, as though he were staring through a window at the horizon. Jess Wilentz swung the pencil down in a swift, decisive arc, and called, "Lights!" He stepped to one side as Fred Thirkell began to speak.

"My name is Sennacherib Sayer," he said to the invisible window on the brightly lighted stage. "You may not know who I am. That is why I sit here in England writing my memoirs. It is important to me that you should know who I am. For only in you, a total stranger who reads this page, can I find what all of us—every human being—seeks: my fragment of immortality."

Jess Wilentz again swung the pencil downward.

"Dimout!" he called. "Music!"

Fred Thirkell rose and walked off stage. Irving Ireland started to play the piano.

"Lights up!" Fred Wilentz shouted. Then, to nobody in

particular, but loud and clear, he intoned: *"Scene, a school-room in the Children's Guild at Deucalion."*

Members of the cast started entering, some of them carrying benches. Jess Wilentz said, *"Time, a June afternoon in nineteen twenty-nine."*

The cast members set the benches in rows and sat down. Jess said. *"At rise, the schoolmaster is working out an arithmetic problem on the blackboard. The children on the benches watch him intently.*

John Sayer leaned forward. When he leaned back, Ellie was looking at her wrist watch.

"One hour and twenty-five minutes," she said. "Sounds like the perfect length for a first act."

"Yes, just about," John said. "Listen, Gwen Quill asked us to meet her next door in Willie's for a drink, so let's hurry. We've only got fifteen minutes."

They went like Indian scouts in a silent movie, working their way single file around the chattering groups that, like clumps of sagebrush, dotted the aisles, the lobby, and the sidewalk.

"I've been reading about this place in the columns for years," Ellie said. "But I've never been in it."

"Personally," John said, "I don't usually like these places that specialize in knockwurst and Löwenbrau on tap. All the waiters look as though under their breath they're humming the Horst Wessel Song. But duty before pleasure. If we can *get* into this place."

"Follow me," Gwen Quill said, coming up beside them. They did, edging through the crowd just inside the door. Here a huge man with a shaved head took Miss Quill's elbow and led her to a round table at the back. He took up the small "Reserved" sign and slipped it into a pocket under his apron. He bowed, and hurried away. Gwen Quill waved them to chairs and said, "I've ordered champagne because there's not enough time for individual orders, and I've noticed that even people who don't like champagne are afraid to say so because they think it makes them sound boorish. Besides, we want clear heads for sitting through the second act, don't we? I see now, Mr. Sayer, why you keep her cooped up at The Nebraska."

John said, "What?"

Gwen Quill nodded toward Ellie and said, "She's pretty."

"Why, thank you," John said, and he performed the introduction. By the time he finished, the waiter had returned, set out the glasses, and was circling the table with the champagne bottle. "You've certainly got this organized," John said. He raised his glass and said, "Is it bad luck in the theatre to toast a show at this stage? I keep bumping into these traditions and superstitions all the time, things I didn't know about."

"Let's drink to the Sayer family," Gwen Quill said, raising her glass. "From Sennacherib to Ellie. Is that short for Eleanor?"

"No, it's a family contraction for Leonora Ewing," Ellie said. "Ewing was my mother's maiden name. She hated to see it disappear from the records, I guess, so she thought by giving it to me for a middle name she'd preserve it."

"I'm glad she did," Gwen said. "Here's to Eleanor Ewing, or L.E., or Ellie, the prettiest Sayer of them all."

She took a sip from her glass. Norman Saul appeared at her elbow. He looked harassed.

"Excuse me," he said to the table, then dipped down and whispered hurriedly into Gwen's ear.

"Oh, shit," she said, setting down her glass. "Excuse me," she said, getting up. "Crisis."

Norman Saul pulled back her chair, said "Sorry" to the table, and followed her across the restaurant to the door.

"I take it back," Ellie said.

"What?" John said.

"She's not pretty at all," Ellie said. "It's the Bergdorf suit and the twenty-dollar hairdo."

"Come on, drink up," John said. "We've got to get back for the second act."

When it was over, and while the audience was applauding, Norman Saul came down the aisle and tapped John on the shoulder.

"Gwen's called a meeting at her apartment right away," the press agent whispered. "She'd like you to be there."

John nodded, said "Fine," and stood up to help Ellie with her coat. They made their way, as before, around the chattering groups in the aisles and lobby. John thought he saw Arnold Zucker, but the plump figure disappeared in the crowd. Out on the sidewalk, John and Ellie both looked at their wrist watches. John's showed twenty minutes to six.

"It's too late to go back to the office," John said. "Let's grab a taxi."

After they had, John did not feel it necessary to make small talk, so he didn't. Neither did Ellie. They were both

waiting. When they got home, she went down the hall to see
Sam and Jim. John went to the kitchen to get the ice. By the
time he had their drinks ready, Ellie had come into the study
and closed the door. John gave her a glass. She went to her
favorite chair near the window and took a sip. John sat down
with his glass in the chair facing her and took a sip.

"Okay," he said. "Start."

"Aren't you supposed to be at a meeting?" Ellie said. "I
thought I heard that press agent man tell you Miss Quill had
called one?"

"During the past year I have been to a dozen of those
meetings," John said. "I know exactly what everybody is
going to say. It's you I want to hear from."

"Not that I know anything about these things," Ellie said.

"Come on, now, none of that," John said. "Ten, eleven
months ago, when this thing started, you said you were going
to stay out of it completely so at least one member of the
family could keep their sense of perspective. You've kept it.
Now apply it."

"Well, first of all, I'm confused," Ellie said. "Confused, but
with a positive feeling. First, I think Thirkell is excellent. I
never knew your father, of course, but I've heard you talk
about him, and I've seen pictures, of course, and this man
gives me the feeling of Sennacherib Sayer. He was nervous,
of course, and wearing those foolish things actors wear,
sweatshirts and blue jeans, didn't help the illusion, but I think
Mr. Thirkell is fine."

"Good," John said. "I like him, too."

"Another thing I like is the music," Ellie said. "Some of
those songs are enchanting, and I'm sure the others will show
up better when they're played with a full orchestra. Mr. Ireland is a fine composer, but not a very good piano player.
Even so, I think the music is excellent. That very first song?
'Good News,' is it?"

" 'Great News,' " John said.

"Yes, well, it's lovely," Ellie said. "And that one in the second act? At the church bazaar? In England? When he's dancing with his wife? And the children join in?"

" 'Happy is a Word.' "

"That's it," Ellie said. "It's simply beautiful. No, I think it's
a wonderful score."

"Get to what's not wonderful."

"I will," Ellie said. "But first one more wonderful thing.
The wife. In the first act. Your mother. You know, she's al-

ways puzzled me. Partly because of what you've told me about her. Partly because of how little you talk about her. Partly because of that small snapshot you have in the silver frame on your dresser. The picture I've had in my mind for years is just like that snapshot in the silver frame. It's been fuzzy. As though somebody moved the camera just as the photographer clicked the shutter."

"They did," John said. "Wade Duhart took the picture. He was the head of the Music Masters' Guild and something of a shutter bug. He was taking pictures at one of our Outdoor Sings and just as he took Mother's, Charlie Devon pushed his kid sister Michelle, and she fell against Wade Duhart's leg. Funny, I never remembered that until this minute."

"Well, it's all association," Ellie said. "I once broke my wrist when I was a little girl, and I had to wear a plaster cast for a few weeks. During all that time it seemed to me people never talked about anything but broken bones. Their own. Bones broken by friends, members of the family, and so on. The same with this snapshot of your mother. As I said, all these years she's puzzled me. I had this fuzzy picture of her. A sort of strait-laced, puritanical woman, vaguely Teutonic in background—"

"Swedish," John said. "She was born in Stockholm."

"Yes," Ellie said. "A not very well educated girl who became a nurse and married an older man, a brilliant man, married him when he was sick, perhaps for his money, perhaps for social position. I don't know. Just a sort of vague, unpleasant thing that seemed to surround the marriage. As though after she pulled it off, she got scared. She didn't know how to handle it. And perhaps your father didn't, either. So they remained together, keeping up a front for the world, as it were. But secretly, in real life, so to speak, they were miserable."

"I don't think that was true," John said. "I'm not sure, either, and I'm not rejecting that interpretation because it's unpleasant, but I really don't think it was true."

"I *know* it wasn't," Ellie said. "I mean I know it now. That's the other wonderful thing I learned from this run-through today. I don't know whether it's that girl who plays the first Mrs. Sayer?"

"Irene Faulk," John said. "She's good, I think."

"So do I," Ellie said. "Or whether it's the way Miss Quill has written and directed her. Or whether it's that extraordi-

nary ballad she sings just before the fire at the end of the first
act. 'Go to School to Your Heart.' "

"I guess that's my favorite, too," John said.

"Well, I don't know that it's my *favorite*," Ellie said.
" 'Great News' and that other one, 'Happy is a Word,' those
are going to get a lot of humming in the next few weeks
around this house. But it *is* a marvelous thing, that song.
Anyway, it helped give me, after all these years, it helped
give me this wonderful, touching picture of your mother.
This frightened girl. Absolutely terrified at falling in love
with the older, wonderful man. Scared to death it wouldn't
work, yet powerless to stop what was happening. Succumbing
to her love, then living a dozen terrible years in secret, *behind* this front of efficiency and toughness. And then discovering, at the end, when it's too late, although of course she
doesn't *know* it's too late when she sings the song, since she
doesn't know the fire is about to happen and she is about to
die, but discovering, at that moment, that her love was *not* a
secret. Her husband had known it all along, because he had
loved her all along as she had loved him. In *secret*. Because
all the time he had been afraid of the same thing she'd been
afraid of. That he was not good enough for *her*. That moment of revelation, the moment of discovery, that's a wonderful moment, John. It makes that first act wonderful. If the
second act could even approach that, it would be a wonderful
play."

"But it doesn't," John said.

Ellie shook her head and took a sip of her drink.

"It doesn't even come close," she said. "And that's what
confused me. But in the taxi ride home, I've sorted out some of
my confusion, and I think what's wrong, for me, anyway, are
two things."

"I am waiting," John said.

"Don't be so impatient," Ellie said. "I want to phrase this
correctly. The first thing, I think, is somehow technical. The
play seems to end at the end of Act One. When Act Two
started, I felt a whole new story was starting. With different
people, about a different problem, and so on, and I didn't
really care. Not after what I'd just seen and heard and, by
God, *lived* through. I mean emotionally lived through in the
first act. I was still wrapped up in the people of that first act,
and I wanted to be back with them. When I found out, as the
second act progressed, that I wasn't *going* to be with those
people, I lost interest. Okay?"

"Yes," John said. "I see that clearly. I mean, I don't know how to solve it, but I see it. What's the second thing?"

"The second thing that's wrong, I think, is the actual *content* of the second act," Ellie said. "After the excitement, the stuff that goes on in the first act, the second seems very flat. I won't say that nothing happens. There are all those scenes. The fight with the publisher of the memoirs. The church bazaar. The scene where he reaches the decision to write the memoirs, as a record for his son. The visit from the American ambassador. All that is interesting, but it's interesting the way a pageant is interesting. You stare at one scene. Then you stare at another. Then a third, and so on. But you don't carry any accumulated emotion with you from scene to scene, the way you do in a story. You don't feel the tension mounting inside you. There's no final explosion or climax. It just meanders along until that perfectly charming final number, the one where they sing, 'A book you're writing is a dear old friend, You must say good-bye when you scribble The End.' Then the play is finished, and you don't really care. You haven't been touched at all. And the reason, I think, is that there's no conflict in the second act. In the first act he was fighting suspicion, jealousy, the accusations of that English schoolmaster, the threat of exposure, scandal, the ruin of his career. It's terribly gripping stuff. You're rooting for him. You're hating his enemies. You're all involved. Act Two? Nothing."

"I felt that, too," John said. "But I'm damned if I can figure out why."

The phone rang. Ellie reached across, picked it up, and said, "Hello? Who? Oh, hello. Yes, he is. Just a moment." She held out the phone to John. "Mr. Howe."

John took the phone and said, "Hello."

"John?"

"Yes."

"Vinnie."

"How are you?"

"Why aren't you here? At Gwen's? Didn't Norman Saul tell you she'd called a meeting?"

"Yes, he did, but there was something I had to do first," John said.

"Gee whiz, fella, this is important," the producer said. "The company goes up to New Haven tomorrow and we open on Monday."

"I know that."

"Well, are you coming over?"

"Vinnie, you're surely not holding up the meeting for me," John said. "I told you there's something I had to do first."

"You'll be over later? That what you mean?"

"Yes."

"How much later, fella?"

"I don't know," John said. "As soon as I can get there."

He handed the phone back to Ellie. As she replaced it on the hook, she said, "Perhaps you shouldn't keep them all waiting?"

"There's no point in my going to a meeting to which I can't contribute anything," John said. "As it stands now, it'll be Roger Benjamin and Norman Saul and Jess Wilentz and Mannie De Leon. All of them sounding off. Saying the way to fix it is to add more dancing, or more costumes, or more furniture to the sets, or more ads in the *Times*. Depending on what their function in the project is. What am I going to tell them? The way to fix the show is give my firm a larger fee? Because that's *my* province? I'm the lawyer? They've worked almost a year on this play. By the time it comes in, after the next four weeks out of town, a year out of everybody's life will have gone into the damn thing. You saw it this afternoon. Unless something drastic is done soon—soon, hell! At once!—the thing doesn't have a prayer. That gang in Gwen Quill's apartment right now, I've listened to them for most of this past year. The something drastic that this play needs is not going to come from them."

"What about from Miss Quill?"

"Well, she might, but I doubt it," John said. "She's very good, as you saw for yourself this afternoon, but I've learned from watching her that she's very good only when you give her something to work with. I suspect that's true of all directors. They're not really creative. Nothing comes from inside them. You give them something from inside somebody else, somebody who *is* genuinely creative, and they can add to it or improve it. Miss Quill is not really a writer. She's a director. That's why the first act works. It's based on real material. The creative aspect of the first act was lived by real people. Her research dug up these real things. With these real things, her talents as a director were able to function. She was able to shape, to add, to improve. And she came up with a first act you found moving and impressive. The second act poses a different problem. Miss Quill's research dug up nothing. Just a few facts without flesh and blood. Dates and so on. In short, she had nothing creative to work on in the second act. So she couldn't shape it, or add to it, or improve it. That's why the second act is neither moving nor impressive. That's what's missing. The creative core, so to speak. The real thing for her directorial talent to work on."

"Well, then," Ellie said, "I would say the only person who can supply what's missing is you."

"I think so, too," John said. "I don't know how, but I feel I should. That's why I don't want to go to that meeting. Not until I've got some hint of what it *is* that's missing."

"It seems to me it could be something very simple," Ellie said. "When you stop and think about it for a moment, the motive power for the first act is almost childishly simple: the jealousy of that English schoolmaster for Sennacherib Sayer. It's not even very fresh or original. Maybe that's what makes it so powerful. You accept jealousy as a motivation without question. Anyway, from that small thing, the jealousy of the schoolmaster, look at all the exciting complications that boil up. If you could find a simple thing like that for the second act, all those scenes, the pageant-like quality, it might all fall into place."

"If," John said.

"Well, let's review what we know about the real facts," Ellie said. "I mean what really happened to your father during the intermission."

"During the intermission?"

Ellie laughed and said, "Take that look to the bar, please, and refresh these drinks." John stood up and took her glass. "The first act takes place in Dutchess County in nineteen twenty-nine," Ellie said. "The second act takes place in England in nineteen thirty-nine. During the intermission, therefore, the hero becomes ten years older. What happened to him while the audience was out having a smoke?"

"You know all that," John said. "I've bored the bejesus out of you often enough with the details."

"Well, then, let me do the boring this time," Ellie said. She took her glass. "Thank you. Listen carefully, and interrupt me only when I get something wrong."

"Okay," John said. "But knock off that public prosecutor's look, please."

Ellie laughed again.

"I was just concentrating," she said. "Curtain on first act. Audience goes out to smoke. Deucalion was burned down. Your mother has died. Your father decides to live abroad.

You, age ten, decide you do not want to live abroad. The reasons seem fairly obvious. The death of your mother, to whom you were very close, has hurt badly. You have never been close to your father. He has always been something awesome and impersonal. A Public Figure. A Great Man, in capital letters. In your grief you turn to the only person you ever loved, aside from your mother. You turn to Ike Ten Eyck. Your father, being a perceptive man, understands what is happening, even if you, age ten, do not. He takes appropriate measures. He sends you to prep school, and he subsidizes Ike Ten Eyck to keep an eye on you. Ike settles down in Wellesville, where he devotes himself for the next few years to some concentrated drinking and keeping an eye on a boy named John Sayer, student at one of America's finest preparatory schools, Norcross, located four miles from Wellesville, just across the New York State line in Connecticut. The boy grows older. He sees Ike at regular intervals. They spend holidays together, summer vacations, go on trips. There are regular letters from the father abroad. Presents. Christmas cards. That sort of thing. The boy graduates from Norcross and goes to Harvard. Ike Ten Eyck remains in Wellesville, and the boy, now a young man, goes to visit him now and then. Wellesville is the place the young man thinks of as home. He doesn't do much thinking about anything else except his studies and he does very well at Harvard. Ike is proud of him. The boy is pleased Ike is proud of him. The letters from abroad indicate his father is proud of him. The boy never questions whether or not he's pleased his father is proud of him. In his last year at Harvard, the question of a profession comes up. The letters from abroad suggest law school. Ike agrees. The boy, the young man, however, he's undecided. He graduates with honors, still undecided. His father, as a reward for graduating with honors, offers him a trip abroad for the summer. The boy, the young man is undecided about that, too. He and his father have not seen each other for almost ten years. He is edging up to his twentieth birthday. Sennacherib Sayer writes that the reunion would please him very much. Aside from his selfish eagerness to see his son, Sennacherib Sayer writes, he knows his son will have a good time. London is lovely in the summer. The English countryside is at its best. The English people are—"

"No," John said. "Not England."

Ellie said, "What?"

"You told me to interrupt you when you got something wrong," John said.

"What did I get wrong?" Ellie said.

"It wasn't London," John Sayer said to his wife. "It was Sydney. It wasn't England," he said, "It was Australia."

The troubled smile on Ellie's face reminded him of something.

"I don't understand," she said slowly. "All these years we've been married, all these years you've told me about your father, you always said he spent the last ten years of his life in England. You said that's where you visited him in the summer of nineteen thirty-nine, when you graduated from Harvard, just before the war began. You said—"

John suddenly remembered of what it was her frown had reminded him, and he lost track of Ellie's voice. Fifteen years ago, when Ike Ten Eyck had come up to see him at Cambridge a couple of weeks before graduation, the old handyman had frowned in exactly the same way as they sat facing each other across their beers in the Crimson Tavern.

"You keep saying why the hell should you go," Ike had said. "All right, I'll tell you why the hell you should go."

"Better have another one of these," John said. "I can see you're winding up for one of your lectures. They're thirsty work." He held up two fingers to the waitress, then said to Ike, "They're thirsty listening, too."

"Don't get so snotty about my lectures," Ike said. "That time your freshman year? You thought you had the clap? It hadn't been for my lecture, you'd have been in hock to some quack son of a bitch for years, not to mention the permanent damage he might have done to your shooting iron. So have a little respect."

John laughed and said, "God, I was a scared kid that time, wasn't I?"

"You sure were," Ike said. "And now you're a dopey one."

"Hey, now, don't let's get carried away," John said. "That's no way to talk to a cum laude edging up to his twentieth birthday. Thanks, Elaine."

The waitress nodded and moved away. Ike Ten Eyck, reaching for one of the two beers she had set down, twisted his slanted body to watch her go.

"You been in there?" he said.

"None of your business," John said.

"Wouldn't mind making it mine," Ike said. "Always was a

pushover for the kind of ass that gives you something to hang onto."

"I know," John said. "And the kind of tit you can pitch a quoit at."

"I see my lectures have not gone in one ear and out the other without leaving a little something behind," Ike said. "I hope I have the same luck with my lecture on why I think you should spend your twentieth birthday in the great and glorious city of Sydney, Australia."

"How do you know it's great and glorious?" John said.

"Sennacherib Sayer wrote and told me so."

"You believe everything he writes you?"

"I should hope to smoke a Sicilian salami I do," Ike said. "He's a great man and a smart man. Smartest I ever knew. Wish I could say the same for his son." John grunted and took a mouthful of beer. Ike Ten Tyck, very quietly, said, "You've got to have it out with him some time, Johnny. This is the best time."

"Have what out?" John said, addressing his beer mug. "Why don't you quit talking in riddles? Why don't you shut up and drink your beer?"

"You've never forgiven him," Ike said, just as quietly. "All these years. Ten years you were first at Norcross, then here at Harvard. All those years you've held it against him. That's why you never wanted to visit him during school vacations. That's why you never talk about him. That's why when you were a kid I had to hound you to answer his letters. That's why now you're stalling about deciding do you go to law school in the fall or don't you. Everything he wants, you do the opposite. In the long run the only one who's gonna get hurt that way is you."

"I told you to shut up."

"Not now," Ike said. "Not any more. I've shut up for ten years. Because I figured you were a kid. Because I figured you were too young to face it. You're not a kid any more, Johnny."

"Will you shut up?"

"Another six weeks you're gonna be twenty. You're a man, Johnny. Or almost. And it's never gonna be better than almost till you get this thing straight with your father."

"If you don't shut up, I'm going to——"

"No, you won't, Johnny. You're going to face this thing you've been ducking for ten years. There's only one way to face it, and there's only one place to face it. There's a ship sails from San Francisco on the eleventh. That's eight days after graduation. I've booked you a passage, Johnny, and I've bought your train tickets to San Francisco."

"You know what you can do with them."

"No, you're going to use them, Johnny."

"I don't want to go, and I don't have to do any God damn thing I don't want to do."

"It's no longer a question what you want or don't want," Ike Ten Eyck said. "It's the old fork in the road, Johnny. You go the right way, or you go the other. You'll sure as hell go the other unless you face him with what's eating you."

"Nothing is eating me."

"It won't stop there," Ike said. "Because you're not in the bush leagues any more. You're coming into the majors, Johnny. Up there, if you don't stop it from eating you, it'll kill you." Ike Ten Eyck pulled an envelope from his pocket and pushed it across the table. "There's the tickets," he said. "The *Lurline* sails on the eleventh."

She sailed on the thirteenth because of a wildcat stewards' strike that took forty-eight hours to settle. John didn't mind the delay. He had never been to San Francisco, and he had never seen a world's fair. The combination kept him from thinking. On the *Lurline* what kept him from thinking, at least as far as Hawaii, was a Radcliffe girl going home for the summer to her family in the pineapple business. After Honolulu it was more difficult. The other passengers seemed to be American businessmen and their wives on their way to do something about the Australian market, or Australian businessmen and their wives returning home from having done something about the American market. All were friendly, and most were pleasant, but none was totally absorbing. Even while playing ping-pong or shuffleboard with them, the thinking, or part of it, went grinding on. Wearing deeper and deeper the ruts of troubled uneasiness that led nowhere because they moved in a circular pattern, away from Deucalion, out into the ten years that followed the colony's destruction, then back to Deucalion, the horror in which it ended, and once again out into the time of comparative peace that was, with each passing moment, drawing to a close. The most troubled part of the thinking was the knowledge that it was drawing to a close because of his conscious act. Nobody had forced John Sayer to board the *Lurline*. Why was he sailing to Australia? Because Ike Ten Eyck had insisted? Or because John had known there was no escaping the truth of

Ike's insistence? Over and over again, unable to find an answer to his questions, John found himself retreating into the pointless wish that he had not set out on the trip. Or that there was some way to turn back. Then, on the dock at Sydney, it all came right.

He was standing at the rail, holding off the circular pattern of thought by checking and rechecking the mental disembarkation list he had put together at breakfast: *passport, landing card, traveler's cheques, inoculation certificate, purser's office to pay bar bill, customs declaration, key to large suitcase, say good-bye to Mr. and Mrs. Washburn, passport, landing card traveler's cheques, inoculation certificate, purser's office to pay bar bill, customs declaration, key to large suitcase, say good-bye to Mr. and Mrs. Washburn, passport*—then the meaningless syllables stopped droning through his head as though the needle had been lifted from a phonograph record.

John's glance, swinging casually across the dock below, had been caught and held by a familiar sight. What made it familiar was not the white hair. John had more or less expected that, even though he had not, he realized, given it any special thought. What made the sight familiar was the way the tall, slender figure in the three-button pepper-and-salt tweed jacket seemed to be separated from the crowd in which he was imbedded, as though he was surrounded by an invisible guard rail.

This was due, John realized, not to what was happening on the dock but to what had happened to himself. Into his mind, as it did when he was a boy at Deucalion, had come the huge, shapeless, fiery glow that used to be a part of being reminded by some kid in the Children's Guild that his father was a great man. And, as he used to do when he was a child, John now found himself bringing an image of his father into the front part of his mind. Also, he found that even though he had several images to choose from, he chose the one that had always been his favorite. The image that showed Sennacherib Sayer on the stage in the Barn Meeting Hall, addressing the assembled Deucalion colonists on some matter of policy or reorganization or discipline.

The image still went very well, John found, with the fiery glow in the back of his mind. The combination showed the tall, handsome figure, with the thin lips, sharp nose, and white hair parted in the middle, the way the figure of George Washington used to look in Mrs. Loring's mural on the walls of the dining room in the Deucalion Main House. There had always been something about that jutting jaw, those thin lips, the sharp eyes, even the white hair that could almost have been a colonial wig but wasn't, that made John's heart beat a little faster. It beat a little faster now, and it continued to beat faster until, the ceremonial details of disembarkation finally completed, John walked up to the white-haired man on the dock.

"Happy birthday," John's father said.

"Thank you," John said.

Their hands met, and held, and John examined his father as frankly as Sennacherib Sayer was examining him. He knew the statistics, of course. His father was sixty-eight, and sixty-eight was not young. But statistics had never had anything to do with the image John had just learned he was still able to bring to the front of his mind. The image was ageless, so that it seemed quite proper for the tall, slender, white-haired man whose hand John was holding to look now almost exactly as he had looked when his son had last seen him ten years ago. He said now, quietly, with a small nod, "Ike's done a good job."

"He sends you all his best," John said.

"Instead of sending it, I wish he'd brought it with him," Sennacherib Sayer said. "His health really bad?"

"Oh," John said, surprised. It had not occurred to him until this moment that his father had asked Ike to come along to Australia. "Why? Is that what he writes?"

"Not exactly, but he did say he didn't feel equal to so long a trip. Here, let me take that."

"No, no, thanks." John swung the small bag out of his father's reach, and said, "It's not really my birthday. Not until tomorrow."

"I know," Sennacherib Sayer said. "But we thought it would be nicer to have the party tonight. To celebrate not only the eve of your being twenty, as it were, but also to celebrate your, ah, arrival." He paused, then took John's arm, and said, "I almost said reunion. Come." When they came out into the street, he said, "Are you warm enough in that?"

"Oh, yes, fine," John said. "I thought it would be colder."

"It usually is," his father said. "But we're having a very mild winter. I never wear overcoats myself." He laughed. "I remember when we first came out here, eight years ago, how odd I thought it was. People wearing overcoats in June. Dwight, this is my son John."

"A pleasure to meet you, sir," said the tall, broad man in

chauffeur's uniform. John had another moment of surprise.
He had always known in a vague way that his father had
money. It had not occurred to him until now that his father
might have quite a lot. The car at the curb was a Rolls limousine.

"I see you got the big bag," Sennacherib Sayer said.

"Yes, sir," Dwight said. "I'll take that, sir."

"Thanks," John said. He handed over the small bag.

"Is that all the luggage, sir?"

"That's all," John said.

"Very good, sir. I'll just stow this in the boot, sir. Shan't be
a moment."

John watched him with a small feeling of puzzled discomfort. He felt as though he had wandered into a British movie
that was not being screened properly. Everything seemed a
little out of focus. Sennacherib Sayer laughed.

"It's the accent," he said in a low voice as he opened the
rear door of the car. "It bothered me, too, when I first came
here. It's part cockney and part American. Pretty much
everything is. The architecture. The clothes. The manners. I
like it. Being an Anglophile, and like all Americans who are
Anglophiles being a little ashamed of it, I find here in Australia I get the illusion of being both at home in America, and
also in my favorite country, England. No, you first. I want
you to sit on that side so I can point out the sights."

Dwight came around from the boot. He climbed in behind
the wheel. The large car rolled off into a city that reminded
John a little of Boston. His father was right. There was something vaguely British about everything, and yet basically
everything was unpretentiously, almost seedily, American.

"The city is built around the harbor, as you can see," Sennacherib Sayer said. "The harbor is a sort of huge saucer, except that it's not round but long. Miles long, really, and it's
protected from the sea by The Heads, through which you
steamed in this morning. A sort of pincers arrangement at the
sea end of the saucer, you might say. When we pass this next
corner, you'll get another glimpse of—there. The old Coat
Hanger." Sennacherib Sayer laughed. "To you and me it's
just another bridge across a harbor, and by comparison with
some of our New York bridges, and the San Francisco
bridge, it's neither very pretty nor very long. But to the citizens of this quite wonderful city it's what Big Ben is to London and the Eiffel Tower to Paris and the Statue of Liberty

to New York. It *does* look like a huge coat hanger, doesn't it?"

"Yes," John said. He wondered whether his father was playing the tourist guide so industriously because he wanted to convey information, or because he wanted to avoid having to talk about other matters. Not that John knew very clearly what those other matters might be. Most of the basic facts about both their lives during the past ten years had been covered in their correspondence. Even the still-unsettled question of John's career—should he enter law school in September or should he look for a job—had been debated in almost eighteen months' worth of letters. He had expected a certain amount of awkwardness when they first met but, now that he realized the awkwardness had not occurred, John also realized that the expectation had been based on things he had read and heard about the meetings of other parents and their children. Sitting beside his father in the Rolls limousine at twenty, John realized he felt exactly the way he used to feel at ten when he sat beside his father in the Deucalion Ford pickup truck: not quite believing the man beside him was real or was really his father.

"In over back there, that's Woolloomoolloo," Sennacherib Sayer said. "The nearest thing Sydney has to a slum area. The more exclusive residential areas are on higher ground, as they usually are in most cities, especially if the cities are on the sea. The human animal has always liked to look out on water, and has always been willing to pay for the privilege. This section, in which we live, is called Point Piper, and for the privilege of looking out on the old Coat Hanger and the water it spans, I must confess I paid a good deal more than I intended when we first arrived here. But it's a nice house, we think, and I hope you agree."

"Yes," John said. "It's very nice."

It seemed a curious word for the architectural oddity toward which the Rolls was carrying them along a carefully raked gravel driveway. The house, which sat on a low hill surrounded by complicated gardens, reminded him of two match boxes, one somewhat smaller than the other, that had been joined together. The larger section, on the left, seemed more delicate and fussy. When the car stopped, and Dwight came around to open the door, John saw why: the smaller section of the house was a replica of the old Main House at Deucalion. John was not surprised, as he walked with his fa-

ther toward the figure on the lawn, by the delicately pleasant
stab of recognition that raced through him.

"Dinah," Sennacherib Sayer said, "here he is, at last."

"Yes," she said, looking up into John's face. "He's—" She
paused and, with the back of her hand, as she tipped her
head to one side, she brushed the long brown hair from her
forehead in a gesture that had identified her, years ago, in
John's mind with the weeping willows on the bank of Aaron's
Brook back of the Children's Guild building. Her whole
body, as slender and reedy as when he had first known her as
a young bride of seventeen, seemed to sway with the gesture,
as though she had been moved by a gentle breeze. "He's
taller and heavier," Sennacherib Sayer's second wife said.
"But he's the same."

"So are you," John said. Then he felt his face grow hot. "I
don't mean that you're taller or heavier. I mean—"

Sennacherib Sayer laughed and said, "We know what you
mean, don't we, Dinah?"

"Yes, I think so," she said. But she did not laugh. A faint,
troubled look seemed to hover around her green eyes, like a
bee buzzing around but never actually touching a flower. And
then, like the bee darting off to hunt elsewhere, the troubled
look vanished. She did laugh, very gently. "He means I'm ten
years older," she said. "And of course I am."

"Well, you don't look it," John said. Her hand came up
again. Her body moved in the delicately swaying motion as
she brushed the hair from her forehead with the back of her
hand. And the thing he had forgotten for ten years came up
and hit him. "I mean nothing seems to have changed much,"
John said awkwardly. "Except the background."

"Well, let's get you upstairs to your room where you can
wash and get into something more comfortable than that,"
his father said, "and then we'll fit you into the background,
too."

"If you'll do that," she said to John's father, "I'll see about
lunch."

She went into the house. John's father said, "We've put
you in what we call the Old Part. That's this." He waved toward the stone section of the house. "It's what was on the
place when we bought it, and so it has all the remodeled
bathrooms and conveniences, because we did that first. This
part—" He waved toward the salt box cottage, "—came later.
I don't much care where I work, and there's a perfectly good
study in the Old Part that does me fine. But Dinah is dif-

ferent. Or perhaps I should say writing poetry is different from writing memoirs. So we built this wing as a sort of place for Dinah to work in. Not that it's used *only* for that. It has two bedrooms and a kitchen in addition to the central room Dinah works in, so we also use it as a guest house, but I thought you'd be more comfortable in the Old Part. It's more American."

It was, and it wasn't. Like the city itself, the house seemed to be a cross between things familiar and things foreign. The bathroom, for example, was equipped with the sort of fixtures John had lived with for ten years at Norcross and Harvard. But the bathtub was pink and, in order to get into it, John had to climb four elaborately decorated pink marble steps.

"That's because Australian plumbing is a comparatively new trade," Sennacherib Sayer said in the drawing room a half-hour later when John mentioned his reaction. "They're still too pleased with it to keep it strictly functional." He held up a crystal decanter. "By the way, I've taken to drink in my declining years. Will you have something with us?"

"He makes it sound so evil," his wife said with a smile. "Actually, it's doctor's orders. He prescribed a nip before lunch, and another before dinner, and I must say your father hasn't found the medicine too difficult to take, have you?"

"On the contrary," John's father said. "It's made me wonder whether my years as a teetotaler were not misspent. I usually take mine in the form of a gimlet. What would you like?"

"What's a gimlet?" John said.

"Gin with a dash of lime and a splash of water."

"Ike would approve of that," John said. "Yes, thank you, I'll have one."

His father's wife said, "Oh, I don't recall that Ike knew about gimlets."

"I don't think he does," John said. "But he knows all about gin. Four years ago, when I first went up to Cambridge, he told me I'd probably be running into a lot of drinking, so I might as well learn how to do it, and he recommended I bone up on gin and bitters."

"What an odd drink for Ike to favor," she said.

"Not after he explained it," John said. "He said it was better to learn to like gin than whiskey because gin gave you more alcohol for your money. And while gin was admittedly bad for you, bitters were a stomachic, so you came out about even."

His father and his father's wife laughed. John wondered when they would stop walking around each other, with light conversation about plumbing and drinks, and get down to the serious business of the visit. They did not get down to it at lunch, which was served by Dwight, now wearing a black alpaca coat and white cotton gloves.

"I always nap after lunch," Sennacherib Sayer said when they were having coffee. "Would you like to rest, too? Or perhaps, if you're not tired you might like a bit of sight-seeing with Dinah?"

"I'd like that very much," John said. He turned to his father's wife. "That is, if—if—" He paused, embarrassed by the realization that he did not know what to call her. He got out of it by saying, "If *you're* not tired, that is?"

"Not a bit," she said. "I like to get out for some fresh air after lunch."

They got out in a bright red Humber roadster which she handled with an easy dexterity that took John by surprise. His memories of her were all rooted in Deucalion, where she had been the shy, awkward wife of the head of the Children's Guild. A girl not much older than John himself who took long, lonely walks during which, she said, she composed poetry. The only motor transport at Deucalion had been Ike's aged pickup truck. It was difficult enough to associate Mrs. Tristram with that vehicle, even though John remembered being in it with Ike on the day they pulled up beside the schoolmaster's wife on the Wellesville Road and the handyman offered her a lift. Now she was his father's wife, and somehow that difficult fact was made more difficult for John by the way she handled the little red Humber. It was as though his own mother, whose quiet, composed housewifely presence still lived in his memory as the yardstick of beauty and the meaning of love, had appeared before him dressed like Amelia Earhart, ready for a take off.

"You're wondering, of course, why we came to Australia."

John looked down at the slender girl on the seat beside him.

"Yes," he said.

It was only one of the things about which he was wondering.

"It seemed wise to get out of the country and then, two years later, out of England," she said. "You were too young to remember all the fuss in the press. Or perhaps that's not quite right. I'm sure you do remember. I mean that you were too young to understand the impact of the fuss. You were only ten."

"You were only seventeen," John said.

She nodded at the windshield.

"Yes, but the difference at that age is enormous." She nodded down toward the harbor. "I suppose your father told you all about the bridge."

"The old Coat Hanger," John said.

"It's so ugly, and yet it always moves me," she said. "I don't know why. It's sad, I suppose. Like an ugly little girl. She breaks your heart because you know what's in store for her when she grows up into a world where ugly girls get very few of the prizes. I wrote a poem about the bridge when we first came here. That was eight years ago."

"I'd like to read it," John said.

"Oh, it's not finished," she said. "Do you really want to sightsee?"

"What do you want to do?"

"I'd like to drive out into the country for a bit."

"So would I."

She gave him a short, glancing look. It seemed to emerge from beneath the hand with which she made the curious little swaying gesture that never failed to move him.

"Do you hate him?" she said.

"Who?"

"Your father."

"Of course not."

"Well, he worries about it," she said. "He's worried about it for ten years."

"You can't hate a statue," John said.

Again she gave him that short, glancing look.

"You do hate him," she said.

"No," John said. "What it is, it's that I don't connect with him. When I was a kid I was told he was a great man, and I believed it. I was proud of being the son of a great man. But I had no feeling for him as a human being. The way I had feeling for my mother. When he wanted me to come away with him ten years ago, I couldn't do it. Where I was, where my mother had been, where Ike Ten Eyck still was, that was my place. It was home. I wanted to keep on staying there. Going away with my father scared me. It would have been like going away with a statue. It was a nice statue. Smiled, held my hand, gave me spending money, all that. But still a statue. I preferred to stay where I knew where I was, with Ike. All these years, at Norcross, at Harvard, Ike and Wellesville, they were home. They were family. Far away, at the other side of the world, there was a statue. A nice statue. Sent me letters. Paid my tuition. Gave Ike money to feed me, buy me clothes, give me spending money. All that. But still a statue. My mother, a hundred times a day, her face, her name, just the *word* mother, they cross my mind. And the way I felt about her then, that feeling is still there. My father? It's still the way it always was. No feeling at all, yes or no, for or against, pro or con. I'm glad he's happy. I'm glad he's well. But it's the way I'd be glad about anybody I'd met or heard about. I'd have no reason *not* to be glad they're happy and in good health. Feeling that way, or I guess *not* feeling is more accurate, how can I hate him?"

"Then why did you come all the way out here?"

"I don't know."

"You *must* know," she said.

John turned again on the seat of the speeding roadster to look down on her. My God, he thought, she *can't* be twenty-seven. She looked like a classmate of the Radcliffe girl who had caused him all those restless nights on the *Lurline* until she left the ship at Honolulu.

"You sound as though *you* want to know," he said.

"Yes," she said. The single syllable emerged with a naked directness that surprised and embarrassed him. It reminded him, he couldn't imagine why, of a letter an English prof had read aloud to his class at Harvard. It was a letter Anne Boleyn had written to Henry VIII the night before she was beheaded. The letter had been a plea for mercy.

"Partly I came because Ike said it was right," he said. "Partly it's because I've had the feeling seeing my father again would lay the thing away. The past. What happened. It would finish it off. Like cleaning out the icebox before you go on a trip. So there won't be anything to spoil. So you can start off clean and fresh when you come home. Okay, statue. No hard feelings. You keep smiling down on the people in the park. I'll go try to be a whatever it is people try to be who don't yet know what they want to be. I don't know if I'm making any sense. But I do know there's no hate in it."

She shook her head, beeped the horn, and swung the roadster around a large black car which unexpectedly lunged toward them. She swung clear without effort or comment and stepped on the gas.

"My God," John said. "Are they drunk?"

"Probably," she said. "It's Sunday. No, the thing about hate is that often you don't know you're feeling it. Love, too, I suppose. But not knowing you're feeling it doesn't stop the danger or the damage. All that fuss ten years ago. The death of two people. The end of the colony. The shattering of all your father's hopes." She shook her head. "When the disaster came, I had nowhere to turn, and nobody to turn to. Your father was in a somewhat similar state, except not financially, of course. His first thought was Europe, but the only country he likes is England. My family were in Kent. His had come from Wales and there were surviving relatives. Aside from his fame, the fact that the disaster had occurred just as he had been appointed to the Supreme Court and the appointment was withdrawn, all that made the fuss even worse. The papers in England were full of it. Two years after we got there, the thought of coming out here struck him, and we both knew it was right. There had been some things in the Australian papers, of course. Months after we arrived, I went to the public library and checked the files. But it had not been much, and by the time we got here, it had all been forgotten. The name Sennacherib Sayer meant nothing in Australia."

"How about now?" John said.

She shook her head.

"Not a thing. The things he did, his trust-busting days, his work for President Wilson, the peace treaty, all that was America and Europe, you see. Very little of it penetrated here. I gather from Ike's letters, he's very bitter about it, that the name Sennacherib Sayer has been completely forgotten in America."

"Pretty much," John said.

"Well, then," she said. "How much more understandable, isn't it, that he should be forgotten here where he was never really known."

"Does he mind?"

"Not a bit."

"You're just saying that, aren't you?"

She shook her head again.

"No," she said. "You don't know him, of course."

"God knows that's true."

"I know him," she said. "Completely. I think what happened ten years ago came at just the right time. He was ready to ring down the curtain, as it were, even though he may not have known it, and he most certainly would have chosen some other means to do it, if he'd had the choice. We live a very quiet life here. We have absolutely no friends and don't want any. It's truly seclusion, which is not always possible, of course. But he's wealthy enough to be able to arrange it. We do a great deal of talking, and over the years much has become clear. The drives of his younger years, the lust for fame, the championship of the underdog, all that, he feels, was a desire to pay back the sort of people who had exploited and, he believes, killed his father. The paying-back process, however, is a rather sterile activity. He feels that at Deucalion, toward the end, he was beginning to go dry. The satisfactions of revenge are short. His life was beginning to feel empty and wasted. He brooded a lot about it. Perhaps that's what made him seem so distant to a small boy. A statue. Although I must say he didn't seem that way to me. He seemed to sense at once that I was troubled and unhappy. He helped me enormously. Life is not *supposed* to be easy, he says. When it is, if you do achieve happiness, it's a pleasant dividend. But most people don't achieve it, and it's most people who make the world tick. That's why, he says, one's primary job is to work at making oneself fit to do one's share of the ticking, and never mind fripperies like happiness. When we came here, he felt he had done his share of the ticking. Not, mind you, because he didn't want to do any more. No. What came clear after a while out here was that he was no longer capable of doing good work. He'd worn it out. I remember, when I was a little girl in Kent, we had a sick dog, and he disappeared one day. I was shattered, but my father said not to worry. The sick dog, he said, crawls off by instinct to eat grass. I think that's what your father did when he came here. He sensed he was sick. He crawled off to eat grass, and it's made him well. He's happy."

"Are you?"

"Very."

The crisply asked question, and the even crisper answer, seemed to hang between them, as though they were both surprised that they had been capable of uttering the words without hesitation or surrounding them with the cotton batting of apology.

"Doing what?" John said.

"He has his memoirs," she said. "I have my poetry."

"Ten years of memoirs," John said. "Napoleon didn't take that long."

"Napoleon's problem was different. So were his motives, as you must surely know."

"Will they ever be finished? My father's memoirs? Will they ever be published?"

The glancing look flung up at John a moment of surprise that made him feel ashamed, as though he had said something she had assumed he was too bright to have asked.

"Of course not," she said.

"He's told you that?"

"Certainly not," she said. "But I know what he's doing, and he knows I know it."

"What's he doing?"

"What all people do who write memoirs," she said. "Reliving the part of his life that mattered. Making it come out on paper the way it should have come out in real life. The way he knows now, now that it's too late, it should have been lived. Only a rich man has the time to do that. Only a great man knows, as he's doing it, precisely what he *is* doing. Your father happens to be both."

"I'm going to say something you may think is smart alecky or even insulting," John said. "It's not intended that way. I really mean it. May I?"

"Of course."

"It's just beginning to dawn on me that, in addition to being a very beautiful girl, you may very well be a damn smart one."

"At the moment I also happen to be a thirsty one," she said. "Would you shout me a spot?"

"I beg your pardon?"

She laughed and said, "Buy me a drink."

He laughed with her. "I'll buy you two, if you'll let me drink the second."

"Done."

She pulled the car off the road into what looked like a corral in a Western film. It was jammed with vehicles parked without plan or regard for any other car. Making their way through the tangled mess, toward a low building over the door of which a neon sign kept winking on and off the word "Lithgow's," John took her arm. It was like taking the handle of a baseball bat. Her arm was as thin as his wrist. Inside the door a tall, heavy man with a shallow but toothy smile said, "Sign the book, please."

It lay, like the Bible in the assembly hall at Norcross, on a lectern in front of a wooden rail. The rail separated the area just inside the door from the functional part of the tavern, which was as alive as an anthill. Every table was crowded with drinkers, most of them wearing their overcoats and hats. The tobacco smoke hung thick, like steam in a locker room shower. The voices had a desperate urgency, as though the speakers were not conversing with friends across a convivial glass, but telephoning for reservations on the last train about to leave a doomed city.

"What's the book?" John said.

"A bit of legal nonsense," she said. "By law, drinks are not allowed to be served on Sunday except to travelers whose journeys take them at least thirty miles. Before you can get your drink, therefore, you must sign the book, and write next to your name the point of your departure and your destination. Needless to say, all of it is invented, but neither the government nor the owner of the pub cares, so long as the spaces are filled in. Here, write." John took the pencil dangling from the lectern at the end of a piece of string. "Your father and I always write we're on our way from Cessnock."

"What's good enough for my father is good enough for me," John said. "How do you spell it?"

She told him and he wrote it and she said, "And we're on our way to Edesboro."

"Oh, you, gee, aitch?"

"No," she said. "Just bee, oh, are, oh. And the name we always use is Mr. and Mrs. Nicholas Mancini."

After he had written all that, and the man with the toothy smile had passed them through the gate in the wooden rail, and a waiter had found them a table for two and gone off to get their gimlets, John said, "You said always. Do you two go racing around the country like this every Sunday?"

"Not every Sunday," she said. "But when we do, it's usually in the morning. And when it gets on for lunch, we stop at one of these places for the nip prescribed by Dr. Ryan. Is there anything wrong with my hair?"

"No, no. I'm sorry. I was thinking, not staring. Your hair is fine."

"Thinking about what?"

"Your poetry," John said. "You said my father has his memoirs and you have your poetry. I'd like to read some of it."

"None of it is finished."

He said, "None of it?" She shook her head. He said, "I don't understand. You've been writing poetry for a long time.

At least ten years, probably longer. I remember that day my father was appointed to the Supreme Court? Ike and I were driving down to Wellesville to meet him at the train? We met you walking near Stonecraft Farm? And you said you were composing an ode to celebrate the good news."

"That's not finished, either."

She made the gentle, swaying motion. It carried her several inches away from the table, far enough to allow the waiter to set down their drinks in comfort. When he disappeared into the mixture of tobacco smoke and voices, John said, "Aren't you a little young to be reliving the part of your life that mattered?"

"Not really," she said. "It isn't the number of years. It's how far you've traveled in the time you've had. You can't fake that, the way you fake the distance you've traveled to sign the book out there so you can get a drink on Sunday. Your father was fifty-eight when he found out. I'm twenty-seven, but I found out long ago."

"Found out what?"

"I'll never have a child."

"Oh. I'm sorry."

"Yes, it *is* a matter for sorrow. For most people, that is. I thought so, too, for a long time. It was at the root of the trouble between me and Francis. He didn't want any, you see. Then, when your father and I came out here, and we both wanted one, the doctor said no. It's something about the way I'm put together inside. It would kill me, he said, and so did all the other doctors, and for quite a while I felt sorry for myself. Then I did what most human beings do when they find themselves forced to live cheek by jowl with a cloud."

"What's that?"

"I found the silver lining." She paused, took a sip of her drink, then said, "Or you might say I invented it. Anyway, I've got it."

"Got what?"

"My poetry. Whatever value it's ultimately going to have, it will have it because of my sorrow." She smiled. "Do I look sorrowful?"

"Not very."

"That's because you're here."

"Oh, sure. Just a bundle of fun and games. So far all I've done is get off a ship, eat a lunch, and sit in a car."

"You could do something else."

"Such as?"

"You could go to law school."

"That would cure your sorrow?"

She laughed and took another sip.

"Heaven forbid. That would be the end of my poetry. No, I don't mean me. I mean your father. When I asked you in the car if you hate him, it was because he thinks that's at the bottom of your refusing to go to law school."

"Couldn't I go to law school even if I did hate him, which I don't?"

"Yes, of course, but what troubles him is that he knows you wouldn't."

"He could have saved me a trip across the Pacific Ocean if he'd explained that in the letters we've been writing to each other for eighteen months on this particular subject."

"How could he?" she said. "Don't you see, he feels you were made for the law. He's talked about it many times. You say he was a statue to you when you were a boy. Perhaps. But he was a remarkably observant statue. He's told me endless anecdotes, things you did and said under all sorts of circumstances from the time you were an infant. Things that add up to his conviction you have a brilliant career ahead of you at the bar. But because *he's* a lawyer, or was, you refuse to enter the same profession. The refusal makes no sense, he feels, unless you hate him, and it's the hatred that makes him feel guilty."

"You're asking me to go to law school, you want me to enter a profession to which I'll have to devote my whole life, just so my father should stop feeling guilty about something that doesn't exist?"

The hand, coming up to brush the hair from her forehead, again seemed to fling at him a flicker of surprise.

"Oh, no," she said. "No, no. I want—" She paused. The delicate, shallow hollows below the cheekbones filled with a dark flush, as though she were embarrassed by the realization that the denial, however worded, could not help sounding like a lie. "All I want," she said with a smile, "is that you be nice to him tonight at the party."

This proved to be a mistake. In his effort to comply, John had a second gimlet before they went in to dinner. It made him feel so good that he urged a second on his father. Sennacherib Sayer hesitated, but his wife said she saw no harm in it.

"After all, it's a celebration," she said. "One's twenty only once in a lifetime. I'll have another with you."

Somehow the second led to a third. John didn't quite know how. He did know, however, when they sat down at the candle-lit table, that he was drunk. It did not occur to him, until Dwight had served the champagne and his father rose to propose a toast, that Sennacherib Sayer was also drunk.

"Once, ten years ago, on a similar occasion," he said, "I had an opportunity to say a few words that seem singularly appropriate now."

The tall figure swayed slightly. Sennacherib Sayer put his hand on the cloth to steady himself. His wife moved her chair back.

"Dwight!" she said sharply. But the big man was ahead of her. His white-gloved hand was under Sennacherib Sayer's elbow before she could stand up. When she did, she said pleasantly, but with a look of terror in her eyes, "Why don't you sit down, dear?"

"To say what I am about to say?" Sennacherib Sayer said. "Nonsense." The white-haired head moved slightly. "I'm quite all right, Dwight, thank you. Go fetch the cake."

The butler-chauffeur glanced at Sennacherib Sayer's wife. She nodded.

"Yes, sir," Dwight said, and left the dining room.

"You may sit, my dear," Sennacherib Sayer said to his wife. She did. But John could still see the look of terror in her eyes as his father continued. "On that other occasion," he said, "I was addressing not merely, as now, my wife and son. I was addressing a group of friends and neighbors who had come to congratulate me. A great honor had that day been conferred upon me. As I faced my friends and neighbors, I said that the pattern of comment a man makes on an occasion like this has been laid down by other and better men, on other and greater occasions. If I seemed to slight that pattern now, I told them, it was not because of disrespect for tradition. It was because I could not believe any man before me had ever been granted the gift of being able to say what I was about to say then."

Again the tall, white-haired figure swayed. But this time Sennacherib Sayer's hand was resting firmly on the cloth. The only result of the interruption, it seemed to John, was that his own head started to clear.

"What I said then, ten years ago, is equally true today," Sennacherib Sayer said. "The circumstances are different, true. We are no longer at Deucalion, among the friends who had cast their lot with me in an effort to transform a corner of God's earth into something worthy of Him. No. We are in a foreign land at the other side of the world. But I am today, as I was then, at the side of the woman I love. And it is a day, as it was then, that we have set aside as a time of joy and celebration because it is my son's birthday."

The hinges of the swinging door from the kitchen groaned softly. Dwight came backing into the room, carrying on a silver tray a pink and white birthday cake with lighted candles. He brought it across the room and set it in front of John.

"Dinah," Sennacherib Sayer said with a smile, "as Peter Midden, the head of our Actors' Guild used to say at a moment like this, I think this is your cue."

Smiling, so that the fear in her eyes seemed to fade, she stood up, holding her champagne glass. She said to John, *"Not a drop of sugar. Egg white, strawberry syrup for coloring, and whole wheat flour."*

John laughed. Without effort or even thought, Mrs. Loring's next words came back to him. He said, *"I put two extra candles to grow on. One for John, and one for Deucalion."*

Sennacherib Sayer joined the laughter and said, "Much has changed but our memories, thank God, remain green." A few drops of champagne slopped over the side of his glass as he raised it higher and said to John, "Ready?" John nodded. As he had said ten years ago, John's father now said, "Blow!"

Exactly as he had done ten years ago, John pulled in his breath, held it while his father and his father's wife smiled encouragement, then hurled it out with all his strength. Again, as had happened ten years ago, a curious thing happened now. The blast reduced the tiny flames to a small mass of writhing smoke. But the blast seemed to flow on, across the cake, down the table, and catch Sennacherib Sayer like the tongue of a storm catching an unfastened shutter. John saw his father whip sideways, as though one of his feet had been kicked out from under him. He clutched at the air, then crashed forward onto the table.

"Dwight!" his wife screamed. That was the last word John heard her speak until, perhaps twenty minutes later, she came back downstairs and joined him in the library. "He's all right," she said. "Sound asleep and no damage done, except perhaps for a bit of a head in the morning." She giggled. "Poor dear, he's as drunk as a coot." The giggle simmered down to a rueful smile. She said, "Sorry to spoil your party, but it's the drink did it, you see. He's not used to taking more than his medicinal nip."

"It's my fault," John said. "I never should have asked him to have that second gimlet."

"Nonsense," she said. "It's a party, or rather it was, and we were all feeling fine. I still do, rather, in spite of the interruption. You?"

"I must say I feel pretty good," John said. "Now that I know he's okay."

"Perfectly okay," she said. "I wish there was something I could do to make it up to you."

"There is," John said.

"What's that?"

"I'd like to hear some of your poetry."

She brushed the hair from her forehead with that swaying movement of her body.

"You don't really, do you?" she said. "You haven't even opened your presents yet."

"It's the only present I really want," John said.

She hesitated. She glanced at the door as though worried about eavesdroppers, then said, "Well, if you're really serious—"

"I am," John said.

"In that case," she said, "come along."

"Where?"

"My workroom," she said. "I couldn't possibly read it anywhere else. You see, as I told you, none of it is finished."

He followed her out into the hall, and through an arch that led to the Deucalion wing of the house. Stepping into the large, central room, John had a feeling that he had been here before. The fact that he couldn't possibly have been did not change the feeling.

"Sit here," she said. She touched the back of a heavy chair near the fireplace. John sat down. She said, "What would you like to hear?"

"The poem you were working on that day my father was appointed to the Supreme Court. Ike and I were driving down to Wellesville to pick him up at the train? We ran into you on the road? You said you were—"

"Yes, I remember," she said. "I'm afraid it didn't come out very well. In addition to not being finished, I mean. Wouldn't you rather hear something else?"

"Only if you don't want to read me that one."

"It's not a question of wanting," she said. "It's simply that I don't think it's very good."

"I don't care about that," John said. "I just want to hear it."

"All right," she said.

She went to a table against the far wall and pulled out a drawer. She shuffled through some papers. Watching her, John realized this was the first time he had ever looked at her from the rear. A moment later he realized something else: she was wearing black velvet slacks. A moment after that he was wondering why it did not shock him to realize he was certain he could, while the tips of his fingers touched, encase both her buttocks in his cupped palms. Still wondering about that, he tried to remember if she had worn the slacks at cocktails and in the dining room, but he couldn't. It seemed to him she had been wearing something pink when Dwight had brought in the cake. But that could have been an impression created by the icing. Then she turned with a sheet of paper, and for the first time he saw she was wearing a sweater. He crossed his legs to hide what was suddenly happening to him.

"You're sure you want to hear this?" she said.

"Positive," he said.

"All right," she said. "But do remember it's not finished."

"I'll remember," he said.

She dropped into the chair at the other side of the fireplace. She bounced around for a few moments, until she had herself adjusted comfortably. When her body stopped moving, she was sitting on her crossed legs, as though posing for an illustration in a book of yoga exercises, with a sheet of paper resting on her calves. Had she changed into the slacks and cardigan when she had gone upstairs with Dwight to put John's drunken father to bed?

"Ready?" she said.

"Ready," John said.

"Remember him when you are gone away," she read, and that was the last of the poem John remembered. He could hear her voice rolling out the words, gently, with a rhythm that seemed to match the beating of his heart. But the words made no sense to him. Watching the nipples move up and down with her breathing under the red wool, he felt himself close to an answer he knew he must have been seeking for a long time. John did not realize he had found it until her voice stopped and then, not quite terrified, but not unafraid either, she said, "What are you doing?"

"Returning something," he said.

She reached out and took the Georgian silver grape scissors. He had been carrying them in his pocket ever since he had sailed from San Francisco.

"Why, what—?" she started to say, then stopped. She snipped at the air with the scissors three or four times, then said, "But I gave this to you on your birthday ten years ago. It was a present."

"I know," John said. "Now I want to give it back to you."

As he dropped to his knees beside her, she said in a frightened voice, "No, don't, please!" But he could not stop. He knew at last not only why he had urged the second gimlet on his father, but also why he had come to Australia.

7

FIFTEEN YEARS LATER, in his New York apartment, discussing with his wife the run-through of Miss Gwen Quill's musical play from which they had just come home, John was puzzled by his inability to answer Ellie's question about why he had left Australia so suddenly.

"It wasn't really sudden," John said. "Booking a return passage to San Francisco, buying some souvenirs for Ike, packing, and so on, all that took a few days."

"Well, that's sudden enough," Ellie said. "Considering that you had gone out there in June, right after graduation from Harvard, to spend the summer with your father."

"That wasn't really the purpose," John said. "Spending the summer, the holiday aspect of the visit, that was an incidental. What I'd really gone out there for, the actual purpose of the visit was to decide whether or not I was going to enter law school in the fall. Once it was decided the night of my birthday party, that, yes, I was going to be a lawyer, it became important for me to get back to America as fast as possible. I had to set the ball in motion for getting into Harvard Law School. You see, most men who were going, they'd applied months and months before. Getting in for the fall semester, I mean *deciding* as late as June to try for the fall semester, well, it posed certain problems. My father happened to know the dean personally. Or anyway, he *had* known him back in the days when the name Sennacherib Sayer meant quite a lot in American legal circles. The morning after my birthday party he cabled the dean at Cambridge, explaining that family circumstances had prevented my applying earlier, but would he, the dean, would he use his good offices and so on and so on. Then I went off to Cook's to find out about ships to San Francisco. Luckily, the *Lurline* was going back a week later, and even more luckily, they had some space, so I booked passage. A week after I arrived in Sydney, I left Australia, and that was the last time I ever saw either my father or his second wife."

Ellie looked thoughtful for several moments, then said, "You know what's funny about all this?"

"My somehow giving you the impression all these years that my father spent the last ten years of his life in England rather than most of it in Australia?"

"No," Ellie said. "If I had a better memory, or if I'd been a better student, I'm sure I could now remember some helpful mumbo-jumbo from my psychology courses at Radcliffe to explain that. I don't know. Nor do I think that matters. What I mean is that, yes, I'm surprised to learn it was Australia rather than England. But I'm not bothered. What does bother me is that your father never made an attempt to come back to America. If in 1939 the scandal was as completely forgotten by the public as you say, I would think the desire to come back to his native land, if only for a visit, would have been almost irresistible."

"Not if you look at the circumstances," John said. "I left Sydney in June. In September the war broke out in Europe. My father's letters gave some hint of the hysteria down there. The Australians expected the Japs to attack and invade at any moment. The whole country was on a war footing at once. I mean at the time when I was peacefully beginning to work my way through *Williston on Contracts* in Cambridge, my father was writing from Australia that they were digging bomb shelters, and working out food rationing, and forcing aliens like himself to register."

"All the more reason to come home," Ellie said. "After all, America didn't get into the war until more than two years later."

"Yes, but that's hindsight," John said. "The Australians didn't know then that we here in America still had more than two years of peace ahead of us. Frankly, it never occurred to me that I'd have enough time almost to complete my work for a law degree at Cambridge before Uncle Sam would send me those Greetings. Down there in Australia it must have seemed that the whole world, including America, would be involved at once. Anyway, that's pretty much what my father's letters said, and being the sort of man he was, he felt it would be dishonorable to desert the country that had sheltered him for eight years. On top of all that, there was his wife's health."

"I've never heard you mention anything about her health," Ellie said. "I always assumed she was a blooming number of twenty-six, or was it seven?"

"Almost twenty-seven, as I recall," John said. "Oh, yes, she was healthy enough. But she'd been warned about not having children, as I told you, and while I certainly got the impression while I was there that she and my father took the warning seriously, they apparently decided later to take a chance. I remember it was one of those horrible, cold, snowy, nasty March days in Cambridge when I got the word from Ike. She'd miscarried at a very late point in the pregnancy. Either the doctors couldn't do anything, or she refused to let them. That part of it has never been clear. Or why, knowing her condition, the doctors even allowed her to carry the baby that long. They could have done something, it seems to me. Caesarian, or, I don't know, *something*. But they didn't, and she and the baby died, and a month later Ike got the second cable. They say people don't die of broken hearts. Well, Ike and I know different, and he's a tough old buzzard."

"He must have loved her very much," Ellie said. "Your father."

"Yes," John said. "He loved her more than he ever loved my mother."

Surprised, Ellie said, "How do you know that?"

"Know what?" John said.

"What you just said," Ellie said. "That your father loved that girl, Dinah Tristram, that he loved her more than he loved your mother?"

"Did I say that?" John said.

"Of course you said it," Ellie said. "What's the matter with you?"

"Nothing," John said. "If I said it, then it's true."

The phone rang. Ellie reached across, picked it up, and said, "Hello? Oh, yes, one moment, Mr. Howe." She held out the phone to John. "For you, and he sounds upset."

"After what we saw on the stage of the Carnegie Theatre this afternoon, he should be," John said. He took the phone and said, "Hello, Vinnie."

"Listen, fella," Vincent Howe said. There was no doubt that he was upset. The slant of country bumpkin joviality had vanished from his voice. His words were coming out standing straight up, spikey with anger. "We're waiting here for you. This meeting at Gwen Quill's. You said a little while ago—"

"I said I'd come over if I felt I had something to contribute to the meeting," John said. "I haven't."

"But—but—" Mr. Howe's voice stopped. He was clearly pulling himself together. "Look, fella, this show is as much yours as ours. You've got just as much to lose as we have."

"I don't agree," John said.

"What? What's that, fella?"

"I have more to lose than you have," John said.

"The hell you have." The anger in Mr. Howe's voice had a slightly unreal quality. His manner and appearance were those of a man totally incapable of anger. "You haven't put a God damn cent into this show. All you've done is draw some fat fees as the lawyer for the project. Now we're in trouble, we're going up to New Haven tomorrow, we open on Monday, the least you can do is give a little help."

"You're wrong," John said. "The least I can do, or the least anybody can do, will not help at all. What I saw this afternoon on the stage of the Carnegie Theatre is absolutely hopeless. As to what I've got to lose, it's a hell of a lot more, Mr. Howe, than your investors' money."

"You mind I ask what's that, please?"

"The memory of my father," John said. "His reputation. What Miss Quill has written, and what you have produced, in spite of some good things in the first act, all it can do is make my father's memory a shameful joke. I feel now it was a mistake for me to give you permission to go ahead. If you feel my firm has not earned the fees you have paid us thus far as lawyers for the project, say so now, and I will put a check in the mails to you tomorrow morning when I get to the office."

There was silence at the other end of the phone. It lasted several moments. Then Mr. Vincent Howe said, "Johnny?"

"I asked you never to call me that."

"Sorry. I meant John. Then you're not coming to this meeting?"

"Absolutely not."

"How about New Haven? You going up with the company tomorrow?"

"No," John said, "I am not."

"How about the opening Monday night?" Vincent Howe said. "Will you be there?"

"No," John said, "I will not."

The fact that he wasn't seemed to bother nobody but Ellie.

"Your play is opening in New Haven tonight," she said on Monday. "I don't see—see, *hell!* John, it is driving me crazy! —how you can sit here in New York and not go up there to look at it?"

"What would be the point?" John said. "What people in New Haven will see tonight is what you and I saw five days ago at the Carnegie Theatre. Except that in the first act the actors will be wearing nineteen-twenty-nine-style clothes instead of sweatshirts, ditto nineteen thirty-nine in the second act, and the whole thing will be done with scenery. Surely I don't have to tell a girl as smart as you are that neither the clothes nor the scenery are going to change the words the characters speak. You heard them. Maybe you honestly believe you would like to hear them again, but—"

"John, I *do*," she said. "I honestly do. Even though I agree with your opinion of the play, I honestly—would—like—to —see—it—again—under—the—conditions—that—will—prevail—in—New—Haven—tonight. Don't you see? I really and truly and honestly *would*. That's the *point*."

"No, it's not," John said. "It may be the point for *you*. But not for me, Ellie. You're not emotionally involved. I am. This God damn piece of crap Miss Gwen Quill had cooked up happens to be about my father. It's a piece of my life, Ellie. Sitting through that run-through, the second act, it was absolute agony. I wanted to get up and run. I thought I was going to be *sick*."

"Good God," Ellie said. "The way you sound—I mean I didn't realize that you felt *that* way about it."

"Well, I do."

"Do or did?"

"What?" John said.

"You say you feel that way about it now," Ellie said. "But did you feel that way about it five days ago, when you were watching it?"

"I suppose so. How could I not? I mean why do you ask?"

"Because it's possible something has happened to you unconsciously since the run-through five days ago."

"Oh, for God's sake, Ellie."

"Okay, but one thing I've learned, John, is that a lot of things happen to a person, and we all do a lot of things,

things that you are totally unaware *have* happened to you or that you have done."

"Just a moment, young woman," John said. "Let's just stop right here for a moment. Are you trying to tell me I could break a leg and not know it?"

"Oh, well, break a *leg.*"

"Are you trying to tell me I could rob a bank and not know I did it?"

"Look, John, if you're going to turn this into a cross examination, I'm going to have to call one of your partners and retain him as attorney for the defense."

"Ellie, darling, you have just made a statement, and I feel I must ask you what your statement means. If I accept your premise that the unconscious reacts and also acts independently of the rest of the human brain, I want to know what I'm accepting."

"I honestly don't know if a limb could break without your knowledge, without your knowing it in your conscious mind, I mean," Ellie said. "I honestly don't know if you could walk into the Chase Manhattan with a loaded gun and walk out with a briefcase full of twenty-dollar bills and be unaware in your conscious mind that you robbed a bank. Those are extremes."

"Extremes of what?" John said.

"Extremes of the sort of things we all have happen to us, and the sort of things we all do," Ellie said. "Example. I believe you can be bawled out by a traffic cop and be so ashamed of the things he calls you that your conscious mind will blot out the incident. So when you get home at night and I say what sort of day did you have, dear, you will have totally forgotten the incident with the traffic cop."

"How totally?" John said.

"As totally as forever," Ellie said. "Other example. I believe you could walk past a pushcart and, because the peddler's back is turned, steal an apple, then feel so guilty or ashamed of the theft that your conscious mind will block out the incident forever."

"What about the apple?"

"What?"

"The apple," John said. "My conscious mind has blocked out the act in which I was a crook. But here I am, holding an apple. How does my unconscious mind explain that apple to my conscious mind? Assuming they're on speaking terms, that is."

"They're not, dear," Ellie said. "That's the whole point. You'd look at that apple in your hand and believe you bought it. Or you'd be convinced it came to you in the mails as a Valentine's Day present from the United Apple Growers Association of Wisconsin. Now stop being so damned legal. Broken legs and banks, for heaven's sake. All I'm trying to say is five days ago, when I was sitting next to you in the theatre during that run-through, I knew you didn't like the second act. Today, five days later, when you explain to me why you refuse to go up to New Haven to see the opening, you make your reaction to the second act during that run-through, you make it sound like they were firing on Fort Sumter. Now, John Sayer, boy. I have known you lo these many years. If you had reacted to the second act at that run-through as though it was firing on Fort Sumter, I think I would have known it. You didn't react that way, John. Therefore I conclude something has happened to you between that run-through and today to convert what was no more than a reaction of disappointment to a reaction damned close to violence."

"You're quite right," John said. "What has happened to me is the realization that I am a horse's ass of rather large dimensions. When I met Mr. Arnold Zucker a year ago, every instinct told me—all right, call it *not* instinct, call it my unconscious—call it Fateful Freddie or Willie the Warner or just plain Elmer—call it whatever you damn please, but it warned me to avoid this whole thing. I did not heed the warning. I then met Mr. Vincent Howe. Again a warning, much louder, and again unheeded. Then I met the prize in this box of Crackerjack, Miss Gwen Quill, and I received a loud, screaming third warning. Did I listen? No, dear. Eyes open, pockets bulging with misgivings, I walked into the project. My intelligence told me there could be only one result of dealing with these three people. I gave my intelligence a good swift kick in the pants, told it to keep away from me, and went on to deal with these three people. A year later, five days ago, you accompanied me to a demonstration of the result. If what you're saying is that my unconscious has a sluggish liver, and it took the damn thing five days to make me realize how big a horse's ass I am, then I agree. But I'm not going to make myself a bigger horse's ass by going up to New Haven tonight. I *know* what's going to happen in New Haven tonight. If you don't believe me, Ellie dear, some time tomorrow, probably in the afternoon, you go over to that newsstand in Times Square, the one where they sell out-of-town newspapers, and you buy the New Haven papers, and read the reviews."

As he came into the apartment the following night, she said, "Boy, John, were you right. You want me to read them to you?"

"Certainly not," John said.

A strange tone came into Ellie's voice as she said, "You know, you're a funny one."

"Oh, I know," John said. "In my lecture tours across the country, I leave behind me a swathe of busted guts."

"I don't mean funny funny," Ellie said. "I mean odd funny."

"In what way?"

"I would never have suspected that the man I've lived with for the past ten years was capable of being so tough."

"Tough?" John said. *"Me?"*

"You, buster," Ellie said. "Yesterday, when you were explaining why you wouldn't go up to New Haven, I thought okay, I'll buy that. He's not me, watching a play. He's watching a play about his father. There's a difference. But *this?* Not even wanting to *hear* the reviews? I've got them right *here!* No effort involved. All you have to do is listen. That's being but *real* tough."

"I don't see why," John said.

"Because it's a matter of simple, ordinary, garden variety curiosity," Ellie said irritably. "Something *no* human being could resist. Or so I would have thought until I found one who could, and that one my husband yet."

"I'm sorry," John said. "I didn't mean to make you angry. If it will make you feel better to read them to me, go ahead."

"Don't be a dope," Ellie said. "How could it make anybody feel better to read obituaries like these? It's just that for a moment, there, I felt you were—"

Her voice stopped. John said, "You felt I was what?"

"Oh, the hell with it," Ellie said.

"No, please," John said. "Tell me."

Another pause, then, "For a moment I thought I was talking to a stranger." Ellie laughed and said, "Must be the effect of reading these things. They all advise the management to close the show right now and not try to bring it into New York."

"They won't," John said.

"Well, they say you can never be sure of anything in the theatre."

"This is the exception," John said. "If they don't have enough sense to close it out of town, I'll close it for them. I may not have had the brains to listen to my unconscious screaming warnings at me to stay out of this little pogrom," John said. "But I had the brains to get myself a good agent. As you know, Mr. Arnold Zucker put a clause in my contract that gives me the right to close the show at any point along the line. I doubt that I'll have to exercise that right."

On Monday morning, John's doubts took an unexpected turn.

The out-of-town schedule for *Deucalion* had been set more than a month ago at a meeting attended by John in Vincent Howe's office: one week in New Haven, three weeks in Boston, and five days of paid previews in New York before the official opening.

John had been certain Vincent Howe would close the show at the end of the week in New Haven. To take it to Boston in the vain hope that a hopeless situation might improve, would have made sense only if money had not been involved. But money *was* involved in moving the show to Boston. A good deal of money, John had gathered. And among the lessons he had learned from his year of involvement with Vincent Howe and his colleagues, the strongest was that money is to the theatrical decision as the law of gravity is to aviation engineering: in the end, despite other factors, it is the only *controlling* factor.

Sunday morning, while shaving, it occurred to John that some time during the day he would receive a call from Arnold Zucker telling him that the show had closed in New Haven the night before. John was certain his agent would imbed this piece of dismal news in a nest of worldly observations, all British-accented, about the rub of the green, the luck of the game, the manner in which the ball bounced or the cookie crumbled, and better luck next time.

Late in the afternoon, coming home with Sam and Jim from a stupefying visit to Mr. De Mille's version of *The Ten Commandments*, John was aware of a sense of, first, surprise, and then puzzlement. Ellie, who had remained home to paste up her recipe book, did not report that Arnold Zucker had called.

Slowly, all during the rest of the evening, John could feel inside him the surprise and puzzlement changing and building

up, like a snowdrift, into a rather large case of uneasiness.
He was ashamed to mention this to Ellie. So he waited until
Monday morning, when he had finished dictating to Miss
Faille and was alone in his office, before he called Arnold
Zucker.

"Oh, yes, hello," Mr. Zucker said. "Isn't that odd? I'd just
been about to pick up the phone and call you."

"About what?" John said.

"Why, the *Deucalion* situation, of course," Mr. Zucker
said. "What else would I call you about?"

"Oh, I don't know," John said. "Another project perhaps.
Would I like to become the lawyer for a proposed musical
show based on the life of Millard Fillmore? The *Deucalion*
venture having gone so well, why bust up the team? Why not
keep the same jolly gang together, and knock out another little gold mine?"

Mr. Zucker laughed. It had not occurred to John until this
moment that his agent's laugh had in it something of the
quality of a traffic cop's glance as he listens to the answer to
his question about the location of the fire.

"I see you've picked up some of the jargon of the theatre
this last year," Mr. Zucker said.

"I wish instead of jargon I'd picked up some of that money
we all saw on the horizon when I was induced to join this
venture," John said.

He had used the word "induced" deliberately. He could tell
from the tone of Mr. Zucker's reply that the word had not
gone unnoticed.

"There are no guarantees in the theatre," the agent said.
"As I pointed out when I first talked with you a year ago, it
is probably the most speculative business since the invention
of roulette. Nonetheless, it is just possible that some of the
money we all saw on the horizon may still be coming your
way."

"Out of a show that closed in New Haven last Saturday
night?" John said.

"That's what I was just going to call you about," Mr.
Zucker said. "The show did not close."

"Oh," John said. It was hardly a brilliant retort. But it
served its purpose: it gave him a moment in which to sup-
press the upsurge of uneasiness and concentrate on what he
wanted to say. "You mean Vinnie Howe has taken it to Boston?" he said.

"No," Mr. Zucker said. "That would have been financially

foolhardy, in view of the New Haven reviews and the amount of business that resulted, or rather didn't result. Vinnie had every intention of closing the show Saturday night, but then an unexpected thing came up. *The Teddy Boys* folded in Philadelphia."

"What's *The Teddy Boys?*"

"It's an English review that was booked to follow *Deucalion* into the Shubert in New Haven," Arnold Zucker said. "The Philadelphia reviews, however, were savage. They did no business all week, and the producer ran out of money. So he decided to close the show in Philadelphia."

"He seems wiser than the producer of our little number," John said.

"That remains to be seen," Mr. Zucker said coldly. "The point is that the demise of *The Teddy Boys* left the Shubert in New Haven with an open week, and Vinnie Howe decided to grab it."

"With what end in view?" John said.

"I should think that's fairly obvious," Mr. Zucker said. The temperature of his voice dropped with each syllable. "It means that without incurring the expense of moving on to Boston, he can keep the show running before an audience for another eight performances, see if they can't find out what's wrong, and perhaps fix it. It's happened before, you know."

"It won't happen to *Deucalion,*" John said.

"I must say I find it puzzling, this attitude of certainty on the part of someone who must be described, at least in relation to the theatre, as a novice," Mr. Zucker said.

"Not nearly so puzzling as I find the attitude of optimism, Mr. Zucker, on the part of a man who is clearly an expert."

There was a pause during which it became clear, as soon as he spoke, that Mr. Zucker had shifted his mental gears. He said, almost affably, "Oh, well, hope springs eternal, you know."

"When it does, there's usually some rational reason for it," John said. "At least to a rational person like yourself, Mr. Zucker. Is there any reason for your optimism?"

"Only my confidence in Vinnie Howe's capacity to pull chestnuts out of the fire," Mr. Zucker said. "He's done it before, you know."

"Never with Gwen Quill," John said.

"They did *Fig Leaf* together."

"I've heard a good deal about *Fig Leaf* this last year," John said. "That show was one of those rare miracles. Everything ticked along like a Swiss watch from the very beginning. There was no trouble on the road. The reviews in New Haven were raves, and business was wonderful."

"Well, as long as Vinnie wants to take the risk and give the show another week of life in the hope that it will find a method of survival," Mr. Zucker said, "I believe he should be allowed to do it."

"Don't you think I should have been consulted?" John said.

Again there was that curious pause at the other end of the line.

"Consulted about what?" Mr. Zucker said. Then, apparently unwilling to hear the answer to his own question, he hurried on with: "Mr. Sayer, do you *object* to Mr. Howe giving the show this extra week of life?"

"I object to not being told about it," John said. "Aside from being the lawyer for this project, Mr. Zucker, I happen to have a contract that you wrote for me. It gives me the power of life and death over the show."

"Perhaps that's why you were not consulted," Mr. Zucker said.

John repeated the agent's answer in his head without the word *perhaps*. The shaded areas of his uneasiness cleared up at once.

"Will I be consulted at the end of this week?" John said.

"If you want to be," Mr. Zucker said.

"What makes you think I don't want to be?"

"Your attitude," Mr. Zucker said. "After the run-through you refused to come to the meeting in Miss Quill's apartment. You refused to attend the opening in New Haven. And all during the run last week, you did not come up to see the show. Surely you do not think it unreasonable that the feelings of everybody connected with the production were hurt?"

"Yours, too?" John said.

"Let's say I was disappointed," Mr. Zucker said.

"I wouldn't want that to happen again," John said. "To make sure it doesn't, I wonder if I could ask you as my agent to do something for me?"

"If I can," Mr. Zucker said, "of course."

"You will undoubtedly be in touch with Vinnie Howe all during this week?"

"Several times each day," Mr. Zucker said.

"Will you call me Friday night and tell me what the situation is in New Haven?"

"I'll be delighted," Arnold Zucker said.

He sounded far from delighted when, late Friday afternoon, he did call.

"Well," Mr. Zucker said. Even though John was taking the call in his office, a mile or more from Mr. Zucker's living room in the Hotel Stanton, John felt from the weariness in the agent's voice that he could almost see the look of exhaustion on the round face under the painting of angry seas. "I'm afraid I must confess, Mr. Sayer, that the amateur was right and the expert wrong."

"You've been to New Haven?" John said.

"I went up late yesterday afternoon," Arnold Zucker said. "After the performance, I sat up with Vinnie and Gwen until four this morning. After a late breakfast, we had another session from noon until it was time for me to catch the two-thirty train this afternoon back to New York." The pause at the other end of the wire was filled by a long, exhausted expulsion of breath. "None of it did any good," Mr. Zucker said. "Vinnie is closing the show tomorrow night."

In his mind John experimented with a few traditional words of condolence—"Too bad," "I'm sorry," "What a shame"—but somehow he could not utter them. He was being swept by a very special feeling of relief. He had not experienced it since he had lived with the buzz bombs in London during the war. It was a feeling that used to take the form of an unspoken but very clear statement that would appear like a winking electric sign inside his head after an explosion: Well, *that* one didn't have my number on it!

"Mr. Sayer?"

"Yes?" John said.

"I thought you'd hung up," Mr. Zucker said.

"Oh, no, I'm right here."

"Did you hear what I said?"

"Yes, and I don't mind admitting I don't know how to make any sort of reply that's not either pointless or stupid."

"No, it does seem a time, I always find, when the ordinary resources of language seem hopelessly inadequate," Mr. Zucker said. "You have one consolation, at any rate."

"Have I?" John said.

"You can now take your holiday."

"Holiday?"

"Didn't you say, at the meeting in Vinnie's office months ago, when the New York opening date was set, I seem to recall your saying it came right in the middle of the skiing vaca-

tion you and your wife had planned to take with your sons
during their winter holiday from school?"

"Oh, *that*," John said. "Yes, I'd forgotten that. Now that
there won't *be* any opening, I guess we can go skiing after all,
can't we?"

"You've certainly earned it," Mr. Zucker said.

"If the play hadn't closed," John said, "I'd have earned the
money with which to *pay* for the holiday."

"I shouldn't let that keep you and the family at home,"
Mr. Zucker said. "You know what the ads say. Go now, pay
later."

"It seems a sensible rule for people in the theatre," John
said. "By the way, how are Mr. Howe and Miss Quill taking
it?"

"Oh, well, they're old campaigners," Mr. Zucker said. "If
you'll let me know where you're going to be, I could give you
a ring or drop you a note."

"About what?"

"The final figures on the production," Mr. Zucker said. "It
will take a week or more to sort them all out, by which time
you'll be up in Vermont or some such place, and I thought
you might want to know."

John started to say, "It will certainly keep until I get back."
But he sensed that this was not what Mr. Zucker wanted to
hear. All at once, still aglow with the very special sense of
relief, John felt the compulsion to be nice to Mr. Zucker. Instead, therefore, he said, "My wife makes all the vacation
reservations in our family. I don't even know where we're
going. Stowe, I think, but I'll call you before we leave and
give you the name of the hotel."

"Very good," Mr. Zucker said. "Have a good time and
please don't think me stupid or banal for saying what I am
about to say, since I mean it most sincerely."

"What's that?" John said.

"Better luck next time," Arnold Zucker said.

For several moments after he hung up, John sat with his
back to the room, staring out at the huge new office building
at the other side of Lexington Avenue. Almost exactly a year
ago, John remembered, on the day when he had talked to
Mr. Zucker for the first time, what he had stared out at was a
gray skeleton to the top of which a couple of enormous
cranes had been hoisting buckets of concrete. A sense of uneasiness, even of danger, had threaded through his thoughts
on that day a year ago. The uneasiness had sent him out to

Stamford to talk with Ike Ten Eyck in the Dogwood Lane Rest Home. It was the talk with Ike that had caused him to say yes to Mr. Zucker and Mr. Howe and Miss Quill and their project. Now that the project had fallen apart, John wondered if Ike, who had always been able to explain everything to a boy of ten, would be able to explain to a man of thirty-five why the wreck of Mr. Zucker's and Mr. Howe's and Miss Quill's hopes should fill John Sayer with a sense of triumph as palpable as the shiny new office building across the street. Then echoes of his conversation with Mr. Zucker started to come back to him, and John turned from the window and picked up the phone.

"Get my home, please," he said to Miss Faille. He wondered why the sense of triumph was fading slowly, like the sugared pictures on the hard candies he used to buy in Jenson's Drug Store in Wellesville, after they had been in his mouth for a while. By the time Ellie came on the wire, the feeling of triumph was all gone. John said, "Listen, I've been thinking. When do the kids get out of school?"

"Christmas vacation starts next Friday," Ellie said. "Why?"

"Are we going anywhere?"

"Are we going—?" Ellie's voice stopped, then came back on the wire more sharply. "No, of course not," she said. "We did talk about going to Vermont, but that was months ago, before the opening date of the show was set, and we canceled. Why do you ask?"

"I was wondering how would you like to take a short trip?" John said.

"How short, and where to?"

"Just for the day," John said. "To New Haven."

"To see the show?" Ellie said.

"That's right," John said. "Zucker just called me. He says it's hopeless, and Howe is going to close it tomorrow night, which is Saturday, so there are two performances. I thought I'd rent a car, and you and I could leave around ten, stop at Stonehenge for a big fat lunch, arrive in New Haven in time to see the matinée, then get back here to New York by six-thirty, or a little later, just as Sam and Jim come home from dancing class."

There was a pause. Then Ellie said, "John, why do you want to do this?"

There was another pause, and then John realized he was responsible for this one.

"I don't know," he said, which was true. So true that at

once he felt the compulsion to qualify the statement. "Curiosity, I guess," he said. "Or maybe I feel guilty about staying away the way I have. Zucker said last week everybody resented it. I didn't mind last week. Today I sort of do. It's all over. Why leave a lot of hard feelings?"

"You mean you want to go backstage after the matinée and congratulate everybody on their individual and collective contributions to the making of a three-hundred-thousand-dollar disaster?" Ellie said. "Or is it three-hundred-and-fifty-thousand?"

"Hell, no," John said. "I have no intention of going backstage. It's just my curiosity, I guess."

"Well, I'll go along for the lunch," Ellie said. "I haven't been to Stonehenge since we moved back to New York from Stamford."

She didn't get the lunch because the next morning Sam awoke with the sniffles and a fever of a hundred and two.

"I've called Artie Steinberg," Ellie said when she came out of the boys' bedroom. "He says it's probably a touch of what everybody else in town seems to be down with. But he wants to come up and look at Sam to make sure, and he can't get here until after office hours. Which means one-thirty or two, so why don't you go on up to New Haven by yourself?"

"Because I'd been counting on going up with you," John said.

"Well, I can't go," Ellie said. "So if you really want to see the show, you'll have to go alone, because today is the last day it will be able to be seen by anybody."

"All right, then I will," John said. "But I won't stop at Stonehenge. We'll save that and drive up and have lunch there next Saturday. Okay?"

"Good, yes, that will be fun," Ellie said. "And will you please, darling, for God's sake stop feeling guilty?"

"Guilty?" John said. "Me? About what?"

"This thing," Ellie said. "The play."

"What makes you think I feel guilty about that?"

"Oh, come on," Ellie said. "If you want to fool somebody, try Miss Faille, who seems to believe everything you tell her. You're wasting your time on your wife. If you didn't have a sense of guilt about this, you wouldn't be going up to New Haven. The thing to remember is you're not the one who is responsible for closing the show. You haven't exercised the clause in your contract that gives you the right to close it.

Mr. Vincent Howe, the *producer, he's* closing it. Because not enough people are paying money for tickets to see it. And not enough people are doing that because Miss Gwen Quill has written a not-good play. We all knew that when we saw it at the run-through. The New Haven critics confirmed it, and quite clearly the New Haven public agreed. If you want to drive up there, fine. But there's absolutely no reason to do it looking like Lord Jim baring his breast to the advancing native spears."

All the way up to New Haven, John wished Ellie had not said that. The image bothered him. Until she had reminded him of it, he had been able to convince himself that his decision to go up and see the show had not been prompted by a feeling of guilt. Now the capacity to fence off his recurring uneasiness with that particular conviction was denied him, and he had to face the fact that he did feel guilty. But about what? And why should his inability to answer that question seem housed with such distressing aptness in Ellie's reminder of the way Lord Jim had found *his* answer?

Thinking about that caused John to miss the parkway exit he and Ellie used to take in the days when they lived in Stamford and, now and then, went up to New Haven to see a play. Doubling back cost him almost twenty minutes. So that by the time he reached the parking lot around the corner from the Shubert Theatre where, in those Stamford days, he used to leave his car, John did not have time for the drink with lunch to which, he discovered to his surprise, he had been looking forward.

The surprise intensified his uneasiness as he ate a hamburger in the coffee pot on the corner. He was not a heavy drinker. At least it had never before occurred to him even to consider whether or not he was. Considering it now, John realized that a man whose intake consisted of two or three drinks every night before dinner, could probably say with honesty that he was *not* a heavy drinker. But to look forward eagerly to a drink at noon, which he could not remember doing since London during the buzz bombs, was not reassuring on a day when his wife had accused him of feeling guilty. John was glad, as he paid for his hamburger, that he *had* missed the parkway exit. Whatever it was that had brought him to New Haven, he felt better about facing it with the knowledge that he was not leaning on alcohol for help.

Coming around the corner into College Street, John saw

the marquee of the theatre. Abruptly, he stopped moving. There had been dozens of moments during the past year when the project that had started with a conversation in Arnold Zucker's living room on Park Avenue had moved out of the discussion phase and become, unexpectedly, an exciting, sometimes an upsetting, three-dimensional reality. The day John attended his first audition had been such a moment. The hiring of Fred Thirkell to play Sennacherib Sayer had been another. The first sight of Mannie De Leon's drawings of the sets. The first day of rehearsal. The first poster Norman Saul brought from the printer. All had provided John Sayer with a sudden, intensified awareness that the people with whom he had for so long been talking had really meant what they were saying. The talk had been interesting. The reality was unsettling.

It was like those moments in law school when he would walk into an examination room to face a question paper for which he had been cramming for days or even weeks. John had never been able to avoid wishing those moments could be postponed. So it had been with each of these moments in the *Deucalion* project that had brought closer the reality of an opening night. Now that he knew there was not going to be an opening night, it seemed odd to John that the sight of the theatre marquee here in New Haven should arouse in him the same feeling of uneasiness, the feeling that a preparatory phase was over, and the time of judgment had arrived.

How could it? John wondered as he walked down College Street toward the theatre. Whatever judgment *Deucalion* was going to earn had already been passed, by the New Haven critics. There would be no further judgments. The show would never face the New York critics. *Deucalion* was closing here in New Haven tonight.

Twenty or so feet from the theatre, John stopped again. Spelled out in lights on the side of the marquee were the words:

D E U C A L I O N
Directed by
GWEN QUILL

John moved on, under the marquee, to the other side of the theatre. He turned and looked up. On this side of the marquee the electric lights read:

DEUCALION
Book by Gwen Quill
Music and Lyrics by Irving Ireland

John crossed the street, and, from the far sidewalk, read the words on the front of the marquee:

Vincent Howe Presents
DEUCALION
A New Musical Comedy
With
Fred Thirkell and Irene Faulk

Wondering why he had made this careful inspection of the marquee, John suddenly remembered his visit to Ike Ten Eyck at the Dogwood Lane Rest Home in Stamford a year ago.

"He was a great man," Ike had said about John's father. "No matter what happened in the past, that fact can't be changed. Sennacherib Sayer deserves to be remembered. He deserves they should do this show about him. Here's a chance for the world to learn the truth. No matter what happens, Johnny, he's earned that."

Ike had been right, of course. That was why John had said yes to Vincent Howe and his colleagues. Remembering the puzzling hesitations of a year ago that had surrounded the saying of that yes, John was glad now that the decision to close the show had been made by Vincent Howe, or rather by the New Haven critics and theatregoers, rather than by Sennacherib Sayer's son. Mixed with the relief that his had not been the hand that had signaled the death sentence, was a feeling of sadness for what might have been. The chance for the world to learn the truth that Ike had urged had also been the chance for John Sayer to learn the truth. Now both chances were gone.

A surge of bitterness toward Gwen Quill, who John suddenly realized was responsible for the failure, carried him across the street and into the theatre lobby. It was almost empty. He went to the box office and asked if the curtain was up.

"Not yet," said the man behind the grille.

"One in the balcony, please."

John put a five-dollar bill on the marble ledge.

"There's plenty downstairs," the man said.

"No, I'd rather sit in the balcony," John said. He did not want to run into any members of the company who were not on stage. To make sure he didn't, John waited in the lobby until, through the gap between the doors, he saw the house lights begin to dim. Then he pulled the door open, gave his ticket to the surprised man who had already started to empty the stubs out of his slotted box, and moved quickly toward the balcony stairs. The shocking sight revealed by a swift, guarded glance toward the stage was confirmed when John found his seat upstairs. It was in the first row, so that he could peer across the guard rail down into the orchestra: only the first six rows were occupied, and they were not occupied completely. Beyond the sixth row, the orchestra was empty. John turned for a quick look at the balcony. There could not possibly have been more than fifty people around him. He turned back to the stage.

On it, wearing the kind of *lederhosen* John had himself worn as a boy at Deucalion, half a dozen members of the Children's Guild were singing Irving Ireland's enchanting song "Great News." Even at the early rehearsals, when there had still been a good deal of stumbling over the words and the only accompaniment to the childish voices had been a badly tuned piano, the opening number had never failed to move John Sayer. Now, with a full orchestra, it moved him again. So did the rest of the first act. John had found it impressive at the run-through. He saw now that he had underestimated the contribution of scenery and costumes. It was even more impressive today. In the final scene, when Fred Thirkell and Irene Faulk sang their duet, "Discovery," John was not surprised to feel the tears come up in his eyes.

The applause at the curtain, which seemed to him inadequate, was also surprisingly loud from so small an audience. It was clear that they, who were not emotionally involved, as John was, with the true story and the real people behind the characters in the play, nevertheless liked it as much as he did. Knowing the disappointment waiting like a coiled trap in the second act, he could not help feeling sorry for them. It was a shame to destroy the glow of pleasure by which they were now suffused. Only because he did not want to run into anybody associated with the company did John decide not to leave before he was himself subjected to the same disappointment. Gwen Quill had undoubtedly already gone back to New York. Even Vincent Howe had probably left town. But Norman Saul and Jess Wilentz, as well as some of the others, would probably be mingling with the audience in the lobby, still hoping to pick up reactions that might prove helpful. John decided to remain in his balcony seat until the second act got under way, and then leave.

A few minutes after the curtain went up, he was sorry he had not taken the risk of running into the press agent or the stage manager or anybody else connected with the show. No embarrassment of that nature could have been as bad as this stabbing renewal of the disappointment he had felt at the run-through. The scenery and costumes, which enhanced the emotional content of the first act, merely underscored the emptiness of the second. John could feel the shock spreading, like spilled wine on a tablecloth, among the few people near him in the balcony. And he knew why, in spite of the brilliant first act, the reviews had been so devastating and business so bad.

When he read something uniformly mediocre, or saw a play that was all second-rate, John rarely commented on it unless he was asked. "Yes, I read it." Or, "Yes, I saw it." Had he liked it? "Oh, not too much." When he read or saw something that was first-rate at the beginning, or even no more than promising, but then fell apart, or failed to keep its promise, his reaction was not passive. In such cases John had a feeling that he had been cheated. He wanted to complain to somebody, and he did, making it a point to raise the subject of the book or play with a friend, and then stating his opinion. Or rather, since it is difficult to feel cheated without feeling indignant, John was aware that he overstated his opinion. This had obviously happened to *Deucalion* in New Haven.

The critics, outraged by the mediocrity of the second act, had clearly found it difficult to be fair to, or perhaps even remember, the first act. The way a biographer of Jack the Ripper might find it difficult to see much virtue in the fact that, as a young boy, he had spent most of his time helping old ladies across busy thoroughfares. And if it was true that what made a hit, as Vincent Howe kept insisting, was word of mouth, it seemed equally clear to John that the New Haven playgoers who had sat through *Deucalion* had not been apathetic about the experience. Instead of waiting to be asked by friends and neighbors what they thought of the play, or even forgetting to mention the experience, they had clearly gone out of their way to buttonhole people and say angrily, "Don't go to this damn thing!"

The few who had gone either had heard nothing about

the play or were, in Vincent Howe's phrase, theatre buffs, people who went to see certain plays for no better reason than a boy, trailing his hand along a picket fence, will go back and touch one of the uprights his fingers may have skipped: they did not like to miss anything.

When the curtain descended John moved to the aisle and walked downstairs with a feeling of relief. The small, nagging uneasiness he had refused to acknowledge, the reluctant thought that his judgment of what he had seen at the run-through might just possibly be wrong, had been laid at rest. There could no longer be any doubt. Painful as the decision must have been for Vincent Howe to make, the producer had made the right one. So had John Sayer, in coming up to New Haven. The feeling of satisfaction and relief carried him out of the deserted lobby.

On the sidewalk, it occurred to John that he had never seen a marquee immediately following a performance with no sign of life under or near it. There were no stragglers lingering to look at the posted photographs of the performers. No groups stood chatting about the play as they turned up their coat collars and prepared to move off toward taxis. True, there had not been many people in the theatre. But those fifty or so men and women by whom John had been surrounded in the balcony, and those he had seen in the first six rows of the orchestra, must have left in an awful hurry after the curtain came down to create so vivid an impression of desolation. John was wondering if they had all walked out before the curtain came down, a possibility that made him flush with embarrassment for the performers, when he saw a familiar figure coming toward him. John stopped short. The figure had ducked into the theatre. John could feel the uneasiness moving with him, and growing heavier. It was so unlike the portly, slow-moving figure of Arnold Zucker to make the swift, furtive movement John's mind had automatically classified as ducking, that he took almost half a block to adjust to the idea. When he did, John's mind was free to contemplate the troubling questions beneath it. What was his agent doing in New Haven three hours before the final performance? When he had talked to Zucker in New York on the phone yesterday, the agent had said he had just returned from New Haven, where Vincent Howe had made the decision to close the show. What had brought Arnold Zucker back to New Haven? John turned and hurried back to the theatre.

The impression of desolation, which had struck him halfway down the block from the theatre, assailed him more strongly as he climbed the stairs. It reminded him of a slip of the tongue Fred Thirkell had made six months ago, the day John met the man who had just been hired to play Sennacherib Sayer. Conversation had been difficult, and the actor, perhaps out of nervousness, perhaps because he thought John was interested, had wandered into a humorous account of his first appearance on Broadway, playing a minor role in a production of *Richard II* that starred a famous British interpreter of Shakespeare. The reviews had been disastrous. Thirkell, in trying to convey to John their effect on business, had said, "People stayed away in groves."

The actor had caught himself up as soon as the word was uttered, laughed at his mistake, and corrected it. But the image it evoked in John's mind was vivid: men and women cowering behind clumps of trees, some of them handcuffed to the trunks and branches, to prevent themselves from even the remote possibility of being exposed to the production by wandering into the theatre accidentally.

There was, John thought as he came out at the top of the balcony, that same feeling in this theatre of active emptiness. A void created not merely because nobody was there but because, somewhere beyond John's range of vision, armed guards stood at attention to make sure nobody approached. The feeling lasted until John reached the seat from which, less than two hours ago, he had watched *Deucalion's* delightful first act. Leaning across the guard rail, John saw that the theatre was not empty.

Spaced about on the first few rows of the orchestra he could see not only Arnold Zucker's gleaming, naked scalp but, to his astonishment, Gwen Quill's close-cropped, slicked-back red hair; and Vincent Howe's thinning tan strands spread carefully across his narrow skull. It was an odd view of the three people who had come into John Sayer's life a year ago with so many bright promises and were going out of it tonight with none of those promises fulfilled. It was almost as though, despite their awareness that what had brought them into this vast, semi-dark chamber was a common cause, Mr. Zucker and Miss Quill and Mr. Howe were equally aware that the common cause had not really bound them together; and so it was more appropriate to sit, not side by side, but with plenty of space separating them one from another. It seemed, all at once, equally appropriate to John that he should have arranged, even though unconsciously, to have the largest space between himself and the other three.

They, at least, were citizens of the same world. He was not. They had invited him in. They had given him a visitor's visa with the clear implication that, if he enjoyed his visit and wanted to remain permanently, all he had to do was ask: his request for naturalization would be honored. He had not made the request. Now, at the end of his visit, John was aware that he had not even exercised fully his visitor's rights. He could have attended all the rehearsals. He had gone to only a few. He had been invited to every editorial conference. He had accepted a mere fraction of the invitations. His approval had been requested before every performer had been hired. Except for the two main roles, he had granted his permission over the phone, without taking the trouble to see the performers in person. He had been urged—Vincent Howe had pleaded with him—to attend the meeting in Gwen Quill's apartment after the run-through. He had refused.

Why?

Seated in the balcony, staring down at the heads of Gwen Quill, Arnold Zucker, and Vincent Howe, John Sayer began to see more clearly the composition of the uneasiness he had carried back with him into the theatre. There was something about this project that had frightened him. Something beyond the fear for his father's reputation that, a year ago, had sent him out to Stamford to talk with Ike Ten Eyck in the Dogwood Lane Rest Home. John saw now, in the most shadowy way but still more clearly than he had ever seen it before, that part of his fear came directly from the people with whom the project was involved.

I have never met people like these, he had told Ellie shortly after he met Arnold Zucker and Vincent Howe and Gwen Quill. The statement had seemed adequate at the time, even to his wife. John began to grasp now that it had not really been adequate. Any more than it would have been adequate if, at the end of an average day, he had made the same statement about any three of the many new clients who were constantly moving through the firm's offices.

So what? If you are in the business of serving the public at large, Ellie would have said, whether as lawyer or doctor or grocer, it stands to reason that some of the people who call upon you to serve them will be unlike all the other people you have previously met. Is that in itself a reason for refusing to serve them? Obviously not. And yet, in the case of Mr.

Zucker and Mr. Howe and Miss Quill, Ellie had not made these statements.

Had she understood at once what John was beginning to understand only now? That it was not these strange people and their strange world he had feared? They and their world were merely catalysts. What he had feared, John Sayer felt now, was what these people were capable of setting in motion. Understanding that, he understood something else: why the run-through which had disappointed him, had also relieved him. Why, even though he regretted losing the money that would have come his way if *Deucalion* had been a success, he was pleased that the show was closing tonight. It was part of the feeling John had come to know in London during the buzz bombs and, later, the rockets: the closer the near miss, the more acute the elation over the narrow escape.

"Okay, Jess, let's go."

The feeling of elation collapsed like a pricked bubble. Gwen Quill's nasal voice rose to the balcony like an unpleasant smell. Leaning forward over the guard rail, John saw the stage manager come out of the wings. He was carrying a looseleaf notebook. Ten or fifteen feet from the wings, Jess Wilentz stopped.

"Stage directions, too?" he said. "I mean, there's no sets yet?"

"The works," Gwen Quill said from her seat down in front. "Mr. Zucker hasn't seen or heard any of it."

"Yes, ma'am," the stage manager said. He dipped his head over the notebook and read aloud. "Act Two, Scene One. Time, summer nineteen thirty-nine. Place, the customs shed and part of the dock at Sydney, Australia. Visible in silhouette at stage left, the side of a Matson liner, its name clearly painted on the bow: *Lurline*. Off-stage noises: the hustle and bustle of passengers disembarking. At Rise, enter from right Sennacherib Sayer."

The curtain rose slowly behind Jess Wilentz. Out onto the bare stage, peering about eagerly, came Fred Thirkell. Jess Wilentz continued to read from his notebook.

"The ten years that have elasped between the end of Act One and the beginning of Act Two have left their marks," the stage manager read aloud. "He is not an old man, although in actual years Sayer is not far from seventy. The difference between the man we saw singing 'Discovery' when the curtain came down on Act One, and the man we now see, can be summed up in a single word: happiness. There is a serenity about Sennacherib Sayer that we have not seen before. It makes itself felt in spite of his obvious eagerness, even agitation, as he peers about. Enter behind him a man in chauffeur's uniform. His name is Dwight."

As the actor, a man John Sayer had never seen before, came out on stage, Jess Wilentz started to move backward, toward the wings, like a subject leaving the presence of his sovereign at a royal levee.

"Mr. Sayer, please," said the actor dressed as a chauffeur, speaking with a Cockney accent. "There's no need to get so worked up, you know. 'Eel be along, sir, as soon as 'eez finished with customs."

"I'm perfectly well aware of that," Fred Thirkell said irritably. "What you don't seem to be aware of, Dwight, is that the person getting off that ship is my son, my only son, and I haven't seen him for ten years."

To John, in the balcony, it seemed longer than that before Jess Wilentz jolted him from the state of numbed shock by appearing from the wings and calling down into the darkened theatre, "The music rises to a crescendo as Slow Curtain."

Gwen Quill swung around in her seat. She said, "What do you think, Arnold?"

"I think it's great," Vincent Howe said. "I think she's licked it."

"I'm not asking you," Gwen Quill said. "I'm asking Mr. Zucker."

The gleam on his naked skull moved, as though it were a small pool of water into which a pebble had been dropped, and Arnold Zucker carefully unfolded, then just as carefully refolded, his plump fingers across his paunch.

"Didacticism is, of course, almost impossible in so chancy a medium as the theatre," he said in a murmur that rose clearly to the balcony. "There is no denying that this new approach has a certain quality, a vigor that was lacking earlier, a unity of emotion, so to speak, that blends the hitherto disparate elements of the first act with those of the second in a way that leads one to suspect there is a possibility, perhaps even a probability—"

"For God's sweet sake, Arnold, will you cut the shit?" Gwen Quill said. "I have worked my ass off for a week on this new second act. So has the cast. We've been rehearsing all day and giving a performance at night. Wednesday and today, *two* performances in addition to the rehearsals. We're punch-drunk. We don't want any more fancy talk about how the scenes in the peripheral areas violate T. S. Eliot's twin polarities. We want the answer to a simple question. If Vinnie closes the show here in New Haven tonight, the investors lose their entire three hundred thousand and that's that. If this new second act is good enough, if it does the trick, Vinnie is willing to take a chance and bring the show into New York. But that will cost an additional fifty thousand bucks. Vinnie and I are willing to put that up out of our own pockets, twenty-five thousand each. We're willing to take the chance if we feel reasonably certain this new second act works. Vinnie thinks it does. So do I. But we want another opinion. That's why we asked you to come back to New Haven. Arnold, what do you think?"

John shoved away the last of the numbness. He seized the guard rail, pulled himself out of the seat, and shouted down into the orchestra, "It doesn't matter what he thinks!"

The red hair, the naked scalp, the tan strands laced across the narrow skull, all vanished and became faces.

"Oh, Jesus," Vincent Howe said. "It's that schmuck Sayer."

The involuntarily spoken word, the single syllable uttered without thought, tore away a year of carefully constructed amiability. The slanting face of the Norman Rockwell scoutmaster had fallen back into the lines and creases among which it obviously rested in repose: the face of a killer.

"Not as big a schmuck as you think," John said.

Zucker, he could see, was gathering himself, assessing the damage, putting together swiftly a structure of plausibility on which he could take an untainted position. It was Gwen Quill, her eyes beginning to glow with the insane rage John had come to recognize and could now see all the way up in the balcony, who asked the pertinent question: "How long you been up there?"

"Long enough to tell you this," John said, hearing his voice rise, wondering if he should check it, then figuring to hell with it. "You and Mr. Howe can save your fifty thousand dollars," he said. "This play is not opening in New York."

He turned and ran up the steps to the top of the balcony. He paused to look back. He saw Jess Wilentz and Fred Thirkell peering worriedly into what must have been for them almost total darkness. Then John turned and went pounding down the stairs two at a time. At the bottom, he stopped, hesitated, and went back up one step. They were waiting for him in a group.

"Mr. Sayer," Arnold Zucker said, "where are you going?"

"Back to New York," John said. "I've got a registered letter to write, addressed to Vincent Howe. According to my contract, that's all I have to do to close this show. I didn't think I would have to do it, since you told me in New York yesterday that Mr. Howe had already decided to close it himself. But that was obviously a lie, since I see now why you were so anxious yesterday to have me go off on a holiday with my family. While we were away skiing, you and your friends here would be sneaking the show into New York. Well, I'm sorry to spoil your little game. This show is not coming into New York. That schmuck Sayer, if I'm quoting your pal correctly, is on his way to close it right now."

"Listen, you jerk."

Vincent Howe took a step forward. John saw that his analysis of the folksy Norman Rockwell scoutmaster had not been inaccurate. The homespun man in tan may not have known it himself, but he was about to commit murder.

"I will," John said, "when you get back to calling me fella. Right now, just get out of my way."

"You watch that stupid tongue, you dopey ass hole, or I'll see it's rammed down your throat," Mr. Howe said with icy calm. "We've taken a lot of crap from you this last year, my friend, but this is the end of the line."

"For both of us," John said. "And you don't seem to appreciate how good a friend of yours I am. I'm about to save you twenty-five thousand dollars."

Gwen lunged at him. Without turning, John took another step back up the stairs. The flailing arm missed him, but the group pressed forward, as though John had released a barrier against which they were pressing.

"Gwen, now, look, really," Arnold Zucker murmured. He placed a hand on her arm.

She flung it away so fiercely that, for a ludicrous moment, as his uncontrolled arm described a perfect half-circle in the air, Mr. Zucker looked like a policeman at a busy intersection signalling a change in the flow of traffic.

"Get the fuck away from me," Gwen Quill snarled. "All of you." She shoved Vincent Howe aside. She came to the foot of the stairs. John took another step backward. The face of the killer emerging from behind the mask of the scoutmaster had been unpleasant. But the watery eyes of the demented jockey were terrifying. "Okay, tell me," Gwen Quill said. "Why you closing this show?"

"Because I've got a contract says I can," John said.

"Fuck that," the savage thing in front of him spit out. "Why you closing the show?"

"Because you lied to me," John said. "You tried to slip in this new second act behind my back."

"What's wrong with this new second act?"

"It's not appearing on any New York stage," John said. "Not while I'm alive to write that registered letter."

"Stick to the point, you devious little bastard," Gwen Quill said. "What's wrong with this new second act?"

"It's a pack of lies," John said.

"A pack is a lot," Gwen Quill said. "Name one."

"Australia," John said. "My father never set foot in Australia."

"You cheap, doublecrossing son of a bitch," Gwen Quill said coldly. She turned and rapped out, "Fred?"

Nervously, Fred Thirkell came forward.

"Yes, Miss Quill?"

"Tell this bastard where you met his father."

The actor, who had told John when they were introduced that he was still on the bright side of forty, suddenly looked ten years older.

"Don't you remember, Mr. Sayer?" he said worriedly. He pinched the corners of his mouth back and forth with thumb and forefinger, as though to help get the words out. "The day we met? I told you I had toured the Pacific during the war with a USO troupe? Doing a cut-down version of Hamlet? And one day, in Sydney, a man came to see me at the hotel? He knew we'd been touring all over the world, and he wondered if possibly I had run into his son? The boy was in the Air Force, based in England? He hadn't heard from him for a long time? And how it didn't dawn on me for some time that the man who had come to see me was the famous Sennacherib Sayer? Who, when I was a younger man, had been the great—" The actor's flow of anxious words stopped. Fred Thirkell shook his head, as though he couldn't quite believe what he had just heard himself say. "But surely, Mr. Sayer, you remember all that?" he said. "We talked about it at great length. The day I was hired for the part. I told you how pleased I was and I said—"

"You didn't tell me anything," John said quietly. "And I didn't say anything to you."

His manner seemed to add to the actor's dismay. Thirkell turned to Gwen Quill.

"I—" he began. "Miss Quill, I don't know what to say."

"I do," she said quietly. Now it was *her* manner that seemed to upset Fred Thirkell. She pushed him aside with a curt, "Forget it, Fred." She came up to John, took his hand, and said, "Come with me a minute."

The others stepped aside as she led him to the doors at the back of the theatre. She pushed through into the lobby, and opened the door of a tiny office under the stairs. Inside, at a small desk under the slanting ceiling, Norman Saul was poking at the keys of a typewriter.

"Hi, kids," the press agent said cheerfully. "Just getting out a release saying we're not closing tonight as announced but will be taking the show to New York, with a brand-new second act, for a series of paid previews instead of going up to Boston, so that we'll—"

"Beat it, Norm," Gwen Quill said.

The press agent looked startled. He darted a glance at John, another at Gwen Quill, and rose quickly. He stepped out of the office, and pushed the door shut. She reached across and turned the key in the lock.

"Okay," she said quietly. "I accept your statement. Your father never set foot in Australia. Now tell me this. What difference does it make to you if the second act is set in Australia?"

"None at all," John said. "Set it in Timbuktu for all I care."

"But you do care."

"Not about Australia," John said. "I care about what you say happened in Australia."

"Didn't it?"

"Of course not."

"Then what are you afraid of?"

"Miss Quill—"

"You can call me Gwen."

"I'll make that decision myself," John said. "I don't understand your use of the word 'afraid.' I object to the story you tell in your second act. Under no circumstances will I allow it to appear on a public stage. I am, therefore, exercising my contractual right to prevent such an appearance. If you choose to treat that as an exhibition of fear, go ahead. But don't waste my time. I have to get back to New York."

He reached for the key in the door.

She said, "Wait, please." John turned back. Gwen Quill said. "You haven't told me what it is you object to in the second-act story."

John hesitated. He stared at this strange creature in a man's pants and a woman's sweater, wearing a man's haircut and a woman's nail polish, staring at him with a murderous savagery that did not quite conceal her pleading desperation. The compulsion to pay a debt, a debt John had not known he had incurred, became overwhelming.

"Your story makes my father a monster," John Sayer said. "It all seems very moving and sweet on the surface. Sennacherib Sayer's son comes to Australia to see the father he has not seen for ten years. The plot says the boy comes because he wants his father's advice about whether or not he should study law. The boy gets the advice, and father and son are reconciled. All this comes about through the qualities in both, as well as memories they have forgotten, that are evoked by Sennacherib Sayer's new young wife. That's on the surface. But underneath, what comes through, we get a picture of the boy paying back the father for what the father did to the boy's mother, Sennacherib Sayer's first wife, ten years ago, in the first act. Worse than that, the story makes it clear that the boy, to revenge himself on his father, does not hesitate to use the father's innocent, young, and completely vulnerable second wife as an instrument of his revenge."

"Did you?" Gwen Quill said.

"What?" John Sayer said.

"I see," Gwen Quill said. "You've conveniently forgotten that, too."

"I haven't forgotten anything except my rights," John said. "And I mean to exercise them."

Again he turned to the door. Again she pulled him around.

"What about *my* rights?" Gwen Quill said.

She said it so softly that he was caught and held. John watched her run both hands along the sides of her head. He remembered his second visit to her apartment. The day he told her he would not permit the last half of the play to contain a lover who comes between Sennacherib Sayer and his second wife. Gwen Quill might have been smoothing her boyishly cut red hair into place. But John knew better, as he had known it the first time he saw the gesture. He was again watching the disturbed mind catching itself up, warning itself back from the abyss, whispering: *Be careful, tread easy, hold onto yourself, or they'll find out you're crazy*.

"What rights do you think you have?" John said.

"The rights of an artist," Gwen Quill said. "Do you think, when you granted me permission to write this play about your father, you were hiring a tradesman? You hereby have the right to grind out one hundred and twenty pages of dialogue, Miss Quill, and if I like it, I will allow it to appear on a stage?"

"I didn't think of it that way or any other way," John said. "You asked for certain rights, and I asked for certain controls. We both got what we wanted."

"No, Mr. Sayer," Gwen Quill said. "We didn't. Anyway, I didn't, and I won't get it until what I have written appears before a New York audience."

"I don't understand what it is you want," John said.

"I want what Joyce wanted, what every artist wants," she said. "I want to find myself."

A year ago, John would have thought she was making a joke. Now he knew that what to the world at large was a burlesque of reality was to the actor and his allied artists the core of truth. Gwen Quill was deadly serious. She was ludicrous and serious.

"You expected to find yourself, whatever that means, in showing a New York audience this distorted accumulation of falsehoods about a man you've never met and don't know?"

"I know him better than you do," Gwen Quill said. "That's why I was drawn to Sennacherib Sayer's story from the beginning. Knowledge of people has nothing to do with consanguinity or even proximity. Knowledge is the result of emotional communication. That sort of communication is timeless. It transcends geography. It laughs at age. It is possible for you and me to know Alfred the Great or Attila the Hun far better than their contemporaries knew them. All we need is to feel. As soon as I read the first few things about him, I knew Sennacherib Sayer was the end of my quest."

"All right," John said. "You've found your answer. You've written it."

"You God damn fool," Gwen Quill said. "What you don't understand is that the answer doesn't exist until it is put on a stage where the whole world can see it."

"I've got to close it," John said. "It's my life or yours."

Wondering what the words meant, astonished that he had uttered them, John saw that they had turned the brain behind the demented eyes in a new direction.

"That's right," Gwen Quill said softly. "I hadn't thought of that. One of us has to die." The hands came up again, to smooth the boyishly cut hair against her temples, but the eyes had narrowed. "You've got it worked out pretty good," she said, even more softly. "What you don't like, you don't remember. But me, I remember everything. I can't stop remembering. That's why I live in hell, while you live in a Brooks Brothers suit." She paused, and her head tipped to one side. "Let's see if it really works," Gwen Quill said. "Remember this?" she said, putting her arms around him. "When Vinnie Howe went for crullers?"

Disgusted, his face burning, John slid aside, away from the typewriter and this crazy woman, and he said, "Miss Quill, I think this has gone far enough."

"My God," she said. There was a touch of awe in her voice. "I believe it really does work."

Her claws darted toward him again.

"Keep your dirty hands away from me," John Sayer said, fumbling his buttons back into place. "What you need is a doctor."

He stepped to the door and turned the key.

"Oh, no, I don't," Gwen Quill said from the floor. "It's you who need the doctor. But it's too late for doctors." She rolled up onto her knees. "What you need is an undertaker," Gwen Quill said. "One of us is going to die." Through the closing door, to his departing back, Gwen Quill screamed, "And it's not going to be me!"

John kept right on going. Through the group of now only vaguely familiar faces clustered near the box office window. Out of the lobby. Up College Street. And around the corner to the parking lot.

"I got into my car and started back for New York," John said to Mr. Mancini on the seat beside him. "Going through New Haven, the roads through the suburbs on the way to the Turnpike, I didn't realize what was happening. Inside my head, I mean. When I hit the Turnpike, though, the minute I came out on the Turnpike and started down toward New York, everything fell into place. All the pieces. I saw the whole thing. My whole life. From that day at Deucalion when I was ten years old, to that day in Australia when I was twenty." John shook his head slowly. "She was right," he said. "Miss Quill."

The policeman stirred on the seat beside him. Mr. Mancini blew out his breath in that small, tired sigh.

"Was she?" he said quietly.

John nodded.

"It's a hard thing for a man to admit," he said. "But pride

doesn't matter. Not any more. Now that I've got only seventeen minutes left to live."

The policeman glanced at his wrist watch.

"No," he said. "Only seven minutes left. You don't have much time. You've got to get it right, all of it, before—"

John shook his head again.

"I've got it right," he said. "All of it. Miss Quill made sure of that. What I've done, what I've been doing for fifteen years, ever since I left Australia, I've been living a double life. Or maybe I should say a second life. From the minute I met Ellie, everything that happened to me before then, everything I did that was bad, I just blocked it out. It hadn't happened. That's why—" He paused, gave the policeman a short glance, then turned back to the windshield with a tired shrug. "What's the difference?" John said. "You might as well know. When you said I was impotent? When I said you were a liar? I'm sorry. You were right."

"No need to be sorry," Mr. Mancini said. "What counts these next few minutes is the truth."

John nodded to the deserted road rushing up toward and under the car he wasn't really driving.

"I wasn't impotent all the time," he said. "Aside from being a father, I've also managed a reasonable sex life. But only reasonable. I think what's been happening, every time the past started to come back, if it happened when I was with Ellie, I'd get blocked. It didn't happen all the time, but often enough to be a problem." John released a short, mirthless laugh. "Because Ellie was so wonderful about it," he said, "I could keep on kidding myself even through a thing like that, a thing that would drive any other man crazy. But tonight, back there in New Haven, when I saw the parts of my life that I'd carefully hidden from myself, the parts that Gwen Quill had guessed at and put into her second act—" He paused, closed his eyes for a moment, then opened them. "When I saw the whole thing, all the pieces in place," John said, "I knew I could never go back to Ellie, to the children, to any kind of life worth living. If I really loved them, if I really wanted to be fair to them, there was only one thing for me to do," he said. "I didn't really make the decision to kill myself," John said. "The decision made itself. A couple of minutes after I recognized it, I saw your flashlight winking up ahead. I stopped the car, and picked you up and, well, here I am. You know all the rest."

The policeman nodded.

"Yes," he said. "But there's one thing you left out."

John turned his head, and saw Mr. Mancini watching him with a small, troubled frown.

"I don't understand," John said. "What have I left out?"

"You told your wife that after you left Australia in June of nineteen thirty-nine just before the war began, you never saw your father again." Mr. Mancini shook his head slowly. "That's not true," he said. "You did see your father again," the policeman said. "Once more, five years after his wife died in childbirth."

"But that's impossible," John said. He frowned as he pulled the dates, one by one, out of his memory. "I left Sydney in June of nineteen thirty-nine. I entered law school in September. In March of nineteen forty, nine months after I left Australia, Ike Ten Eyck got the cable about Dinah's death. A month after that, I remember it was a raw, blustery day in April, Ike came up to Cambraidge with the news that my father had died."

Mr. Mancini shook his head.

"No," he said. "You're getting things mixed up. Here's how it went." The policeman put up his left hand, fingers spread wide, and ticked off the items one by one with his right forefinger. "You left Sydney in June, nineteen thirty-nine. True. You entered Harvard Law in September. True. Ike brought the news of Dinah's death to you in Cambridge in March of nineteen forty. Also true. But now come the parts you've left out. Ready?"

John nodded.

"Yes," he said.

Mr. Mancini's right forefinger moved back to the thumb of his left hand.

"Graduated from Harvard Law in June of nineteen forty-two," he said. "Drafted into army in July of nineteen forty-two, Officers' Candidate School, second lieutenant commission, February, nineteen forty-three. Assigned to Eighth Air Force in England, August nineteen forty-three. Served with Eighth Air Force until V-E Day, May, nineteen forty-five. Transferred to Pacific Theatre, June, nineteen forty-five."

"Now, wait a minute," John said.

"There's not much time," Mr. Mancini said. "Please listen. Your unit, which was scheduled to be based on New Guinea, flew into Sydney on a Friday late in June," the policeman said. "Shortly after lunch, while you were taking a nap in your hotel room, you had a call from a man named Dwight.

He was downstairs in the lobby. He said he was your father's
chauffeur. Do you remember that?"

"No," John said.

"You changed your shirt and went downstairs to meet
him," Mr. Mancini said patiently. "You recognized him at
once. It was the big man in chauffeur's uniform who had met
you at the dock in the big Rolls six years before, in nineteen
thirty-nine, when you first came to Sydney on the *Lurline*.
Do you remember that?"

"I remember the first time," John said. "Yes. I don't remember being in Australia any time after that."

"Dwight said your father had heard your unit was being
transferred," the policeman continued as though he had not
been interrupted. "Through friends, he was able to trace your
movements. Dwight said your father was not well, so he had
been unable to come to the hotel himself, and had sent
Dwight to fetch you. He led you out to the car. It was the
same big Rolls. You got in and Dwight drove you to your
father's house on Point Piper. Do you remember that?"

"No," John said.

"You will," Mr. Mancini said. "As soon as the car turns
into the driveway."

The policeman was right. The moment the big car made
the turn, and John saw the house on the low hill, it all came
back to him. He remembered the complicated gardens that
surrounded the house, and the way the structure reminded
him of two match boxes, one somewhat smaller than the
other, that had been joined together. He leaned forward eagerly. The car pulled up in front of the smaller of the two
match boxes, the section that was a replica of the Main
House at Deucalion, and John saw his father standing in the
doorway.

Dwight came around to open the door of the car, but John
beat him to it. He jumped out and ran up the walk, hearing
the gravel kick out behind his shoes, and he threw his arms
around the white-haired old man. Even as he held his father
in his arms, John knew that now it would have been wrong
to use any word but old. Not only because what he was holding was a fraction of the bulk that John remembered, but
also because all the control had gone out of it. The emaciated
body in his arms was trembling. John came out of the em-
brace gently, easing the trembling body forward, as though
he were setting a fragile doll back on a shelf.

"Well, Captain," Sennacherib Sayer said.

John laughed and said, "No, sir. Major, sir." He touched the gold leaf on his khaki shoulder and said, "They gave it to me as an inducement to come out to Australia."

"Did you need an inducement to come?" the old man said.

"No, sir," John said. "A man isn't exactly a free agent when he's in uniform, especially if there's a war on, but I've been trying to wangle this for some time."

His father seemed surprised.

"You have?" he said. "I thought you didn't like it out here?"

"Well, I wasn't here long enough to make any permanent judgments," John said. "But I did have a good time and, after all, you are my father."

"Yes," Sennacherib Sayer said. "That's true." He turned and said, "Come in, John."

John followed his father into the central room that had been Dinah's study. The old man pointed to the heavy chair beside the fireplace. It was the chair in which John had sat after his twentieth birthday party and listened to his father's second wife read aloud the poem she had composed at Deucalion a decade earlier for Sennacherib Sayer on John's tenth birthday.

"Sit here," Sennacherib Sayer said. "Dinah once told me you liked this chair."

"I did," John said. He sat down and then said, "When did she tell you that?"

"After you left," his father said. "Several months after. Ah, yes, thank you, Dwight. Put it here, please."

The chauffeur, who was now wearing his white gloves and butler's uniform, set down the tray of glasses and bottles.

"Will that be all, sir?"

John remembered his old reaction on first hearing Dwight talk, the feeling that he had been caught in the sound track of a badly filmed British movie.

"For the moment, yes," Sennacherib Sayer said. Dwight backed out of the room and John's father said, "What's your tipple, Major?"

"We get scotch pretty cheap in England," John said. "So I've learned to stick to that."

"That's the whole trick of getting through life," his father said. "Learning lessons from everything that happens to you. Even the price of liquor." He poured the drinks, handed one to John, and lifted his own glass. "To the fates, or to God, whichever has been responsible for keeping both of us alive for this moment."

"Yes, sir," John said. Then, as he put the glass to his lips, he thought about his father's toast. "How is your health, sir?" he said.

"Not good," Sennacherib Sayer said. "I should have died five years ago. When Dinah died, and my heart broke."

He said it so casually, as though he were directing a passer-by toward a bus stop, that for a few moments the meaning of the words did not catch up with John. When they did, he could feel the short, closely-shaved hairs at the side of his jaw begin to rise and tingle.

"I'm sorry, sir," he said.

"I wonder if you are," Sennacherib Sayer said. "After all, five years ago, when you came here, you did accomplish your mission."

John set down his glass. Something was happening that he did not understand.

"Father," he said.

"Don't use that word," Sennacherib Sayer said.

John reached for his glass, changed his mind, thought about his next words, then realized his father had clearly indicated the ones he wanted his son to speak.

"Why didn't you die five years ago?" John said.

Sennacherib Sayer nodded. He might have been indicating his appreciation for John's understanding that these were indeed the words he had arranged to hear.

"Because I couldn't go until this meeting took place," the old man said.

John thought about *that* for a few moments. But he couldn't make it come clear in his mind.

"It might never have taken place," John said. "There's a war on. I might have been killed."

"I prayed that you would not be." The handsome old face twisted in the merest hint of a sardonic grin. "It seems to have worked," he said. "It kept you alive for this meeting."

John wondered about the times during the past three years when he had felt the clutch of death's hand. Would he have known those moments of terror if he had known about his father's prayers?

"Why did you want this meeting?" John said.

"I had accepted a task," his father said. "I wanted to perform it. I could not go without performing it. Also I could not go without making a statement. I had to make it." He reached into his pocket and pulled out what looked like a piece of twisted wire. "Just before she died," Sennacherib Sayer said, "Dinah gave me this. She set me the task of giving it to you. Dinah said you would understand."

His hand moved toward John, who reached forward and took what he had thought was a piece of twisted wire. It was the pair of Georgian silver grape scissors Dinah Tristram had given him on his tenth birthday at Deucalion, the scissors he had returned to her on his twentieth birthday in this room.

"I'm sorry," John said. "But I don't understand."

"You will," his father said. "Now I've performed the task, all that remains for me is to make the statement. Waiting to utter it in your presence has kept me for five years in bondage to this life I have loathed since Dinah died." Sennacherib Sayer drew a long, slow breath. "As you know," he said to his son, "Dinah died in childbirth." The old man paused, drew another breath, and said, "As you may not have known, I contracted the mumps during my mission for President Wilson to the Peace Conference in Paris. The illness struck me a few months after you were born at Deucalion. Ever since that time, for a quarter of a century, I have been sterile."

Ten years later, seated beside Mr. Mancini in the car that was carrying them to Edesboro, John could still hear the three sounds that until this moment had come back to him only in nightmares: the gentle bump as his father's glass, slipping from the wax-like fingers, hit the rug beside the fireplace; the slithering crash as the frail body fell across the fire screen and carried it down on the brass fender; and the sound of Dwight's heavy footsteps coming up the hall on the run.

"I'm sorry I had to remind you," Mr. Mancini said.

John watched the road in silence for a few moments.

"You didn't really," he said finally. "Miss Quill had that in her second act, too."

"She did?" the policeman said.

The surprise in his voice gave John a moment of bitter pleasure, as though the executioner, carrying the headsman's axe toward him with pompous majesty, had stumbled and fallen in a foolish tangle of flailing limbs.

"God knows where she got it," John said. "Maybe she invented it. Maybe she guessed it. Or maybe——"

The pause caused Mr. Mancini to turn.

"Maybe what?" the policeman said.

"Maybe what she said is true," John said slowly. "Tha

what really happens to us in life isn't real at all," he said. "That it only becomes real when an artist takes the real facts and rearranges them in a pattern. She said art is the only reality. She said what she had written was the real truth. What I remembered, she said, was only part of the truth. It was only the surface. The part I could face and handle." John shook his head. "This last piece, the piece you thought I'd left out, no man could handle that, and go on living."

"You tried to handle it," Mr. Mancini said. "By trying to block it out even at this late stage, when you have only—" He paused to glance at his wrist watch. "Less than three minutes left to live."

"But I couldn't block it out," John said. "Even you, you who want me to change my decision, even you had to remind me."

The policeman nodded. He moved the brim of his Swiss mountaineer's hat up on his head, and he blew out the small, tired sigh.

"Yes, I had to," Mr. Mancini said. "It's the part of my job I don't like. I always feel, when a man or a woman makes the decision and I show up to help them through whatever time they have left, I always feel maybe, maybe, maybe if I can keep that one last thing from them, if I can make them forget that final straw, so to speak, maybe they won't—" The policeman paused and shook his head. "It never works," he said. 'Because the decision a man or woman reaches to end his life isn't really a decision at all. I mean it's not something arrived at here, now, this minute, the way you think you arrived at it back there on the Turnpike near New Haven." Mr. Mancini shook his head again. "No," he said. "The decision is your whole life, the way you've lived, the total of all your acts, that's what adds up to the decision. By the time I get to you, it's all over. Nothing can be changed or undone." The policeman paused, looked anxiously at John for a moment, then said, "Everybody ends up understanding that. Do you understand it, John?"

"Yes," John said. He had a curious moment of reassurance, almost of pleasure: Mr. Mancini had finally addressed him by his first name. "I understand."

He wanted to say something else. He wanted to say that now that he and the policeman were friends, it wasn't as awful as he had always thought it would be. But there was no time for extraneous remarks. The car had picked up speed. The "Edesboro" sign up ahead was rushing toward him.

"You're scheduled to hit the Turnpike rail between the third and fourth posts beyond the sign," Mr. Mancini said. "The cables are weak at that point, so you'll go through without any difficulty. You'll fall thirty-six feet, hit the river, and be pinned in the mud at the bottom for eight hours and eleven minutes. That's how long it will take for the dredgers to pull the car out of the water. Got all that?" John nodded. The policeman said, "Good luck," opened the door, and stepped out of the car.

John wondered why he did not hear the door slam shut behind Mr. Mancini. But he did not wonder about it very long. He was hunched over the wheel, squinting through the windshield, aiming the speeding car like a gun for the slack cables between the third and fourth posts.

John did hear the tearing crash when he hit. He had a stab of pride for his accuracy. Then everything was as he had wanted it: out of his hands.

FAWCETT CREST BOOKS

ON TOP WITH
THE BIG BESTSELLERS

A MOST PRIVATE INTRIGUE by Leo Rosten (T1116) 75¢

OTHER PEOPLE'S MONEY by Jerome Weidman (M1117) 95¢

WINTERWOOD by Dorothy Eden (T1104) 75¢

FATHERS by Herbert Gold (T1107) 75¢

THAT QUAIL, ROBERT by Margaret A. Stanger (R1090) 60¢

WHO DO YOU THINK YOU ARE, CHARLIE BROWN?
   by Charles M. Schultz (D1097) 50¢

PHYLLIS DILLER'S HOUSEKEEPING HINTS
   by Phyllis Diller (R1082) 60¢

THE LAST ONE LEFT by John D. MacDonald (T1085) 75¢

CASTLE UGLY by Mary Ellin Barrett (T1076) 75¢

THE COUNTRY TEAM by Robin Moore (M1069) 95¢

APPENDIX TO THE I HATE TO COOK BOOK
   by Peg Bracken (D1063) 50¢

NO ONE HEARS BUT HIM by Taylor Caldwell (T1054) 75¢

GILES GOAT-BOY by John Barth (P1052) $1.25

SATURDAY THE RABBI WENT HUNGRY
   by Harry Kemelman (R1036) 60¢

COLUMBELLA by Phillis A. Whitney (T1037) 75¢

ECSTASY AND ME by Hedy Lamarr (T1035) 75¢

I, THE KING by Frances Parkinson Keyes (T1021) 75¢

THE DOUBLE IMAGE by Helen MacInnes (T1013) 75¢

THE SOURCE by James A. Michener (C1122) $1.95

THE RABBI by Noah Gordon (M954) 95¢

THE I HATE TO HOUSEKEEP BOOK
   by Peg Bracken (D830) 50¢

THE I HATE TO COOK BOOK by Peg Bracken (D777) 50¢

A Fawcett **Crest Reprint**

Wherever Paperbacks Are Sold

If your dealer is sold out, send only cover price plus 10¢ each for postage and handling to Crest Books, Fawcett Publications, Inc., Greenwich, Conn. Please order by number and title. If five or more books are ordered, no postage or handling charge is necessary. No Canadian orders. Catalogue available on request.